Lifelong romance a
New Zealand. Writ
with happy ending
create. You can fo
Facebook.com/jcharroway, ...
jcharroway and Twitter.com/jcharroway.

New York Times and *USA TODAY* bestselling author
Cathryn Fox is a wife, mom, sister, daughter, aunt
and friend. She loves dogs, sunny weather, anything
chocolate (she never says no to a brownie), pizza and
red wine. Cathryn lives in beautiful Nova Scotia with
her husband, who is convinced he can turn her into a
mixed martial arts fan. When not writing, Cathryn can
be found Skyping with her son, who lives in Seattle
(could he have moved *any* further away?), shopping
with her daughter in the city, watching a big action
flick with her husband, or hanging out and laughing
with friends.

If you liked *Forbidden to Taste* and *On Her Terms*
why not try

Make Me Yours by Katee Robert
Take Me On by Dylan Rose

Also by JC Harroway

A Week to be Wild
Her Dirty Little Secret
One Night Only

Billionaire Bachelors

Forbidden to Want

Discover more at millsandboon.co.uk

FORBIDDEN TO TASTE

JC HARROWAY

ON HER TERMS

CATHRYN FOX

MILLS & BOON

First Published in Great Britain 2019
by Mills & Boon, an imprint of HarperCollins*Publishers*
1 London Bridge Street, London, SE1 9GF

Forbidden to Taste © JC Harroway

On Her Terms © Cathryn Fox

ISBN: 978-0-263-27379-3

MIX
Paper from
responsible sources
FSC® C007454

This book is produced from independently certified FSC™ paper
to ensure responsible forest management.
For more information visit www.harpercollins.co.uk/green.

Printed and bound in Spain
by CPI, Barcelona

CHAPTER ONE

Kenzie

I HOVER IN an alcove just outside the kitchen, unstable on the modest heels I'm wearing as part of my impromptu waitress uniform. I take a second to drag in a bolstering lungful of air. Now I'm here, my plan seems crazy. Audacious. But I need to capture his attention somehow.

I spent the whole day perfecting the desserts precariously balanced on my arms in the tiny, ill-equipped kitchenette of my one-bedroom flat. I even carried them here in a catering box on the Tube. Seeing them splattered on the plush carpets of the Faulkner's fine-dining restaurant because I'm having scaredy-cat second thoughts… Not an option.

The mental slap works. I straighten my shoulders, poised on the brink of my opportunity. I watch the waiter leave the table of interest, a rage of nervous energy jolting me into action—chin up, strides bold, and an air of *I totally belong in one of London's most upmarket eateries with four dessert plates balanced on my arms.*

My teenaged waitressing experience keeps my jittery body upright, my serene facial expression in place and my thumb out of the salted-caramel cheesecake as each step brings me closer to the man with the power. But the short walk, which had seemed like a marathon, is over in seconds, and I arrive at his table breathless and adrenaline-depleted.

The sight of Drake up close rattles my bones so hard I have to clamp my jaw to prevent my smile becoming a grimace full of chattering teeth. Not that the four diners would notice—they're deep in conversation, each handsome brother focussed on his date.

And I've always been invisible to Drake, hence tonight's subterfuge.

I slide a surreptitious glance his way, using the seconds before I'm spotted to assess the ways he's changed in the three years since the funeral—his face a little more angular, a sprinkle of telltale grey disrupting the inky blackness at his temples, perhaps a few more laughter lines—his appearance familiar but reminding me that we're strangers.

He'd been a soldier three years ago, every forbidden inch of him lean and buff and rigidly disciplined. Not that I'd looked too closely. But photos Sam had sent from wherever they were posted always featured the handsome duo—my husband and his best friend.

I shudder at the exposed memories and the unexpected surge of heat. I'm only human, and Drake Faulkner is eye candy personified for any woman.

The woman with him now, presumably his date, laughs, her possessive hand on his forearm and her smile wide and captivating.

I swallow the sour taste in my mouth—Drake and I have never had *that* kind of relationship. We've never even been friends. Not really. Yes, he's sent financial assistance in the regular cheques over the years, but our relationship was cordial at best, a fact that gives me a moment's hesitation as to what I think I'm doing, about to interrupt what is obviously a double date.

I lift my chin, remembering I only want one thing from Drake Faulkner and it's not his charity or his seduction. It's the only reason I'd seek out anyone's help: Tilly. My sister needs me close by in London—not as much as she used to need me, admittedly—and I need this job opportunity to get my life back on track.

I hold my breath and pray Drake's past friendship with Sam will grant me that chance as I place my offering in front of Drake's date. Her attention is firmly fixed on him, earning me a few more seconds of anonymity to deposit another two desserts in front of the other couple at the table, who are similarly oblivious to my presence. I recognise Drake's brother, Kit. Last I'd heard, he, like the other two Faulkner brothers, was single, but this woman is clearly more than a date. Heads close, non-verbal communication in the form of heated looks, fingers toying with each other's on his thigh and a cloud of barely repressed lust permeating the air—I flush, a voyeur to their intimacy.

I look away, eyes burning with envy, and place the last plate before Drake. And wait. My blood roars through my head at my barefaced effrontery. At this point a real waitress would leave, but I hover at Drake's elbow, my own stomach so knotted I doubt I'll ever eat again.

Without turning to look at me, Drake eyes my dessert and says, 'Miss, this isn't what we ordered.' His voice is older, too. Or perhaps it always carried that rich baritone timbre, which slides over me like bittersweet chocolate sauce…

Drake's companion flicks a look of barely concealed contempt my way, probably at my interruption of her dream date with one of London's most eligible bachelors. But the thing foremost in Horny Helen here's mind is the last thing I'd want from Drake of all people.

I smooth my damp palms down my black skirt. 'Compliments of the chef, sir.'

Horny Helen sweeps her gaze over my waitress-style outfit, a derisive curl to her lip. Has she noticed that my plain white blouse doesn't bear the Faulkner monogram of the other waiting staff uniforms? I don't work here. Yet. And I'm not here for a waitressing job.

The other two occupants of the table join the staring contest Drake's date has instigated. Kit's brow furrows, presumably as he tries to place me. But we've only met a handful of times. I hope his amnesia will last long enough for Drake to taste my dessert.

Taste it. Give me a chance.

Horny Helen pushes her plate away. 'Could I please have what I ordered? Es-press-o.'

She enunciates every syllable slowly, as if she assumes English isn't my first, or even my second, language. *Condescending cow.*

My eyes dart to the back of Drake's head, snagging on the golden skin between his shorn hairline and the top of his collar, while my head swims at the spicy masculine scent of him—so close, but permanently out of bounds.

Tense seconds stretch, and an ominous silence crawls over my skin.

I mentally rehash my bold, perhaps foolhardy plan and reach the same conclusion—I'm desperate. If I want to be close to my sister *and* chase my own dreams of one day taking charge of my own kitchen, I'm all out of options.

Drake turns his head.

'Kenzie...?' His shocked eyes latch on to mine from underneath his frown. Then surprise clears, replaced with the inscrutable distance of every look that has ever passed between us since the day we met.

Cool, distant, polite.

'Hi, Drake.' My voice is breathier than I'd like. I tell myself it's the high-stakes gamble of my mission. 'Good to see you. Please try the dessert.'

Drake blinks, as if I've asked him to solve world hunger in the next thirty seconds. He doesn't even look at the exquisite creation on his plate, which took me most of the day to prepare—the curls of dark Belgian chocolate, the flecks of gold leaf, the shiny smear of decadent salted-caramel sauce against the crisp white china... I might as well have served up school dinner's congealed semolina pudding with a blob of jam.

The curious looks of the rest of the party burn the exposed parts of me like the heat of the industrial stoves in the kitchen. I lift my chin, likely seconds away from an escort from the premises by Security.

Drake pushes his chair back and stands, swiftly followed by Kit, who has either finally placed me as the widow of Drake's best friend, or shares his older brother's innate good manners.

'What are you doing here?' He frowns, his hands hanging at his sides. Touching, even the polite social pleasantry of a peck on the cheek, wasn't our norm. While Sam was alive, and considering the amount of time the two spent together, on and off duty, I fought hard not to resent his cool indifference.

And then Sam died, and with the exception of a few stilted words at his funeral we've had no contact beyond those uncashed cheques.

Until now—my botched plan.

'Are you here to see me?' He looks around, still trying to explain my unorthodox presence.

'No…yes.' Colour rages up my neck. The small white lie I told his PA informed me of his dining plans. But I'm supposed to be seizing the day, making my own luck, not bungling my best chance at my dream job. I tell myself my muteness is simply fatigue—days spent job-hunting in this unfamiliar city, an inbox full of rejection emails, lonely evenings waiting for my break—and nothing to do with seeing him again.

'I see.' His frown cuts into me, making my feet shuffle, about to run for the kitchens. But giving up on my fresh start, my dream, my future, is not an option.

'Do you…do you work here?' says Drake.

My throat constricts, making my swallow almost painful. I hadn't considered a public interrogation. 'No… I… Not yet. I just… I'd really love for you to try my dessert.'

The proof really is in the pudding. Outside of credentials, there's no better way to show him I have the skills required to work at the Faulkner.

I take a deep breath, preparing to explain myself, even in front of an audience, when the real waiter returns carrying a bemused expression, Horny Helen's espresso and three affogato. He stares between Drake and me, his professional smile slipping to one of confusion.

I look away from Drake as the flames reach my

face. What was I thinking? Worst plan ever born of *carpe-diem*-style desperation.

'May I have my espresso, please?' Horny Helen says to the waiter, who places his offerings on the now crowded table.

'Should I bring an extra chair, Mr Faulkner?' He addresses Drake, looking slightly nervous for his job no doubt, although he wasn't the waiter on a ciggie break out the back that I managed to con earlier. Dressing the part, faking lateness and a cocky smile earned me access to the staff entrance past the security lock even without the monogrammed uniform.

Drake lifts one brow. 'Would you like to join us?'

My face must be singed by now. Certainly my stomach is on strike and trying to flee my body. Lonely, desperate gooseberry, Kenzie. I shake my head and squeak out a no.

Drake, his confusion raking me in a way that makes me want to check my blouse buttons haven't popped open, takes control of the bizarre situation I've created. 'Kit, you remember Kenzie Porter.'

Kit smiles, kisses my cheek and introduces me to his girlfriend, Mia.

'And this is Ashley Morris,' says Drake, his stare cool but persistent on me. Ashley offers a sickly-sweet smile and sips her espresso, her attention returning to Drake as if staking her claim.

She needn't worry. He's obviously just shocked to see me. From the very first time I met him and Sam in that bar all those years ago, Drake's never looked at me in *that* way.

I look away from the woman, who is exactly Drake's type. Although I'm only here for a job, my ribs pinch as if I've run a marathon on a full stomach, the second-best feeling confirming I shouldn't have come to once more have my face rubbed in *you're not good enough*.

I struggle to swallow the surge of bitterness. What was I thinking? Drake is no friendlier than when Sam was alive. Less so, in fact. The idea he might help me would be laughable if my eyes weren't already hot with humiliation.

A familiar helpless panic closes its fingers around my throat. I bite the inside of my cheek, chasing away the stray emotion. I haven't cried for three years and I have no intention of breaking my dry spell. Forcing the brightest smile possible, I scan the group, latching on to Mia's open, friendly face.

'Well, it was lovely seeing you again and great to meet you, Mia, Ashley.' I need to get out of here before the burn in my eyes becomes liquid, before I'm forced to relive the rejection to my application for the Faulkner's sous-chef position in person and with Drake's date for an audience.

'Sorry for interrupting.' I back away. In the light of my and Drake's less than cosy reunion, my long shot now seems ludicrous. I spin on my heel, ignoring Drake's 'Wait!', my strides weaving between the elegant tables as fast as the tightness of my skirt will allow.

I push through the kitchen doors, duck past several actual waiting staff collecting their orders and grab the denim jacket I'd stuffed behind a stack of empty produce crates next to the walk-in freezer.

By the time I hit the alleyway behind the hotel and suck the freezing air into my gasping lungs, my whole body trembles with the spent adrenaline of futility.

What an idiot. Why did I think my reception from Drake Faulkner of all people would be any warmer, any more personal, than the two-line rejection email?

We're looking for someone with more experience... wishing you luck in your career...

I bite the inside of my cheek, staving off the well of emotion, unsure which rejection has my stupid eyes scalding—that of Drake's head chef, or that of the man himself.

I scuff the toe of my shoe at a blob of welded-on chewing gum on the road, the shame directed inwards. Drake had greeted me with all the warmth of the strangers we are. Just because I thought I could convince him to take a chance on me with my dessert stunt doesn't mean he'd be anything but consistently distant and frosty.

With my chest tight and my jumpy muscles cooling in the bitter November chill, I shrug into my jacket and drag my feet in the direction of the Underground.

The slam of the door bouncing off the brick wall behind startles me. I spin, clutching my chest. Drake, his face slashed with a scowl, heads my way with singular purpose and an intent expression, his suit jacket billowing out from his trim torso.

My previously defeated heart picks up the pace. Not only did my deflated soufflé of a plan fail, I've also ticked off the man with power to grant me a shot at my dream. When I fled, trailing my dignity, I was counting on him making some excuse for my unexpected appearance and continuing with his date. Now he'll want an explanation, and, with the humiliation pounding through my bloodstream and facing a wall of his imposing but unfriendly manliness, I'm in no position to present my best argument.

I blurt the first thing that comes to mind, attack being the best form of defence. 'What are you doing? Aren't you on a date?'

He ignores me and strides closer, his long, muscular legs filling his dress trousers to perfection, each ominous footfall a clip from his tan leather brogues. My belly takes a nosedive—I've always loved brogues.

When he comes to rest in front of me I inhale a gulp of the damp air, wishing it were a shot of Dutch courage.

His thick brows dip over incredulous eyes. 'What

am *I* doing here…?' His harsh expression could back me up a couple of paces but I stand still for the face-off. 'That's my question for you.'

I gape wordlessly. His chest seems twice as broad as he slings his hands in his trouser pockets, the fabric stretching across his hips. I lift my stare from his crotch, swallowing the heat in my throat. Hopefully it's too dark for him to see my blush, and I can always blame the sub-zero temperatures.

'What was that all about? The dessert?' He nods at my outfit. 'You pretending to be a waitress?' His nostrils flare, his mouth tight with annoyance.

My shoulders sag. I've disrupted his date with the delightful Ashley, his bollocks are probably starting to freeze and my pathetic dream for a fresh start lies in tatters.

The adrift feeling, which has plagued me these past few months, returns with stinging force that makes me want to run or hide or fight. But which is the best tactic to convince Drake?

'I…I hoped to get your attention.' Hoped he'd see *me*, not just Sam's widow or Tilly's sister—but a woman with her own skills, aspirations, ambition. 'It seemed like a good idea at the time, but now I see it was a mistake.' Drake's undivided focus, him looking at me in this new, disconcerting way, is potent—like standing too close to a bonfire.

'Forget it. Go back inside. She doesn't look the type who'll wait for ever.' The damp air has turned into a mist of freezing drizzle—the kind that seeps into your bones. I belatedly fasten the buttons of my jacket, although the front of my blouse has already become transparent.

'Well, you have my attention.' His eyes narrow, as if he finds my bullshit decidedly suspect. 'And what type *does* she look like?'

Why would he care what *I* think of his date? Or perhaps she's his girlfriend. It would be a first for him, but then what do I know? This man is a virtual stranger—despite all the years we've known each other. And would he leave a girlfriend to chase after a woman he barely tolerates and hasn't seen for years?

'She looks like *your* type, Drake. Sorry for the interruption. Goodnight.' My tight smile sticks on my frozen face as I spin away. But then I'm brought to a halt by the touch of his hand on my arm.

'For fuck's sake—you can't just leave like this.' He peers down at me, his irritation lessened but still brooking no argument. 'Not until you explain what's going on.' He drops my arm, pinning me in place with the force of his intense stare alone.

I tilt my chin, my humiliation already complete. 'It was a stupid long shot. I should have remembered that you owe me nothing.' Absence, it seems, doesn't make *this* man's heart fonder. I cross my arms and grip my elbows in an attempt to conserve some heat and hold myself together.

'Explain. What was a long shot? And why did you run out?' He waits, his jaw tight and his breath whitening the air as his order echoes in the alleyway.

I press my lips together. I've nothing left to lose. I came here determined to seize the day but, now I'm face to face with this somehow different but equally stand-offish Drake, I'm not sure I want to expose myself or justify my fragile fledging dreams to his cool indifference. If he'd treated me to one whiff of welcome, a hint of pleasure at my appearance, perhaps I'd find the extra courage.

When my teeth rattle he sighs as if abandoning his search for answers, shrugs out of his suit jacket and drapes it around my juddering shoulders.

'Thank you.' I look down, too cold to protest, and tug the lapels across my chest. And then I'm hit with his scent, a waft from the fabric, a heady cloud of deliciousness that's foreign and yet vaguely familiar.

I look up, my breath caught in my throat. We've never stepped this close before. A rare, awkward, one-armed hug constitutes the sum of our physical contact.

But he doesn't back away.

'You're welcome.' His voice drops, low enough to sound seductive to my rusty eardrums, although the remnants of the scowl linger behind his eyes.

I roll back on my heels, my frozen toes protesting at the surge of blood with a vicious throb. I should abandon the fight. Walk away from further explanation. But my feet have forgotten the way. I'm frozen with indecision, clinging to the lip of my coveted new life. Not a great position for a woman on an audacious mission...

In a last-ditch attempt to save myself the shame of exposure, I toss out, 'You know it's rude to keep a woman waiting, right?' Since when did fleeing the effect his stare has on my pulse trump talking my way into a life-changing opportunity?

He grins a humourless grin and looks away, shaking his head as if he can't believe my obstinacy. And yet here we are, his evening in tatters, my plan abandoned, standing in the rain at a stalemate.

'Come back inside. We'll talk in the warm.' He scoops up my elbow in one of his big hands and directs my stiff form towards the kitchen's entrance.

I dig in my heels, heart hammering. The last thing I want is to return to the scene of the crime. To explain my sad, lonely, unemployed status to both loved-up couples... But I'm too cold, damp and bone-weary to put up much of a fight beyond backtracking.

'Look. I'll call you tomorrow. Explain everything then. That's probably what I should have done in the first place,' I wheedle. Yeah, that would have been a better plan. Why didn't I think of it sooner? 'Go. Enjoy what's left of your evening.'

He sighs, casting me a withering look. 'I sent her home. I sent them all home.'

I gasp. 'Why?' A stupid flare of hope flickers in my chest, gooey and warming.

'Because dinner's over and I want to hear your explanation.' He pauses on the top step and I want to look away from his semi-transparent shirt, which clings to the defined muscle he hasn't lost since leaving the army.

He wants to hear my sob story—isn't that why I came?

Of course, now my elevated heart rate and clammy palms have less to do with nerves or humiliation and more to do with hormones. Because his hand on my elbow, even through two layers of fabric, is deliciously alien enough to remind me I'm a woman.

A woman on a mission to reclaim her life.

All areas of her life…?

I bite my lip, stifling a groan. His innocent, non-sexual touch—strong, in control, commanding—is *that* good. Because it's been three long years, and something about Drake—his confidence, the control he wears like the discipline of the soldier he was—it's sparked my long-dormant body to life.

I slide my arm free of his hand, my fickle stomach rolling at my traitorous turn of thought, and he keys in the entry code on the panel beside the door.

The breath judders into me, delivering another dose of warm, Drake-scented air from his jacket. But there's no margin for whimsical flights of sexual fancy here. I'm here for a job, and he'd never think of me in *that* way.

He's Sam's best friend.

Sam, my dead husband.

I swallow acid. I'm simply overwhelmed, my body's reaction to his dismantling looks and his warm touch a product of too long without any sort of male contact. Or perhaps I can blame the stress of formulating and then executing my plan, the chance of new purpose in my life now my sister is grown.

The electronic click sounds and he swings the door inwards. 'Let's get you inside.' His stare slides over my face and then dips lower, taking in my sodden clothes. 'Get you warmed up. And then we'll talk.' Those green eyes of his penetrate. '*You'll* talk.'

My belly rolls again, bossy, commanding Drake not something I've ever experienced. That it warms me more than irritates makes me snappy. 'Huh? What is this, an interrogation? Gonna shove bamboo skewers under my fingernails? You're not in the army now.' My petulance forces heat to my stinging cheeks. I need to get a grip before I blow this chance to smithereens. The ultimate in self-sabotage.

'Yes, but I still have the moves.' Drake smiles, an unguarded twitch of his lips an expression I've rarely seen directed my way.

My breath turns to thick syrup. Is he…flirting?

The flare of warmth in his eyes and the mischievous twist to his full mouth thrusts my neglected body into meltdown. I expect a cloud of steam to start rising from my head.

He holds the door open, the welcoming light and warmth beckoning. 'It's your call, but we can do this in comfort or out here where it's pissing down.' A shrug. 'I'm happy with either.'

He waits, as if he has all the time in the world. As

if he's immune to the sub-zero drizzle. As if he's still used to the discomfort and discipline of the army.

Now I'm not certain if the shivers racking my body are temperature-related or a tug of war between my conflicted urges—to run from his dark, unfathomable looks or to follow him and prolong the conversation, which is already our longest and most addictive.

I step inside, dragging my attention from the wet shirt plastered to the contours of his chest. I shouldn't find this man in any way attractive. He doesn't need me, would never want me, and just acknowledging his good looks and the effect they have on my only-human pulse floods my throat with the bitter taste of betrayal.

But Sam's not here. I'm twenty-eight. This reaction to Drake proves I'm not immune to the charms of the opposite sex…or at least the charms of *this* man. Am I going to remain celibate for the rest of my life?

Yes, I haven't wanted anyone else these past years, but I'm a woman and Drake fills his suit the way he used to fill his uniform—fit, virile, a man at the top of his game. I'd have to be dead to not feel the zing of electricity through the cobweb-strewn parts of my nervous system.

And there's no escape from him. From his deep stare, dark and penetrating, from the past we share, convoluted and confusing, or from my aborted plan and the explanation I owe him.

I try to slow my breathing as I follow his long strides, his broad shoulders and dominating height obscuring our direction. This is what I wanted—his attention. All I have to do is plead my case and hope to salvage something, even if it's just my dignity. So why do I feel ready to concede the fight and flee the ring?

CHAPTER TWO

Drake

MY PULSE SPRINTS like an excited fucking puppy as I lead her from the staff entrance and along the corridor towards the lift and the Faulkner's private suites. That I'm even taking her to the hotel rooms I only use if I've been working late or if I'm entertaining a date sounds an air-raid siren in my head.

A warning the glutton for punishment in me shuts out.

But Kenzie and I going upstairs *isn't* a date. The selfish part of me wishes 'us' were that simple.

In truth, there is no 'us'.

The achingly familiar visceral blow provides a perfect reminder to my dick, which had perked up the minute I'd seen her in the restaurant.

My army discipline helps to dispel images of all the filthy sexual things I'd like to do with her—things she'd run from if she knew. As it is, I'm tempted to drop to the carpet and pump out a hundred push-ups to put myself on the safe side of exhaustion.

Because the woman standing across the narrow corridor from me, her guarded hazel eyes shooting me cautious looks, may as well be a nun, she's so untouchable.

And pissed.

I'm a bossy bastard when the need arises, and McKenzie Porter ignites that need like no other. I slowly inhale. A fucking stupid move that drags her subtle feminine scent into my head, where it has no place being and maximum potential to test my restraint.

Why is she here, in the flesh? Not just the dream version—the one I've spent considerable time with over the years. And what the hell was tonight about?

I open my mouth to ask again and then clamp my lips together. She's freezing, her body still trembling. At least I can no longer hear her teeth chatter.

Instead I scrub at my hair and try to work out her stunt with the dessert. She'd wanted to get my attention, she'd said. Well, all she had to do was walk into the same room. If I were a heat-seeking missile, she'd be the sun…

'I'm sorry I messed up your date.' A flash of vulnerability, of bravery, ghosts her eyes and I want to tell her she can gatecrash all my dates.

Whoa… I haven't spent all the years I've known her keeping her at arm's length just to screw it all up in one move.

'You didn't. It was pretty much over.' She interrupted the tail end of a satisfactory evening of good company, excellent food and the potential for meaningless sex. Pity a five-minute conversation with Kenzie eclipses a hundred meaningless encounters, as evidenced by the surge of testosterone I'm currently battling, my body as attuned to her presence as high-voltage power lines to an approaching rainstorm.

I force my mind to the mundane, willing my libido to obey orders. Sharing army barracks and tents with thirty other men helps to master control of the body parts that have a life of their own. And the technique, one I've practised a thousand times in her presence, reminds me of the first time I saw her, a mere thirty seconds before my best mate caught her eye.

I swallow the bitter taste with a silent curse. I've tried, but I've never been in control of my feelings for this woman—the intervening years, her falling for and then marrying Sam, and then losing him, may as well count for zilch.

I want her.

I've always wanted her.

And it's *never* been an option.

That's why I've stayed the hell away. Not only have I always coveted my best friend's woman, but Sam is no longer here to punch me in both of my two faces, as I deserve.

And what I definitely *don't* deserve is Kenzie.

The guilt and self-disgust turning my stomach deals with my hard-on. *Yeah, not happening, bud.*

The lift arrives and we step inside the brightly lit and mirrored cell. I lock down my trapped-inside emotions behind the neutral facial expression of my reflection while I wonder how the fuck I'm going to manage the next thirty minutes until I can get rid of her without taking a cold shower.

'Have you and Ashley been dating for long?' she asks, leaning up against one wall, her beautiful eyes huge and tinged with doubt. 'I hope she'll forgive you for cutting things short to…deal with me.'

Deal with her…? Can she read my fucking mind? See all the filthy ways I'd like to *deal with her*? Does she know that she stars in dreams that jerk me from sleep, leaving me soaked in sweat and harder than steel? I've had stern words with my subconscious, but it's persistently twisted.

'We're not dating. Just casual.' All my interactions with women over the years can be classified that way. Anything more serious would have demanded comparisons I knew deep inside would only highlight the gaping chasm between reality and the fantasy of what might have been with *this* particular woman.

I look away, feigning fascination in the digital display that tells me I only have thirty more seconds to endure being this close to her in an enclosed space, which may as well be a torture chamber. I slow my breathing to ward off the head rush and slide my eyes over the source of every erotic fantasy I've had since the day we met, forcing myself to look beyond the perfection of her combination of features.

'You're pale.' With cold, fatigue or something else? I curl my fingers into fists to stop me from pulling my jacket tighter around her frame and buttoning it up to the neck to protect her from my lecherous stare. I grip the handrail. I only have so much self-control—another reason staying away was easier.

She shrugs. 'I'm okay.'

I scour her face for clues. Then my stomach plummets as if the lift were descending, not ascending. Is she ill? Is that what she's come to tell me? She could be dying for all I know. Outside what I struggled to ignore while Sam was still alive and what I've pieced together through social-media stalking in the three years since his death, she's a stranger.

Because I've kept her that way in order to atone and for self-preservation.

Panic subsides as I remember the dessert. She came with a mission. I know she had a passion for cooking. But she and her autistic sister, nine years her junior, live in Bath. A long way to deliver dessert.

Another surge of adrenaline traps my breath. Is Tilly sick? Do they need help? Money? Am I the only person she can turn to? I swallow razor blades. Have I neglected her? She must miss Sam. She's far too young to be a widow. And too fucking beautiful.

My heart stutters frozen as another thought occurs: I have no idea if she's seeing someone. Three years is a long time for celibacy. I fight the urge to make fists, the idea of some worthless bastard laying his hands on her souring a perfectly satisfactory Michelin-starred dinner.

Enough.

One glimpse of McKenzie Porter and my regimented life turns to chaos. I suck it up. Repeat the mantra: *thoughts, eyes and hands off. She's Sam's.*

I'm about to bang my head against the wall of the lift to knock some sense into my libido-ridden brain when it slows, releasing an electronic ping so welcome, I'm mentally fist-pumping the air at surviving the journey.

'We could have talked downstairs in the bar, you know,' she says, a flash of admonishment in her pretty eyes reminding me of the times she bawled out Sam for some bawdy, barrack-room joke.

The doors glide open.

'Three years is a long time.' A lifetime. 'I'd say that warrants a…private reunion, wouldn't you?' I hold out my arm for her to exit.

Her mouth thins with censure. 'I've only just moved to London; if you'd wanted to find me sooner, you knew where I was.'

The urge to kiss that sensual mouth slams into me with previously unexperienced force. How can this woman do that to me? Is it just the forbidden thing…? I never considered myself such a puerile arsehole, but hey…anything that helps me keep my hands off her.

She pauses outside the lift. I indicate the direction, and she precedes me down the hallway with a sexy flounce of attitude.

'I did.' She's right. I've known where to find her all these years, but couldn't be a part of her life. 'And if you needed me, you could have called.' The lash of guilt slashes between my shoulder blades. Have I punished her, too, in punishing myself for wanting her, for keeping secrets, for plunging her into a life without Sam? I bite back a wince, my jaw aching where my teeth grind together.

By castigating myself and avoiding temptation, I've neglected my obligations—the promise made to Sam when neither of us believed it would need to be honoured.

It was better to keep my distance. Better for her because she wouldn't have wanted to hear what I had to say, and better for my unscrupulous conscience. Because even when I oh, so briefly held a sobbing McKenzie in my arms while she grieved for another man—a man we *both* loved, a man I made promises to, a man I kept secrets for—my thoughts weren't wholly innocent.

At the suite door, the only one at this end of the corridor, she turns, big eyes finding me in the gloom, burrowing through my self-protective skin. 'Yes, well, I wouldn't be here either if I wasn't desperate, believe me.' She flushes and blinks, looking away.

Desperate? My mind races with possibilities, turning my stomach. I let her down, but it was better for her this way. And the sooner I warm her up and get her talking, the sooner I can send her on her way.

'Great,' I bite out. 'You don't need me and I've done a shit job of keeping in touch.'

Her glare dissolves into mocking humour. 'Fair assessment.'

I unlock the door and activate the suite's lighting, swallowing the real reasons I stayed away from this forbidden woman. Those damaging words are locked deep inside, out of harm's way. Harm to Kenzie, to the memory of Sam and to any hope of being in her life in the future. Distant acquaintance is better than nothing. Distant acquaintance keeps me sane.

'So, coffee? Tea? Something stronger?' Fuck, I need something stronger. I unbutton my cuffs and roll up my rapidly drying shirtsleeves, the previously comfortable ambient temperature in the suite now stifling, thanks to her presence.

'Do you have any wine?' she asks.

I nod, reaching into the cupboard off the entrance-way for a spare towel, holding it at arm's length in offering.

'Thanks.' She takes it with a grateful smile and towels the ends of her hair. She's still wearing my too-big jacket. A mark of possession that pumps my blood faster. How would she look in one of my shirts and nothing else? How would her skin react to the scrape of my facial hair, a map to every place I've been lucky enough to run my mouth?

'Take a seat and I'll get you a glass.' And a bucket of water for my own parched throat…

I head to the kitchen, activating the sound system for the distraction of some background music. I select a bottle of wine from the rack, not that alcohol is a good idea around her but I need to keep my restless hands and hungry mouth occupied until she leaves.

Silently, I give myself a talking-to—I can handle a little self-discipline: I'm an expert around Kenzie's particular brand of temptation. And just because she's turned up on my doorstep, *nothing* has changed.

I carry the wine and glasses into the lounge, finding Kenzie holding her hands out to warm in front of the fire.

'I switched it on. I hope you don't mind?' she asks, hesitant.

'Of course not. It's put some colour in your cheeks.'

She smiles, shrugs out of my jacket and places it on the chair. I look away, telling myself that, when she's gone, I will under no circumstances inhale the fabric to catch her lingering scent. But then she removes her own denim jacket and my fucked brain fries.

Her white blouse is partially see-through from the rain. I'm gifted a flash of lace straining across the fullness of what I'm a million per cent convinced are spectacular breasts, before I look away to pour wine with a trembling hand.

Damn, don't think about her breasts.

'Would you like to borrow a change of clothes?' I ask. 'A robe?' A scream sounds in my head. The last thing I need is her removing any more clothing, even in another room. Fuck, another country is too close for comfort. I swallow, tearing my thoughts away from her naked, crying *my* name as she comes on my tongue…

'I'll be fine, thanks.'

I hand her a glass. Her smile widens as she scans the bottle. 'Mmm… Pinot Noir—my favourite.'

'Oh…?' I shrug, pretending I didn't know that tiny detail. Despite the nuclear meltdown happening inside my body, I turn up the fire, the small gesture worth the sweat it will cost me when she gifts me another of those killer smiles.

She takes a seat and I slide onto the sofa next to her. I can do this—keep things PG. Foster a relationship of fond acquaintance, connected by our love for Sam.

Remembering my manners, I raise my glass, touching it to hers while I force my face to conceal the turmoil tumbling inside, like jagged rocks before the hard edges have been polished. 'Cheers. To… chance meetings.'

Not friends. Never that.

I take a sip, the wine tasting acidic. I should have toasted Sam. Perhaps he's the reason she's come to talk. My temples start to pound, the conflict in my head seeking an escape route.

She covers her small frown with a big gulp of

wine. 'So I take it you left the army?' She crosses slim legs covered with sheer black stockings.

I look away from her legs, grateful for the perfect distraction. 'Yeah. I'd done two tours. And… after…' I clamp my lips together, the wine now burning through my internal organs.

Her expressive eyes freeze, and my tongue sticks to the roof of my mouth. The last thing I want to talk about is *that* day—the worst day in both our lives, I suspect.

'I needed a change of direction. The timing felt right.' I release the rest of the breath I've been holding. I'm not ashamed that I suffered PTSD—most people would under the same circumstances—but opening that can of worms will lead to more questions than I want to answer. Time to find out why she's really here. 'So what about you? You needed something from me?' Another slash of guilt pierces.

She swallows, nods, looking down at her lap, where she finds a fleck of fluff on the hem of her skirt. 'I am sorry I interrupted your evening.' She snorts a mirthless laugh. 'Looks like neither of us will be getting laid tonight, although for you, I guess, it hasn't been as long.'

I practically spurt wine. Is she deliberately trying to torture me with images easily accessed in my vast Kenzie-themed spank bank? And does that mean she hasn't had sex since… Sam?

I swallow the brick in my throat, too turned on to think straight and too scared to ask, in case I'm wrong and the answer brings up my dinner. 'So why did you come? You have my attention.'

Round eyes settle on mine, a hint of vulnerability shining there, although she's the strongest person I know. 'I…I wanted you to try my dessert.'

'So, you made that dessert?' Before Sam died, she worked as a teacher's aide, helping kids with special needs, a job that allowed her plenty of time and flexibility to care for a teenaged Tilly.

Of course, she'd been a fantastic cook, always trying out new recipes on Sam, Tilly and me, her 'guinea pigs', on the few occasions I couldn't get out of an invitation to their home without looking like an arsehole. Her roast beef with homemade horseradish still haunts me… Sam was a lucky bastard in many ways.

'Yes. I had a crazy plan to surprise you so you could taste it.' Her eyes dip to her lap.

'So…you're what? In catering? A pastry chef?'

She shakes her head, her face rosy. From the wine? The fire? Or is she embarrassed she's been forced to come to me, of all people? Someone who, despite being her husband's best friend, abandoned her after his death?

'After Sam I…I needed a new direction. Something for myself.' Her stare clings, as if begging me to understand.

I nod, my own shell cracking to let a tiny confession free in solidarity. 'I understand—I was lucky to have a job here to fall back on, after the army.' I don't add how it saved me—stopped me from going mad with grief and guilt, and stopped me from going to her and confessing bottled-up feelings I had no right to own.

She smiles and continues. 'Tilly is a woman now.' Her eyes soften at the mention of her sister and she swallows hard.

I freeze. If she cries, I'll have to give in to temptation and hold her. I won't be able to stop myself.

'She doesn't need me quite so much as she did growing up.' She collects herself, brightening. 'So I retrained in a field I love.' Excitement turns her eyes alive with golden spangles. 'I've always wanted to cook professionally. And I'm not bad. I never once poisoned you, did I?' Her mouth twists, a flash of sass that evokes a hundred convoluted memories.

I offer her a genuine smile, my first since I turned to find her behind me in the dining room downstairs. 'That's fantastic. You always sent the most amazing cookies. Every guy in our unit buzzed around Sam when those parcels arrived like flies around sh…'

I break off.

Kenzie laughs then smiles, a bittersweet offering that tells me she's thinking about Sam.

I lean away from temptation. 'Well, it looked delicious. You're a great cook.' Is she after my approval, a reference, a recommendation?

'Thanks.' Her eyes are full of doubt, of hesitancy. 'I guess I thought if I just came to you and asked, you might feel obliged…you know…because of Sam. This way, I hoped my food would speak for me. It was a stupid stunt.' She takes a glug of wine and I want to reach out and touch her, comfort her, certain she's never done anything stupid in her life, even as I discreetly glance at my watch and wonder how quickly I can see her on her way.

'Tell me how I can help?' I'll give her anything I'm able to give. Make up somehow for the lonely years of hardship I caused her.

She chews her lip, looking momentarily lost.

My thumb moves rhythmically over the stem of my wine glass as I battle the urge to touch her. Would her mouth be as soft as it looks? What would those expressive eyes tell me if I crossed the line? To fuck the hell off? That she's never ever once thought of me that way…? That I'm betraying Sam's memory, just by thinking of *her* with anything beyond cold, consolation-prize friendship?

Nothing I don't already know.

She collects herself, holding my eye contact with a tilt of her chin. 'I hoped if you tasted something I'd made, you'd see how serious I am now I'm free to pursue a career, not just…pacify me because of our…past connection.'

Connection… Fuck, that's a passionless and depressing descriptor. But accurate.

'And, having already been declined, I knew it was a long shot.' Her shoulders droop as she watches the flames of the fire.

All my protective instincts flare to life and my fingers make a fist around the stem of my wine glass. 'Declined?'

She nods. 'It's no big deal.' A gut-twisting, sad little smile. 'Breaking into the top restaurants is hard, even outside London. Believe me, I'd have stayed in Bath if I had the choice. But Tilly moved here to study at the London School of Economics and, even though she wants her independence, some days… she still struggles. It made sense for me to be close, for…emergencies.'

Then it registers in a single icy deluge. She lives here now. On my doorstep. I tamp down my increased breathing. This is bad news. How will I sleep at night knowing she's somewhere in my city, but not in my bed? Close, but still out of bounds?

My lust-addled brain finally slots it all together. 'You applied for our sous-chef position?'

Another nod, the excitement back in her eyes. 'I know I'm inexperienced in a restaurant of the Faulkner's calibre.' She turns her body to face me, perched on the edge of the sofa. I zone back in to what she's actually saying rather than just the way her luscious mouth forms the words. She's so animated, her breaths come in soft pants.

'I told myself to grasp my big chance, now that I'm free to focus all my energy on what *I* want. I just need a shot. A trial even. A chance to prove I'm up to the job and willing to learn.'

This is her passion. Something she's put on hold

while she raised her sister. Something she might have achieved sooner, if my actions hadn't made her a widow.

Yes hovers on my lips. I clamp them together. She's enough of a temptation across the country, but in my space every day... And the glimmer of hope behind her guarded, afraid-to-dream expression may as well be a shower of hurled knives.

Euphoria drains away, slashed to shreds. I stiffen to hold myself in place and clear my throat. 'Well, I believe we already have a trial set up for someone else—a Dominic Brown.'

She shakes her head, her eyes dulling but her chin lifting with grit. 'I see. Couldn't we take it in turns? Work alternate shifts. You'll get two for the price of one.'

Every beat of my heart hurts. It's in my power to help her. But it's too dangerous. She sees the refusal forming on my tongue and jumps in.

'I'd put in the hours, more than the hours. I have great references, and if I'm not up to it, if it doesn't work out, no hard feelings.' Her cheeks flush as she grows increasingly hopeful.

It's a physical blow under my ribs to see that look on her face. This means more to her than a job. More than taking care of Tilly. It's personal. She lost her parents, stepped into the role of Tilly's caretaker, sidelined her own dreams. That she's come to *me*, of all people...the last person who deserves her trust...

'I don't think it's a good idea.' Fuck, that's lame.

I have to do better than that. 'Our executive chef can be difficult to work for.'

Her lips thin. 'I'm not asking for a freebie or special treatment.' She rushes on where I would have interrupted. 'Just an opportunity to see if I have what it takes. The same as Dominic.'

I stroke my chin, juggling the pros and cons of Hobson's choice. Unless I find somewhere else to eat, I'll see her all the time. I could work at the Faulkner Group offices with Reid and Kit. Then I'll most likely only bump into her on the days I meet with Rod, our temperamental head chef, who has a large say in the hiring and firing of those in his kitchen. But I'm a Faulkner. The bosses' boss. If Kenzie wants a trial, I could make it happen.

Then I wince as my gut twists. Rod is a notorious ladies' man. He fucks all the single waitresses and half the married ones. He's the very reason we have a sous-chef vacancy. The idea of him working day in, day out with Kenzie…

No. I'll have to send her away. Crush her dream. It won't be the first time I've ruined her life. I put down my wine before I hurl it at the wall.

'I'll work hard, I promise. I'm not asking for handouts,' she adds, her eyes wide as she reaches for her denim jacket and rummages in the pocket. 'In fact…' she holds out an envelope '…I also came to return these.'

I stare at her offering as if it's packed with plastic explosives, the hairs prickling on the back of my neck. 'What is it?'

When I don't take the envelope from her, she huffs and places it on the sofa between us like a barrier.

'The cheques you sent.' Her eyes harden.

My stomach rolls. She may as well have kneed me in the balls. I temper a sigh while I process what feels like a slap in the face. 'But that money is for *you*.'

Guilt money.

She looks away as if she knows what's coming and wants to hear it less than I want to utter it or admit the ugly truth.

I say it anyway, because if she hasn't cashed a single one of the cheques I've sent her over the years I need leverage. Blackmail. 'I promised him I'd look after you.' I force the words out, inviting Sam into the room—a major cock-block for me and a reminder for her: *some* promises still apply. 'And I want to help.'

My stomach rolls—of course I made promises to Sam, too. The promise of time to sort his shit out, get his house in order and come clean to Kenzie.

One look at the wistfulness in her beautiful eyes at the mention of his name tells me he didn't, and my burden doubles in weight as if gravity no longer exists.

A determined pout forms on her soft, plump lips. 'I appreciate that, Drake, I do, but I don't want your money. I don't need it. And you can help me by giving me a chance to get a job.'

There it is—her steel, her independence. Fucking attractive qualities I've always secretly admired.

'I know you don't need it.' She's the strongest woman I know. Facing her losses with the bravery of a whole squadron of men.

Her eyes dart away, perhaps finding the carpet, this particular shade of charcoal, fascinating. But she's right not to trust me. Right not to need me. She's unaware, but I'm a snake in the grass. I'd never have played my hand—in my mind, she'll always be Sam's—but thoughts can betray as much as actions. Did my thoughts make me as complicit as Sam, who had everything I dared to crave, but failed to honour its value?

I aim for nonchalance with my shrug, ignoring the colicky twist of my gut that remonstrates. 'I just wanted to ease your burden. Help the only way I could.' The money helped me to keep my word without losing my mind.

I should have stayed in touch. Should have worked harder to fight my attraction from day one so I could uphold my promise to my friend with more than financial assistance. She would have needed more than money these past three years—solace, company, practical help. Sam's army pension probably covers her mortgage, but not much else. And now with London prices… And besides, I swore. Made a vow to look out for his woman and her sister. If Sam were here, he'd tell me straight up—I'm a shitty friend. But then, at the end, he was a shitty husband…

'Why are you so stubborn? A promise is a promise.' Every married soldier has his brothers at his back and I had Sam's back.

Every time except that last time. The only time that counted...

'I prefer determined. That's why my plan was supposed to entice you—I don't want your money. So, do I get my shot?' The set of her jaw tells me she isn't going to back down and, if there are three years' worth of cheques in that envelope, nothing I say tonight will change her mind and convince her to accept what I can easily afford.

I close my eyes, wishing I could close my mind to the dilemma as easily. Of course, the only thing my brain latches on to is the delicate scent of the woman next to me on the couch. The warmth of her body seeping across the pathetic slice of space between us.

I drag in air. It would be so easy to reach out. To touch her. To have all my fantasies confirmed in the flesh.

I snap my eyes open and sit a little straighter, sucking on my discipline.

I groan aloud at my lack of options, rub my hand over my face, the length of the day and its unexpected turn finally draining the last of my energy.

But she's done waiting for my answer. 'It's okay. I understand.' Kenzie stands and places her glass on the table. 'Don't worry. Just forget I came.'

Forget? Not fucking likely. I'll probably relive

every second throughout a long, sleepless night. I stand, too, my thoughts tripping over themselves to break free as coherent sentences.

'It was great to see you.' I wince. Is that the best I can do?

'Thanks for the wine,' she says, grabbing her stiff, wet denim jacket, the defeat in her eyes buffeting my resolve.

She's reached out to me after all this time. It's my fault she needs a job.

'Wait.' I can offer her a chance. I'll just have to double my morning gym routine so I'm completely exhausted if and when I do run into her in the corridor. Yeah, no amount of burpees or pull-ups will counter the urges she inspires.

She's halfway to the door when I catch up. This time when I touch her elbow, there's no fabric barrier to block the potent lust that thrums through my blood. My hand slides down the smooth length of her bare forearm until my fingers encircle her delicate wrist.

My pulse rate doubles. I was right—her skin is as soft as my imaginings. She looks up from my hand, her face so familiar, but foreign at this proximity. My fingers twitch involuntarily. With one small tug she'd be in my arms...pressed against my aching chest... her mouth on mine...

I swallow the watermelon in my throat. I have no right to touch her. No right to make her any promises, the ground I'm on so shaky I may as well be standing on a fault line.

But she's not asking for promises, just a chance. I'll just have to steer clear.

'I want to help…with a trial in the kitchens,' I say. It's the least I can do. *All* I can do. Everything else in my head is strictly prohibited.

'Really?' Her smile rearranges the organs in my chest, each jostling for space in the too-small, confined space.

I nod. Control fraying. If she's going to look at me like that…

'Drake… I… Thanks.' Her voice is husky, tentative, my name decadent on her beautiful lips.

Blood whooshes through my skull. She's too tempting, my intentions too grubby. And I'm still touching her. Why hasn't she snatched her hand away?

'It's nothing.' So much less than she deserves.

'It's something to me.' The gratitude in her eyes fades, replaced with something else. Something that makes my breath catch. Something I must imagine. She'd never look at *me* that way. Never trust me enough. Not if she knew everything.

I should move. Let go of her wrist. Tell her it was great to catch up after all these years and send her home in my car.

But I'm frozen.

Frozen in time, to our first meeting. Frozen in those heady seconds of possibility when all three of us—Kenzie, Sam and I—were strangers in a bar. Then, I planned to buy her a drink, invite her out, get to know if we had anything in common beyond attraction, which, for me, was pretty instantaneous.

The medieval-torture device strapped to my chest cranks another notch tighter. Breath strangled. Without stepping back I release her wrist, waiting for the tension to snap, but if anything the air around us thins.

She tilts her head. 'I'm glad I came...' A small sigh blows over her plump bottom lip, her gorgeous mouth perilous temptation. And closer than ever before.

The urge to kiss her roars back to life, hijacking my brain, my body and my sanity. I'm steel-hard now, straining the fly of my trousers. Her eyes suck me in. Muscles primed to break the restraints, I'm about pull her close, to cover her mouth with mine, when she emits a nervous laugh.

Steps back.

Shakes her head.

'I'm sorry.' She covers her heated face with her hands.

I'm doused head to toe with ice. I scrub a hand through my hair, a fist forming. What the fuck...? I must have imagined the last few seconds—that look on her face, her rapid breaths and dilated pupils. There's only regret in her eyes now.

My mouth opens and then closes. Do I play the

gentleman, breeze over what my body is desperate to interpret as…a moment? Our first.

She drops her hands from her face and looks away with a snort of embarrassment. 'Clearly I need more help than a job.' She's bright red now, braving it out with a flash of humour and a roll of those expressive eyes. 'If you want to help me out beyond giving me a chance in the kitchen,' she looks at her shuffling feet, 'perhaps you could help me over my dry spell.'

My brain impulses blink in and out like static. *WTF…?* She made light of those momentous words, which have hurled us into a forbidden, previously uncharted no-man's-land.

'I…' I'm gaping, synapses firing so hard I'm surprised my head doesn't explode. Surely she doesn't mean what my brain and dick have concluded?

'What are you saying?' I croak out, too dazed by testosterone for subtlety. Does she mean for me to help, personally—*hell, yes*—or is she asking me to set her up with some other dickhead? *Over my dead body.* But, even if my libido has made the correct interpretation, nothing can happen between us.

Can it?

Kenzie looks down and buttons her coat. The amusement leaches from her face, leaving only the pallor of earlier. 'I'm sorry, Drake—that was unfair.' She raises her wide, vulnerable stare from the carpet and takes in a shuddering breath, eyes full of remorse.

Unfair? Nothing about our circumstances is fair.

'God, I'm such a desperate idiot. Forget I ever came here.' She yanks at the door handle, the metal slipping from her frantic fingers in her haste to flee.

'No… Wait.' I want to rewind the last minute. Have a rerun. Hold her captive until she clarifies *exactly* what she meant.

A metallic click warns me she's succeeded with the door.

I snap to attention.

'Kenzie, wait—'

'I'm sorry.' She's off out of the door and halfway down the corridor before I've pumped enough blood back into my head for my nervous system to work.

'Wait.' I yank my phone from my pocket, everything I want to say locked in that secret place I've guarded for so long, it's like a fucking panic room. 'I'll call my driver to see you home.'

She turns, her breathing still fast, shakes her head. 'I'll be fine.' She trots down the corridor like she can't get away from me quick enough.

I take off at a run, skidding to a halt just as the lift doors close.

I wedge my arm into the closing space. 'He's waiting at the main entrance. Please—it's late.' She can run—she *should* run—but I won't have her in danger.

She nods, eyes wide.

I lock my knees, balanced on a knife-edge. One step and I'd be inside with her. One word and I'd know to hope or to try to rein in the fantasy her comment unleashed.

Static clears. Restraint returns.

I think of Sam. Remove my hand. Wait for tense seconds.

Kenzie's emotions mirror mine, the doors closing on the regret on her face.

CHAPTER THREE

Kenzie

I'M THIRTY MINUTES early for my first shift at the Faulkner, despite the nerves riding me, threatening to make me flee back home. I believed I'd blown my chance by my behaviour, but Drake's text yesterday shows the strength of his loyalty to Sam:

Come to the Faulkner at nine sharp tomorrow.

That he would still offer me my shot after I practically propositioned him… My face heats again at the memory of my confession that it's been too long since I was intimate with someone and my suggestion *he* might be the one to help.

I'd almost made a fool of myself.

Almost kissed him.

Drake Faulkner of all people.

A man who was practically a brother to Sam. A man of honour and integrity. A man who'd never think of me as anything but Sam's widow… He showed me that by keeping his distance all these years, and his cool reception in the restaurant two nights ago proved nothing has changed.

Was I *that* lonely, *that* sexually frustrated or just curious to explore the flicker of attraction that, had I not once been married to his best friend, had potential to flare like a blowtorch…?

I worry at my lip, shake any notion that isn't strictly professional from my head and focus on filling out the Faulkner's paperwork. I'm going to cook my arse off, wow the restaurant's Michelin-starred head chef and stay the hell away from Drake. Clearly my lonely, neglected libido can't be trusted around hotness of his calibre…

Why has it chosen now to come out of hibernation? Not once in the past three years have I looked at a man in a sexual way. Not even during the rocky last year of my marriage to Sam, when I had the perfect justification had I wanted, was I tempted by another.

Why now? Why Drake? Yes, I'm ready to get my life back on track, but am I ready to embrace intimacy again?

I add my signature to the bottom of the form with a flourish of finality. This is my chance to build something for myself, a career I've been too busy to pursue, here, close enough to Tilly to support her burgeoning independence. I cannot screw this up. Especially not with any further ideas of kissing Drake Faulkner, sex with Drake Faulkner or making Drake Faulkner see me as more than the wife of his friend.

I take a cleansing breath and hand in the forms. The Faulkner's Human-Resources manager passes me a temporary security card and leads me upstairs. In the stairwell, the scent of onions and garlic and red wine waft to my nose. My stomach clenches, but with excitement. I touch the pristine chef whites folded in my bag, buzzing to get started.

'The boss wants to see you. He'll introduce you to the rest of the kitchen staff.' The woman from HR swings open the door and points me in the right direction down a nondescript corridor. 'Second door on the left.'

Behind the scenes, the luxury of the Faulkner the guests see persists with the same plush carpet and soothing decor. I suck in a deep breath, a little intimidated by meeting Rod for the first time, which is probably why I come to an abrupt standstill in the doorway when I find Drake sitting behind the desk, talking on the phone.

Heat shunts my entire body up in flames as my eyes latch to his moving mouth. I almost kissed him. Almost begged him for the sex he would have probably treated his date to, had I not gatecrashed.

Drake's green eyes land on mine, pinning me to the threshold.

No smile of welcome. Just that impenetrable stare, which could mean anything from *I'm seconds from tearing off your clothes* to *I'm still smarting at your inappropriate behaviour.*

I lift my chin and stare back. There's no shame in

admitting you haven't had sex for three years. That you've been busy rebuilding your life, regaining your confidence and changing career paths. And I made myself a promise, packed it safely in the boxes with my belongings when I moved to London—no more putting myself last. Time to make something happen.

Of course, kissing Drake hadn't been one of those promises.

Drake's brows slant downwards and his mouth tightens. 'I'll call you back.' He disconnects the call while I dither in the doorway, torn between running to the nearest fast-food restaurant advertising a vacancy and riding out my mortification.

I stand tall. We're adults. I've been looking after myself and my sister since the age of twenty-one, since the death of our parents in a car crash. I can handle one inconvenient little sexual attraction…

'Hi.' I didn't actually touch a single hair on his glorious head. I can laugh off the rest—hypothermia and too much wine… Not that we've ever teased each other, as if we both subconsciously knew playing it straight guaranteed the boundaries stayed in place.

Drake stands, beckoning me inside and showing off his broad chest in another of his crisp shirts. 'Good morning. Are you all signed in?' I guess we're not going to talk about my overt proposition. He's right. I, too, should pretend it never happened and get on with proving myself worthy of the vacancy.

I nod. Perhaps women come on to him so often, he didn't even notice. A flash of foolish disappointment clouds my buoyant mood. But then, what was I expecting from the ice king? *Hi, Kenz. I've thought about what you said and I'd be happy to break your sexual dry spell—now, then, doggy or missionary first...?*

I swallow at the lurid images my shrivelled ovaries have helped me create and press my thighs together. The man standing in front of me dressed for a boardroom fills his suit like he belongs on a billboard, but clearly my interest isn't reciprocated.

I drag my eyes away from the open neck of his shirt, deciding it's best to forget I all but pestered a man who could barely tolerate a cordial conversation with me for sex.

'Thanks for this—I really appreciate the opportunity.' I rub at my wrist, remembering the illicit heat of his fingers on my skin. I must have imagined the way his eyes dipped to my mouth and his head lowered a fraction as we invaded previously uncharted personal space.

He grimaces, as if he's recalling the fool I made of myself. 'No need to thank me. Have you been to HR?'

I nod, my head wooden.

He's definitely not going to bring up my confession. Rather than congratulate my escape, that he couldn't have noticed me mooning up at him, it feels like a backwards step. Last night, talking with him by the fire... I've never felt closer to this man I've known for years, but don't really know.

My feet shuffle backwards, embarrassment a thread tugging me to a safe distance. 'Well. I'm sure you're busy enough without welcoming the newbie. I'll just…head to the kitchen…'

'Not so fast.' He cuts off my nervous over-talking. 'I'll show you the way.' He waits for me to vacate the doorway and indicates the route, while he shrugs back into his suit jacket.

My pulse may as well be a ping-pong ball bouncing all over the place. This is stupid and hardly the behaviour of a grown woman with her shit together. I suck in a breath, preparing to reveal the elephant in the room.

But Drake interrupts. 'I told you Rod is…temperamental.' He holds open the fire door and ushers me though. Professional. No touching. A perfect gentleman.

'But we don't tolerate harassment or bullying here at the Faulkner.' He shoots me a serious look. My steps inch closer to his, as if of their own accord. A fraction closer and our arms might brush. I exhale through pursed lips—I'm playing with fire, but can't seem to stop. Is this loneliness or liberation? Grasping the possibility of moving on with my physical life as well as my professional one?

'Anything of that nature—I want to hear about it, understood?' He pauses to hold open another door.

I've never seen him so…protective.

An almost giddy bubble of laughter rises up to escape. 'I can handle myself, don't worry.' I'm warm all over, a foreign feeling I know better than to trust. But I can surely enjoy the concern he probably offers all new employees for a few heady seconds…

He pauses, turning to face me, giving me the decadence of his undivided attention. My clothes, a sweater and jeans, cling too tight at the look on his face, which reminds me once, not so long ago, this urbane man was a soldier.

'I mean it, Kenzie—I want to hear about any misdemeanours, verbal or…physical.'

His concern washes me with heat. Mmm…misdemeanours. Then nerves spoil it, causing me to snort out a laugh. 'What's he going to do? Dice me into tiny pieces with a chef's knife? Hide me in the walk-in freezer?'

Drake's mouth flattens as if he's smelled something unpleasant, but he doesn't elaborate. And then we're off again. 'I'll show you where the chef whites are kept and then I'll take you to the staff changing rooms.'

'I have whites.' I force my eyes away from the clench of his muscular arse as he walks. I shouldn't notice, but there must be something in the London water. I can't decide if I prefer him in his tailored suit or his combat dress.

Drake opens another door, flicking on lights, and I follow him inside a long, narrow storeroom lined with shelves.

'The Faulkner whites are monogrammed.' He

strides to the back, his hand rifling through the piles of crisp white laundered uniforms.

'I can find the right size, if you want.' I know the Faulkner brothers have a hands-on attitude when it comes to running their chain of London-based hotels, but his attentiveness seems above and beyond, even for the widow of a friend. 'I'm sure you have more pressing things on your agenda?'

Drake turns, thrusting the garments at me with a grim expression, his obliging orientation now a distant memory.

I glance down.

He's guessed my size correctly.

When I smile up in thanks, his brow is pinched in a frown, his dark eyes unreadable. His hands fist in his pockets, the bumps of his knuckles showing through the fabric. He's wary, looking at me like he expects me to strip right here and beg him to shag me out of my desperate state.

I sigh. Here is as good a place as any. No more chickening out. He deserves a thorough apology and more of an explanation—time to clear the air. I put him in a shitty position that night, just because I'm embracing my new life a little too thoroughly, and he handled it with the levels of discretion and integrity I'd expect.

'Look, Drake, about the other night—'

'I can't stop thinking about what you said.' His confession rushes out, his words clashing with mine, his voice low, gruff, and his eyes the emerald colour of a wine bottle.

The tiny room shrinks, compressing the air. The fluorescent tube buzzing overhead replicates the buzz in my nervous system, every sense on high alert.

My head vibrates the loudest, filling in the blanks. He's furious I crossed the line. I've messed this up, before I've even started. I should never have gone to that hotel suite with him—my reaction to seeing him again in the restaurant on a date with another woman provided enough of a clue that I have chemistry with him.

But why is his stare filled with heat?

'I…I was inappropriate—I'm really sorry. It's just that it's been a long time since I've felt desired.' Even before Sam's death. 'Can't we just…forget it?' I'm happy to plead, not just for my potential job, which is literally slipping through my fingers like grains of rice, but for the intact memory of his friendship with Sam. I made this mess—time to clean up after myself.

'Did you mean it?' His mouth is still grim. He's not even going to cut me a little slack, even for old times' sake.

My shoulders collapse and I look at our feet, my Converse toe-to-toe with his brogues. 'That I haven't had sex for three years…?' My voice trails away to a whisper. I clear my throat. 'Of course I meant it.' I'm not sure which mortification is worse—that I'm admitting my pathetic lack of a sex life to a man I don't share a confessional kind of relationship with, or that, when I brought up a solution that night, I was deadly serious.

But neither matters.

He's shown me over and over that he doesn't see me that way. 'I'm just lonely, probably. I haven't had any time for making…friends yet.' I should take a leaf out of his book. I should remember who he is—Sam's friend—and that he's the last man on earth likely to want something physical with me. No matter how temporary.

'I mean…' He steps closer. The toes of his shoes touch the toes of mine, and his body heat warms my breasts, my downturned face. '…About helping you out of your dry spell—did you mean it?'

The air thins. My lungs catch fire. I brazen it out, lifting my chin and latching on to his heated eye contact, only inches away. I shouldn't want him. But I do.

My knees almost buckle with need to feel something other than second best.

I nod.

A single decisive gesture.

'I—' I don't finish. Drake's hands cup my face.

With a strangled whimper, I drop the whites and my bag and reach for his shoulders. He swoops his mouth down on mine, my feet straining on tiptoe so I can get closer to his kiss, which is hot and possessive and so welcome, the head rush gives me vertigo as he drags a sob of relief from me.

So long. So, so long since I've felt this heady physical connection to a man. So long since I've felt desired, wanted.

With an unintelligible growl, Drake's lips encourage mine open, his tongue surging against mine before my brain has even registered I'm kissing Drake Faulkner. And he's kissing me.

Madness.

Euphoria.

I need to stop.

But as soon as I pull away I'm right back there for a second addictive taste, my mouth seeking his once more as he walks me backwards and presses me up against the shelves at my back.

My mind, all my faculties, actually blink out for a few seconds, so heady is the feel of this big, strong man before me, his large hands tangled in my hair, his broad chest colliding with my nipples, his breath gusting in and out and his erection a rigid length against my belly.

Heat pools between my legs and my blood sings. It's as if I've locked my femininity into a box and he's turned the rusty key, setting me free. Three long years of doubt dissolve for a few giddy seconds.

When I open my eyes he's looking down at me, his mouth still dragging moans from my throat. When he boldly palms my breast, as if he's thought about doing it a thousand times, and thumbs my nipple into a hard peak through my shirt, I want to weep.

So good, I'm on the verge of combusting.

I gasp and pull away from his mouth, needing more oxygen to handle his touch. But I want more— this is too good to pass up. I push his jacket over his shoulders and slide my hands down his back, savouring every bump and ridge of muscle I skim over on the way to his arse. I cup his toned backside, shunting his hips forward until the hard tip of him nudges my clit through my clothes and I bite my lip, I'm so close to coming. From just a few forbidden kisses and an ungainly dry hump.

Drake dives for my mouth once more as if he knows what my body craves, and I tangle my hands in his hair, revelling in the contrast of the shorn strands at his nape, which scrape the sensitive pads of my fingers, and the longer, silky strands on top. And then I'm being hoisted onto the shelf and Drake is between my thighs, his mouth on my neck and his hand rubbing me through my jeans.

'Fuck, Kenzie…' he rasps against my skin, his stubble scraping.

'Yes…' I all but hiss. I gyrate my hips against his hand, all arguments about why this is the worst idea in the world drowned out by the hormones raging through me and how right this feels, which is heightened tenfold by the magic wielded by Drake's hand and his mouth.

I need this. I want this, with him. Just one time. The perfect antidote to the years of feeling inferior. I deserve this, don't I, just like I deserve to chase my dreams?

It's not until this moment that I realise the shaky feeling deep inside is vulnerability. I trust Drake. My body chose him, seemingly independently of my psyche. He's decent and considered and earnest. He's not going to use me, dump his load and run or want anything from me that I can't give.

Perhaps that's why my subconscious chose him. Drake won't want anything beyond the physical.

It's an addictive, heady realisation. I lose myself in his kiss once more, blotting out reason, memories and any other thought that might drag me from the quicksand of desire I'm in up to my neck.

Voices on the other side of the door see Drake springing back like he's been scalded and me helping him get there with a hefty push to the chest.

'Fuck.' He looks at me, panting. His mouth is red and his hair fucked by my fingers. He adjusts his cock and reality douses me like an ice-bucket challenge.

What did I do? To Sam's friend Drake? I kissed Drake. I dry-humped Drake. I rode Drake's hand. At work. On my very first day.

My thighs judder, the remnants of delicious pleasure tendrils fading to be replaced by the momentarily forgotten doubts.

Drake clears his throat and swoops down to collect my things from the floor. I take my bag from him with trembling fingers, eyes downcast. Shame lashes my skin, a million pinpricks, making way for the hollow swell of loneliness, twice the size of the burden I arrived with.

My throat is too tight to speak. I busy myself with folding the pristine white uniform I've already sullied. Not only have I just jeopardised my one chance at a job—in other words, even if I'm good enough, I've shown willing to shag the boss—but I've also just kissed a man. A man that isn't Sam. Almost done more than simply kiss him, although there was nothing simple or innocent about what just transpired.

Would we have stopped, but for that interruption?

I bite my lip, my burning eyes flitting to anywhere but him. I fiddle with my ponytail and wipe the lip gloss from my chin in lieu of blurting out another pointless apology, or freeing the hot sobs clogging my throat.

Drake turns his back, silently giving me some seconds to compose myself, and then he opens the door. Drake is back together. His jacket donned, his tie straightened and his hair tamed.

As I pass him on the threshold he blocks my exit with his arm.

'I'm in a board meeting until six tonight. Don't leave until we've had another discussion.' And with that he lowers his arm and strides back the way we came, leaving me shell-shocked, my good intentions ripped in two.

CHAPTER FOUR

Drake

'WHAT DO YOU MEAN, she's not here?' I scan the chaotic kitchen, which is bustling with the prep for early-evening dining, my body temperature boiling over.

Rod slices shallots at the speed of light and shoots me a grin laced with malicious delight. 'First day and already she's upsetting the boss, eh? Shame...she's not a bad worker.' His lip curls like he wants to say more. Like he's thinking more.

I make a fist, already teetering on the edge at finding Kenzie gone. One word. That's all it would take for Rod to walk away from his position here minus his front teeth. But he must sense the quality of the ice he's skating because he quickly amends his response.

'She left an hour ago.' He shrugs and turns back to his sizzling-hot pan.

But I've heard enough.

She's gone. My plan to put a line under what happened and ensure it never happens again, even if I have to gouge out my eyes with a wooden spoon or chain myself to my office chair, peters out.

I should have shown better control. She's probably devastated by the whole fan-fucking-tastic kissing thing. Mortified that a man who is supposed to be her husband's best friend would stoop so low. Perhaps even grieving anew over Sam because of my behaviour…

My own stomach gripes. What was I thinking? I certainly wasn't thinking about Sam.

Abandoning the kitchen, I storm back through the hotel and into the lift for the underground car park. The mirrored interior of the lift mocks me with my reflection. I wince, looking away from my own stupid face. I crossed the line so badly, fucking sprinted over it, in the end, for all my talk about keeping my distance, keeping my promises and despite every other excuse I'd invented to keep my hands off Kenzie Porter.

Every reservation frittered away like sand through a sieve, the moment I touched my mouth to hers. Not that kissing her hadn't surpassed every single one of my fantasies of how she would taste or feel—soft lips moving against mine, the slide of her tongue, first hesitant and then voracious, as if her need consumed her as much as mine controlled me. Better than I'd ever imagined. And I'm an expert on Kenzie fantasies.

No—I took advantage. I need to make this right. Not for Sam, or for my own fresh well of guilt.

But for Kenzie. She deserves her chance after everything she's been through.

I reach my car, gun the engine and roar from my parking space, the squeal of the tyres on the concrete welcome and matching the noise in my head.

I idle at the security barrier, cursing the seconds it takes to rise, but also wishing it would trap me inside for good. Because I should stay away and simply send a brief message—*It will not happen again*...

As today progressed and away from her temptation—the apple scent of her hair, the cute way her nose wrinkles and the sexy sound of her voice—I found perspective.

The kiss had been a vile imposition, a huge mistake—one of weakness on my part and, as she said, for her, one of loneliness. I slap the steering wheel. Of course she'd be lonely—she's just moved to a new city. That she came to me for a fresh start fills me up and dries me to a husk in the same breath, I'm so conflicted. And what did I do? I fucked it up, at the very first hurdle. In one stupid, reckless move, I doubled my own guilt and put her in a compromising position, blurred the personal-professional line until it was little more than a grey smudge.

No wonder she ran out.

Sam's best friend...?

I wince, hating that I took advantage of someone

vulnerable. Someone I'm supposed to be looking out for. Someone I let down. But *my* role in this mess could be rectified with better control—I managed to keep my distance for three years; a couple of weeks should be a doddle. It's not too late to forget that kiss. To forget that fantasy paled against the reality.

I grip the wheel like I'm trying to snap it in two, breaking a few speed limits. If my behaviour has tarnished the memory of Sam for her in some way, I'll have to live with that knowledge. Another weight strapped to my back.

When I realise I've driven to Kenzie's address, I sit in the car for five minutes until I have clarity.

Apologise.

Assure her that the fucking astounding kiss won't happen again.

Leave and keep my distance.

The rap of my knuckles punctuates my resolve. She opens the door, flushed, hair damp from a shower and dressed only in a robe.

Shit. This is my punishment.

I suck it up, calling on deeply ingrained military training to keep my hands by my sides and my eyes from scouring the body I'd felt every inch of up close and personal earlier.

'Are you going out? We need to talk.' My voice, curt, gruff, is snagged somewhere between my brain and my tight vocal cords.

She shakes her head. 'I just had a shower after work. It's been a long day.' Her eyes narrow at the arsehole standing on her doorstep wearing a scowl and berating her, when all he should be doing is swearing he'll never touch her again and walking away.

I scrub a hand over my stubbled face and glance around the freezing, dingy hallway, which is decorated with linoleum that dates back to the seventies. My shoulders lift until they practically touch my ears. 'Shouldn't you be more safety conscious?' I can't help myself. That she lives here, in what looks like a tiny, one-bed, ground-floor flat, physically pains me. It's not the dodgiest end of London, but neither is it the palace she deserves.

She crosses her arms over her chest and the robe slides open a fraction. 'I have a spyhole—I saw you.'

That fraction, that sliver of creamy thigh, is all I need to send my pulse and blood pressure through the top of my head.

A bad fucking idea. Don't go inside. Say what you have to say and get the fuck away from her.

She lifts her chin. 'Are there any other reprimands, Lieutenant, or are we done?'

When I stay silent but also stay frozen in the doorway, she sighs. 'Why don't you come in so we can do this without my neighbours listening?' She opens the door and, like an idiot, I step inside, taking in the flat in one swoop.

It's minuscule but clean and homely. Kenzie has clearly given it a once-over, imprinting her style on the space with some art on the walls, coordinated cushions on the couch and soft lighting coming from several lamps. The tiny kitchen resembles a workspace, with equipment lining the bench and utensil racks on the walls. Something smells delicious—my stomach growls, reminding me I haven't eaten dinner. But the way my gut twists and turns, food is the last thing I want.

'Do you want a drink? I was just having one.' She points to an open bottle of red on the coffee table. I drag in a calming breath. She looks tired, her eyes a little haunted. Because of the kiss? Have my actions reopened her grief?

I shake my head, wound too tight by the memories of her mouth on mine to tempt fate. My inhibitions are low enough. Despite the speech I'm about to deliver, I want to peel open the silky robe separating me from what I'm sure is nirvana, lay her back on the couch and plunge my tongue inside her and then suck on her clit until all I can think, taste and feel is Kenzie.

'I've come to apologise. I won't be staying long enough for a drink.' Certainly not long enough for the stuff-of-dreams couch scenario…

Kenzie rounds those eyes on me and takes a generous sip of her wine. 'For what?' She stares over the rim and then her tongue catches the wine on her bottom lip.

I swallow, my balls rising up, ready for action. 'For what happened this morning—it won't happen again.'

But fuck, I'm not sorry.

If that was my one taste, I'll take it, happy to pay the price for eternity. My only regret is that I might have caused her pain by betraying Sam's memory.

Instead of sitting, she takes another slow swallow while she watches me, her lips parted and stained red. I want to kiss them so bad, taste her again, lick the wine from her mouth and then explore every inch of her hiding under the robe.

'Okay.'

Okay...? No accusations? No demands? No slap in the face?

She places her glass on the table and skirts me, giving me a wide berth. I keep my distance, swivelling on the spot to watch her path while my scalp prickles.

She opens the door and leans her hip on the edge. 'So you don't want a drink and you've apologised. I guess all that remains is to say goodbye. See you around some time.' Sparks glitter in her eyes. Challenge and provocation.

Yes. Time to leave. But like this...?

She's still angry with me. I'm half tempted to call her bluff and leave with a polite nod. That's exactly what I *should* do...

'I know you're angry and you have every right— I shouldn't have touched you.'

'I'm not angry, Drake.' Her voice is glacial. 'I get it. You think you crossed a line. You think you took advantage of me—'

'Didn't I?' Breathing actually hurts. Doesn't she sense the danger, see what a terrible…fucking awesome…idea this is?

She rolls her eyes. 'Don't be stupid. I'm not a child.' Her stare blazes, all woman.

Some sort of poltergeist has control of my vocal cords. 'Were you looking for a relationship? Because I don't do that.'

Not with you, and you don't want that from me.

She laughs, the sound hollow. 'Don't tell me what I'm looking for and don't flatter yourself. Perhaps I was lonely for physical contact. Perhaps the new me chose to seize the day. Perhaps I just wanted sex. No empty words. No promises. Just to feel wanted again. But if it's not going to work for you…' she shrugs '…no hard feelings.' She glances out into the gloomy hallway while the seconds beat shock waves through my brain.

'My door is still open.' Her lips part, her chest rising and falling.

'Are you baiting me?' I step closer, my temperature soaring and my control fraying. She's too close. Her warm, womanly scent a potent aphrodisiac.

She shakes her head, her hair sliding over her delicate shoulders. 'Not baiting. But what else is there to say?' She sucks in air, her breasts shifting under the silk. Then she releases a breathy sigh I want to swallow up. 'No one has touched me in a sexual way for a very long time, Drake. *I'm* not sorry about kissing you. In fact, I want more. I want it all.'

I practically swallow my own tongue. Throughout her speech I've grown increasingly hard. Now my dick is ready to burst through the zip of my trousers.

I slide my eyes over her bare, shapely legs poking from the bottom of the robe. Damn, even her feet are sexy, her toenails painted blue to match the robe.

'This isn't a good idea. You know this isn't a good idea. Too much shared history.' Too complicated. Too forbidden. I've already taken this further than I should. I try to recall my prepared speech and plan... Nope, not a single fucking word...

She shrugs. 'Maybe not. But it doesn't have to be complicated. Just temporary. I know you won't hurt me.'

She's right—I won't cause her any more pain than I already have by making her a widow. But if only the rest were true. If only I could give her what she wants. Act on my attraction, without consequences. I curl my hands into fists, torn between the need burning in Kenzie's eyes and the escape of the cold, empty foyer beyond her door.

I should take the escape route.

I'm two steps away from doing the decent thing. The self-preserving thing. But my feet may as well be encased in concrete.

I want more... It doesn't have to be complicated... Just temporary.

Fuck, I want to shackle myself, not flee.

I look at the woman I once knew only from a self-imposed distance, forcing myself to look closely.

Her hungry eyes boldly hold mine, her pulse flutters in her neck and her breaths practically pant in her chest. She's excited, perhaps even sharing the near-combustible desire turning my resolve to ash. One thing is clear—she knows exactly what she wants. I was a fool to forget she has steel running through her skeleton.

I suck in air, dragging my mind from the erotic scenarios involving Kenzie naked and me meeting all of her needs until neither of us can walk and try to imagine what it's been like for her these past three years. Try to put myself in her shoes. Could I have survived without sex for so long? I snort. Stupid fucking question.

'Look, I'm a big girl.' She lifts her chin. 'If you're not interested, just say so. I can take it.'

Not interested…? If I weren't focussed on keeping my heart beating, I'd laugh. She won't wait for ever. And there'll be a queue of willing candidates around the block. With a roll of my guts, I recall the look on Rod's face when he talked about her earlier. She's a beautiful woman. She's kind and funny and caring. The whole package. A keeper for some lucky bastard. But if she's ready to be intimate with someone again, fuck if I want it to be with anyone but me.

My voice emerges, strangled. 'This isn't a good idea.'

She shrugs, but the stakes, the longing, are written all over her beautiful face. 'You said that. Look, I'm not asking for anything more than sex, one time, two… Clearly my body has decided it's time to cast off celibacy.' She swallows, her eyes darting away. She has no need to feel embarrassed. That she's chasing what she wants makes her twice as tempting. Another show of her strength—making herself vulnerable, admitting she has needs that aren't being met because of circumstance.

Because of me. Because I let Sam down. I let her down.

She looks directly at me. 'I don't have to explain myself to you, or persuade you—'

'Fucking right you *don't* have to persuade me.' I'm practically drooling. Only fear of making this mess worse keeps my feet still.

She continues as if I haven't spoken. 'It would just be good to get past what feels like a hurdle with someone I know… To get my confidence back without having to expose myself to fifty bad dates with strangers.'

Of course, if not with me she might rush into this with the wrong man.

'Perhaps then, one day, I could think seriously about…dating again.' She pins me with a stare that lets me know she's deadly serious, determination that pulses heat through my engorged cock.

'I'm twenty-eight, Drake. I'm not a nun.'

No, more's the pity. Fuck, this woman tests me to the limit, always has, even when the conversation between us has been about the weather and included Sam. But now…talking about sex…with the taste of her kiss still fresh in my mouth and the memory of her sexy little moans in my head as I teased that hard nipple and stroked her heated centre through her jeans…

She may not be a nun, but I'm sure as shit no saint either.

Still, restraint tightens my muscles.

I move in front of her, placing my hand above hers on the open door and holding her eye contact. 'You're sure you want this?' The words release a torrent of endorphins. I'm so close. But the stakes are a slap of reality.

'There's no margin for error here. If we cross this line we do it together, eyes wide open.' I have so much regret where she's concerned, I don't need another layer of guilt that I somehow duped her or took advantage.

She nods, a shuddering breath lifting her perfect breasts into my peripheral vision, although I keep my eyes glued to hers, needing to be certain I'm seeing the truth, and not just what I badly want to see.

'No feelings…' I can't risk more than sex, not that she'd ever want more from me. But I can give her this, can't I? I can lock down everything else and enjoy a tiny part of what I've craved as long as I've known this astounding woman. I should feel euphoric that I'm seconds away from finally exploring something I've fought long and hard to deny, but need steals all my oxygen.

'Just temporary,' she says, her hand sliding from the door, releasing it to my decision.

I swing my arm back, the sound of the door clicking closed both exhilarating and a seal to our shared fate. Because seconds after that click registers she's in my arms, her mouth frantic on mine and her hands tangled in my hair.

This kiss makes a mockery of our first, because this time I anticipate the elation that pounds through me the minute our lips connect. I shelve doubt and embrace every second.

I swivel us around, pressing her into the back of the closed door, and crush my aching dick between our bodies so I can slake some of the need eating me alive.

I grind into her, my mouth picking up where we left off this morning. Kissing Kenzie is everything. Kissing her the way I've done in my imagination over and over again almost buckles my knees.

She takes what she needs, her tongue meeting mine, her hands roughly angling my head so we can plunder deeper and her body writhing against me like she's trying to simultaneously stimulate every nerve in her body.

Reality is so much better than fantasy.

And then I groan, because the heat from between her legs registers against my thigh, burning through the fabric of my trousers like molten metal. She's scorching hot and damp enough to leave a wet patch and I fucking love that I've done that to her. Love that she's ready for me. Love that she was standing here getting turned on just by my presence, even as she showed me the door.

I pull my mouth away, rearing back from the tight hold she has on my hair. 'You're sure, Kenz? Tell me.' There can't be any doubt. She's too precious to me to fuck around. If I could stop dry-humping her for one second I'd get her to sign a contract. But I can give her this—great sex. Drag my mind away from the betrayal, from the secrets trapped inside me and simply be what she, this brave, ballsy woman, needs right now.

'Yes… Drake…' She nods, as if she's too overcome to utter another sound, but it's all the encouragement I need. How long have I yearned to hear her speak my name with passion, longing, almost delirium? How many times have I dreamed of rendering her incoherent? How many nights have I lain awake, wondering what it's like to touch her, to hold her, to make her come?

I kiss her again, lifting her bare arse and wrapping her legs around my waist so I can align our bodies more effectively. She cries out and her heat covers my dick, adding to the delicious friction that's shunting towards unbearable levels with every grind. If I don't get some skin-on-skin soon, I might start ripping at fabric…

I nibble on her lip and kiss along her jaw until my nose is buried in her hair, where the scent of apples is strongest. I suck the delicate skin of her neck into my mouth, making her back arch and her hips buck into mine, writhing on me with a wildness I've felt a million times in my dreams, and her noises…

Fuck, her mewls and sighs as she takes what she wants, takes what she needs from me, make my balls boil until I have to ease back to control the delirious attention my dick is receiving.

I take a second's reprieve from simply enjoying every fantastic second to wonder at the location of the nearest condom.

Then the icy deluge covers me, head to toe.

Shit.

I have nothing.

I was so adamant I wasn't going to touch her, I've sabotaged the best moment of my life.

I rest my forehead against hers, stilling the movement of my hips and sucking in calming breaths while I try to rein this back a thousand notches. 'I didn't bring any condoms.'

I want to cut out my own tongue. What a fucking idiot. Tomorrow I'll buy a jumbo box and stash two in the pocket of every pair of trousers I own. No, make it three. Damn, I'll scatter them like confetti…

Kenzie sobers enough to look up at me with lust-filled eyes. And then she grins, her neck flushing. 'I have some. I bought them on the way home from work…just in case.'

My heart soars into my throat. 'You did?' She's been thinking about this? All day? Our minds are aligned. But where I tried to talk myself out of this, she prepared.

Wonderful woman.

She nods and I cover her mouth again, hitching her arse higher so I can nudge open her robe with my face and get my mouth around one of those tasty nipples. I can't contain the groan that leaves me at the sight of her naked breast—it's too much. But I'm quickly swamped by the taste of her skin and the hard bud on my tongue and the way her cries fracture as I press it between my flattened tongue and the back of my top teeth.

I press closer. Even if I were a contortionist, I couldn't get enough contact for satisfaction. I hoist her higher. Couch or the bedroom?

I release her nipple, chuckling at her wail of outrage, and slide my mouth over the curve of her breast. Her skin is baby-soft, her scent a shot of heroin to my neurotransmitters. I kiss and lick and suck my way across her chest and back towards the heaven of her mouth. Then I hoist her around my waist and carry her towards the bedroom.

The flat is so small we're there in three or four strides—perfect. I've reached my limit of impatience where Kenzie is concerned. I lay her down on the bed, loosen the belt around her waist and peel the robe open so I can see her perfection laid out before me.

Time stutters to a halt. She's wondrous—her nakedness surpassing my imagination a millionfold.

'Drake…?' She must interpret my sudden still-ness as hesitation.

'I'm looking.' That's when I spy the mark I've left behind on her breast—redness from the scrape of my facial hair and a purplish bruise at its centre. Fuck, a hickey…? The primal roar in my head warns me how badly I want this. Want her.

I close my eyes, the sight of my possession on her skin too much.

When I open my eyes I trace the bruise with a fingertip. 'I'm sorry. I marked you.' The Neander-thal in me isn't one bit sorry. In fact, he's running a victory lap around the stadium wearing a shit-eating grin while his loincloth flaps in the breeze…

She looks down, her pupils dilating as if she, too, likes the sight of my possession. 'Good.'

I shrug off my jacket and loosen my tie, my eyes still gorging. How did I get so lucky? My throat closes—a good thing because I want to say a whole lot more. I could wax lyrical all day on the visual feast laid out on the bed. I bite my cheek and unbut-ton my shirt. Tossing it on the floor, I allow my stare to linger on the pink, pouty lips between her legs. I undo my belt and the button of my trousers, slip off my shoes and drop to my knees.

She raises her head off the bed and peers down at me, her face breathtakingly vulnerable, eyes wide with questions. Hesitations.

I slide my hands up her thighs, too impatient to get my mouth on her but needing to savour every second of this. If this is my one time with her, I need to make it count. To make it good for her. To force every touch, every sound, every taste into my long-term memory for all of eternity.

I breathe through my nose, sucking in her womanly scent, the best aphrodisiac known to man.

She props herself up on her elbows, covers my hand with hers, guiding me to cup her breast. Our hands slide in unison over the perfect curve. 'Touch me,' she whispers. 'Feels so good.'

She's killing me.

I'm done fighting.

I keep one hand at her breast while I slide the other between her thighs to her slick centre. She's drenched. I look down and she spreads her thighs, letting me in. I part her and push first one finger and then a second inside.

Watching my fingers disappear into her tight warmth is the single most erotic moment of my life, especially as her hand presses mine closer to her breast, her thumb bumping mine around her taut nipple as we grapple to inflict pleasure. She whimpers, husking out my name again as I plunge and withdraw my fingers with a twist of my wrist.

I look up. Her rapture-slack face is too much. 'Fuck, you're beautiful.' I abandon her breast and scoop my arm around her hips and tug her arse to the edge of the bed. 'I have to taste you.'

I'm all out of patience. Without withdrawing my fingers, I cover her soft pink folds with my mouth.

She cries out, her hands gripping my face as she looks down at me with wonder and lust. That look, like I'm saving her from a fate worse than death, makes all the years of denial seep away.

Her scent and taste coat my mouth, her moans drench my eardrums, filling up my senses with Kenzie. She's mine in that second, filling all the empty places in me.

I slide my tongue up to her clit, laving and sucking while I keep my eyes locked on hers until she's gasping and tugging at my hair with erratic jerks. I don't want to miss one second of that wonder on her face, her pleasure intense. Because of me.

I prime her clit for a few strokes and then I switch it up, my tongue replacing my fingers inside her and my drenched fingers sliding over her swollen clit. It's so good I can't decide which way I prefer, but Kenzie can. She gasps, grips my hair by the roots and bucks her hips up to meet my face, her thighs buffeting my head with the ecstasy she can't contain.

'Drake, oh, Drake... I'm going to...'

She doesn't finish, because I finish her. I spear my tongue as deep as I can, my fingers rubbing her through the convulsions of her orgasm as she comes on my tongue. My growl joins her broken cries and I prolong the best head I've ever given with a few more thrusts.

I'll never get enough. I want more. To claim every inch of her with my touch.

She pushes at my shoulders and I withdraw with

reluctance. Kenzie has just become my favourite meal. I could eat her for hours, now I've tasted her; I'm ruined…

'Oh, my fucking hell…' She flops back on the bed, her breasts rising and falling with her laboured breaths. I shed the rest of my clothes and climb above her, capturing her pants with my kiss. She grips my cheeks and sucks herself from my lips and tongue. 'That was incredible. Drake. I need you to do that to me again. Oh…wow…'

I smile past her nibbling kisses. 'Anytime, gorgeous. Condom?' I can't wait any longer to get inside her tight warmth.

She twists beneath me and reaches under her pillow, her cheeks joining the pinkness of her chest and neck from her orgasm. 'I rushed to stash them there before I opened the door. Spyhole, remember…?'

'Fucking fantastic plan—well done.' This woman will be the death of me. They'll have to cite her name on my death certificate:

Cause of Death: extreme sexual frustration relating to McKenzie Porter.

The best way to go.

She tears open the condom and rolls it over me before I've had a chance to clear my head of the implications of what she did. But then my mind is blank again because she tugs my mouth down to her kiss and pumps my already weeping cock in her hand.

I wince, the raw pleasure of her touching me like this too acute.

'Drake. I need you inside me.' She squeezes me, her pupils so big her eyes are black.

'I need that, too.' I take her hand from my cock and press it beside her head on the mattress, our fingers interlocked as I slide a kiss over her parted lips. While her tongue duels with mine I spread her thighs wide with my knees and then angle the tip of my erection to her opening. Kenzie raises her hips and the head of my cock, the most sensitive part, is swallowed by the clasp of her tight heat. I groan. It's too good. Too everything. Something I've only dreamed.

I rear away from her sensual mouth. To make this last I'm going to need every scrap of control I possess, and her kisses drive me right to the brink.

With both her roaming hands pinned down, I sink into her eyes as I push all the way inside. She gasps, her throat exposed as she pushes her head back into the bed. I bite my tongue, the slice of pain distracting my strung-out body from the intense pleasure of Kenzie's sex sucking me in, inch by inch.

'You feel so good.' She bites her lip.

'Don't stop.' A low moan.

'Drake, I need this.' She untangles one hand from mine and touches her own nipple, fingers tweaking until the peak is dark and elongated.

The erotic sight burns into my brain.

I squeeze the fingers of her one hand, powering into her again and again, my jaw clamped tight. Savouring, slowly worshipping, making love—I tell myself that's not my role. Not what she wants from me. But I can give her what she said she needs.

She wanted a leg back up into the saddle. That's all. And it has to be enough.

Sweat breaks out on my neck and chest. The bed thumps the wall and I'm about to pull back, to lessen my pounding hips, when she cries out, her legs wrapping around my waist so she can cling, lift her pelvis from the bed and angle her sweet pussy up to meet my thrusts.

'Drake, I want to come again. Take me there.'

Her demand thrills me. I'll give her anything in that second. Sucking deep on a well of previously unknown stamina, I give her my all, hips pistoning, one knee braced on the bed to provide a twist of my pelvis that must bash her clit because she grips my cock tighter. I just have time to clamp my lips on that nipple she's torturing, adding flicks of my tongue to the roll of her fingertips, before she explodes, coming with a hoarse cry, her stare blazing into mine until pleasure overwhelms her and she closes her eyes.

I could happily die in that moment. But I'm right behind, fire racing down my cock as I fill the condom. I ride out the convulsions, my face in her wild hair as I suck the essence of her into my lungs and christen this moment the best of my life.

CHAPTER FIVE

Drake

MY VISION SHARPENS into focus as the incredible high fades. I'm on my back, staring at the ceiling; Kenzie's at my side, her head heavy on my arm—a weight I feel in every part of my body.

What the fuck have I done?

Her breath tickles the hair on my chest and I tense, my stomach in knots of my own making, trapped by the magnitude of what just happened.

I lie still, breathe, testing my conscience.

Do I regret it? Hell, yes. But also, hell, no. Because, fuck, it couldn't have been better, every fantasy pale and lifeless in comparison to the vibrant reality we've just created. But is perfection perfect if you can only experience it once?

Kenzie stirs, pads softly to the bathroom and then returns with a wad of tissues, which she hands to me with a sheepish smile on her flushed face. 'Fancy that glass of wine now?'

She's breathtaking with afterglow, the skin of her chest and neck and cheeks red from the scratch of my beard. Even her inner thighs are a little dusky where she writhed against my five o'clock shadow.

Fuck, yeah!

I nod, taking the tissues. The thought of leaving hollows me out, even though I should get the hell away before I have the urge to do that again and again and again... It's already there, a flicker in my softening cock and an obsession in my Kenzie-craving mind.

I shut down the thoughts, convinced one time with Kenzie will never be enough.

She slings on the robe and moves to the kitchen, while I remove the condom and clean up.

'Have you eaten?' she calls. Her place is so small I hear her clearly from the bathroom, where I'm washing my hands.

'No.'

Just you—all the sustenance I'll need for a while.

My still-hard dick perks up and I grit my teeth, willing the erotic replay of the last half an hour from my mind. I'm tempted to splash the greedy fucker with cold water, not that it would help. I've done it now—tasted forbidden fruit. Too late to go back.

By the time I emerge, she's back, relaxed on the pillow, her glass of wine in her hand and one for me on the bedside table.

Her smile is sad, as if she sees the conflict in

me as clearly as the colour of my eyes. The idea that she feels similar turmoil smacks me in the solar plexus. She must be thinking about Sam and regretting what we just did to his memory. I don't think I can hear what she's about to say... *Well, that was great, Drake, but we should never have done it...*

It's only what's pinballing around inside my skull, but I'd rather tear off my ears than hear confirmation when I'm still aroused, still reeling from our incredible intimacy and chomping at the bit to make the same mistake again.

My stomach twists again—it's like fucking emotional macramé in there. I paste neutrality onto my face to hide my confusion, for her sake and my own sanity.

Kenzie taps the bed and I join her, manning up to the consequences of my actions. I had my perfect, once-in-a-lifetime moment and now she's done with me. I should feel relief but I taste bile.

She's made a platter of cheeses with what looks like crumbly homemade-looking crackers, quartered fresh figs drizzled with oil and dollops of tapenade. I grab some cheese, grateful for her efforts, dousing it with a mouthful of wine. If I'm going to throw up I'll need something in my stomach.

'Did you make these crackers?' They're good—walnut and some sort of herb, perhaps thyme, perhaps what I smelled when I arrived.

She nods, slathering a cracker with tapenade and licking some stray olive oil from her fingers. 'And the tapenade—it's my favourite.' She hums with appreciation, the sound calling directly to my balls. I watch her eat for a few heartbeats—savouring every bite with gusto, vocal in her pleasure for food, her tongue lapping up any stray morsel.

My body rouses, a glutton for punishment. I hide the urge to touch her behind a compliment. 'You're an amazing cook—never doubt that or let anyone in the industry steal this—' I hold up the cracker '—your passion for food.'

She flushes, finishing her swallow. 'Thank you.' She looks away, as if my words prick her vulnerability more than all the physical intimacy we've just shared. 'I guess I'm not used to focussing on myself, my goals. I'm trying, though.'

My hand twitches in my lap with the need to cup her breathtaking face. A bigger need shifts in my chest—one to protect her from arrogant arseholes like Rod. 'Good. There's nothing wrong with prioritising your needs.' Of course she's not just reclaiming her dormant sexuality. She's rebuilding her life, coming to terms with Tilly leaving home, fighting for the career she wants...

I relax. Perhaps I'm over-complicating this, allowing my guilty secrets to cloud my judgement. She said she only wanted sex, all I can give, and the no-strings variety is my forte. But this is Kenzie. Normal rules definitely do not apply. Because even a casual one-off comes with a price—it was *that* good.

My zone-out must have lasted a while because she breaks the silence. 'What about you—do you miss the army?'

I stiffen, so many topics between us fraught with triggers. 'Sometimes. At first I missed the camaraderie… But without Sam…' I shrug, thinking of my friend while reeling from the best sex of my life, which happened to be with his widow, twisting me up like hot metal. I rush on. 'Working with my brothers has brought us closer, and the family business needed me—we've taken over more and more from Dad, who has largely retired and spends most of his time on the golf course.'

She studies me, brushing a crumb from the corner of my mouth. 'Yes, you're lucky to have Reid and Kit. Tilly is my rock—I don't know what I'd do without her.' Tension tightens her mouth.

I want to kiss it away. Instead I ask, 'How is she doing?' I recall a socially isolated teenager that looked a lot like Kenzie, with a love of animals and all things Harry Potter.

Kenzie smiles. 'She's good. It's so awesome to see her spread her wings. Make friends.' Her eyes glaze and she traces the pattern on the duvet cover with a finger.

'You miss her.' They're close. Tilly has been Kenzie's focus for most of her adult life. A constant.

Unlike Sam…her parents…

A half-shrug, half-nod. 'I'm just adjusting to her not needing me quite so much. This is the first time we've ever lived apart. But I'm so proud of her overcoming some of her everyday challenges. Mum and Dad would be proud, too.'

I reach out and take her hand. She's lost so much. No wonder she's struggling with her new role in Tilly's life. No wonder she's keen to carve out her own path.

'Of you both—you weren't much older than Tilly is now when you stepped up to the caretaker role.' And now Tilly is naturally breaking away from Kenzie, too. An ache settles under my ribs, my own guilt compounded. I tell myself I ate too much cheese.

'Anyone would have done the same.' Her eyes stay downcast.

'Not everyone—some people are all about themselves.' The burn in my lungs returns, Sam's secret and my own breath-stealing. My friend was a good man, but he would have hurt her, too, if he hadn't died. Just like I've caused her pain, but can't ever confess.

Kenzie prepares a cracker with tapenade and holds it up to my mouth with a questioning brow. 'Try my tapenade…'

I'm not hungry, but she wants to change the subject. Me too, the veer of my thoughts never far from dangerous when she's around. And I want her again. Stuffing my face seems as good a plan as any to stop me touching her once more.

The ferocious need is still there, undiminished.

She smiles, desire lingering behind her wary eyes.

'So, I'm not going to thank you for sex.' She grins. 'But thanks. You have no idea how badly I needed that.'

I grip her wrist, steering the offering a little closer while I stare at her over the back of her hand. 'You are most definitely welcome.' I smile, despite myself, happy to be her prize stud. Her breath shudders as I wrap my mouth around the bite-sized cracker, my lips grazing and then licking her fingertips clean.

'Delicious.' I'm not talking about the food.

Her pupils flare and she leans in, pressing salty lips to mine. She tastes of wine and sharp cheese and the sex we just enjoyed.

Curiosity gets the better of me. 'So you haven't met anyone else?' She's too young to be alone and has so much to offer. Of course, the cheese and crackers take an expected trip around my writhing stomach—I may not like her answer.

She shakes her head. 'For a long time just thinking of the possibility didn't feel right—I still felt married to Sam.' Her eyes flick to mine and then shift away. 'And I didn't want to expose Tilly to any of the dodgy randomers filling the dating apps, which seem to be the only way to meet people these days.'

I tense my muscles, telling myself it's relief that she avoided meaningless hook-ups with potential psychopaths, not jealousy, that makes me shudder. But isn't a meaningless hook-up exactly what we've just had?

No—I care about this woman even though it can't be more than sex.

Her next question knees me in the balls. 'I…I know I put you in a horrible position. Are you thinking about Sam?' A small frown pinches her brows together.

The cheese curdles. I *should* be thinking about Sam. I feared she'd want to talk about him. Perhaps she needs to process what we've just done in the context of moving on. I swallow. I'd rather tear out my own vocal cords than talk about Sam while I'm still naked in her bed, the scent of sex all around us. Because I'm half tempted to drag her under me or over me and go again. At least we won't have the breath to talk. Her delicious crackers may as well be razor blades in my stomach.

'I…'

I don't want to lie, but neither can I offer complete honesty. But she's intelligent. Perceptive. Senses my shifty demeanour. I'm considering excusing myself to the bathroom so I can get my nausea under control, when she touches my arm.

'It's okay.' Her eyes grow sadder, any hint of the spent passion I put there long gone. 'You were such a good friend to him.'

No, don't say that… I betrayed him with thoughts of her. I let him down. I made her a widow.

I want to clamp my hands over my ears like a fucking toddler who doesn't want to hear the word *no*. But listening is my penance.

'And, although I asked you to cross a line, I hope…perhaps *we* can be friends…'

I hold in a splutter. Friends…? Is that how she sees me? I wince at the hypocrisy. Temporary fuck buddy is no better, especially now I've had a taste of what I've always wanted and I'm struggling to remember who she was, who she is.

Sam's wife.

'Of course.' I smile despite the feeling I've been cleaved in two. Because, while I've just enjoyed the single best sexual encounter of my life, it's payback time. I've always craved more than her friendship, but that's exactly where my head *should* be and clearly her end goal.

I can try. But friends are there to make life better, not worse. Friends don't keep secrets. Friends don't inflict pain. She trusted that I wouldn't hurt her.

'Do you miss him?' she whispers.

I keep my gaze steady on hers, my nod almost physically painful, because it's true. 'Yeah. He was my best friend.' We shared laughs, tears, a love of craft beers and fast cars. We argued over fuck-all and ribbed each other mercilessly. Missing him never fades, the ache wrapped up in years of tortured, convoluted feelings.

Her wobbly smile slides from her face and I feel like I've physically struck her. I grip her hand, my fingers curling around hers, which are cool to the touch.

If Sam were still here, I wouldn't be. I wouldn't be in Kenzie's bed. Wouldn't be touching her. Wouldn't be having this conversation—the most intimate one we've shared.

He'd rip my head off for touching his woman. For even thinking about her… I've always chastised myself for wanting Kenzie.

'Me too,' she says. 'I think the hardest part is not idolising him in my memories—he wasn't perfect. But he's not here for me to find irritating or argue with.'

A creep of apprehension crawls up my back. Does she know about his affair? Sam and I only talked about it one time. He confessed his indiscretion and I slated him, making him promise that he would come clean to his wife during his next leave.

But then he died, leaving me to juggle the slippery, leaden burdens of his secret and my own. My skin writhes, raising every tiny hair—I'm no angel. I've just shit on my dead friend's memory, broken my promise to him by being with this woman, and I'd do it all again in a heartbeat.

'No. None of us is perfect.' Especially me, although she's pretty fucking close. I swallow bile and search her face for a sign she's figured out Sam's infidelity, certain the confirmation will scour the inside of my skull like acid.

I'm torn.

If I tell her he cheated, I'll always be the bastard

who tainted his memory. If I keep the knowledge to myself, I'm complicit. As good as a liar.

I'm fucked either way, as I deserve.

'Do you remember his coin?' Her eyes shine when she returns them to mine and I'm trapped anew.

I nod, my neck so brittle it could snap. 'Of course. I lost many a bet to him with it.'

I lost the possibility of you. I lost him.

Sam's lucky fucking coin is the reason he's not here and I am. The reason she's his and not mine.

'Yeah, me too.' She smiles and I'm certain the crackers will make a reappearance. 'He carried it everywhere—bloody drove me crazy.'

I swallow past the brick trapped in my throat and nod. I force my breathing to slow, force myself to stay and listen even though I want to pierce my own eardrums rather than hear fond memories of the man she loves. But this is the price of sampling nirvana. Atonement for acting on my attraction.

'Tea or coffee—a coin toss.' She rolls her eyes. 'Movie or pub—a coin toss. Spain or France—a coin toss.' A sad twitch of her beautiful mouth.

My free hand, under the duvet, makes a tight fist so my nails bite my palm. I've been a selfish prick by staying away. I was his friend—his best friend. With the exception of this woman, I knew him better than anyone. She clearly needed to talk about Sam before today and who better than the man who'd always been by his side? The man there at the end?

As if she's read my tortured mind, she says, 'Do

you think you could…?' She looks away and then looks back. 'I'd like to hear about it…some time.'

My blood freezes in my veins. My face must reflect the horror I feel.

Her hand squeezes mine. 'Not now. Just some time…when you're ready. If you want to.'

I swallow, my throat on fire, and tug my hand from hers. 'I should go. It's late.' I look away from the pain still glimmering in her eyes—pain for the loss of another man, pain I put there, pain I share because, despite his shortcomings, I miss him, too, and it's my fault he's gone.

I slide from under the duvet and reach for my boxers with wooden movements.

'You don't want to stay?'

Her voice catches, with a vulnerability that gives me a second's pause.

My heart thuds against my ribs. I can't. Not when I feel like I've just survived the best night of my life, and one of the worst, all wrapped up together in a sickening swirl of doubt and remorse. Not when waking up with her in my arms tomorrow would be like Christmas morning, until it hits me with the force of a sledgehammer that this particular gift isn't mine to keep. Not when I need to grapple this thing between us back under control.

I turn, cup her face, press a soft kiss to her mouth, one I hope softens my rejection. This isn't her fault. It's about me. The shitty choices I made and have to live with. 'I should go.'

Her teeth plunder her lip and her eyes dart to the floor. 'Did…did I guilt you…into…that?' Even now she's thinking about me, when I'm the fraud.

She thinks she coerced me into the best sex of my life? She thinks I'm *that* loyal to Sam, that it was little more than a pity fuck…? I wince, her misconception the polar opposite of the truth. But I lock down my inner feelings, which are only succeeding in tying me in knots.

She loves Sam. Whether she knows he cheated or not.

How would she feel to hear the man she just slept with, the first man she trusted with her body since him, was so caught up in his own cravings, he gave not a second's thought to his best friend…? That the same man is the reason her husband, perfect or not, isn't here?

Nothing's changed.

'Absolutely not.' I slide my boxers up my thighs and cup her face once more. 'I had a great time.' *Understatement of the century.*

'So did I.' But doubt lingers in her eyes.

I kiss her because if I say more I'll likely say everything. When I pull back the storm behind her eyes has settled.

'I'd like to take you to breakfast tomorrow, or lunch,' I say. 'Catch up properly.'

In a public place, with all our clothes on, so I stand half a chance of being a fucking gentleman.

She nods, her smile like sunshine. Then frowns.

'Shit, I can't. I forgot—I have to help Tilly put flat-pack furniture together.' She pulls her hair back from her face and secures it with a hairband from her wrist. 'I promised, and if we don't do it tomorrow she'll get anxious. And after that I'm on the late shift at the restaurant.'

I tug on my trousers, a boulder expanding in my chest. She's been through so much. Her life thrown into upheaval so many times. But here she soldiers on, caring, independent and uncomplaining. She's so amazing. She'll soon heal her massive heart and want more than sex, to be in a relationship again.

Will I be able to stand by and watch for a second time…?

'I can help put furniture together.' I make a show of finding my shirt rather than look at her, cursing the stupid impulse offer and the protective urges she inspires. If she's done with me, doesn't want my help or my company, I don't want to see it on her face—that kind of shit stays with you, eats you alive…

'You can?' She's risen from the bed and is holding out my tie and jacket.

I shrug. 'Sure. And then we'll do brunch. I have a place in mind, although I doubt their food will be up to your standard.'

She laughs and I scoop my arm around her waist and drag her up to my kiss. I can't help myself.

Just one more taste.

Kissing her occupies my mouth before it can run

away with itself any further, but gives me another problem.

I walk the five minutes back to my car with a dwindling hard-on, the delicious scent of her all over me and a swarm of guilt and regret buzzing through my head like the throb of toothache.

CHAPTER SIX

Kenzie

THE RAP AT my door signalling Drake's arrival sends my pulse into overdrive. I'd offered to meet him at Tilly's place, but he insisted on us travelling together. My hand hovers on the doorknob while I try to settle on one of the myriad emotions giving me nausea.

I clutch my stomach. Last night I blurred the lines. Demanded the amazing sex, so desperate to feel wanted, needed, safe in the knowledge Drake would treat me with respect and care, I didn't stop to think beyond the orgasms.

I didn't anticipate feelings. His or mine.

As soon as I'd come back down to earth, I sensed his withdrawal, his regret. Oh, he made all the right noises for my sake—he's that kind of man—but his poker face isn't as good as he thinks.

I just hope mine is better.

I rest my forehead against the door, my hand on the catch, debating opening it at all. I shouldn't have pried when he clearly wanted to escape. I thought talking about Sam would give him peace of mind, show him that, just because we'd given in to chemistry, things could return to normal.

I scrunch my eyes closed, blocking out the guilt—did he feel used?

He knocks again.

I suck in a breath. *I* asked *him* for sex. Time to make this right. Not awkward as hell. Drake is one of very few people I know in London—it would be good to have a friend. A friend with incredible benefits...

I plaster a friendly smile on my face, one that hopefully hides the heat in my face, and open the door. The sight of him in jeans and a sweater that looks soft enough to snuggle against mocks every single vow of restraint I've made since waking up alone, recalling the fight he put up before I coerced him and the cagey look on his face the second it was over.

'Hi.' He has a scarf wrapped around his neck, his hair dishevelled as if lifted by the wind. Scrummy.

'Morning,' I say, the pitch of my voice evidence I still want him.

He presses a kiss to my cheek, his devilish smile kicking up, and I remember the same mouth on me, greedily eating me out with such devastating proficiency that I forgot how to breathe.

I clear my throat and look away, the brush of his lips reminding how right our connection felt—better than chemistry alone, because I was free to explore what, for the previous three years, seemed like an alien act. But then came crushing guilt. I tried to sound out where Drake's head was, but he retreated, illustrating how little I really know him, despite the way we seemed to slot together.

I'm clearly confusing amazing sex with something more.

'I'm almost ready.' I busy myself with a search for my keys, my phone, my bag—anything to keep my hands from Drake. Because now I've broken my dry spell it's as if I'm addicted, craving, ravenous.

'It's cold out.' Drake takes my bag while I hunt for a scarf, that flutter his caring side ignites back in my belly.

He's so honourable, last night—indulging my sexual request—must have cost him dearly. Sam was his friend, and I asked him to set that aside.

He tried to hide it, but I saw how his conflict mirrored mine—I've spent the last three years grappling loneliness, inadequacy, but above all discord. I loved Sam and he cheated. I never had a chance to ask myself what I'd have done, because he died before the inevitable confrontation. Two blows in quick succession, each shoving me in opposite directions and providing no answers.

And now a new question—did Drake know? Is that the explanation for his wariness? I hide the pain in my chest by rummaging through a drawer.

Sex with Drake has complicated everything.

Things I thought I'd reconciled years ago have sprung up, roadblocks.

I can at least right one wrong—I can clear the air, apologise and promise I won't put him in a compromising position again.

I suck in a breath that feels too big for my lungs. 'Look. I've been thinking…about last night. Despite what you said—I feel…bad. I feel like I…coerced you.'

He frowns and presses one cold finger to my lips. 'You didn't, understand?' I nod, his finger bumping over my lips. 'We're on the same page.'

Instead of the relief at his reassurance, I collapse a little inside, as if my entire skeleton has dissolved in a puff of smoke. But this is what I wanted, isn't it? To move past last night?

I breathe. Wait under his dark stare.

His finger slips down my chin.

Was that the same one he pushed inside me last night? The same one he used to torture my clit as he made me come the first time…? I catch my breath as he takes away his touch and mentally slap myself. Thinking of Drake and sex has to stop. I've had my moment in the sun.

Time to focus on my fresh start and Tilly.

'Great.' I cover the disappointment I'm sure is all over my face by shrugging into my coat. At last I locate my scarf, exactly where it should be on the coat hook. 'Let's go.'

On the street we fall into distant and silent step.

Not only does this leave me to wallow in the new-found awkwardness I've created, it also allows my mind to wander back to last night.

How sexy, alive and feminine I felt. How Drake made something potentially embarrassing, amazing. Three years of doubt and soul-searching, feeling unloved and second-rate, silenced in the first heartbeat of his kiss.

Until doubt roared back to life at Drake's obvious regret the minute the sweat dried.

I look down, a fresh wave of heat burning my throat. No matter how good the sex, how badly I wanted it, the taste of betrayal lingers, tied up in the complexities of my feelings for Sam, this man beside me and their deep, lasting friendship.

A silent scream builds in my head at the growing enormity of my actions.

I fucked Sam's best friend.

Did I do it to get back at Sam in some twisted way, therefore betraying Drake, too? My eyes burn—I selfishly loved every second, giving not a thought to how Drake might feel, how his integrity and loyalty to Sam might tear him up, how his own demons might surface...

I walk on autopilot, half tempted to fake a stomach ache and rush back home. But I can't let Tilly down. I throw out a mindless question. 'Where did you park?' Anything to break the stilted silence.

Drake looks my way then sidesteps an oncoming mother with a pushchair. The move shunts him into my side and he puts his hand in the small of my back, steadying me as our bodies accidentally collide.

'I didn't drive.' His voice is low, close enough that his breath ruffles through my hair, leaving a warm patch on my scalp. 'I thought it would be quicker, easier, to take the Tube.'

My pulse, reeling from his touch and proximity, throbs between my legs. Conflicted about last night and gutted that he accepted my apology and suggestion we steer this backwards so readily—this last nugget scrambles my mind completely.

'*You* take the Tube?'

He grins, shrugs.

It's too good an opportunity to pass up. 'You, Drake Faulkner, CEO, hotel-chain owner, use the Underground?'

He rubs his eyebrow, his mouth twisted in that sexy way that makes me aware I'm a woman with a reawakened sex drive. 'There's plenty about me that might surprise you.'

I flush. Yep—his phenomenal orgasm-delivering skills, his belief in my culinary skills and the fact he's helping Tilly and me lug furniture around today, when he could have told me to piss off and never see me again after my proposition.

My belly ignites with curiosity to learn more about Drake. 'I'm sure. Perhaps we should rectify that.'

'Perhaps.' He smiles but then his face shutters and he looks away, creating another slice of distance that reminds me there'll be no more orgasms. Not with Drake. And, it seems, no more surprising facts.

'So what are we making today?' he says.

'One of Tilly's flatmates moved out and took some of the furniture,' I say. 'She's bought a replacement bookcase but asked for my help with the construction. It shouldn't take long.' I glance at my watch.

'Are we late?' asks Drake, taking my elbow to guide me through the Saturday morning throng.

'No. But time is important to Tilly. A routine, knowing when things will happen—it helps to reduce her anxiety.'

'Well, let's get a move-on, then.' He smiles and quickens his pace.

We arrive at the Tube station and I pause to allow him to lead the way. 'I bow to your superior knowledge of the Underground. I still get lost on a semi-regular basis.'

We laugh—friendly, uncomplicated laughter—and something inside me settles, a hidden splinter working free. We're going to be okay—I feel it. Yes, from now on things will be strictly platonic.

A gust of wind from the labyrinth of underground tunnels beneath London wafts a hint of his cologne my way and my internal muscles clench as I recall falling asleep last night, alone, but with his Drake scent all over me and my pillow.

Platonic...? Good luck with that.

Tilly's in a great mood when we arrive, because

Drake navigates the London Underground like he uses it every day, meaning we're on time.

As I reacquaint Tilly with Drake—they've only met once before when Drake spent a rare Christmas with us—I feel a flutter of apprehension in my chest. I'm overprotective of Tilly, and I haven't had a chance to explain the exact nature of my relationship to Drake. Probably because, beyond *temporary*, I have no idea how to label it. My doubts settle at the genuine warmth in my sister's smile and the way Drake treats her like he does everyone.

'Right. Let's get started,' he says, taking the bag of tools. I offer to make tea while Drake carries the first box into the living room. Their soft murmuring conversation and occasional laughter reaches me from the other room. Hearing his laugh, I remember his roguish smile. I press my thighs together, recalling Drake's face between my legs and above me as he pounded us both to oblivion.

Can I really forgo a repeat?

I snap my eyes open and pour boiled water into the pot. Only ten hours after two spectacular orgasms and a mere hour since I made a vow to stop thinking about him that way and I'm craving him still. How could I survive three years? But somehow, three more hours seems like eternity.

No. It can't happen again. This way is better. A friendly face for Tilly and me in our new city. And maybe Drake needs a friend, too, one who knew Sam. He clearly has unresolved issues over his death.

He said Sam was one reason he left the army. I swallow, trying to imagine the horror of watching your friend die.

Did he suffer PTSD? Did his life change because of what happened to Sam? Would he still be in the army today if it hadn't happened?

When I carry the tea into the room I see Drake and Tilly have unpacked all the pieces of the bookcase and Tilly has lined up the correct screws in the order they'll be required.

She looks between us, her mind working. 'Your Sam's friend from the army?' she asks, clarifying Drake's relationship to our family. She knows the answer, but repeating questions is another way my sister handles the unpredictability of her world.

Drake smiles. 'Yes, he was in my platoon.' His stare finds mine and I hold my breath. With a single question Tilly has brought up the one subject that highlights every obstacle littering our path to the continued uncomplicated sex my body still craves.

'But Sam died,' she says, glancing my way.

I nod, keeping my emotions from my face for my sister's sake. We've done this routine a thousand times. Death can be an abstract concept for someone with a concrete and literal mind.

'So…now you're Kenzie's friend.' Tilly hits the nail right on the head in her direct way. My throat clogs with doubt and perhaps hope.

Is he? He certainly won't be more than a friend.

'That's right,' I say, injecting my voice with a

fake breezy tone and taking the heat from Drake, who looks a little green around the gills. 'And once he's helped us make this I think Drake will be your friend, too, don't you, Tills?'

She shrugs—she's not easily won over—and launches into a Q&A on one of her favourite subjects: all things Harry Potter, including Hogwarts and JK Rowling.

Drake answers every question, his patience endless. We assemble the bookcase, a team. For the first time in a month, my shoulders dislodge from around my ears and the weak November sun seems a little brighter. With Drake's 'friendship', London might work out for Tilly and me after all.

'Here.' Drake offers me a bite of his chicken waffle, which drips with maple syrup.

I hesitate. 'I'm sorry—I always want to try everything on the menu and then when I make a decision I want what the other person has ordered.'

He grins and holds the forkful up to my mouth. 'I knew you'd love this place. It's Chelsea's newest, hippest eatery. Already won a handful of awards.'

I take the food, the intimacy of being fed by him almost as good as the sweet and salty flavours on my tongue. 'Thanks.' I swallow, but it's an effort. The erotic vision of him eating from my fingers last night, with that look on his face and his smoky voice...

'Stop feeding me—I'll split my jeans.' I shoo away another forkful and relax back into my chair.

This is nice, this morning's awkwardness all but disappeared. With the sex business over, I can focus on Tilly and my potential new job. Perhaps we're exactly where we're meant to be.

I look up to see Drake's smile fading.

'What?' Unease creeps over my skin.

'Nothing. I…I'm surprised Tilly didn't want to join us.'

I look away, swallowing back the feeling of being adrift that's never far away. 'No, she has her new routines. Saturday is food-shopping and the movies with her flatmates.'

'And you used to do those things together?' he asks.

I nod, blinking the sting from my eyes, torn between happiness for my sister and a feeling of redundancy. 'She's growing more independent.'

Drake lowers his voice, leans closer, creating a private bubble in the bustle around us, as if he senses my turmoil. 'You've helped to raise a great young woman. I'm glad you have time to focus on you a bit more.'

Despite his considered words, he doesn't look glad. He looks a little rattled, distracted. But I have no time to query.

'So do you see yourself working in a restaurant like the Faulkner in five years? Head chef? A couple of Michelin stars under your belt?' His change of subject could be interpreted as diversionary, but his expression is serious, as if he really believes me capable of those incredible pipe dreams.

I take a swallow of water to combat the flush his scrutiny and his compliments induce. 'Actually, I do have a plan.'

'Good—tell me.' He pushes his plate aside and rests his elbows on the table.

'Okay...' I hesitate. With the exception of Tilly, I've never told anyone my dream. 'But promise you won't...laugh.' Now I'm about to say the words aloud, they sound naïve, far-fetched, unrealistic.

Drake frowns. 'Why would I laugh?' His piercing frown penetrates my layers. My body floods with heat, just like it did last night when he took his time looking at my naked body.

I shrug. 'I've been so focussed on raising Tilly, I guess I'm just rusty when it comes to demanding something for myself.' My bones turn molten at the reminder of what I demanded from him last night. And how thoroughly he obliged...

I plough on, the harsh 'it's over' in my head providing focus. 'One day, I'd like to have my own restaurant—nothing grand. Just an everyday, wholesome-food kind of place.'

He nods, his eyes full of warmth and encouragement. 'Sounds good. I can see you responsible for expanding waistlines all over the city.'

My stare drops to his lithe torso, his muscular

bulk visible through the fine wool of his sweater. I can't help myself.

'Thanks.' I roll my eyes and toss a packet of sugar at him from the selection in the centre of our table. 'Only I'd love to employ adults with special needs. Adults like Tilly.'

He nods, perceptive eyes probing. 'You miss your old job as a teacher's aide?'

He remembers I worked at a special educational-needs school. I smile, the flush reaching my face. 'I got made redundant shortly after Sam died.'

Shock streaks over his face and his skin pales. 'I'm sorry.'

I laugh, taken aback by his reaction. 'You weren't to know. It's hardly your fault.'

He swallows hard, his eyes a little haunted. 'I'm still sorry you had to go through that on top of everything else.' His fingers curl into a loose fist next to mine on the table.

I hold my breath—I can almost feel his touch, but the moment passes. 'It's okay—I used my redundancy pay to pay for chef school. And here I am.'

His smile builds, forcing the corners of his eyes into a fan of creases. 'Good—I'd say you're at least halfway to your dream already.'

For a moment I'm overcome with an unnamed emotion. This is what I wanted when I came to him—someone to believe in me enough to offer me a chance.

His eyes are still on me, so I try to pull myself together. 'So, if we're going to be fiends now, tell me one of the things I'd find surprising about you, apart from your impressive, encyclopedic knowledge of all things Harry Potter.' I stop myself from prying about a wife and kids. I don't want to know if Drake has aspirations for future marital bliss.

He laughs, but the laugh doesn't reach his eyes. It's hardly a difficult question. He's still cagey. Still doesn't want to talk about himself.

'Let's start with work. Do you enjoy being a hotelier?'

His smile grows into that boyish twist. 'I do, actually. A complete change of pace has really helped. Of course, I have to spend quite a lot of time at the gym to counter the delicious food, and my degree wasn't much use, but I learned the ropes quickly—couldn't have Kit and Reid outsmarting me.'

I laugh. All three Faulkners are savvy businessmen who grew up learning the family business. I doubt either of his brothers could outsmart Drake, and they definitely don't out-suit him.

'And your father is almost retired?'

'Yes. A good thing.' He grins and my belly flips. 'He's getting a bit forgetful. Too many G and Ts at the golf club, probably.'

To distract my wandering mind from that smile, I check the time. 'Bugger. I need to go. I don't want to be late.' I stand, tugging on my coat and untangling my scarf from the strap of my bag while Drake pays the bill, despite my protests.

He puts his hand in the small of my back as we leave the warm, crowded restaurant. 'Don't worry—we'll take a taxi.'

Inside the cab, it hits me like a lead weight: his kindness towards Tilly, the passion we share for good food, his belief in my fledgling dream—now we've reacquainted, I can't mess this up with something as trivial as…lust, no matter how great the sex and how much I'd love a repeat. I have few enough friends, or even contacts, in London.

Sucking in a breath, I pull up my big-girl pants. 'Thanks for everything today. So—we're good? You and I?'

His stare lifts from my mouth, inscrutable, where all morning it's been clear, open and friendly. 'I'd say we're good.'

'So, friends?' The term chokes me but I force a smile, letting him know I won't be pawing at him for any more orgasms.

Before he can confirm our new-found status, my phone pings, covering my erratic reaction with an incoming text.

I show Drake the picture from Tilly, who declined his invitation to brunch in order to fill her new book-case with her Harry Potter collection.

Drake laughs—a deep rumble coming up from his chest. 'Gotta love Harry.'

His laugh, like his smile, gives me butterflies, the tense moment of seconds ago likely a figment of my imagination. 'Yes, who knew you were such a nerd…?' I bump his shoulder with mine and then instantly regret touching him—my body wants more than *friends*.

'Has she been to the Harry Potter studio tour?' he asks.

I roll my eyes, grateful he's steering us back to safety. 'Six times, but it's on her birthday wish list.'

'Perhaps we could all go together—I haven't been for years.'

I nod, my chest hollowed out. My determination to shelve the sex solidifies. Tilly and I have a new friend.

'It's a date,' I say as we pull up outside the Faulkner, my blush flaring when I realise the phrase I've tossed out.

He nods. 'A date.' Drake pays for the cab and we head in different directions, while I try to see his friendship as something more than a consolation prize.

CHAPTER SEVEN

Drake

I CLOSE MY laptop and fist my hands on the desk, finally admitting no amount of work can distract me from the thoughts that have dogged me for the past twenty-four hours.

Kenzie.

I expected the brush-off the minute she opened the door to her flat. She was right to steer this away from the murky waters of no-strings sex, because that only works for people with no prior feelings. Kenzie and I…we have history. We're complicated. And spending today with her was a mistake.

Discovering she lost her job just after Sam died and seeing first-hand the impact of Tilly's growing independence left my stomach so contorted I could barely swallow a morsel of the food I'd raved about.

She needed me, needed someone, and I wasn't there for her because of my burden of guilt and my need for self-preservation.

And don't get me started on the sex…

I don't begrudge her the safe space to help her back into the intimacy saddle, and being friend-zoned where I belong should offer relief. Instead, I'm crawling out of my skin.

If we're going to be friends now…

So, friends?

I think Drake will be your friend, too, don't you, Tills?

I push away from my desk with enough violence to send my chair crashing to the ground four storeys below but for the reinforced glass that gifts me a view of Sloane Square.

I should be happy. I had one night to slake my long-held attraction. Of course I pretended we were on the same page—the last thing I want is to make her feel guilty for what we did. And friendship is the logical and mature next step.

Except I've always wanted more and now I know—one night with Kenzie won't be enough.

I don't blame her for slotting me into a platonic role. I'm her husband's friend. Of course she would regret what we did. And I aided her decision by shutting down with the finality of a fucking mousetrap.

My stomach lurches as guilt robs my breath.

She deserves better than a man with secrets. A selfish man who caused her dire predicament three years ago and then walked away, leaving her to deal with the fallout alone. And she's more alone now than ever. She needs a friend. The last thing I can be.

Because a real friend would be honest.

I scrub a hand over my tired face, so torn the floor should be littered with my pieces. I groan aloud and thump the arms of my chair, impotence dragging my twitchy body upright with the speed and grace of a man three times my age.

I can do this. Be her fucking friend.

I can keep my guilt hidden and do it for Sam.

I can do it for Kenzie.

Snagging my jacket, my phone and my keys, I start to head down to the lift for the underground car park. As I pass the foyer my eyes stray to the staff entrance leading to the kitchens.

Kenzie's domain.

I busied myself with some paperwork this evening, deliberately staying away from the kitchens. If Rod gets any whiff of my connection to Kenzie, it might jeopardise her fair shot at the sous-chef position. One I made happen, despite knowing I'd somehow end up in my current untenable position.

I dawdle in the foyer, picturing Kenzie at work and ignoring the odd looks I'm attracting from the night manager behind the front desk. How is she faring under Rod's brusque tutelage? Did she make any part of the delicious beef Wellington I had delivered to my office four hours ago?

My stomach growls, the tender meat and rich mushroom and red-wine sauce a distant memory. I skipped dessert, as I always do. But perhaps there's some delicious concoction left in the fridge. It's

2:00 a.m. The restaurant closed two hours ago. But I have nothing at home to appease this uncharacteristic sweet craving, the only craving allowed. It's as if my body knows it can never have another taste of Kenzie, so it's compensating with common or garden sugar.

Fuck it; if I want a midnight snack instead of driving around to Kenzie's flat and knocking her awake for more sex, I can damned well have one. I can spend an extra hour on the treadmill tomorrow.

Decision made, I head for the kitchen, certain whatever I find will taste sweeter just knowing Kenzie might have had some hand in its creation.

At the door to the kitchen I come to a standstill. The lights are still on. I catch movement through the glass.

My pulse races. She's still here.

Her back is to me. She's busy. Concentrating. My tired arse forgets the time, my hunger banished. One glimpse of her and I could run the London Marathon.

I push open the door, rearranging my face to hide ninety per cent of my delight.

'Why are you still here this late?' I let the door swing closed at my back.

She jumps, startled, spinning to face me, one hand covering her heart. The piping bag she's holding spurts out green icing onto the stainless-steel bench.

'Sorry, I didn't mean to scare you—'

'You scared the shit out of me—'

We talk together and then laugh together.

'I'm going to throttle Rod if he's pushing you this hard.' The urge to go to her, to kiss her, leaves me brusque.

'Whoa, there's no need for *that* look. Rod doesn't know I'm here.' Her eyes dance in the lights focussed on the bench and on the cake she's making.

'Which look?' I stand taller, preening and fucking peacocking under her inspection.

She waves the piping bag in my direction, mirth flashing in her eyes. 'You know, that scary regimental sergeant-major look.' Wisps of hair have escaped from her ponytail to kiss her flushed cheeks and she has a smear of icing sugar on her forehead. I love that she's comfortable enough to tease me.

'I'm not scary.' *Unlike wanting you or envisioning never touching you again...* Heat boils in my belly and I succumb to the roar inside my head— forget *friends.*

I want her.

Same as always.

This sexy, sassy woman. A woman who's had to fight to make life for herself and her sister better. A woman who dunks biscuits in her tea, tries to hide the sheen of moisture in her eyes when she's proud of Tilly and pretends she's Slytherin when really she's Hufflepuff.

Kenzie quirks one eyebrow. 'I think you could be. And you're still here, too. Working late?'

'For my sins.' Her corner of the kitchen is a bomb site. Cake tins fill the sink, bowls filled with different-coloured icing are spread over the bench and the floor is dusted with flour.

'I'm sure you don't have any.' She laughs and my smile threatens to slide from my face.

If only…

She looks around at the mess, as if seeing it for the first time. 'Oh… I'm going to clean up. I'm almost done.' She returns to the cake, piping rosettes of icing around the base of the three-tiered creation with expert speed. 'I'll be out of your hair in ten minutes.' She looks up, eyes uncertain.

'I don't care if you're moonlighting. As long as you don't burn yourself out.' I step closer to watch with fascination as she swirls and pipes with proficient accuracy. Then I take in the whole cake. 'You made Hogwarts!'

The cake has a castle on the top, turrets, flags, a quidditch pitch, the whole shebang. 'She's going to love that.' Of course—Tilly's birthday.

Kenzie grins, nodding and swirling the cake around on its stand with a flourish. 'I know, right? Her birthday is Thursday—today was my only late shift and I thought no one would mind if I stayed behind to use the kitchen.' She rolls her eyes. 'You've seen my tiny flat…' She trails off while she twists the icing bag tighter, looking uncertain. 'I…I bought all my own ingredients…'

Clearly our 'friendship'—fuck, I hate that word— is still so new, she thinks I'm checking up on the Faulkner storeroom.

'I don't give a rat's arse that you're using the Faulkner kitchen to make Tilly's cake.'

She smiles and laughs at me in the same breath— it's a heady combination that makes me want to smear her lips with icing and then kiss it off... Then I remember the time. See the fatigue behind her eyes and the mess in the sink.

'But pulling an all-nighter and traipsing across the city alone in the early hours—that requires a scary sergeant-major look, I'm afraid.' I remove my jacket and roll up my shirtsleeves.

Nervous laughter. 'What are you doing?' Her eyes widen.

'I'm helping you so you can get to bed. Have you eaten dinner?'

She shrugs, retuning to her piping, and I growl under my breath.

She laughs off my reprimand. 'I planned to, but we had ninety-six covers tonight. Then I started baking and...I forgot.'

'So the last thing you ate was my chicken waffles this morning?'

'Yeah.' She abandons the cake and fists her hand on her hip.

I curl my fingers into my palms to stop myself reaching for her, to stop myself pushing her hair back from her face, wiping that smear of icing sugar from her forehead and holding her until everything battling inside me calms.

Instead I stride to the fridge, yanking open the

door to peer inside. 'Finish the cake. I'll make you some food and then do the dishes.'

This is what *friends* do. They look out for each other. Minus the great sex.

Kenzie huffs, but she's already distracted with her piping once more. 'Don't be ridiculous. I'll clean up and then I'll head home.'

'Ridiculous…?' I take eggs and mushrooms from the fridge and grab a pan from overhead. 'I'm not the one who hasn't eaten since brunch.'

Even tired, she shoots me an insolent smile. '*You* cook?' Swirl, pipe, swirl, pipe.

Her provocative tone imbues me with vigour. I forget cooking, her tiredness, even breathing, and stare as if seeing her for the very first time. When she's concentrating, the tip of her tongue touches her top lip. Fucking adorable.

I viciously crack the eggs into a bowl to stop myself taking the piping bag from her hand and reminding her of the innumerable benefits to our friendship like I've wanted to all day.

'I'm not bad.' Certainly better than nothing. 'When was the last time someone made you a simple meal?'

She shrugs. 'You're right—I have no idea.' She watches me whisk eggs. 'Thanks.'

I grow another inch taller. 'You know, you don't have to do everything alone, right…?'

Let me take care of you.

Whoa, where did that come from? She's not mine to care for. Never can be.

She stops what she's doing, sobers, a small wrinkle forming between her brows. 'I've been doing it for so long—just me and Tilly.' She shrugs. 'I guess it's just easier not to rely on other people.'

People who let you down? Hurt you? Leave you?

She looks away and I swallow bile. She doesn't know it, but I'm on that list. I let her down in the worst way. Sam and I went to some war-torn hellhole overseas and only I returned...

Losing my own appetite completely, I focus on her midnight snack. The mushrooms may as well be cardboard for all the finesse of my slicing, but at least all my fingers are intact by the time I've finished. I need to pull my head out of my arse.

Wanting her again is selfish.

If only I'd stayed strong. Turned down her life-changing proposition. Now I've had one taste—I'm ruined.

Kenzie groans, stretching out her back muscles. I grit my teeth and toss the mushrooms into the pan, the spatter of too-hot oil on the back of my hand a reminder of what is at stake.

She tosses the piping bag down, removes her chef's hat and adjusts her hair. 'There, finished.'

I take a second to admire her arse in the white trousers, which are covered in smears of chocolate, and then I tear my eyes away and tip the egg mixture into the sizzling pan. 'Good. Come and sit down.' I place a stool at the bench. This is bad... I'm acting like her friend, but I have no right. She's open and caring and wants companionship and I'm a closed book, keeping things from her, and lusting.

She looks at my omelette. 'That smells delicious—I had no idea I was so ravenous, thank you.'

I freeze. She's too close, too tempting, and then she steps closer still and reaches up. 'You have a splash of something, right here,' she says, brushing one finger over my cheek and then stepping back with a satisfied smile. 'Kitchens are messy places.' She indicates her splattered chef whites as evidence.

'Thanks.' I breathe, but it's a struggle.

She leans back on the bench and watches me finish making her meal with a small, slightly mocking smile. 'So, you're handy with a screwdriver, you're Gryffindor, know the rules of quidditch *and* you cook.'

Is she flirting…? My smile is feeble. She's looking at me like she'd love nothing better than a session of verbal foreplay, culminating in a round or two of high-calibre fucking, right here on the stainless steel, but her eyes are red-rimmed and she's pale, probably about to drop with fatigue.

Plus, I'm no hero.

'I have a few skills.' The pan sizzles, breaking the tension and splattering my shirt.

'You should let me make that—you don't want to get grease on your suit.' I feel her stare slide down my body to my toes.

Fuck my suit.

'I'm tough. You haven't lived until you've eaten

lukewarm boil-in-the-bag stew in the middle of no-where.'

She wrinkles her nose. 'I'll take your word for that.'

I slide the eggs onto a plate and add some milled black pepper with a flourish. I disguise my turmoil with a dash more of bossy. 'Now, eat my substandard omelette and then go home, have a bath, work out all those kinks with a long, hot soak.'

Stop. Don't imagine her naked and wet, water running down her phenomenal body... Thank fuck she can't read the one-track nature of my far from friendly mind.

She rolls her eyes, covering a yawn with the back of her hand. 'Sounds like heaven.' She reaches for the fork. 'But I only have a shower—bathroom's too small for a bath.' She takes a bite of the omelette, moaning with pleasure.

'I have a bath,' I say, surprising us both. 'Why don't I take you home to mine—it's just around the corner—you can have a soak and sleep in my spare room?'

Damn and fuck it all to hell.

She looks up. Swallows.

Say no.

Say yes.

I hide behind clearing away the ingredients and wiping down the stove. Why am I so set on littering my own path with the ultimate in temptation?

When I look up she's staring, but quickly covers

her indecision with a smile. 'Sounds like a plan…if you…don't mind.'

I shrug like it's no big deal, while my heart beats its way into my throat. She'll be in my house. In my bath. Sleeping in my spare room.

I fall back on my old mantra: *hands, eyes and filthy mind off.*

She covers another yawn. 'Excuse me. I have to be back here for the early shift in five hours.'

'Great, it's sorted.' While she finishes the omelette, her little moans of appreciation pulsing my dick, I keep my back to her, don rubber gloves and begin to wash up the bowls and cake tins filling the sink.

'How had you planned on getting that home?' I tilt my chin at the cake, which is at least thirty centimetres high—not the easiest thing to transport across London on the Tube.

'I hadn't thought that far ahead… Taxi.' She shrugs, washing down omelette with a sip of wine I poured. I scrub at the cake tin, my attack on the burnt-on dollop of cake mixture doing little to distract me from the sight and sound of Kenzie enjoying my food.

'I didn't really have much time to make a birthday cake this year, and Tilly's getting a little old—'

'Can you ever be too old for a birthday cake?'

She points her fork at me. 'Good point. Anyway, I've been making them for Tilly for years, since Mum and Dad died. It's a family tradition, one Mum started and now I continue—can't mess with tradition.' Her eyes lose focus for a second, and I dry my hands on a tea towel, fighting the urge to go to her, hold her, kiss the sadness from her lips. To tell her we—her, Tilly and I—can make new traditions…

'That's a nice tradition.'

She nods, her eyes darting away, but I've already seen the sheen in them. 'I tried to keep those family times alive for Tilly. Birthdays, Christmas—Mum and Dad always made them special.'

I turn away, an intruder to her private moment, even when every cell in me wants to comfort her for the things she's lost. 'I'll have the cake delivered tomorrow.' She starts to protest but I hold up my hand, silencing her assertions that she can cope. 'Just let me do something for you, take care of…this simple thing.'

Take care of you.

I step closer, my chest so tight the words I manage to push out surprising us both. 'Let me keep my promise.' Try to be your friend. Try to make up for what you've been through because of me. 'Please.' The last is a gruff whisper, my throat closing on the word. Because not only am I the shittiest friend alive, to both Sam and her, but I also have the grubbiest intentions where this beautiful woman is concerned.

She nods, her big eyes round.

The victory leaves me so conflicted my chest aches. I knew she'd be the death of me…

* * *

Having Kenzie in my home is akin to an eternity locked in the London dungeons, every lash to my raw back a sentence, because I can almost taste how different my life might have been if I'd approached her instead of stepping aside for Sam.

I *saw* her first. Saw her the second we walked into the club, at the bar with her friends, her stunning face hard to ignore and her laugh infectious. The next time I looked her way, scoping out her ring finger, Sam had spotted her, too. And then she looked in our direction, catching his eye and quickly looking away. I should never have taken his wager, literally putting my fate in the outcome of a coin toss.

She's so tired, I take her straight to the spare room, every step she takes at my side a self-inflicted flogging. Hiding my mistake, I turn down the covers on the bed, silently praising Fiona, my housekeeper, for keeping everything shipshape. I catch Kenzie eyeing the huge bath in the en suite with longing, so I detour there, robotically turning on the taps and adding half a bottle of bubble bath to the steaming stream of water.

'There are fresh towels on the warmer and a new toothbrush in the drawer.'

Kenzie nods and smiles like I've handed her a winning lottery ticket. She heels off her shoes and removes her coat.

I'm still standing here, probably with drool on my chin, waiting to be invited into the bath, the bed…

I force my body into submission and force my eyes away from the swell of her breasts beneath her simple white T-shirt.

'Well…goodnight.' I make for the door, clearing the tightness in my throat. 'I'm going into the office early tomorrow, so I can drop you off for your shift.'

A small smile. 'You don't need to do that.'

'I'm going anyway.' A lie. Who goes into the office at seven on a Sunday morning?

She nods, her eyes heavy… I tell myself it's with fatigue, rather than the longing I hope to see. 'Thanks, Drake.'

I'm in my own bathroom cleaning my teeth when I look up into the mirror and see the smear of vivid green icing she must have rubbed on my cheek back at the Faulkner. She's managed to talk to me all evening with a straight face. My bark of laughter breaks some of the tension coiled in me, only for it to be replaced with a profound ache.

Fuck, she's incredible. I glance at the closed bedroom door, every muscle straining to go to her.

I sober quickly, tossing down my toothbrush with disgust.

The blast of hot water from the shower does little to settle my strung-out nervous system. How am I ever going to sleep knowing everything I want is just across the hall? Knowing how good it felt to cross into forbidden territory?

It's three-fifteen by the time my head hits the

pillow, the cool sheets a balm to my fevered naked skin—I always sleep naked.

My last thought, one of wishful thinking, that the chances of Kenzie walking in here and finding me this way are depressingly slim. My dick hates the odds.

What feels like only five minutes later I'm being shaken awake. My heart thunders as reality and sleep merge, images of Sam running ahead of me, just out of reach, lingering. I stretch out my hand—he's so close I see the weave in the fabric of his combat gear, but then he slips through my fingers like the acrid smoke filling my lungs.

I emerge fully into reality. The room is dark, but Kenzie's silhouette and big eyes are easily recognisable in the shaft of light from the hallway.

'Are you okay?' she whispers, releasing my arm.

I sit up, scrub my hand down my face, the roar of blood through my head as deafening as the explosion that took Sam. 'I'm fine—' I clear my aching throat. 'What's wrong?'

'You were having a nightmare—calling out in your sleep. Sorry. I thought it best to wake you.'

Fuck, that's the second one this week.

She rubs her arms. She's wearing her T-shirt and underwear, her bare skin scattered with goosebumps. A chill has settled through the room—it must be close to dawn. I reach for the throw at the end of my bed and drape it around her shoulders, while I try to straighten my head.

Kenzie tugs the blanket across her chest and tucks her bare legs up under herself. 'Was it bad? It sounded bad.'

With a sigh, I switch on the lamp. 'I'm okay. I don't have them anywhere near as frequently as I used to.' But the subject matter is always the same—Sam. Chasing after him, only to watch him get blown up, the knowledge it should have been me slamming home with the predictable inevitability of a high-speed collision.

'Was it Sam?' She reaches out, her touch whisper-soft on my arm, torture and redemption.

I stifle a groan. 'Don't do that.' She snatches her hand away and I quickly intercept, grasping her fingers and holding tight. 'I don't deserve your comfort.'

But I'll fucking take it, suck it dry, if that's the only part of her I can have.

'What do you mean?' Her eyes widen with alarm.

I step back from the edge of the precipice. 'Nothing.' I grip tighter, silently begging her not to push for answers. Not now. When I'm naked and she may as well be. When the vestiges of my nightmare cling, dragging me down into the familiar pit of endless guilt.

'Do you want to talk about it?' It's barely a whisper, as if I'm a frightened animal. But the only thing to fear is keeping control of my burgeoning feelings for this woman. Feelings I'm struggling to contain.

I shake my head, squeeze her fingers. 'I'm fine. I'm sorry I woke you.'

Time to get her out of here.

'You didn't.' She looks down at our still clasped hands. 'I couldn't sleep.'

My pulse soars, but that's not a hangover from the nightmare. 'You should go back to bed.' Now. Before I do something stupid. 'It's freezing.'

She nods but her only movement is her warm fingers pressing against the back of my hand.

I'm trapped by my nakedness and the hard-on that roared to life the minute my body registered her proximity. And by the fact that touching her is exactly where I want to be.

Am I strong enough to fight it?

'Thank you for today,' she says, lifting her eyes to look at me from under her lashes.

'What for?' My throat is sandpaper-rough.

Ask me to kiss you again. Ask me to fuck you again.

'For all of it.' She smiles and my heart pounds. 'Helping Tilly, brunch, washing up, making me food and running me a bath.' Her eyes are searching as a slow sigh gusts out across her lips like she wants to say more but is holding back.

'No problem.' My voice croaks. The only problem here is if she doesn't leave soon, I'm going to do something we'll both regret. Something unforgivable, because she made her position clear today.

Fuck, why didn't I sling on some tracksuit bottoms to sleep in? At least then I could climb out of bed, make her a glass of hot milk and tuck her back into the spare bed, out of reach.

I glance at the door, the slant of light from the hallway. 'I'd take you back to your room…but I'm… kind of naked under here.'

She lifts her eyebrows, her lips parting. 'You are?'

I shrug. Did I imagine the way her eyes sparked? I must still be dreaming, making up the shit I desperately want to see. Because it's over, right…? Friends, she said.

Her eyes cling to mine while we breathe. And stare. And wait. For what, I'm not sure, but I want to break the spell as much as I want to run around the dark-shrouded streets of Chelsea stark bollock naked.

'Do you regret it?' she asks, a whisper.

If I weren't so fascinated with her lips, I'd have missed the question completely.

My pulse thrums painfully in my head. 'Regret what?' All I can think about is how I want her so bad I can already taste her.

Her shoulders rise and fall with rapid, shallow breaths, her tongue darting out to moisten her bottom lip. Her reply is whisper-soft, as if she's afraid to speak any louder in case the words become too real. 'What we did.'

My heart stops altogether. Regret it…? I've fucking replayed it a million times, reliving every incredible second until I'm drunk with its rightness. I shake my head, my tongue thick in my mouth.

'No.' I scrub a hand through my hair, tempted to

tear it out at the words formulating in my head. 'But I don't want to hurt you, either.' *Hurt you any more than I already have.* 'You've been through enough. And I…I made him a promise.'

Her eyelids lower, taking her eyes from wide to sultry, heavy with want, as if she needed to hear confirmation I'd do it again in a heartbeat. But that can't be what she's saying, can it? Because we agreed, only this morning… A mere thirteen hours, ten minutes and forty-three seconds ago.

I can't look away, even though I should. I can't speak, because what I'd feel compelled to say is 'go back to bed' and, right now, I'd rather cut out my tongue.

When she speaks again her voice is breathy, but with a firm enough tone that speaks of her sincerity. Her certainty. Her need. 'You can keep your promise to him.' Her breath shudders out and then back in. 'But don't make me a promise you can't keep, Drake.'

My name on her lips, husky, uttered on a breathy sigh, punches me in the chest and makes my blood sing through my veins and pool in my groin. How does she know me so well? Better than I know myself? Because right now, with her scent in my head and her eyes on mine, I couldn't swear on the life of my brothers which way this will go. Which way *I'll* go.

She's temptation personified.

But I'm strong. Practised at self-denial and tolerating discomfort.

The *friends* mantra loops through my head.

'You wanted friends—I can keep that promise.' The words tear at my throat. Her hand is still in mine. One lunge, one tumble and she'd be under me. Where I want her, her mouth on mine, her wet heat clamped around my cock while I drive us both to oblivion, drive away the memory she was ever anyone else's but mine.

Her eyes glow, their depths full of things I must be dreaming, or concocting in my mind.

'Don't,' she says.

One word.

One meaning.

All it takes to seal my doom.

She slides the blanket from her shoulders and I tug her under me in one move, as I imagined. A move so perfect, there's a fanfare sounding in my head. My mouth covers hers, my hand sliding under her shirt, up her smooth belly to her breast, and I succumb, my weakness for her obliterating every resolution and mocking the friend, the disciplined soldier and the man for a liar.

CHAPTER EIGHT

Kenzie

JUST LIKE THE first time, his touch rains down liquid lightning on my skin. I gasp into his kiss as he rolls my nipple between his fingers with the perfect degree of pressure to leave me panting. His erection, hot and bare, digs into my thigh and I spread my legs, angling the hard length where any shift of my hips will rub him over my clit.

'Drake.' He swallows my ragged cry and then rears back, his hips rocking into mine, reproducing the exquisite friction I crave, over and over.

'Say it again.' His stare glitters, the bite of command telling me how close he is to the edge.

Thrust. Grind. Rock.

He's braced on his arms, looking down at me, and I want to chant his name until I'm hoarse.

'Drake… Drake…' I want my underwear gone. I want to feel the head of his cock sliding through my wetness, waking my hungry clit with every glide. I bite my lip on the urge to voice my desires in case their ferocity scares him off.

How could I convince myself I only wanted friendship? That one time with him would end this yearning?

His mouth silences my thoughts, his tongue surging against mine as a growl vibrates from his throat. His hand is back under my top and I writhe and wriggle until I've scraped the fabric overhead and tossed it to the floor, breaking our deep, drugging kiss in the process.

I slide my hands over Drake's naked chest, his sculpted shoulders and up into his hair, while he grinds against my centre, his chest working hard and his eyes locked to mine with twice the passion of last night.

No matter what we said, this isn't over, for either of us.

His skin scorches me. He's big and solid, surrounding and engulfing me in the best way. Holding me like he's held me all day with his actions and his encouragement and his thoughtfulness.

'Tell me you want this.' He barks out the command as if he's as close as I am to totally losing control. How can this be better than the first time? How is this need nowhere near diminished?

I nod, too pleasure-drunk for words, but then I pull myself together. 'Yes, oh, fuck, yes.' My desire breaks free, starkly honest. Seizing this moment with Drake feels as important as seizing the chance at my dream job. More important. Because with him I feel powerful, capable, strong.

But I shut out the growing emotional attachment we've developed today, telling myself I can enjoy and control the sexual storm he's awoken in me. Telling myself I want nothing from him beyond incredible sex.

Because more than that hurts.

More than that is a temporary illusion.

He leans over me, yanking open the drawer beside the bed. I'm distracted with all that yummy chest I didn't get to explore the way I wanted to last time. This time, even though I'm aching and empty and my underwear is soaked, I lift my head from the bed and indulge, my open mouth sliding over his hot skin. He moves out of reach, so I latch my arms around his back and clamp my mouth over his nipple, before sliding my kisses down the bumps of his ribs.

He rolls to the side and I follow, straddling him and taking the condom from his hand. 'Not so fast.'

He cups my breasts, his hips restless under me as I work my mouth lower, guided by the happy trail of dark hair leading to his proud cock.

'Kenzie… Kenz…'

I ignore the hint of warning in his tone and wrap my lips around the fat head, sucking and breathing him in at the same time.

'Fuck, woman.' His fingers tangle in my hair, his hips rising up to meet my mouth. His thighs are steel under me, his hands so big they practically cup my entire face as he holds on.

Triumph soars inside me. I glance up, the look on his face turning me on more than the last five minutes of frantic kissing and dry-humping combined. His mouth hangs open as he drags air into his lungs, his heavy-lidded stare is glued to the place where he disappears into my mouth and, as I take him deeper, breath hisses from between his teeth and his strong abs contract, shoving him a little further down my throat. Even lost to his pleasure, he can't stop touching me, one hand leaving my hair to roam across my shoulder, my breast, even tracing my lips where they're stretched around him as if he's fascinated by the sight and feel of me giving him head.

This big, sexy, controlled man wants me. He can't stop himself, despite his reservations and honour. Just like I want him. My sex clenches, empty, a new gush of arousal coating my soaked underwear. Then, with a low cry, he yanks me up from my position between his legs and rolls me under him once more. 'Need to come…inside you.'

'Yes! Hurry.' I wriggle free of my underwear at last.

In seconds he's sheathed and then he pushes my knees back up onto my chest and guides himself inside with one hand. We groan together, breath mingling. Drake's eyes roll closed and then slam back open as he lowers his head to my breast, his hot, possessive mouth covering my nipple. I cry out, my internal muscles clamping on him as jolts of pleasure snake down my belly.

He's worked his way inside me, as deep as I think he can go, but then he rears back, his eyes locked to mine, and rolls his hips, pushing in the last delicious inch. He holds still, his hips pressing mine into the mattress.

Our chests work in unison to drag in air.

We lie face to face, joined, as open and physically vulnerable as two people can be.

Neither of us speaks.

I hold my breath, lost in the newness of him—his eyes, his strength, his possession—lost to possibility. Because only now am I really discovering Drake Faulkner. And the more I know, the more I want to know.

Slowly, and without moving his hips, he balances on one arm over me and with the other hand traces an almost reverent path from my cheek, down my neck, pausing to cup my breast and then across my belly to my hip. My breath stalls. I feel claimed. Marked somehow.

A dangerous feeling.

Lifting my leg, he curves my thigh over his hip and his abs contract, providing the barest hint of friction.

It's so good I want to weep.

When he's positioned me just how he wants me, he entwines his fingers with mine and presses our clasped hands into the bed beside my head. 'Fuck, if I'd known it would be this good...' he bites out, his jaw muscles bunched.

My lust-fogged brain scrambles. *What does that mean?*

Then he starts to move in earnest and I tremble, too overcome by my desire and the battle against my own feelings to dissect his words.

'Don't stop.' I don't care that I'm begging. I don't care that I shouldn't want him this way. I don't care that I'm betraying our past connection and potentially jeopardising my future by blurring the lines. All that matters is this. How he makes me feel.

Reborn. Whole. Freed.

It's slow, torturous and thorough enough to make me want to close my eyes, but the almost reverent look on Drake's face is worth committing to my long-term memory, and I can't look away.

'Kiss me, Drake.' His eyes flare.

'Ask me again,' he grits out, eyes feral with what looks like longing.

Hearing his name does something to him. I want to say it over and over until I've cracked him open to see inside. Until everything he's holding on to spills free.

'Kiss me, Drake. Kiss me and don't stop.' Ever.

He growls, his face twisted with agony, and then he cups my face, fiercely lifting my mouth to his kiss. He starts to buck into me, putting us both out of our misery. I want to pull him down so his weight presses me into the mattress, every bit of his skin against every bit of mine. But my hands cling to his, our fingers locked together, a connection I couldn't break if I tried.

I pull back from his ferocious kisses for air. The look on his face, as haunted as just after his nightmare but burning with urgency, shows me what he's held back and how deluded I was to think we could walk away from this physical bond.

I knew he would be an attentive lover, but if he's subjected all those other women to this intense intimacy there should be queues of broken-hearted rejects lining the street outside the Faulkner.

A jab of pain disrupts the pleasure, the sharp slice of possession.

'Kenz… I can't hold on much longer…' There's sweat on his brow, his nostrils flare as he delivers deep, pounding thrust after thrust.

I shake my head and raise it from the bed to kiss his decadent mouth, chasing off my demons and searching for a return of the all-consuming rush. 'Don't worry about me…' I whisper against his lips. I want to witness his release. He gave me so much the first time and I've allowed my head, my pointless jealousy of some fantasy woman in his future, to get into my head.

'Fuck that.' He pulls away and I cry out. But I have no time to lament, because he encourages me to roll over onto all fours, plunges back inside and then scoops one arm around my waist and tugs me up so my back is plastered to his sweaty chest.

'Grip the headboard,' he growls against the side of my neck, his facial hair scraping my nerve endings awake.

I obey. Kind of. Needing to touch him, I hold on with one hand and raise the other over my shoulder to tangle in his hair. The minute he's no longer supporting all my weight, he slips one hand between my legs and strums my clit through my own arousal.

My head lolls back onto his shoulder and he kisses the side of my neck, sucking down on my skin while his hand works me in front and his cock shuttles inside from behind.

'Drake…' I'm losing myself. Too turned on to do anything but cling on tight and accept the free fall when it comes.

He's ruthless, his pants gusting as he drags me back to the edge of bliss.

His growl buzzes against my ear as he slams home time after time, his words incendiary. 'I don't want to be your fucking friend, McKenzie.'

I turn my face to try to capture his mouth, his fingers sliding over my clit and the possessive way he growls my full name dragging a strangled whimper from me.

'Good.' I cry out, twist my fingers through his hair and hold on tight.

His thrusts grow in power, bumping me up and down on his lap. 'I want this—' his arm leaves my waist and he toys with my nipple so I'm a mass of writhing delirium, stimulated from all directions '—you. For as long as you need me. For as long as you'll let me inside you. That's what *I* want.'

It's a stretch to reach his mouth, but as he pushes his tongue against mine I can just see the fierce need on his face from the corner of my eye.

His need for me. Desire for me.

The feeling rushes in, filling parts of me I didn't know were empty.

I drag my mouth free as my orgasm crests. 'Yes… I want that, too…' And then speech is impossible because I'm coming and I don't know how he manages to hold me up in this position, but he grunts behind me, his free hand a vice on my hip as he slams into me and follows me over the edge into new territory.

CHAPTER NINE

Drake

I FIND HER in my living room. The panic thrumming in my throat tells me I'm in deeper than is wise, but my morning hard-on offers a distraction. I adjust myself inside the jogging bottoms I threw on when I found her gone.

She's wearing one of my shirts, the sleeves rolled up to her elbows and the hem skimming the tops of her thighs. Just like I fantasised. Only better. Because it's real. She's real.

Her hips sway to the music she's switched on as she walks around my space, her hand trailing the spines of the books in my bookcase. I watch the sensual way she moves with my elbow resting on the door frame and my head propped on my hand—may as well get comfortable for the show.

I'm loath to interrupt her curiosity. After last night, my declaration still fresh in my head, finding her gone amplified the rawness inside.

But now we've dispensed with *friends* we can focus on the sex.

I drag in a shuddering breath and give free rein to my grin. That I get a chance, even of something physical and temporary, with this wonderful woman makes child's play of the years of denial. And now what I want from her is out there I'm not going back to the friend zone, even if all it can be is fucking fantastic sex.

Kenzie comes to a standstill, her attention caught on something of interest. My gut twists as I figure out what it is she's seen.

It's a picture of Sam and me.

My body veers forward to intercept her before I freeze.

Too late.

She lifts the frame from the shelf.

My smile dies, my happiness draining. The past will never abate. It can never be just us—Kenzie and Drake. The time for that dream was the sliver of possibility just after I first spotted Kenzie and before she spotted Sam.

Fresh regret sours what little progress we made last night in bed.

'Basic training,' I say.

Kenzie spins, the photo still in her hand.

'We'd just thrown up moments before that photo, after a ten-mile run.' We'd bonded over our lack of fitness.

Sam was a great mate and an even better soldier.

Would he have continued to be her husband, had he lived? Would she have forgiven him?

A flush creeps up her chest and neck. From being caught snooping or because the last words we said to each other were ones that propelled our relationship in a new, uncharted direction? 'You're both so young.' She smiles down at the photo, a faraway look on her face.

'He ribbed me all day for being older and less fit than him.' Oppressive restlessness propels me to the kitchen, where I flick on the kettle. 'Tea or coffee?' I ram some bread into the toaster, regretting the fact I didn't go straight to her and kiss her good morning—perhaps then she'd never have spotted the photo.

'Tea, please,' she says, her voice distracted.

I don't decry that I've lost her again to memories of Sam. No matter where we go or what we do, we can't ever outrun our past, our connection through Sam.

My appetite vanishes.

I busy myself with breakfast, but I'm so attuned to the woman whose presence seems to brighten every corner of my home that when she sidles up beside me my muscles tense.

Her hand slips to my hip, just above the waistband of my joggers, her fingers warm, the tips flexing. I turn, automatically slipping an arm around her waist, and tug her up onto her tiptoes until my mouth reaches hers in that good-morning kiss.

Our mouths part, foreheads touching, my voice a husky croak that has nothing to do with the early hour. 'I thought you'd left.' *Changed your mind, regretted what you said...*

'No. But the shift work is messing with my sleep rhythms and I didn't want to wake you.'

I disguise my vulnerability by pressing my erection into her soft belly and slipping my hand over the curve of her hip to the cheek of her arse. She's naked under my shirt. Breakfast, work, meetings all slip from my mind as she wraps her arms around my neck and gusts a soft sigh over my lips.

I hoist her up onto the kitchen bench and slot myself between her thighs, which part readily as she accommodates me, despite her underwear-less state. I kiss her again, silently berating myself for falling asleep at all. I could have gorged on her all night, tried to sate this hunger, or at least died giving it a shot, because something tells me I'll never get enough, not now that we've dispensed with the 'friends' label.

'Do we have time?' she whispers against my ear, making my fingers flex against her arse cheeks, which fill my hands as I grind her onto my hard length.

I drag my mouth away from the soft skin of her neck, which is already red from the scrape of my morning stubble. One look at the clock on the stove turns this morning from *awesome with possibility* to *I wish I had a time machine*.

'Not if you want to be on time for your shift.' I could wing it, make a phone call, tell my assistant to inform Rod his protégée won't be in until she's come at least twice—the first time on my mouth, right here in my kitchen, and the second time while I fuck her in my shower…

Damn.

With a sigh she drops her forehead to my bare chest and presses a kiss there. 'To be continued, then?' Her eyes still carry that dreamy, turned-on glow. I want to sweep the bench clear of breakfast preparations, splay her out and make sure I'm the only man in her head for the rest of the day. Even if that fantasy were possible, my condom stash is miles away and the clock is ticking…

I slide her from the bench with one last kiss and hand her a plate of toast. 'Help yourself to spreads— sorry it's not gourmet.'

She laughs, pouring herself a mug of tea from the pot and snagging some marmalade from the fridge.

'I don't need gourmet. Anyway, you shop at Fortnum & Mason…' She waggles the jar in my face with a roll of her eyes. 'I think you have gourmet covered.'

My smile tugs at my cheeks and I steal another kiss, my mouth sliding to the back of her neck as she butters her toast and spreads a generous helping of marmalade on it.

'By the way…' I bury my face in her hair, hoping the scent of apples will rub off on me '…thanks for the green icing.'

Her lips twitch. 'You're welcome. Thanks for taking care of me last night.' She presses her arse against my still-hard cock and moans as she takes a bite of toast.

I lick a stray crumb from the corner of her mouth, the urge to tell her I'd like to take care of her a whole lot more brewing in my throat when I remember what she told me last night about her family traditions, about all that she's lost.

'How did you do it?' I whisper, respect and awe for her strength pushing my organs aside. 'Take on the responsibility of caring for Tilly after losing your parents? You were so young.'

She stills and I curse changing the mood.

'I had no choice. She's my sister and I didn't want to be parted from her—she helped me grieve for Mum and Dad as much as I helped her. And, for a while, we both had Sam.'

Fresh guilt crushes my windpipe. Only the feel of her in my arms stops my fists from forming.

She brightens her tone, but I hear the forced note. 'Life goes on. It's been lots of fun, too. And look at her now.'

'You are both incredible women.' I struggle to talk past the emotional chokehold. 'Any time either of you needs anything, just let me know.' It's not enough, but it's all I can offer.

She leans back into me with a sigh, crushing my

erection between our bodies and curling one arm around my neck. 'Thank you. I didn't realise how much I needed the simple pleasures of a hot bath and a meal I didn't make myself.'

'No problem.' But, with her soft and warm and wriggling against me, my brain has other simple pleasures in mind. My fingers skate her waist under the shirt, over her belly.

Her head lolls back against my chest and she groans as my hand dips between her legs. 'Drake, yes…' She spreads her thighs a fraction, making room for my hand between her thighs and my cock between the cheeks of her arse.

If I abandon my own breakfast, we shower together and I break a few speed limits, we have time…

'Good…? Shall I stop?' I strum her clit, my slippery fingers circling.

'No.' She abandons her toast and grips the edge of the bench. 'Don't stop.'

'Touch your nipples.' My order makes her whole body shudder.

She clings tight with the arm around my neck and follows my instructions. Her hand covers one breast through the open neck of my shirt, and mine toys with the other nipple—a sight way more satisfying than mere breakfast.

She's so ready, so responsive, she comes with my name on her lips and likely the taste of F&M's finest lime marmalade still on her tongue.

* * *

It's only a few miles to the Faulkner, but driving prolongs the time I get to have her to myself.

'Do you have a shift tomorrow?' I glance sideways. She's distracted, searching for something in the pockets of her bag.

'Yes, but not Tuesday. Why?'

I must be possessed, or my blue balls have poisoned my mental faculties, the only explanation for what I say next. 'Wanna get out of town for the night, go somewhere…hole up in a B&B…have tons of uninterrupted sex…?' I'm practically salivating. And I want another hit of waking up with her next to me.

She looks over, her eyes bright with excitement.

'We can escape as soon as you're finished tomorrow.' I coerce for good measure. 'Just pack an overnight bag, although I don't mind if you spend the whole twenty-four hours naked.'

She scowls. 'Even while I cook?'

'Especially while you cook.' Visions of her laid out and me sampling amuse-bouches from her naked skin blind me so I almost rear-end the car in front.

Her face splits into a breath-stealing smile. 'Yes,' she says, fuelling my fantasies of all the filthy things I'm going to do to her, away from London, away from reminders and memories. A place where we can just be Kenzie and Drake. Perhaps make some memories of our own, ones I can carry long after this ends.

Then she frowns and looks away.

My euphoria plummets and then it hits me—she has responsibilities.

'Will Tilly be okay for one night?' I ask, my heart skipping a beat. 'We don't have to go.'

Kenzie nods, her smile warming me from the inside. 'She'll be fine, and I can check in with her—we won't be that far away, will we?'

I shake my head. 'I'll keep it to a two-hour drive—we can come back any time, day or night. If you want, I can ask Kit and Mia to be on standby, just in case.'

Perhaps I imagine the sheen of moisture in her eyes as she stares at me and nods.

We're nose-to-tail in traffic, the car idling at a complete standstill. I'm about to cup her face and kiss the residual worry from her mouth when she says, 'There's something I want you to have.'

Her bag rummage successful, she produces a small purse.

I inch the car forward, keeping up with the snail's-pace flow of cars, and then look at her outstretched palm.

A coin. It looks like any other coin but the fact she keeps it in a special purse and she's offering it to me confirms my guess: Sam's lucky coin. It may as well be a coiled viper.

I know surprise registers on my face because it's knocked the wind from me. But I manage to cover the nauseating roll of my stomach with my question. 'You still have it?'

She's smiling her sad smile at me as she nods. 'It was returned to me with his possessions.'

I know this. I put it with Sam's personal effects. I had it in my hand when he died.

'I...I want *you* to have it.' Her luminous eyes are round.

I'd rather put my hand in the industrial mincer in the Faulkner kitchen, but I force a smile, knowing the likely import of this treasured token to Kenzie. She carries it with her, for fuck's sake.

'*You* should keep it.' I'm on a knife's edge of white-knuckled panic.

She's shaking her head before I've even finished speaking. 'He'd want you to have it. You know he would.'

I swallow bile, smack what feels like a grimace on my face and reach for the coin. It's not the item itself—it's what it represents.

My failures.

My biggest regrets.

Loss of not only my best friend, but any chance with this woman, too.

I pocket the coin, grateful when the traffic nudges forward and I'm forced to concentrate so she can't witness the storm of emotion I'm not certain I can hide.

She must interpret my silence as one of contemplation, reliving fond memories. If I were alone I'd punch out my own windscreen.

A perfectly timed break in the traffic means I

have to navigate the drive for the last few minutes to the hotel's underground car park.

When I kill the engine and look her way she puts her hand on my arm. 'So I'll see you tomorrow? I'll be finished by three.'

I squeeze her hand, my throat too tight to utter more than, 'I can't wait.'

She nods and then whispers, 'Me neither.' The haunted look for the husband she lost is still at the fringe of her stare—you'd think I'd be used to it by now. Immune. But there's heat and excitement, too.

I console myself with the latter, accepting the scraps she can give. I can do this. I can hang in there. Give her what she needs until she's ready to move on to a forever relationship without our complicated history, untainted by my baggage.

We leave the garage, her for the staff entrance and me for the lift to the executive offices. The symbolism strikes a chord with me like a blow to the chest. No matter how badly I want her, we're moving in different directions.

· CHAPTER TEN

Kenzie

WHEN I'M STARTLED awake it's pitch-black outside the car and we've left London far behind. I know because I smell the sea as the car bumps down some sort of rough gravel driveway.

Beside me, Drake seems pensive. I clear my throat and he flicks me a hastily donned smile. 'I didn't want to wake you.' His hand covers my knee.

I rub at my eyes. 'Where are we?'

Somewhere two hours from London, he said, but it feels like the middle of nowhere. I slip my hand into his, my breath hitching when he lifts it to his mouth and presses a kiss to my knuckles.

'Hampshire,' he says, the look on his face an intimate promise. 'The New Forest coast.'

A shiver runs over me—one of anticipation. 'Sounds like heaven.' Of course, we've had lots of alone time, but away from the Faulkner, away from our respective roles, perhaps he'll open up and we can finally move closer...

He's holding back. I feel it. I saw it when I gave him Sam's coin. And I understand. Losing Sam, witnessing his death—the nightmares prove it must still haunt him. Perhaps he'll never be free, some things too horrific to overcome. My stomach twists with guilt. I had no idea he still suffered, that, while I'm moving on, Drake remains stuck.

His handsome profile, silhouetted in the dark, catches my breath and fills me with longing. I want to help. He's given me so much. He's helped me with my career, given Tilly his time and most importantly he's made me feel desired again where Sam's affair left me feeling second best and doubting everything—my worth, my attractiveness, my very femininity.

I grip his hand, craving closeness. 'I'm sorry I fell asleep. You had no company while you drove.' I want to ask him if he's sought counselling, if he wants to talk through the day of Sam's death. But our bond is fragile, and he's already knocked back my questions once.

'No problem. We're here.' He pulls to a stop outside a whitewashed cottage and winds down the window, allowing the frigid, sea-tinged air into the car. 'This cottage was once a smuggler's inn. The sea is right there—not that you can see it at the moment. But tomorrow...' He lifts a brow, his face relaxed, flirtatious and full of promises.

My heart lurches—perhaps I imagined his reaction to the coin.

Someone has left lights on inside, the cosy orange glow welcoming. Drake kills the engine and collects our bags from the back seat. We locate the key under the doormat and I can't help the giggle that escapes as we enter our seaside hideaway for the night.

I gasp, exploring the living room, my touch trailing over plush throws, soft leather armchairs and comfy cream sofas with sea-coloured cushions while my stare flits between quirky art, whitewashed walls and the crackling fire in the hearth. An open bottle of red wine sits on the coffee table with two glasses.

I turn to Drake, my heart in my mouth. 'It's stunning.'

His mouth twitches. 'Why don't you pour, while I dump the bags?' While he goes in search of the bedroom, I toss my coat over a chair and snuggle by the fire. When he returns he's changed into jeans and another soft-looking sweater.

He settles beside me and takes the glass of wine I offer, clinking it gently to mine. 'To getting away from it all.' His smile is warm, eyes sultry, but he hasn't touched me. *Tons of uninterrupted sex*, he said…but he's clearly in no hurry.

Whereas I—my foot is jiggling, I've already sunk half of my wine and if I get any warmer I'll have to strip off or go for a dip in the black ocean beyond the windows.

'Are you hungry?' he asks. 'The owner filled the fridge for us—I can do cheese on toast as well as an omelette.'

I sip my wine. 'Maybe later. I'm not hungry right now.' Burning with curiosity, full of repressed lust, but not hungry. If we're talking, moving at Drake's leisurely pace, at least I can satisfy one of my urges. 'So, are Kit and Mia serious?'

Drake nods, his stare taking on that slightly wary look he wore when I gave him Sam's coin. 'They've been a couple for a few months, but I'd say Kit's in love. And I'm glad. He deserves a second chance.'

Here goes. 'And what about you? Anyone serious these last three years?'

He laughs, shakes his head and looks away. 'No. Work, life. I'm pretty busy.'

'So you've never…been in love?' From memory, Sam told me Drake has always done casual, never once losing his heart. But he has so much to offer. The idea he's content with so little skates beneath my skin, raising hairs.

He shrugs, giving nothing away.

'Is that a choice, or have you just never found the right woman? Because you have a lot to offer.' I wave my hand around, encompassing the complete package that is him and this idyllic romantic hide-away he's organised.

Even when Sam was alive I wondered at this co-nundrum. But some men aren't commitment types. Not that Drake is a Lothario, but I'm sure he hasn't been a monk over the years.

'Something like that.' His eyes glitter as he

watches me over the rim of his glass, and I grow even hotter inside. Is he going to distract me with sex?

'What about you? One day I guess you'll want another relationship?' His lip curls like the idea of a lasting commitment, of love, is distasteful, and I shrivel a little inside. I don't want to examine why too closely. I shouldn't be thinking about Drake and lasting relationships in the same headspace.

I wince. 'I haven't really given much thought to the future.' I said sex is all I want from him, and it was…in the beginning. 'I've just been putting one foot in front of the other, focussed on taking care of Tilly for so long. But I definitely want to find love somewhere down the track—once Tilly is settled, of course. She's still my priority.'

I loved Sam. We had our issues. He's gone. I can't shut myself down to the possibility of ever finding love again.

His stare heats my face. I shrug, feeling foolish. Romantic.

'You deserve another shot at happiness. You've been through so much. You've bravely steered your little family through adversity most people never have to face.' He lifts my free hand from my lap and raises it to his mouth, pressing the back of my hand to his lips as his searing eye contact delivers a hit twice as potent as the alcohol in my system. 'But don't forget your own dreams.'

I'm too choked to speak, so I nod, wishing I could return the sentiment. He deserves more, too. Just because he said he wanted more than friendship, doesn't mean he wants more than fuck buddies—not with me. But one day…when the elusive *right woman* comes along…

I ignore the flare of jealousy beneath my skin and focus on helping Drake like he's helped me.

I swallow another gulp of wine and lower my voice to murmur, 'Have *you* had some help…talked things through with anyone…?' Is the trauma of losing Sam still buried inside, holding him back?

He freezes. 'Things?'

'Yes. Losing Sam, the nightmares…' I can't stay quiet. I care. I want him to be whole, even if it means he finds love with another woman.

He looks away, scrubs a hand over his face, the moment he decides to let me in heralded by a minute slump of his shoulders. 'I had some counselling for PTSD. Walking away from the army, coming back to the family business, the support of my brothers all helped.'

I cover his hand with mine, needing to touch him. 'But you still have the nightmares…'

He nods, eyes haunted. 'But before this past week, it had been a while.'

His tone is matter-of-fact, as if he's downplaying it for my sake. To save *my* pain. But why?

'Is…is it because I came back? Have I opened things up for you?' I *should* have fought my attraction to him more.

'No. It's nothing to do with you. I'm fine.'

I'm not letting him hide this time. 'Of course it's something to do with me. I charged into your life, asking for your help, and I've stirred up the past.' The inescapable maze of the past, *my* past with Sam and Drake, throws up a brick wall around every corner. 'I was selfish. I'm sorry.'

My throat burns, nothing to do with the wine. 'What can I do? Do you want me to leave the Faulkner? To disappear again?'

'Don't be stupid.' He places his glass on the table and tugs me forward. 'You're the most selfless person I know.'

I clatter my own glass down so I can hold him with the fierceness building inside. His arms drag me closer until we're chest to chest, our heartbeats thudding together.

'The nightmares will pass.' He presses a soft kiss to my mouth, but I pull back, the flicker of doubt in his eyes increasing my unease.

'I want to help.' I cup his face, stroke the hair at his temples with my thumbs. 'You've done so much for me, for Tilly.'

'You are helping.' His kiss is warm and wine-scented, tempting me to trust his assertions. 'We have all night to talk,' he whispers. His hips shift under me and his erection presses between my legs. Another distraction I can't ignore.

But now I have him talking, I won't allow him to retreat. 'Promise. This is important.' He's important to me. 'I want to understand what you've been through.'

'Sure.' He shrugs, kissing me again. 'But I also promised you sex.' His avoidance is bordering on evasive, but his lips on my throat remind me we have all night and all day tomorrow. I can't expect him to spill all his feelings out in one sitting. But I want to know everything he's holding in check. Not just from me, but from living his own life to the max.

His hands are under my sweater now, skimming up my back and expertly opening my bra, single-handed. I succumb to his diversion tactics with a sigh. 'I probably smell like sautéed onions. Do you want to take a shower?'

'You smell like you taste…delicious.' His mouth grazes my neck and his fingers tangle in my hair, tugging my messy bun loose.

I arch my neck, giving him access to all the sensitive spots that curl my toes and thrum my pulse between my legs at the scrape of his mouth.

The usual wave of arousal drags me down, but in the background I'm hollow, empty. It's not enough. I want more of this incredible man than great sex. I want his confidence. His trust. The knowledge that, if he needed someone to talk to, he'd come to *me*, just like I know I could ask for his help or advice.

I try to relax, to enjoy him raining kiss after kiss on my neck, my face, my mouth while I tug at his broad shoulders and thick biceps, loving the size and strength of this big man under my greedy hands.

Soon we're panting hard, my reservations side-lined, our sweaters in a heap in front of the fire. Drake pulls away, all action, dragging me to my feet. In seconds we've made it to the bathroom and we're stripping off the rest of our clothes while the double-sized shower cubicle fills with steam.

We're about to step inside when I still Drake with my hand on his arm. I'm kind of killing the moment, but I know how this is going to go. We're naked, I want him inside me more than I want my next breath, and there are no condoms in that shower cubicle.

'What is it…? Changed your mind?' He hides his disappointment well, his hand gripping mine, his thumb tracing soft, lazy circles on the back of my hand.

'No.' I kiss him, showing him I'm completely in-vested. 'I just… I had a sexual-health check a few weeks back…' I shrug. 'Just in case. I'm on the pill and I—'

He silences me with another kiss, his groan buzz-ing at my sensitised lips. 'Fuck, Kenzie. You're kill-ing me.' He cups my face, his expression earnest. 'Just for the record, as we're being responsible, I haven't slept with anyone since my last screen. I wouldn't have touched you without an all-clear.'

That he's already thought of this, that he respects me enough, is mature enough to take care of the women he's intimate with, seals my decision. Not that I want to think about those women who came before me. And the women who will come after…? I want to think about *them* even less.

I grip his waist, taking a next step with him now imperative. 'If you want…we could forget about the condom.' So he's struggling to open up. I know he cares. He's shown me over and over—his patience with Tilly, his encouragement of my dreams, even feeding me and remembering my wine of choice.

I tug him towards the shower and step under the hot spray.

A feral gleam enters his eyes as he grips my hips and backs me up against the tiled wall. His naked body covers mine, shoulder to hip, as water rains down over his back. But for Drake the subject isn't closed. He tilts my chin with one finger, eyes searching.

My breath catches.

'You sure?' His intense stare brands my skin. Is this moment as momentous to him as it is to me?

Because we're responsible adults. What we're really saying is 'I trust you' on a whole new level.

I nod, words trapped in my aching throat.

'You trust me?' His strength pins me to the tiles where the look of sincerity on his face would buckle my knees. 'To take care of you…?'

'Yes.' No hesitation.

His pupils dilate, swallowing the colour of his eyes.

'Do you trust *me*?' I whisper. That we have each other's backs, even in this small way, makes me feel like there's less room in my chest. Less room, because a new heart—fragile and tender, but with the potential to thrive and overcome—has grown alongside the old.

I don't need his words, because confirmation is written on his face, but they replenish me.

'Of course.' He looks so vulnerable in that moment, I drag him close, wishing we could somehow merge, so I knew his thoughts and there was nowhere for either of us to hide. We don't kiss, simply stare, our foreheads touching, our soft pants mingling as we breathe each other's air.

'Drake…' Forbidden thoughts materialise into words I'm too scared to free. I swallow hard, sidestepping the terrifying admission of emotion I can't trust. 'Thanks for bringing me here.' It's not what I want to say, but he seems aware of the gravity of the moment.

His hands trail over my skin with lazy reverence. 'Thanks for running away with me.'

I want to ask what he's running from but refuse to kill the moment. He promised we'd talk later.

Almost reluctantly, Drake reaches for a bottle of body wash and soaps every inch of my skin, his eyes following his hands as if in fascination. 'You're beautiful. Inside and out.' The husky words scrape my senses like his slightly calloused palms. 'When you're ready, any man would be lucky to have you in his life.' His reference to our earlier conversation hurts my ears.

Any man but you…

I almost say the accusation aloud. Instead I slide my soapy hands through his chest hair, over his muscular shoulders and down his back.

'You're beautiful, too,' I whisper.

His eyes flare with heat and his hips flex, pushing his erection into my belly. A swell of emotion builds like trapped lava inside me. I know first-hand the futility of the 'what if' game, but for a decadent second I imagine a different life for myself, a life shared with Drake.

My heart thunders, the realisation as cold as the tiles at my back. I want more than sex. I want the possibility not just of some future man, but of *this* man. But wanting someone is dangerous. Pain inevitable.

I focus on the physical so the panic squeezing my lungs abates. I kiss him, pouring my conflicted feelings into the slide of my lips against his and the tease of my tongue.

Drake groans against my mouth, his hands cupping my backside so he can grind against me. His fingers roll my nipples and my legs grow weak. I curve one leg over his hip, raising my hips to align my clit with his hard length, my flesh sliding over him making us both moan and break from the frantic kiss.

With a curse, Drake slams off the water and leads me from the shower. We're sopping, leaving puddles on the tiles, but there's no time for drying, because Drake scoops the fluffy white towels from the heated towel rail and strides into the adjoining bedroom, dragging me in tow.

The room is warm, an intimate glow coming from the two bedside lamps. In seconds he's spread the towels over the duvet and lowered us on top as if he, too, has no patience for the trivial.

Drake licks the droplets of water from my breast, his mouth sucking hard on my nipple until I cry out, throw one thigh over his hip and lift my pelvis towards him, seeking the friction I need.

'I want you.' *All of you.* I clamp my lips closed on the latter and tug his hair, cradling his head so he continues the delicious torture that's almost too good to trust.

'I want you, too. So fucking much. You have no idea.' Need brands his features, as if he's reached his limit. His fingers slide through my slickness as he plunges two inside me and thumbs my clit.

But I want more.

'Give me everything, then.' I grip his erection, pumping him until he growls, rises up to kiss me, his teeth scraping my lip.

'Don't say that.' His tongue delves into my mouth, his eyes wide open to capture my reaction to his touch.

I pull away, panting, staring, provoking. Because he may not give me his confidences, but he'll give me his trust this way. 'I mean it. I want everything you've got.' Does he feel it, too? That it's no longer about sex? That every touch, every look, every word tonight seems amplified, bigger than either of us, as deep as the ocean outside our hideaway's windows.

'Kenzie...' His gruff voice holds a note of warning, but he kneels between my thighs, spreading them wide with his big hands.

I roll my nipples, because I've seen what it does to him. 'Drake, you've given me so much...don't hold back now.' I sit up on my elbows and we watch together as he angles his cock to my entrance with one hand and slides inside me, skin to skin, his beautiful, earnest stare and the low growl in his throat giving me everything his words can't.

It's so good, I want him to both hurry and slow down at the same time. But then he's gripping my hips and pulling me towards his thrusts, his lip trapped between his teeth as he watches himself plunge inside my body.

I'm jealous. I want the view he can't seem to drag his eyes from, but then his thumb finds my clit once more and I'm past caring, too focussed on the last ascent and the almost euphoric possession on Drake's face.

I spread my thighs and hook my legs around his hips. He sinks lower, coming to rest fully on top of me, his weight crushing me into the bed and his mouth on mine in kiss after breath-stealing kiss.

'I'm going to come so hard for you.' His fingers lock with mine, squeezing as if he's afraid I'll disappear.

'Yes!' I buck my hips, meeting him thrust for thrust.

'Kenz, come for me.' His eyes cling, pleading something I long to grasp. But his request is easy to grant, because he's powering into me, his thrusts deep and fast and his kisses pushing me over the edge.

'Drake…' My nails dig into his back as the orgasm takes me. But he's only seconds behind me, his groan, buried against the side of my neck, almost feral and his arms banded so tightly around me, for a second I think he'll never let me go.

CHAPTER ELEVEN

Kenzie

WEARING ONLY DRAKE'S T-SHIRT, I pad on bare feet down the hallway, my steps hesitant as I balance the contents of the tray—what's left of the wine and doorstep sandwiches. I expected him to come looking for the post-sex snack I've made, so loud was the rumble from his stomach only five minutes ago.

I pause outside the room, hoping he hasn't fallen asleep. The bedroom door is ajar; I peek through the gap, an indulgent smile on my face.

He's not asleep.

He's perched on the side of the bed, dressed only in his jeans, his attention focussed on the object in his hand—Sam's coin.

The smile slips from my lips.

The expression on his face, like a harsh slap across my own cheek, makes me certain all his previous expressions up to this point have been masks. Defeat drags at his broad shoulders and his teeth scrape repeatedly at his lip as he flips the coin over and over between his fingers.

I'm frozen, my pulse leaping. Interrupting feels intrusive.

I grip the tray, backing up a pace, desperate not to rattle any of the contents and give away my position. And then my feet stall, shocked still.

Drake's face twists with disgust.

He hurls Sam's coin across the room before plunging his hand into his hair with a curse.

The blood drains from my head. I've never seen controlled, caring Drake so upset. My heart thunders, slinking away undetected now the priority, because if he looks up, sees me snooping, he'll know I've just witnessed his outburst. But worse, I'll want answers I'm not sure I'm ready to hear.

Is he angry with Sam? With me? Has my gift slashed open painful memories?

With a frustrated hiss, he jerks to his feet, turns his back to the door and strides in the direction he threw the coin. While he drops to his knees, his hand searching the floor under a chair, I seize my chance.

I scuttle back to the living room as quickly and as quietly as I can. I place the tray on the low coffee table with trembling hands, dragging the whole thing aside so I can spread one of the throws in front of the freshly banked fire and finish the impromptu carpet picnic with a handful of the brightly coloured cushions.

I sit on the throw and pour myself a bolstering

glass of wine, the whoosh of blood through my head deafening.

This is how Drake finds me, moments later.

'Food looks delicious.' He helps himself to a glass and joins me on the rug. He's donned another T-shirt along with a fresh mask and I wish I'd taken the time to dress properly. I, too, could use the armour.

'It's just sandwiches. I think the gourmet fairies have visited, because the food in the cupboards resembles the selection at your place.' I force a smile and hand him a plate. He selects a sandwich, taking a massive bite. He grins but he's too busy eating my pulled pork and watercress to speak.

Perhaps he'll be more talkative with his belly full.

What should I say? He won't want to talk about whatever momentous thing just happened in the bedroom. But I can't ignore his pain. I need more than the parts he's willing to share when we're naked. I brush a crumb from his chin and cup his cheek, seeking his stare with mine, hoping to find the answers I need.

His chewing slows, his hand coming up to cover mine and holding it against his face while he finishes his swallow.

'Aren't you hungry?' He washes down the mouthful of sandwich with a hesitant sip of wine and I take a drink of my own, although I want a clear head for the conversation to come.

I lie. 'I ate one while making them.'

He accepts my answer, but he must sense my

change of mood, because he pushes his plate aside,
settles back against the mound of cushions and tugs
me between his legs so I'm resting on him, back to
chest. His arms encircle me and his chin rests on my
shoulder as we stare at the flickering flames for several silent minutes.

'What is it?' he murmurs against my temple, his
lips whisper-soft.

I draw a deep breath. The last thing I want is to
spoil our romantic getaway. But this has moved past
casual. I care. A part of me always has.

I clear my throat. 'That was going to be my question for you.'

He stiffens.

I'm done letting him run. And the first thing that
springs to mind is something I've often wondered—
that Sam must have confided in Drake about his indiscretion. If Sam told anyone, it would be Drake.

'Did he tell you?' I whisper. 'That he'd cheated
on me?'

He holds his breath because his chest stops moving at my back. I stroke his arm with my thumb, letting him know I understand his torn loyalties. 'It's
okay. It wasn't your place to tell me.' Shooting the
messenger is unfair for both of us.

'You knew?' His breath ruffles my hair as he
presses his mouth to my temple with almost punishing force and sucks in a deep breath. 'He told
you?' His arms tighten around my waist.

'No. But I'm not stupid—he'd grown distant,

cagey, always checking his phone. Sam was a crap liar. And now you've confirmed it.' Of course, the part of me that had lost my parents had somehow expected his desertion; I just hadn't anticipated the permanence of his death to rob me of closure.

Drake's soul-deep sigh reverberates through my bones. 'I only found out at the end. I swear.' He grips me tighter. 'We fought about it. I made him promise he'd confess when we got home.'

I nod, the uncertainty I've carried all these years slipping away. 'I saw a text on his phone before you left on that final tour.' I twist my head on his shoulder to press a kiss to his lips, free at last to kiss him with a lighter burden of guilt at betraying Sam.

He frowns, his eyes stormy, as if he's just been told Father Christmas doesn't exist. 'But you didn't confront him?' A hint of accusation sharpens his tone.

I look back to the fire, the memories of that horrible time, Sam's unfaithfulness and then the finality of his death rising up afresh to burn and shame. 'I didn't want him leaving me feeling guilty or defensive. He needed focus. I thought there'd be time to confront him later.'

We fall silent, the tension in Drake's muscles telling me we're both processing.

Drake's loyalties would be divided between Sam and me, a no-win position. Is that why he threw Sam's coin? New resolve thrums through my veins. My fresh start and any future Drake and I might have is dependent on letting go of some ties to the past. For both of us.

'I know it's not fair to ask,' my voice wobbles, 'but would you tell me…about that day?'

He knows what day I mean. The day Sam died.

Half of me wants to know what Drake went through, the other half curls into a ball at the idea of hearing, from the horse's mouth, how my husband, an imperfect man I loved, died. But perhaps it's a conversation we both need.

I place my hands over his, my fingers tracing the strong tendons and smattering of dark hair on the backs of his hands.

His stillness is ominous, but he says, 'Didn't the army fill you in at the time?' His voice is quiet, measured, as if he's afraid to reveal too much. For a minute I think I've imagined our closeness, because this is distant, disciplined Drake talking.

'Yes, they told me it was quick…that he wouldn't have felt any pain.' I turn my head to the side, pressing my mouth to his. 'Please, Drake. Don't shut me back out.'

He stares at me for so long I think he's going to refuse. His eyes reflect so many emotions—a kaleidoscope. But what comes out of his mouth forces a gasp of air into my lungs.

'It should have been me.' It's barely a croak, rough with emotion.

I turn, facing him so I can see the truth of his words pass over his face.

But my reason fights for him. 'It wasn't your fault. What do you mean?' It was an accident. An act of war. No one was accountable, least of all Drake. 'Tell me how.' The shock on my face must convince him. He's kept this from me for three years.

His jaw hardens. 'It was a routine patrol. We'd done the same thing a hundred times. There was a car alarm sounding down the street. We ignored it for a while, waiting for someone to silence the damn thing.'

His harsh swallow shows what this costs him. I reach for his hand.

'Sam, as usual, was in a playful mood, calling me "old guy"—he never let me forget our age gap. Then this kid alone started crying not far from the car.' He hesitates, his chest working hard while he grapples with the emotions his confession releases. '"Heads I'll go, tails you'll have to drag your old arse down there," he said.' His tortured stare slays me and his swallow distorts his next words. 'He threw the coin and I caught it.'

I'm struck dumb.

Sam died over a coin toss.

It could have been Drake instead.

He grips my chin, his eye contact fierce, penetrating. 'I should have ignored him. Ordered him to leave it. It was *my* patrol, *my* responsibility.'

'You didn't know what would happen.'

His stare grows distant and he releases my face with a shake of his head. 'We saw similar scenes ten times a week.' His breath shudders out, and I feel the blades of his anguish slice my insides.

I want to hold him, but I stay still, waiting for more.

'Something felt off. I should have sensed it sooner, called it in, stopped him…' His throat bobs as he swallows hard. 'I was too far away. The hairs on the back of my neck started tingling and I called out… too late. I came to, deaf, my eyes and mouth coated in dust and Sam's coin still clutched in my hand.' His face is so haunted my eyes burn.

They could have gone together. Died together.

'Sam died instantly. An IED.' He pulls the coin from his jeans pocket, holding it up between us. 'But for this, it would have been me instead.'

My heart must have stopped beating somewhere along the line, because it restarts with a violent jerk behind my ribs. I can't compute his account beyond one clear fact—he may not have placed the explosive device that killed Sam in the road, but he's carrying the guilt.

'You're right to be angry. I stole him from you.' He grips the back of his neck.

My head pounds. I sift my feelings, teasing them apart. 'I'm not angry. I…I didn't know…about the coin. I never would have given it to you.'

He shakes his head, pain evident in the lines around his dulled eyes. His hands rise to touch me and then fall back to his sides, listless. 'I'm sorry.'

I cup his face, forcing him to keep my eye contact. 'Drake, it's *not* your fault.' He's carried this for three years. This sense of responsibility. No wonder he stayed away. He couldn't face me.

He nods, eyes tormented. 'I let Sam down. I let you down. You lost him.'

My eyes burn and I look away from his gorgeous face, the strength and pain I see there suffocating. I lean my head on his chest, dragging comfort from the steady beat of his heart and the rhythm of his breath sounds.

With a final shudder, my weary soul accepts that ahead lies a dead end.

Drake only wants sex, and I'm the last person he could consider loving, not when he's carrying the blame for what happened to Sam.

There's no way past it.

We sit in silence, his strong arms a cocoon around my body, which is trapped somewhere between the languid weight of comfort and the icy shivers of doubt. But now I have new resolve—convince Drake he wasn't responsible, so when this, us, is over he can move on without regret.

CHAPTER TWELVE

Drake

KENZIE'S COLD HAND in mine as we walk along the beach fills the aching void in my chest where last night's sleepless hours of replaying our conversation over and over while she slept at my side failed. Her passion, her honesty, her trust rubbed at the angry scab of my self-doubt, even as I did my best to hold on to my secrets.

Although she woke as the weak dawn light pierced the curtains, turned to me and wordlessly kissed me with growing passion that quickly turned into more, she's been quiet since. We both have. There's a lot to process.

And processing hurts like fucking salt on an open wound.

She knew. About Sam's affair.

I drag in sea-tinged air, breathing through the burn of futility. All these years I've grappled with the shame and guilt of carrying that burden for nothing. She loved him anyway. That their marriage could weather infidelity confirms what I've always known.

I might regret my choice for my own selfish reasons, but stepping aside for Sam was the right thing to do.

I glance sideways, at Kenzie's fresh beauty, her pensive focus on the view of the choppy waters of the Solent beyond our private beach a small patch on the gaping wound in my chest. Her love for my friend was strong. Perhaps she's found a measure of peace from knowing exactly why Sam died.

My stomach twists with guilt and revulsion. Perhaps she does blame me and can't forgive either of my transgressions—keeping Sam's secret and handing his fate over to the pointless toss of a coin.

Either way, her sous-chef trial is almost up. Soon she'll either be a permanent fixture at the Faulkner, a permanent reminder of my failures, or she'll be building her career elsewhere, her fresh start and Tilly her only priorities…

A seagull cries overhead, the sound resembling the plaintive rumble in my head, demanding a solution I haven't quite reached. Now two of my secrets are out, could we continue to see each other on a casual basis?

I'd give anything for her to be more than casual, but there'll always be an enormous roadblock. There'll always be Sam.

But for me, he'd be holding her hand right now. He'd have been the one to make love to her in the early hours. He'd have laughed with her over cooking breakfast: eggs, bacon, all the trimmings—well, she cooked and I tried to keep my hands off her while pretending to learn how to perfectly sauté mushrooms.

I look down at her fingers, which are wrapped in mine. I grip her hand tighter—the simple act a dream come true—then swallow, the taste bittersweet.

Rising panic tightens my throat. I'm falling for her. Fair game with any other woman. But Kenzie and I aren't playing on level ground. While the memory, the ghost, of Sam is always present, he's not here in person.

How can we be together when she's his? How can I enjoy this when it's at his expense? And how can I win her when it's so far from a fair fight?

I look at her and I feel small for my years of yearning and hiding my true feelings. I touch her and I recall the first time I saw her face and I want to scrub my mind free of memories, free of regret. I kiss her and feel like the man I was always supposed to be.

I must utter some bleak sound, because Kenzie turns to me, her face glowing from the chill November wind and her eyes searching. 'Penny for your thoughts…' she says.

Could I tell her every feeling waking up inside? Unburden some remorse over that fateful decision I made? Would she run if she knew how long I've wanted her for myself?

'I was congratulating myself on bringing you here.'

Fucking coward.

I tug her close, pull her inside my coat and turn her away from the wind. 'This has been… Let's just say I haven't felt so content in a long time… Perhaps not ever.'

Does she feel the depth of our connection? Could she ever forgive me? Ever want *me*? Give me everything?

Could I tell her what I've held back from day one? Would my final confession repulse her as much as my regret sickens me?

She smiles, her lips cold against mine as she returns my kiss. 'Good. I'm glad.'

I can't resist teasing. 'And the sex was okay, too.'

She thumps my arm, rolling her eyes.

I grip her waist, sobering. I need to know that hearing about Sam hasn't reopened wounds. 'Are you okay? Can you forgive me…for Sam?'

A sheen covers her eyes. 'Ah… Drake. There's nothing to forgive. If it wasn't him it might have been you, or another member of your platoon. Sam was Sam. You knew him, I knew him. We loved him, despite everything.'

Hearing his name, spoken with such longing, I shrivel a little inside. My arms around her waist tighten, keeping her close in case she turns into a wisp of smoke and disappears on the wind.

'To be honest…'

I hold my breath, bracing myself for the worst.

'I'm a bit worried…about you.' She nibbles her lip. My thoughts reel while I hold myself still. 'Me?'

She nods, her big eyes wary and her own arms tightening around *my* waist. 'I want you to be okay, Drake.' The stare she raises to mine is full of things I want so badly to be more than apparitions. 'I want you to forgive *yourself…*'

'I…' I must stiffen because she rushes on.

'Have you ever visited Sam's grave?' Now it's her turn to hold her breath. I feel her chest expanding.

I swallow razor blades as I shake my head. Admitting I've neglected my friend's memory by staying away strips me bare to the sting of the sea spray. The notion this incredible woman sees so deeply inside me… It's like I've been sandblasted until all my layers are revealed.

Then I pull my head in. We're talking about *her* husband's grave. 'I'm okay—I lost a friend. You lost more.'

'Perhaps you should visit.' She sighs and I press my mouth to the top of her head, both offering and sucking up comfort.

She settles on my chest, as if it's the most comfortable spot on earth. 'I used to go there all the time in the early days and months, just like I'd take Tilly to visit our parents.' Her head rests against my heart, her cheek cold even through the thickness of my sweater. I wrap the sides of my coat around her, enclosing her body in a tight cocoon.

'I'd take a flask of tea, a packet of Sam's favourite biscuits and just sit there, talk to him, imagine his unique brand of sage advice…' She chuckles, the sound vibrating through my chest, and I'm torn in two once more.

She looks up, her sad smile slaying me. It's intimate, like a secret shared between a married couple. Like the smile she must have shared with Sam a thousand times. And if I close my eyes I can convince myself it's similar to the smiles she's shared with me this past week.

A chill hits me like the icy spray behind, spreading to infect every corner and crevice, that makes me understand—she'll *always* be his. Despite his flaws. Despite the passage of time. Despite how we might both want things to be different. She's his because I didn't fight for her the day we met.

I turn us back in the direction of the cottage, my hand tightly clasping hers—if I have to talk I need to move.

But what do I say to a woman I want for my own about her dead husband?

If I talked to Sam, I'd have to confess I've not only been sleeping with his wife, but I'm falling for her, too.

Even if you forgive me, Kenzie, I can't ever forgive myself, because my desire for you mentally betrayed Sam, even while he was alive.

Confessing my true feelings to you might, one day, earn me everything I've ever wanted, but at whose expense? At Sam's expense.

I've stayed silent for so long, Kenzie must assume she's caused offence with her suggestion, because she says, 'I'm sorry—I didn't mean to push… I just… want you to be happy. Sam would want you to forgive yourself. If he were here, you know what he'd say.'

I wince. Sam would toss his fucking coin—*Heads I kick your arse, tails I beat the crap out of you…*

'And I…care about you.' Her arm loops through mine and she leans close.

Her caring should thrill me, but I feel it being snatched away by the wind. I put one foot in front of the other, trudging through the soft sand while my head fills to exploding point. I might lose her for good. But if I stay quiet, I'm risking any chance I might have with her in the future.

At the deck at the rear of the cottage, I take a seat overlooking the ocean, tugging Kenzie down beside me. I suck in a breath tinged with possibility, the momentous words expanding in my throat until they break free. 'Do you know why I held you at arm's length while Sam was alive? Why I was never *your* friend?'

Her understanding expression turns injured as she blinks rapidly and glances down at her lap, trying to conceal her hurt. 'We weren't close, but—'

I press my fingertips to her frigid lips and then cup her freezing cheeks. 'I couldn't be your friend back then for the same reason I can't be your friend now.' The catharsis of last night's confession drags out my final shameful secret. Words pour from me, a tidal wave I've trapped inside all these years. 'I've always wanted you like this. The way we've been since you interrupted my dinner at the Faulkner that evening.'

She pulls back, her face slipping from my hands. It's hard to swallow, to admit my feelings, knowing I'll be less in her eyes, but the truth, concealed for so long, erupts like the crash of waves, needing an outlet. 'From the first day I met you, the very first moment I saw you… I wanted you that day and every day since. It's never lessened.' My self-recrimination is a dark pit, her comfort and forgiveness a foot up onto the first rung of the ladder out.

Confusion streaks across her beautiful face. 'But…' Her frown, the flash of pain in her eyes, chops the ladder from under my feet. 'You didn't speak to me…that night in the bar.' She shakes her head as if trying to clear her thoughts. 'You all but ignored me.'

I wince, admitting a colossal lapse of judgement. 'The minute I walked in I saw you in that red dress. Your infectious laugh, the spark in your eyes, the way you carried yourself—you were hard to ignore.' Her frown only deepens with my words. 'You know the way you look at a stranger, and you just know there's going to be sparks, a click, chemistry?'

She opens her mouth and then closes it again, her eyes shining as she tries to piece everything she thought she knew back together.

'By the time you noticed us, Sam had spotted you, too.' My throat is raw.

Then her hand covers her mouth and her eyes

widen. 'He didn't...?' She shakes her head. 'You didn't...?'

I nod, feeling an inch tall, my nails ragged where I've scrabbled against the grimy pit wall. It's so juvenile to think how I conceded so readily, that I allowed the toss of a fucking coin to seal my fate. To have lived the long-reaching consequences of that single decision.

'Sam tossed it out there—heads he'd earn a shot, tails I would.' I'm weighed to the seat, so heavy I may as well be a part of the timber. 'I was about to tell him to shove it—I already knew I wanted you. And then...' The razor blades are back in my throat, each word taking a little piece of me with it into the damp air. 'You looked over. Looked straight at Sam. Smiled that dazzling smile at him.' I shrug, the action painful, my muscles are so tight with repressed need.

'But... I...' Her confusion, her doubt is a blow to my sternum, smashing the wind from me, as she deflates on a sigh.

I kiss the back of her hand, hating how cold her skin is, hating that I chose to do this here, outside. Or to do it at all.

'You didn't do anything wrong. Neither of us knew you. You might have been engaged or married. You might have told us both to fuck off. You're not responsible for *my* appalling decisions.' No good can come from telling her this. Only that, in some selfish way, I've set my final burden free.

Her smile is brittle, unbelieving.

I grip her frigid hand. 'I was a dick. I threw away any chance of having you and had to live with the consequences. I know this…us…has an expiry date. You'll want to move on, date for real, find someone for the long-term. I'm only telling you this because… you deserve more. Someone without my baggage.' *Someone who can give you everything, love you without guilt.* 'And you're right—I need to work on forgiving myself. Get my shit together once and for all…'

The clock in my head ticks louder. We're expected back in London this evening. Back to reality.

She's still shocked speechless.

I hold her eye contact, make her hear my hoarse words. 'Part of me wishes I'd done things differently, but then I remember you loved Sam, had happy years with him.' I shake my head, the impossible choice no choice at all. 'I can't change a fucking thing, and, aside from losing him, I wouldn't.'

She nods, her brave smile wobbly as reality dawns. Even if we could meddle with the time-space continuum, changes to one scenario have ripple effects for the alternative.

I draw her close, the rhythmic lullaby of the waves my only solace. Because no matter how much I want to rewind time, Sam's still dead, and the woman in my arms is still Sam's.

CHAPTER THIRTEEN

Kenzie

THREE DAYS AFTER leaving our coastal hideaway, I'm struggling to recall the fairy-tale moments—perhaps I made them up. Perhaps I imagined Drake opening up to me, confiding his pain and confusion and his long-kept secrets.

Perhaps he didn't give me everything after all...

Dragging my mind back from the way he looked when he talked about the day we met, I jiggle the sauté pan on the stove with a sigh. I need focus. Rod is in a pissy mood. He's already made the new waitress cry and bawled out the pastry chef. I get it. It's his kitchen. He's right to demand perfection.

I add a glug of cream to the sauce in the pan. Spits of hot oil spatter the back of my hand, snapping me from thoughts of the phone in my pocket, which remains stubbornly silent.

I could reread the last text Drake sent...

Are you free for dinner tonight?

I could scour the non-committal words for hidden meaning, but I haven't fallen that low.

Yet.

I plate up the salmon steak atop a swirl of rich, creamy sauce and scatter a tiny trail of salmon roe as a garnish, my last lunch cover of the day. I take the plate to the pass, where Rod casts a critical eye over the dish, before wiping an imaginary speck from the rim of the plate with a pristine tea towel hanging from his waist and then sliding it forward for the waiting staff.

The Faulkner's maître d' finds me as I'm heading back to my station to clean up.

'McKenzie, you have a customer at table eight who'd like to thank you for their lunch.'

Rod overhears, giving a reluctant nod of approval.

I wait for the surge of euphoria at customer recognition in an otherwise thankless shift, and then offer a flat 'thanks' when it fails to materialise. My mind should be on this, my chance, my future. But…

I wipe my hands on my apron and head for the restaurant. When I see Drake sitting at table eight, I imagine I must have summoned him up from my mind, a hologram.

He stands, takes my elbow and presses a brief kiss to my cheek.

'What are you doing here?' So acute is the urge to touch him, to hold him, I'm tart, the deep trouble I'm

in where my feelings for him are concerned sucking
at me like quicksand.

'I've just finished lunch. Have a seat.' He pulls
out a chair and I eye it with longing. My feet throb
and I have kinks in my back only a ten-hour soak in
a hot bath and a massage will fix—not that there's
any chance of either.

I scan the restaurant before sliding in opposite
Drake, but the lunch rush has dwindled and no one
is paying any attention.

'The salmon tasted delicious. Thank you.' His
smile reminds me of the day I turned up in this restaurant to ask him for a favour.

'You're welcome.' It hurts to swallow. 'You…
you didn't have to do this—why so formal?' I look
around, my eyes struggling to stay on his, which
are haunted, distant. Is he embarrassed over what
he confessed at the cottage? Does he regret trusting
me with his demons?

'I wanted to talk to you.' He straightens his tie.
He's nervous.

A sense of foreboding pounds at my temples. 'I
thought we were meeting for dinner?' Perhaps he's
changed his mind. I fidget, feeling out of place in such
an elegant setting dressed in fat-spattered whites.

Then I look, *really* look, at his face.

My stomach plummets.

I know what's coming.

I know this man now—why did I ever think he
was hard to read? My fate is written all over his face,
despite the warm smile he's forcing for my sake.

His fingers twitch on the table, a few short inches from mine. Is he thinking about touching me? Or just nervous to be the bearer of bad news? Those inches may as well be miles.

'I'm sorry,' he says.

I cringe. Drake has left the building—this is Mr Faulkner talking.

He does touch me then, the slide of his fingers brief on the back of my hand. 'Rod has decided to go with Dominic—he says it's an experience thing and Rod feels he's a better fit.'

'Okay.' I wait for the crush of disappointment, but it's not as profound as I'd anticipated. I'd be lying if I said I haven't struggled under Rod's tutelage. Admitting you've bitten off more than you can chew sucks, but I've come to realise I might be better off at a lower-profile restaurant while I hone my skills and learn to perfect my craft.

'Well, thanks for such a great opportunity.' I'm impressed by the strength of my voice. 'I've learned a lot from Rod.' He may be an arsehole, but he's a talented chef. And I've had what I wanted—my shot at the big league.

And more—I've had my time with Drake.

Is that over, too?

He drops his voice, leans closer. 'Look, if it were down to me—'

'It's okay.' I don't want Mr Faulkner's platitudes. I'm a grown woman. I gave this my best shot and it didn't work. I'm not giving up on my dream.

Trouble is, I still want Drake. But there's no sign

of him. Will he remove me from his life, as well as from his restaurant?

His lips, lips I know are soft and demanding, thin. 'We will, of course, give you a stellar reference.' His eyes soften. He's conflicted, trapped between professional and personal. 'You have so much potential, Kenzie.'

I nod woodenly. I was expecting this—not the marching orders, but Drake's reaction. I seek confirmation that my growing unease is warranted.

But no, his face is unreadable, his mask back in place.

Has he been avoiding me? Not just because he didn't want to be the one to tell me I hadn't got the coveted job at the Faulkner, but because he's withdrawing emotionally?

Now the crush comes. Pressure surrounding my chest as if I'm trapped in one of those industrial compactors. I know, no matter how hard I scream, no one will hear and the space I'm in will continue to shrink, until I can no longer breathe.

If I'm honest, I saw Drake's desertion in his eyes on the beach. My stomach plummets as if I'm in a lift, the sense of déjà vu sucking all the energy from my body, a sickening coming-together of past and present.

Loss.

It pinches my stomach, a physical blow, and my eyes water.

The urge to talk to my parents, to Sam, Tilly—it's

been absent for a while, but it's back now, crushing my hot, aching throat.

I bite the inside of my cheek hard enough to stem the swell of grief. I need to pull myself together. I have to go back to work, face Rod, finish my shift.

I offer Drake a brave smile, seeing only regret in his eyes. All the signs were there from day one. And more fool me for thinking this time would be different. I care, I trust enough to let someone close and I get hurt, left, abandoned. The cycle as predictable as night following day.

I stand, dragging my weary body from the elegant chair. 'Well, thanks for letting me know.' My smile is one of gratitude—I'd rather have heard it from him than Rod. And Drake did exactly what he promised.

He stands, too, reaches for my hand, his Drake voice back. 'I…I'll pick you up at seven.'

I nod but all I want to do is head home and hide under my duvet. Emotionally, I feel like I've lived through an electrical storm featuring every feeling known to the human condition. And I've only myself to blame.

I trusted Drake. I gave too much of myself, hoping we were moving in the same direction. But his confession about the day we met—how he wouldn't change it—and now the sense he's pulling back… I suck in a deep breath, trying to stay rational, but I'm a pinball, ricocheting between emotional extremes.

I return to the kitchen and finish the clean-up, my movements automatic. I thank Rod for the opportunity, change out of the monogrammed Faulkner whites for the last time and head home on the Tube, the rhythmic clank and rumble of the carriage swaying on the tracks a lullaby to my pensive mood.

A headache grips my temples and I consider bailing out on tonight's plans with Drake. If I had a bath at my tiny flat I probably would cancel, wallow, drink wine in bed with a good book. But if the reckoning is coming I won't shy away, and tonight, whatever restaurant Drake has booked, is as good a place as any for a showdown. At least I won't be tempted to touch him, to kiss him, to succumb to the physical us and ignore the train wreck that represents the rest of our relationship.

Making a decision, I exit the Tube two stations early for an impromptu shopping trip. If the time has come to walk away, I want his lasting image of me to knock off his fine wool dress socks.

At home, I shower until the water runs cool and then I blow-dry my hair in soft waves and slip into my new purchase—a red dress, the fabric ruched to cup my breasts and caress the curves of my hips and backside.

If Drake plans to stage a tactical retreat, who says I can't fight dirty?

I top the dress with a faux-fur jacket to ward off the chill and meet Drake at the kerb outside my flat.

His gaze sweeps over me, his kiss to my cheek warm and soft, but his eyes are wary. From giving my marching orders or does he plan to tell me our affair is over, too?

As we crawl along Cromwell Road, Drake pulls my hand into his lap and breaks the silence. 'I'm sorry about the job—I know what it means to you.'

And what do I mean to you...?

'I'm fine. You were right to warn me at the beginning—Rod isn't easy to work for.' We stare, eyes locked, neither of us, I suspect, voicing what we really want to say.

We've barely sat at our table in the very upmarket restaurant and ordered a bottle of wine when we're joined by another man. I smile through my surprise as Drake shakes his hand and introduces us, before inviting him to sit. 'Luke is head chef at La Folie.'

Luke and Drake wait for me to take my seat and then join me. I hide my confusion with a sip of wine. Has Drake piggybacked a business meeting onto our date? I look down, a little hurt—I'd assumed we'd share an intimate dinner at best and a discussion on where this is going at worst. Before I can register what this means, Luke has drawn me into a conversation about my training and experience.

'So, Drake tells me you trained at Newell Academy?' Luke asks.

I nod, drawing upon the sales pitch I could recite in my sleep to appease Drake's charming friend. My hand grips the stem of my wine glass—Drake is lucky he's not *wearing* my glass of Pinot Noir. What the hell is going on? I shoot him a pointed look, earning myself nothing more enlightening than a return sheepish smile.

'Kenzie has a real flair for flavours,' Drake says, 'and, like you, she's passionate about local produce, ethical farming and sustainable agriculture.'

I smile but wither inside.

This is a job interview.

Drake's passing me on from his restaurant to Luke's.

'There's a sous-chef position opening up at La Folie,' says Drake, in confirmation.

This is his idea of a consolation prize. And the only reason I would need a consolation prize is if he's not only nudging me out of his workplace, but also out of his life.

I plaster a fake smile on my face for the easy-going, affable Luke, who's talking shop. If only I'd seen the position at La Folie before Drake thought he could stick a bandage over the gaping wound in our relationship with this act of appeasement, I could muster some enthusiasm.

If only Drake could offer me more than a leg-up, professionally...

I struggle through the rest of dinner. I smile in the right places, say the right things and attempt a laugh or two, while I burn inside. The raw feeling, like I'm a pan that's been scrubbed too vigorously, is familiar. It's the same feeling I got when Tilly told me she was moving away from home to explore her independence. The same feeling I had when my grief over Sam faded and I realised that he'd left me long before he died.

And now Drake has unburdened his guilty secrets, ticked the helping-out-the-widow-of-a-friend box, has he no further need for me, either?

I push away my dessert, my stomach in turmoil. I've fallen for a man who can't ever see me as a woman, because to him I'll always be Sam's wife.

Unless he's prepared to fight for me.

In the car, Drake instructs his driver to take us the short distance back to his place. I'm mute, my resilience at rock bottom—my skin too tight, my head too full and my heart…? Someone has removed that organ, split it in two and replaced it without bothering to sew the halves back together.

We're settled by the fire, nightcap in hand, before I speak my mind. 'Luke seems like he'd be great to work for. Better than Rod.'

He looks like he's tasted something sour, when all he's done is take a large sip of his own Scotch, single malt Glengoyne that's probably older than me. 'Yes. I've known him for years. He's a good man.'

The hairs on my bare arms prickle to attention. 'Like you.'

Drake snorts, shakes his head and downs the rest of his Scotch.

His body language speaks for him, confirming my doubts. *You can't work at the Faulkner, but here's a job at La Folie. We can't work, but here's the prize for runner-up.*

My temperature rises, nothing to do with the open fire.

He wants to move on, safe in the knowledge he's done his bit to take care of my future, as if I'm a goldfish in need of a new owner.

I draw in a mouthful of Scotch. 'So I'm guessing the job's mine, if I want it…' It's an effort to keep my voice neutral, to keep my face impassive, while I wait for his nod of confirmation.

I force a smile that literally hurts my face. 'Well, every cloud has a silver lining.' My blood pressure hits the roof.

I want to slap the bemused frown from his face.

'Are you angry? La Folie is a great opportunity, as good as the Faulkner…'

I close my eyes. Can't he see what he's doing? He's a decent, intelligent man. He probably thinks he's doing the right thing by me, by Sam. And on one level, he is. But we surpassed that level long ago—I want more than a consolation prize. I want him.

'I'm…hurt that you think I'm so fragile.' I breathe, teasing out the strands of this mess, which is twisted up with our pasts, our current predicament and what could be in our future. But only if we're both brave enough to take that leap. 'I can find my own job.' Can't he see it's not about the job?

'I know you can. I just wanted you to have some… security. I have the industry contacts—why shouldn't you benefit?'

'Because I'm a grown woman—I can look after

myself. I've been doing it most of my adult life.' Before you. 'When I came to you, I wanted one thing. A shot. And you gave me that. We're quits.' My words are a crack of a whip.

Of course now what I want has changed. I don't want him to fight for my career; I want him to fight for *me*. But is Drake, so caught up in regrets, in what might have been, capable of the fight?

Drake places his cut-crystal tumbler on the coffee table and nods, his eyes dark and stormy on mine while a muscle twitches in his cheek. 'I know you can take care of yourself. I'm just trying to keep my promise.'

'I know you're still loyal to Sam.' But what about me? What does *he* want? For himself? 'And your solution is to send me money or find me a replacement job?'

'Kenzie…' He growls out a warning, one I'm happy to ignore.

I stand, slapping down my own glass. I'm so done. 'Tell me the real issue here, Drake—be honest for once. Spell it out.'

His brow crinkles with confusion. 'What are you talking about?' Even now he can't hide how much he wants me physically, his eyes raking my body as his chest rises and falls on his rapid breathing.

'You said yourself, we're not friends. So physical is all we have, right? Tell me you don't want me and I'll leave. I'll go and work for Luke.' It's hard to breathe, so I lower my voice to a whisper. 'Tell me.'

I know I'm baiting him to fight for me—it's a low blow, but no worse a tactic than him trying to protect himself with his emotional withdrawal and his pathetic circus show at dinner this evening.

Tired of waiting, I unhook the strap of my halter dress behind my neck, allowing the fabric to peel down to my waist without ceremony. My breasts spill free and Drake's eyes widen with a flare of heat, even as he clenches his jaw and makes loose fists.

I tug at the zip in the small of my back and slide the dress over my hips, tossing it aside until I'm standing before him in nothing but a lacy thong. 'Tell me.' It's a harsh plea, one I barely finish before he stands, tugs me into his arms and crushes my mouth under his in a hot, possessive kiss.

He breaks away, his breath gusting out in pants. 'This is what *you* want? Me? Despite everything?'

'Yes.' At least we're being honest at last.

He tugs at his shirt buttons, a blaze of challenge in his eyes that makes my belly flutter and my knees tremble. I can't wait for him to strip—he's taking too long. I kiss him and then break away to slide my mouth over every strip of skin he exposes, while my hands work on his belt and fly in hurried tugs.

I drop to my knees, yanking at the fabric of his trousers to release his erection. He's still trussed, his trousers around his knees and his arms trapped in his shirt by his cufflinked shirt cuffs as I take in him in my mouth with a greedy whimper.

'Fuck! Kenzie…' Drake grapples his arms free

and grips my head, his hips rocking in time with the slide of my mouth down his shaft. I take him to the back of my throat, humming out my possession and then I suck on the head with a flick of my tongue on the spot that makes him curse and his stare grow hooded.

His fingers curl in my hair, gripping. His eyes follow the passage of his cock in and out of my mouth and his thighs are steel as he braces his legs.

With a growl he pulls back and slips from my mouth and then he tugs me to my feet, kicks off his trousers and lifts me so I'm clinging to his waist with my thighs. He keeps his eyes open while I kiss him so he can spin us around and lower me to the leather sofa, cool at my back.

The heat of his body covers me. I spread my thighs, creating a cradle for his hips. 'Hurry—I need you.' I'm past caring. Ready to beg.

His elbows trap my arms at my sides, his hands cupping my head and his fingers sliding into my hair so he can hold me still to the plunder of his kiss. It's possessive. A deep exploration of tongues and teeth and lips that leaves us panting and gyrating against each other. I keep my eyes open, needing to see the way he's looking at me, the stark honesty of his desire.

His mouth dips to my breast and his hands slide my underwear down and then he's back kissing me again as he aligns himself at my entrance.

'Drake…'

He pushes into me, his jaw clenched and his eyes locked with mine. I open wider, taking him to the hilt, his mouth catching my whimper as he reaches the end and we groan together.

'I want *you*.' He grunts, the rhythmic thrusts of his hips setting off a cascade of fire along my thighs and down to my toes.

I nod. He's showing me all I need to see. Everything I want to hear. I grip his shoulders, lifting my pelvis to meet his thrusts, which grow in power. He watches my breasts jiggle as he pounds me in earnest, swearing as I dig my heels into his backside, urging him deeper.

We kiss, my head lifting up to meet his mouth as I cling to him, riding out the pleasure. I cup his face, tearing my mouth from his as my orgasm builds. He must see it in my face, because he grips my hips and slams home. 'Yes, Kenzie, I've got you.'

The emotional dam inside breaks before the physical release. The realisation I love him. 'Drake!' I gasp out as it strikes, my eyes closing as wave after wave of delirium buffets my body. He's there with me, my name growled out against the side of my neck as he collapses on top of me, pressing me under his weight.

We lie still for a handful of seconds. Endorphins thrum through my blood. I smile into his chest, because admitting I've fallen for him unlocks something in me, allowing me to see a future bright with possibility for the first time in years.

He slips from me, rolling to the side and drawing me against his chest, so my head is tucked under his chin. He kisses my forehead, his arms tightening around my shoulders.

I wait, the steadying thud of his heart mocking the rabbit pace of mine and his slowing breaths gusting through my hair. But the feeling is still there, stronger than before. The real deal. I love him. I didn't expect this when I sought him out, but I'm not going to run from it either.

But what does Drake want?

I lean up on my elbow and look at him. He's relaxed but the tension still brackets his eyes and it hits me like a punch in the stomach—I'm open, I'm fighting, and he's stuck. We're no longer on the same page. Perhaps we never were.

'We've hit a dead end, haven't we?' Heat wells behind the words.

Drake gets that shady look that confirms all my fears. I'm three paces ahead and he's not sure he wants to catch up.

He pushes my hair over my shoulder. 'What do you mean?'

I capture his fingers. Kiss the back of his hand as I let my last wall topple. 'I'm leaving the Faulkner, but I don't want to leave you.'

Drake props himself on his elbows and presses his mouth to mine. But for once, his kiss chills me. 'We can still see each other.'

He's saying the right words, but the truth is in his eyes. 'Drake, be honest—is there any future for us, beyond this?' I slide my hand up his arm, feeling the tension coiled in his muscles. Not to pull me into his arms and tell me everything I want to hear, but to withdraw.

My new heart, the one in training, withers. The pain on his face confirms my fears.

He cups my cheek. 'Kenzie...' His beautiful mouth twists in agony. 'I...I can't. You're Sam's.'

I freeze. I want to pretend I'm deaf to the reminder I once loved his best friend. I'd expected to feel more conflicted, but making love with him, the knowledge I've fallen in love with him, brings clarity and a last flicker of hope. I press my mouth to his, clinging to every scrap of courage I possess as sure as my fingernails dig into Drake's arm.

I suck in a breath, putting everything on the line.

'Make me yours, then.'

CHAPTER FOURTEEN

Drake

MAKE ME YOURS...

The air thins but it makes no difference because there's an elephant sitting on my chest. My vision swims and Kenzie's breath-stealing beauty fades out of focus. I press my mouth to hers, tasting her soft lips and sucking in the faint scent of apples from her hair, which is wild and messed up. I close my eyes, knowing the view of her soft, replete, well-loved at my hands will shred my heart to ribbons.

Because... Of course I've fallen in love with her, fucking idiot that I am. But... The 'but' persists.

I want to rewind to the perfect moment of possibility when we were strangers in a bar. I've denied how I feel where she's concerned for so long...perhaps I don't know how to be any different... Perhaps excavating those feelings is an impossible task. Words and air are trapped in my chest.

She's waiting. But my beautiful, brave Kenzie won't wait for ever.

She sees my turmoil then—it must be carved into my face. She pulls away. Sits up.

Then she looks back. Her honest stare boring into mine. 'Thing is, Drake, I love you—'

'No.' It's a bark, one that shakes us both. But hearing that from her is too much. I've imagined it a million times and hearing it now, when I'm no closer to being able to accept it, is a crippling blow.

I grip her neck, pull her mouth back to mine. 'Don't say that.' The words, spoken against her lips, actually burn my throat. But she can't just toss that out. Not when I want to believe it more than I want my heart to keep beating. Not when it can't possibly be true. Not when I told her how little I deserve that gift.

Kenzie pushes at my chest, breaking our kiss, looking at me with justified hurt in her eyes.

'Listen to me.' I grip her waist tighter. Fuck, I've messed this up. But I have to douse us in cold, harsh reality.

She wriggles to the edge of the sofa and I let her go. I want to stop her, to drag her to the bedroom, to spend the rest of the night, and all day tomorrow and the rest of my life, lost in the fucking awesome dream of the last two weeks.

But I'm still stuck, neck-deep in the reality of what's right and what I want. The fucking no-man's-land I seem to have spent most of my adult life aimlessly wandering.

'It's okay. Don't worry.' Her back is ramrod straight. I reach for her waist but she stands, my fingers sliding uselessly over the curve of her hip. She scans the floor, and scoops on her underwear.

'Fuck, Kenzie, don't go like this.' She's hurt. And I'm the bastard who hurt her. I make a fist, hating that I've done the one thing I never wanted to do.

I have to make this right, to make her see that, in the long run, we'd never work. Too much past. Too many obstacles. Too much regret.

I lower my tone, praying she's not too far gone to hear. 'I promised him. And I betrayed him, right from the start.'

She turns on me, eyes blazing. 'I get it. I promised him things, too, remember. You were there, at the altar. By his side—his best man. But he still left me. He's still gone.' The pain in her eyes slashes a fiery path through the centre of my chest. 'You're just hiding. I opened myself up to something new, to the possibility of us, but you're not willing to do the same. You want to keep everything in a neat box labelled with the past so you can beat yourself up even as you try to do the honourable thing.'

She's right.

Where she's concerned, I've hidden my feelings for years for fear they'd destroy everything I am, everything I have. But what do I really have without her…?

She strides from the room and I jump up, sling on my jeans and follow her to the hall. 'You're right. I am hiding. We have too much baggage, don't you see?' Fuck, she's so angry with me now, the last thing she'll want to hear is how I truly feel. I had my opportunity and it's passed. Not that it would change anything.

Loving her makes no difference.

She tugs her dress up, covering her body from my stare, which is as greedy as ever where she's concerned. She huffs. 'Baggage that *you* keep opening. Not me.'

I scrub my hand through my hair, my own temper rising. 'It doesn't matter. He's still there. He'll always be there. I'd cut off my arm to have it any other way, but that won't change a thing. Even when I tried to take us away, to outrun it, he followed us.'

Kenzie reaches for her phone, her fingers flying across the screen and her eyes downcast. 'Because you invited him.' She looks up at me then, the fire in her eyes snuffed out. 'I understand your guilt and regrets, Drake—I have them, too. But I'm finally moving forward with my life and I refuse to be held back. What you do is up to you, and you alone.'

I grip the back of my neck. How have I fucked this up so monumentally? What she said tonight—I should be on cloud nine…instead I'm on terra firma with a fatal case of foot-in-mouth disease.

'Can you honestly tell me, hand on heart, that a part of you doesn't think of him, every time we touch, every time I kiss you?' The image, the very idea I've tried so hard to banish, floods my mind, forcing bile into the back of my throat. I want to rip out my tongue.

Her hazel eyes glow, ice-cold. 'Do you think of the other women you've been with when your cock is in *my* mouth?'

I've delivered a low blow and I deserve her counter-attack. 'Of course not. Listen…' Shut up. Shut up now before the damage is irreparable.

I drag in air, hating what I'm about to ask. 'Answer me this—would you have chosen me that night?' I hold up my hand, refusing to see the flash of doubt that passes over her face—a look that guts me. 'No. Don't answer. I can't ask you that. Not because it's a shitty thing for me to do, but because I don't want to know. And it makes no difference. You're his. We can't get past that.'

Kenzie freezes while my heart tunnels into my throat. Then she swipes up her shoes and pads to the door. At the threshold she turns, her eyes bright with moisture but her chin tipped up. 'Well, we'll never know, will we? You said you wouldn't change a thing. You wouldn't fight for me then, and you won't fight for me now.'

She spins on her heel and leaves, quietly closing the front door. I yank on my shirt and chase after her barefoot, arriving at the kerb in time to see the Uber pull away, taking everything I've ever wanted out of reach.

CHAPTER FIFTEEN

Drake

I SLAM INTO Kit's office, my feet skidding to a halt at the scene before me. Kit and Mia, making out in the middle of the day. At work.

I cough to alert them to my presence. 'Sorry to interrupt…'

They break apart, completely unapologetic. Mia wipes Kit's mouth and Kit grins at me like a love-sick puppy…

I look away, ignoring the pinch under my ribs. I'm happy for my youngest brother. He deserves happiness.

'Sorry.' Mia climbs from his lap and smooths her hair into place, offering me her wide smile. 'We're going for lunch—want to join us?'

Normally I'd happily accept. But there's no way lunch is going to pass my strangled throat and stay in my stomach. I decline. 'I came to ask if you could give my apologies at the family dinner tonight. I'm not going to make it.' I'd rather rip out my own fingernails than make polite conversation in my current mood.

Kit frowns. 'I think Dad is finally officially announcing his retirement. He'll expect you there.' He offers me a sympathetic smile.

I stuff my hands in my pockets and look out at a grey London, the idea of doing anything other than replaying that last time with Kenzie to work out where we went so wrong rolling my stomach.

Why am I here? I could have sent an email. Made a call. Asked my assistant to send a bottle of my father's favourite port. I face the truth with a sigh—I came for advice. Advice I don't need, because I already know I've ruined things with Kenzie. Ruined my only shot at the kind of happiness I see on my brother's face. Because she's it for me. Always has been, always will be.

'I'll tell him you can't make it,' says Kit, perhaps sensing the storm inside I'm struggling to conceal.

Why did I need to fuck it up monumentally in order for everything to shift into crystal-clear focus? Not that it matters. She's gone. Left the Faulkner. Won't answer my calls and, when I knocked on Tilly's door last night in a last-ditch bid for her whereabouts, I discovered she's gone away from London. For 'a break', Tilly said, while she thinks about her job options.

I wait for the relief to roll in and fill the empty hole inside. Relief she's better off without me. Relief she's probably already moving on. Relief my life can return to uncomplicated.

Trouble is, I fucking love complicated, almost as much as I love Kenzie. I scrub at my hair, tugging a handful until my scalp protests, the impotence currently rendering me antisocial its own form of torture. One I deserve. I chased her away. I made her feel her love was worthless.

Where can she be?

I don't know who her friends are, and what the fuck does *job options* mean? Will she leave London? Return to Bath? Give up on her dream?

No. She's a fighter. Strong. Stronger than me. Just because I screwed up doesn't mean Kenzie will be derailed.

'But, if you can't make tonight, we have something to tell you,' says Kit. He looks to Mia, who rolls her eyes, reminding me of Kenzie.

'We're having a baby.'

I can't help my grin, which slides between my ecstatic brother and a blushing Mia, who simultaneously thumps his arm and kisses him again.

'Congratulations.' I hug them both, genuine joy diluting some of my self-directed fury.

Their happiness, hard-won after fighting their own demons, is contagious. I want a slice of it for myself. A fucking great big salted-caramel serving loaded with cream…

And why shouldn't I?

My mind shakes off the guilty shackles as I realise I'm the only person standing in my own way. I hug my brother again, as he's just given the advice I came here searching for, my limbs practically jerking with the need to act. To stop punishing myself and claim what my brother has won. Before any more time passes and the damage becomes permanent.

I want this. And I want it with Kenzie. I always have. I want to make love to her every day. I want to share her dreams and aspirations. I want to be a husband and a father, if she wants children with me, and to grow some middle-aged spread because of her delicious cooking.

'I have to go.' I press a kiss to Mia's cheek and slap Kit's shoulder. 'Enjoy lunch and dinner.'

'Where are you going?' asks Kit.

I pause, the portent of the last few minutes catching up to me. 'I'm going to visit Sam.'

Kit's bewilderment clears as he guesses my meaning.

'And then…we'll see. Next time I see you, I hope to have news of my own. Thanks for all your help.' I turn for the door, already texting my driver.

'Drake.' Kit's shout breaks through my focus. He looks from a bewildered Mia and grins. 'Good luck.'

I nod. I'm going to need it.

The lights in the distance douse me with hope, impatience hot on its tail. I floor the accelerator, the resulting tyre spins flicking up gravel from the driveway. But from the minute I figured out where she'd be I've been crawling out of my skin to get to her and undo the biggest mistake of my life.

I knock, my knuckles stinging with the force of my rap and the freezing air, which is heavy with sea spray. The seconds it takes for the door to swing open will be etched in my memory for ever. Three times I reach for the door handle, only to snatch my hand away from the foreboding piece of metal.

I refuse to accept it's too late. I can make this right.

Then she's there, wrapped in a blanket with a steaming glass of what looks like some sort of hot toddy in her hand.

Her wary look, one I deserve because I made her doubt, knocks the air from my lungs.

'Kenzie.' I hold up one hand, warding off objection. 'Please let me speak.'

'How did you find me?'

'I hoped you'd come here, somewhere we've been together.' Please let it mean she's still open to forgiving me...

She steps aside and opens the door wider, wordlessly inviting me out of the frigid night. The temptation to reach for her, to touch her, tenses every muscle in my body. I make fists and follow her deeper into the cottage.

In the lounge, she retreats to her seat by the fire, tugging the blanket closer across her chest and taking a sip of her drink. 'Help yourself.' Her stare is wary, but she lifts her chin in the direction of a drinks tray.

'I'm good, thanks.' Something warming would

work wonders about now, but the only thing I want, the only thing I need to warm me, is the woman looking at me like she's done with me.

She's pale, her eyes round. 'Are you okay? Are you ill?' I step closer, about to reach for her, when I remember I threw away that privilege and snatch my hand back to my side.

She shakes her head. 'I can't seem to get warm tonight, that's all.'

'Have you eaten?' There are no signs of food preparation, no delicious smells coming from the kitchen, no snacks. 'I can cook you something. Soup? An omelette?'

Her mouth flattens. 'Why are you here, Drake? I have the cottage hired for the week.'

Of course. I'm way ahead of myself. I shrug one arm out of my coat and then pause. 'Do you mind?'

She half shrugs, half shakes her head and I remove the now stifling garment. Perhaps I won't be staying that long. She hasn't invited me to sit, but bending my strung-out body into a chair seems impossible at any rate. I pace to the rug in front of the fire and face her.

My Kenzie.

I suck in courage. 'I went to see Sam.'

'Okay.' Her eyes are shuttered. She's not going to make this easy on me, and for that I love her a little bit more.

'You were right. I should have gone long ago. Because I miss him. Because I wanted to have a beer with him, like we used to. Because he was my friend and I'll always love him.'

I drag in a shuddering lungful of air, more certain of why I'm here than of anything else in my life.

'Well, good for you, Drake. I'm glad.'

She looks anything but glad. She looks like she's about to kick me back out into the night.

I rush on. 'I told him things I've always wanted to say—how lucky he was to have you, how I'd always secretly envied him, how I wish I'd done things differently the day we all met. Then I realised something.' I reach into my pocket and retrieve Sam's coin, holding it out to her on the flat of my hand. 'His lucky coin is broken.'

She places her drink on the table and leans forward, peering at the coin with scepticism. 'It looks okay to me.' She picks it up, turning it over. The contact of her fingertips on my palm thrums my blood harder, but it's over too quickly.

She looks up in confusion, then looks back to the coin. 'Heads, tails. How is it broken?'

I nod, as if agreeing with her, and drop to my haunches at her feet, taking the coin from her and examining it as if it holds the secrets of the universe. It doesn't. It doesn't even hold the key to my future, my happiness, my dreams. I've always held that. I was just too fucking scared to take my chance after messing up the first time.

I turn it over and over, the constant changing face

reassuring. It's irrelevant. The outcome is always the same. And entirely in my hands.

Mine and hers.

I meet her stare, my fingers continuing to flip the coin. 'I'll show you.' I place the coin with the queen's head uppermost in the centre of my palm and wait for her beautiful eyes to settle back on mine.

'Heads,' I lift one eyebrow, pausing to gain her full attention, 'I'll love you for ever.' I flip the coin over, my eyes never leaving hers. 'Tails, I'll love you for ever. See? No choice at all…'

My words settle into the thick silence, the crackle of logs burning the only sound.

Air is trapped under my ribs.

She looks away, her face blank.

My stomach drops to the floor.

But I did this. I made her doubt. I had everything I wanted and I dismissed it because of our convoluted history. Because of my guilt. Because I didn't fight hard enough.

Swallowing down the boulder in my throat, I take her hand. 'I want you to have it.' I press the coin into her palm and fold her fist closed, cupping her hand with both of mine. Her fingers *are* cold. I never want to let go.

'I don't need it.' My voice is scratchy now, but I push ahead, the words a torrent, stumbling over themselves. 'I know how I feel—it's how I've always felt. I want you. In my life. In my future. As mine. Always.'

Her eyes are shining now, but she's still unconvinced. I know her. She battles alone, because that's what life has taught her. And I added to that lesson.

'I know I messed up. I let you down. I got in my own way. I punished myself needlessly.' I press a kiss to the back of her hand, my lungs on fire. 'I was careless with your astounding words, with your precious love. I'm sorry.'

She pulls her hand from mine, her eyes dipping to the coin. 'It's okay—'

'No.'

She's going to ask me to leave. Tell me it's over.

'It's so far from okay.' I grip the back of my neck so hard, it's a wonder it doesn't snap in two. 'You're brave and honest, and so strong. I was a scared idiot. Scared of your rejection, scared you could never forgive me and scared you could never love me like you'd loved Sam. I thought that staying loyal to Sam meant I couldn't love you. But I share his luck, because from the day I met you I've had you in my life.' I cover my heart with my hand. 'I've carried you here—that's why no other woman stood a chance. And I know you don't need me, but I want whatever way I can continue to have you in my life. Please... don't give up on me.'

The crackle of the fire sounds like a countdown.

I'm frozen. Waiting. Impotent.

'I can't, Drake. I'm not that strong.' My heart aches at the resignation in her beautiful eyes.

She stands. I'm left staring at the throw, which

has slipped from her shoulders and pooled on the chair. I look down, sucking in a deep breath laced with determination. 'Kenzie—'

'It hurts too much to go through it again. I can't...' She's halfway across the room, heading towards the bedroom. If I let her go now I'll never get another chance—I see the confirmation in the set of her shoulders.

'Wait.' In two strides I'm behind her. 'I know I let you down—I took your amazing caring, your comfort, your love and I gave you nothing in return. But I see now I can love Sam, and I can love you.' I inch closer, sucking in the scent of apples. 'You are the strongest person I know, but if you'll let me I'm going to take care of you and Tilly. For ever. I'm going to love you, for ever. Let me show you.'

She sways in the doorway, her back to me.

I step up closer, bend until my lips brush the silk of her hair. 'You're mine,' I whisper.

She shivers, her shoulders twitching. And then she spins to face me, slowly.

I'm lost in the glow of her eyes, mesmerised. I raise my hands with care, cup her face like she's made of blown glass. 'You're mine.' I tilt her jaw and lower my mouth to hers, taking time for my words to sink in. For her to withdraw, if she wants to.

'Yes.' One tiny word. The smallest nod of her head.

Our mouths touch, our lips finding each other's

as if equipped with a homing instinct. Because this is right. *We* are right. Nothing else matters.

I lift her and carry her to the bedroom. She clings to me with arms and legs and lips and then we're peeling away the layers of clothing that separate us, until we're skin to skin.

'Say you're mine.' I run my mouth over every inch of her I can reach as we head for the bed. I follow her down, covering her body with mine, blocking out any residual chill she might feel.

'I'm yours, Drake.'

She claws at me, impatient. But I want her certain. I want her exhausted by the weight of my love. Filled to the brim so there's no space for doubt. I kiss her, running my hands over her body, laying claim. She's equally possessive, her nails digging into my skin, her hands twisting my hair, her mouth leaving kiss after kiss, like brands.

When I push inside her, I know I'm home. 'Kenzie.' I grip her face, direct her eyes to mine. 'I love you.'

'I love you, too.'

With our eyes locked, I rock us both over the edge, my cry the last thing I manage to speak against her arched throat. 'You're mine!'

EPILOGUE

Kenzie

I COVER MY mouth and hide my giggles as I look down at Drake's denim-clad backside, which protrudes from underneath the bottom of the Christmas tree.

'How about now?' he huffs, and the tree shifts a fraction to the left.

It's already perfectly straight, but I can't help but string this out…get my money's worth. Wind him up so I earn some delicious retribution.

'A little to the right.' I bite my lip and try not to drool at the way his butt clenches and his shirt rides up, exposing a strip of muscular back. How can I possibly want him again? We've only been up three hours. If Tilly wasn't due in thirty minutes, I'm guessing we'd still be in bed.

'Now?' he asks, pushing the tree in the opposite direction.

'Left a bit.' I snigger.

There's a curse. More huffing. And then he

emerges, his face dusky with exertion and some pine needles stuck in his hair. 'Are you deliberately winding me up?' Even while he admonishes me, sparks of heat in his eyes, he's tugging me by the hips so he can press a kiss to my twitching mouth. He smells of Christmas. And Drake.

'Mmm.' I run my hands through his hair, scattering the pine needles to the floor as I press my hips forward, finding him hard. A pretty permanent state for my man—I'm not sure how he gets anything done…

He breaks from our kiss, even as he's walking me back towards the sofa. 'Let's just get one delivered from Harrods, already decorated.'

I gasp, but he fills my mouth with his tongue as his hand slips under my jumper. I shove at his shoulders, my fingers curling into his shirt to stop him escaping too far.

'We can't do that. Decorating the tree together is a family tradition—Tilly and I did it with our parents and we still do this every year. We drink mulled wine, decorate the tree and then watch *White Christmas* followed by *Love Actually*. And now our family includes you, so suck it up, trouper.' I flop onto the sofa, tugging him down on top of me. Right now I couldn't give a toss if the tree is straight. Tills will sort it out when she gets here. She has an eye for detail.

'How long do we have?' mumbles Drake against my lips as he unbuttons my jeans and slips his hand inside my underwear.

I glance at the clock, wishing we had a time machine parked in the garage beside the collection of luxury European vehicles I'm always teasing him about. 'Not long. She's always punctual…twenty minutes, tops.' My words pant out because his fingers are between my legs and his kisses are working their way up my naked abdomen towards my breasts.

He looks up, a grin of promise and eyes full of possession and heat, a look I've seen daily—no, hourly—in the last month. 'I can work with that time frame.' His hand starts sliding my jeans and underwear over my hips. There's no way I could resist. I want him. Always. Insatiably.

He's mine. And I'm his.

* * * * *

ON HER TERMS

CATHRYN FOX

MILLS & BOON

To Heather Veinotte, friend, big sister, confidante.

Thanks for letting me bounce this one off you, for helping me get the facts straight and for reading the very first rough draft.

Love you!

CHAPTER ONE

Brianna

"COME ON, COME ON, come on," I say under my breath as the cabbie slowly drives his car. We wind through the streets of St. Moritz, the gorgeous Alpine town where my cousin Tate is getting married—he's no doubt wondering where I am.

I glance at my watch and groan inwardly. I hate being late. Absolutely hate it. I actually pride myself on my punctuality, but divorce court ran late, and that left me running to the airport to board Granddad's private plane. By the time I took my seat, the Learjet had been waiting on the tarmac for hours. Granddad's personal flight attendant gave me the once-over. Probably because I looked like I'd just come from the rinse cycle and had been hung upside down on the line to dry. Although I'm anything but dry, thanks to the turbulent flight and the humid summer air way up here in the Alps.

I pull my damp blouse away from my skin and

steal a quick glance at my watch again. Dammit, the
bridal party dinner started fifteen minutes ago, and
Tate—considerate man that he is—would have held
the meal for me. A double dose of guilt hits at having so many people waiting, because I got tied up,
and now I'm in a cab with a whistling driver who
is moving at a snail's pace. The New Yorker in me
wants to jump in the front seat and press down on
the gas pedal. Hard.

"Relax, we're almost there," the cabdriver says,
clearly picking up on my tension. He waves a hand.
"Look around. Enjoy the view. No one can feel anything but peaceful when surrounded by such beauty,"
he says in a heavy French accent that's almost difficult to understand.

I exhale a slow breath and look out the window.
My God, I'd forgotten just how magnificent the high
Alpine town really is, how it's unlike anywhere else
I've ever been. I marvel at the sun-kissed mountains,
their peaks white, even in summer. My gaze travels
to the towering Palace Hotel positioned over Lake
St. Moritz. I smile as old memories bombard me. As
a teen, I spent a lot of time here with Granddad and
Tate, especially after my dad left and my mom dis-
engaged from life. But thinking of Granddad brings
on another blast of guilt.

Over the last few years, his health has been fail-
ing, which is why Tate recently moved his law practice from Boston to Manhattan to be closer to him.
I've been so damn busy at work, putting in sixteen-

hour days to prove I'm partner material at the firm, I haven't been around as much as I'd like to be. Then again when I am around, Granddad spends most of the time grilling me about when I'm getting married.

I'm not.

Ever.

A garbled sound crawls out of my throat, and I catch the cabbie's eyes in the rearview mirror. Seriously though, I'm a divorce lawyer. I face couples squaring off against each other every day, and I've come to learn that what starts as love always turns to greed and hate. If that's not enough to make me jaded, all I have to do is look in my own backyard. Most of the men in my family have a penchant for younger women and are never able to settle down for very long, hence the ironclad prenuptials they always have drawn up. On top of that, the last guy I dated seriously turned out to be a two-timing asshole. And of course I can't forget the sting of rejection from that one notorious guy during my University of Oxford undergraduate years. A gorgeous Italian god every girl wanted. One incident was all it took for that arrogant stuffed shirt to shake my confidence for years afterward.

Cynical much? Oh yeah, like 100 percent. Now when I'm with a man, it's on my terms. No love. No romance. Just physical one-night stands with no tomorrows. That's how I like it, and whether Granddad approves or not, he has no choice but to accept it.

"We're here," the driver says as he slows his car

down in front of Raydolins Hotel, one of the many opulent resorts my granddad owns here. I grab some bills from my purse and quickly hand them over. The cabbie slides from his seat and pulls my luggage from the trunk, and I slip from the back seat and check my reflection in the car window. When I take in the hot mess that is me—Brianna Carson—I cringe.

My hair is a big ball of frizz, and no amount of spray can fix that in this humidity. I swipe at the black smudges beneath my heavy-lidded eyes and only manage to make matters worse. Great, now I look like an angry raccoon jacked up on pain meds. Maybe a bit of lipstick will help brighten me up. Then again I'm not here to impress anyone. I wish I had time to shower and change, but I'm not about to keep Tate or his guests waiting a second longer.

"Relax. Enjoy it while you can. You'll be back in New York before you know it," the cabdriver says. As he saunters back to his car, I can't help but feel a tinge of envy. My life is fast-paced, hectic and mostly chaotic. I wish I could be so laid-back. Cripes, if I'm not careful, I'm going to end up having a heart attack before I hit twenty-eight next month, and for what, really? Am I really making this world a better place? Doing work that is meaningful?

I grab my bag and head inside. The bellboy opens the door as I approach and the cool air washes over me. I widen my arms and let loose a grateful moan. I hurry to the registration desk, sign in quickly and leave my bag for the concierge to take to my room.

My heels tap on the marble floor as I pick up the pace and head to the dining room where the private function is being held. Before I enter, I take a deep breath, let it out slowly and plaster on a smile. I step inside, work to present a well-put-together woman, and search the long table for Tate. When he sees me, he jumps up, comes over and picks me up in a crushing hug.

"I'm so sorry, Tate. I got tied up, and the cabbie—"

"Hey, stop. It's okay," he says, and when I take in his big smile, my heart beats a little faster. I've never seen him happier, and that warms me from the inside out. Summer Love, his beautiful fiancée, has been so good for him, and he deserves all the happiness life has to offer. Still, there is a small part of me that worries about their future. They've only been together for six months. Is that enough time for a strong bond to build? Lord knows love can become venomous pretty quickly. At least I know Summer isn't marrying for money, and Tate is one of the good guys. That doesn't stop me from throwing up a silent prayer for him, a request that he doesn't end up like the other men in our family, with a long list of exes.

"Come on. Everyone will be so happy to see you," he murmurs over the din of the crowd as he puts his arm around my waist to guide me across the floor.

I glance at the elegant table with its crisp white linen, fine china and crystal glasses. The wine has been flowing, but no food has been served. "Yeah, only because they're starving," I shoot back.

Tate laughs and it's so exuberant, I can't help but laugh with him.

"What's so funny?" Granddad asks as Tate pulls out the empty chair beside him.

"Oh, nothing," I say and give my grandfather a big hug before I take a seat. I glance around, take in a few familiar faces of my relatives and offer up a smile to the table. My eyes track Tate as he moves to the head of the table and drops a kiss onto his fiancée's lips before smoothing his hand over his tie, a familiar habit.

"Where's your plus-one?" Granddad asks, and I suppress a sigh.

"I came alone," I say and smile at him.

He lifts a gnarled, arthritic hand and shakes a finger at me. "I can't wait forever, Brianna. I don't have a lot of time left, you know."

My stomach drops. Honestly, I wish I wasn't so jaded. I wish I could fulfill a dying man's wish, but I'm not about to enter into marriage only to go through the pain of divorce, just to please my grandfather.

"Granddad—"

"I worry about you, Brianna." His once-syrupy voice cracks and he coughs into the crook of his arm. He hacks for a few seconds, and then he turns to me and adds, "It's not natural to be alone."

He would know. He had a slew of younger women over the years. But who am I to judge? After Grandma—his one and only true love—died, it was good to see him happy again, have someone help fill that void.

He frowns at me and my heart sinks into my stomach as I take in the deep lines bracketing troubled eyes. I've never seen him look so old or tied, completely worn out. The trip here must have been hard on him, but he insisted that Tate have his wedding at the resort and that he was well enough to travel. Looking at him now, I'm not so sure he'll last the week. My heart squeezes. Granddad has always been good to me. He was there for me when Dad walked out on us, and again when I lost Mom a few years ago. He taught me the value of hard work and supported me when I moved across the pond to attend Oxford. He even visited me when I was lonely. Jeez, maybe I should tell a fib, pretend I have someone just to please him and ease his worries.

Should I?

I mean, what could it hurt, right? Let him think I have a man, give him peace of mind during the wedding. Like he said, he doesn't have much time left, and I don't want to see him spend the rest of his days needlessly worrying over me.

I place my napkin on my lap and take a big drink of wine after the server fills my glass. Here goes nothing. "Granddad, this isn't the time or place to be talking about this, but you can put your worries to rest. I'm seeing someone, and it's serious. In fact, we're engaged." *What the hell? That was too far, Bri.*

His cloudy blue eyes light up, and weathered lips

curl up into a smile. "Tell me all about him," he says and leans back in his chair.

I open my mouth, ready to spill more lies. Did I mention I hate lying as much as I hate being late? Yet here I am, batting two for two. I'm about to tell him some fabricated story about my Prince Charming when Tate stands and taps his crystal stemware with a spoon. All eyes turn to him, including Granddad's.

Thank God!

"Now that we're all here," he begins, and heat moves into my cheeks as he winks playfully at me. "I'd like to do a round of introductions."

He begins with his beautiful fiancée, who is beaming up at her soon-to-be husband. An invisible band tightens around my heart, and tears prick my eyes, but then I quickly remind myself I want no part of love or marriage. Nope, it's just hit it and quit it for me, as crude as that sounds.

Tate goes around the table, talks about how he met those in his bridal party and adds a fun little story about each person. When he gets to me—the last bridesmaid—I nibble my lip with trepidation. The stories the man could tell about me would be humiliating at best. But instead of embarrassing me, he introduces me as his closest cousin, and goes on to let everyone know that I make a mean apple pie, which is a total lie. Then again the pie might have turned out just fine, if I hadn't burnt the kitchen down baking it.

Granddad laughs at the inside joke as Tate knowingly grins at me. He continues the introductions, and I crane my neck to see around Uncle Bill, who's seated to my right. Tate reaches the last man at the table, the one sitting on his left, and I pick up my glass to take a drink.

"This guy here is my right-hand man," Tate says. "Most of you don't know him. He joined my law firm just a couple of months ago, and not only did we hit it off the first time I met him here in the Alps, I don't know what I'd do without him by my side in the office. He's smart, meticulous and works long and hard into the night to get a job done. I'm happy to introduce Luca Marino, my best man."

Luca Marino!

Wine sloshes over the edge of my crystal stemware as my hand shakes. I forcefully swallow the lump climbing into my throat and set my glass down before I drop it. I must be wrong. I have to be wrong. No way could the man seated to Tate's left be *the* Luca Marino, the Italian jerk who rejected me in college. What are the odds Tate would even know him?

As my pulse beats double time against my neck, I slowly stand to see over my uncle's head, but the bottom falls out of my world when my gaze settles on the most gorgeous man I've ever set eyes on— Mr. Arrogant-Stuffed-Shirt himself.

CHAPTER TWO

Luca

Brianna Carson is Tate's cousin?

Brianna Carson is Tate's cousin!

I try to wrap my brain around that, but I still can't quite believe it. I never put it together before, and why would I? I haven't seen her since our University of Oxford days, and after I walked her home from a party one night, she went out of her way to avoid me. I'm not sure what I did or said to piss her off, and while I would've liked to have talked to her to find out, there was never an opportunity. She made sure of that.

As I meet Brianna's gaze from the other end of the table, my entire body grows tight. Raw energy arcs between us, and I suck in a fast breath as she wobbles slightly, like the sight of me has completely caught her off guard, too. I catch a flicker of recognition in her eyes, but then she offers up a polite, somewhat distant smile and turns away. Wait, maybe she doesn't remember me. Could I have imagined that flash of familiarity? I'm not sure, but I sure as hell would never forget her. She might have lost a bit of weight and changed her hairstyle and hair color, but I'd know sexy Brianna Carson anywhere.

Oh, how I'd wanted to take her to her bed that night, put my hands and mouth all over her curvy body. Do all the dirty things that had been racing around my brain when I first set eyes on her in my senior year. The sight of her now is stirring up all of those hot images and urging me to do something about it. Why again did I walk away, leaving her alone in her dorm room? Oh right—she'd been drinking. I might be a lot of things, but I'd never take advantage of a girl who'd had one too many.

Tate nudges me. I've been so lost in thought, I missed what he was asking me. "What's that?" I say.

Tate laughs. "Where were you?" he asks as a handful of servers begin setting our meals in front of us.

I look down at the roast beef dinner in front of me. "Work," I fib. "Just thinking about some figures I'd like to go over." Okay, not a total lie. I was thinking about Bri's curvy figure and how I'd like to go over it—with my tongue. My dick swells and presses against my zipper.

Cazzo!

Get it together. This is not the time or place to be sporting a hard-on!

"You need to take this week off and relax, my friend. Put work behind you and have some fun.

That's an order." Tate leans closer, his words for my ears only. "What you need is to get laid, buddy."

I laugh. "You're probably right." I recently moved from St. Moritz to New York to help Tate get his law business off the ground. Then I buried myself in work, enjoying life outside my duties back in Italy for a little while longer.

I've been avoiding those for years now, ever since my dad and brother died in a car accident three years ago. Even before that, I hid my identity from the world for a long time. Not even Tate knows who I really am—a duke. People treat me differently once they know, and while I can probably trust my friend, past experiences have taught me every woman wants to be my duchess, not because of love but because of prominence.

I can't avoid duty much longer, though. The letter in my suit-coat pocket is a burning reminder of that. With my father gone, along with my older brother, Matteo, the family legacy falls to me. That includes the dukedom and the family conglomerates. Uncle Giovanni is overseeing things for now, but if I don't meet the stipulations of my father's will and marry his best friend's daughter before I turn thirty this year, the controlling shares of my father's conglomerates will go to my eldest cousin, Marco. I can't let that happen. He'll blow through the entire Marino fortune in no time, destroy everything my father built.

"This looks amazing," Summer says, and with

that we all dig into our meals. Small talk is made as the courses are served one after the other. Over an hour later, after the dessert dishes are cleared, we all head to the bar area for a drink. I search the crowd for Brianna and find her talking to Tate, but every now and then she casts a fast glance my way. Only problem is, whenever she finds me staring she tears her gaze away. At least that gives me the opportunity to blatantly look her over, revel in the way her formfitting skirt clings to her hips, the way she fiddles with the button on her blouse. A nervous little habit I remember from years ago. I'm not even sure she knows she's doing it, but it does beg the question, what is sexy Brianna Carson so damn worked up about?

"Can I get a whiskey neat," I say to the bartender as I shrug out of my suit jacket and place it over the back of the stool before I settle myself onto the plush seat.

Summer comes up to me and puts her hand on my shoulder. I turn to her and she offers up a smile. "Hey, Summer," I say and drop a kiss onto her cheek. "You look beautiful tonight." She angles her head and narrows her big eyes, her curious gaze moving over my face. "What?" I ask and shift a little on the chair.

She taps her nails on the bar top. "Do you and Brianna know each other?"

I shake my head and grin. Leave it to Summer to notice the tension between us. As a doctor, she's pretty good at picking up on subtleties, and there isn't much anyone can get by her. I'm about to open my mouth to answer, when Tate slides his arm around his fiancée's waist.

"I was wondering the same thing," he says, and that's when I notice Brianna coming up behind him, avoiding my gaze as she signals the bartender for a drink.

"Brianna," I say, and she settles a polite gaze on me.

"Luca, isn't it?" She turns to Tate. "Sorry, I was so jet-lagged when you did the introductions, I wasn't sure if I caught the right name."

"Ah, so you two *don't* know each other, then," Summer says, but from the way her gaze is going back and forth between the two of us, I'm not so sure she's convinced of that.

There was a time I would've liked to have known Brianna. A girl like her, well, she could make me forget my responsibilities to my family in Italy. If life were different, I would've gone for her, made her mine. But I didn't date while I was at Oxford, not when I'd have to subject a woman to the rigidity of my title and obligations.

"Why would we know each other?" Brianna asks and smooths her hand over her thick chestnut hair. For a second I envision my hands in that tangled mess, tugging on those long strands until her mouth opens for me. What I'd do to finally taste her, fin-ish what we never got the chance to start all those years ago. But I'm not about to start something I still can't finish. Brianna deserves better than that. She deserves her own Prince Charming, not a duke who's already spoken for. For the last few years, Valentina has been waiting in the wings, eager to walk me down the aisle and become my duchess. I haven't seen the woman in years. Who the fuck does arranged marriages anymore, anyway? I never thought in a million years that my father would put such a stipulation in his will.

"You both went to Oxford Law," Tate says. He gives a shrug of one shoulder and adds, "Then again it's a big campus, and Luca was probably a year or two ahead of you." The overhead lights dim, and the music picks up. Tate turns to Summer. "Dance with me." She smiles up at her fiancé, and I grin. Those two were made for each other. I knew it the first time she came into the bar here in St. Moritz, where Tate and I were working six months ago. He was undercover as a bartender, trying to prove Summer was a fraud who was out to steal billions from his granddad. At the time, I was hanging out in the Swiss Alps, enjoying the commoner's life. For years now I've been travelling around, doing odd jobs, trying to live a full life before duty catches up to me and I have to settle into my rightful position as Luca Marino, Duke of Massara.

Brianna opens her mouth, no doubt to excuse herself, when her granddad's cane hits the floor as he saunters up to the bar. "I'll have a brandy," he says.

"Granddad, I don't think you should be drinking," Brianna says.

He waves a dismissive hand her way. "Foolishness, child. I've got more brandy in these veins than blood. Now, what's this I hear about you two knowing each other?"

I shake my head, having no idea how he could have heard us from the other side of the room. He settles himself onto the stool next to me, and the bartender slides him a drink. He drains the amber liquid in one easy swallow, slams his glass on the mahogany top and then gestures for another.

"We don't know each other," Brianna says quickly, her gaze darting to mine, like she's worried I might claim otherwise.

"Well then, get out there on the dance floor and start getting to know each other, already."

Brianna briefly closes her eyes, and I catch something in Granddad's smile, something that looks an awful lot like mischief. What is the old man up to? Tate told me his grandfather was behind him and Summer meeting and falling for each other. I look him over, take in the statuesque way he carries himself. Something tells me he's not as frail and sick as he lets on. Maybe the others can't see it because they're too close. But I sense there is something more going on with James Carson.

"I'm tired, Granddad. It was a long flight and an even longer day. I just want to go back to my room and call it a night."

"I'm headed out, too," I say, picking up on the tension between Brianna and her grandfather. Wanting to help her out, I add, "I'll walk you to your room."

"That's okay," she says quickly, her smile forced. "I forgot a few things and have to hit up the gift shop." She drops a kiss onto her granddad's cheek and hurries from the room, once again avoiding my gaze and pretending she doesn't know me. Although I'm pretty goddamn sure she does. What the hell is going on with her?

"I guess I should call it a night, too," I say to James as he downs another ounce of brandy. "I have some forms I need to go over."

"I just bet you do," James says to me, an almost sinister smile quirking his lips, like he's been inside my head all night and knows all the dirty things pinging around in my brain. I can't imagine he'd be too happy with my thoughts, considering Brianna is his granddaughter.

Tate and Summer come back to check on their granddad and I use that opportunity to excuse myself. I leave the room and head outside. I've opted to stay in one of the family's chalets instead of the grand hotel. I have always preferred the solitude.

I nod to a group of women as they wave to me, and keep my head down as I make my way to my cottage. The warmth of the night falls over me, and my clothes stick to my skin. Since I know the resort like the back of my hand, I turn left instead of right. Forgoing rest, I take one of the lesser-known paths that leads up the mountain. There are plenty of suit-able swimming lakes scattered throughout the town, but this high up on the hill, most are untouched. The frigid temperatures a bit too much for visitors. The wind picks up as I climb, and I dodge a few puddles, compliments of the afternoon downpour. I start to unbutton my shirt, tug it away from my body, anx-ious to jump into the water to cool myself down. But that's when I realize I left my suit jacket back at the hotel. Good thing I brought a couple of extras.

The path narrows, and up ahead a bunny scurries into the underbrush. The temperature has dropped significantly, but I don't mind. As I approach my favorite private spot, I'm about to unzip my pants, but humming reaches my ears. *What the hell?* Only Tate and I know about this place, and he's back at the hotel. I slow my steps, not wanting to frighten who-ever happened to stumble upon my spot, but when I see a pile of clothes on the ground, my heart jumps into my throat. That skirt. That blouse. A certain woman from my past was wearing those tonight.

CHAPTER THREE

Brianna

I CAN'T FOR one minute believe that Luca and Tate know each other, let alone work together. I dunk myself under the cold water, letting it cool my heated body—which just might have more to do with the man I hate than the humidity of the night. Luca Marino is a complete and utter asshole, but my body can't deny he's as gorgeous today as he was all those years ago. Okay, maybe that's not entirely true. Back in the day he was a boy who looked good in his blue Oxford hoodie. Today he'd fill that sweater out like a man. Damned if I wouldn't like to see that.

Heat trickles through my blood despite the frigid water, and I swim from one side to the other, my mind going back to that mortifying night he walked me to my room and left me there. Alone. Every girl in my dorm wanted Luca Marino, myself included. I'd seen the women he gravitated toward and as a chubby girl, I never thought I had a chance with him. Until that one party.

He'd been wearing that comfortable hoodie, and he had smiled at me. At first I thought he was looking at someone else, but when I turned, no one was behind me. My girlfriend encouraged me to go for it, and I was so damn nervous, I kept drinking. With enough alcohol to cloud my judgement, I sauntered up to him. This was it—I'd finally have a real conversation with him. We talked for a few minutes and he asked where I lived. I totally freaked out, inwardly of course. *The* Luca Marino wanted to know where I lived! I told him and as he walked me back to my dorm, I could barely put one foot in front of the other. Not because I'd been drinking but because I was going to have the night I'd been fantasizing about forever, with the man of my dreams, and come tomorrow I'd be the one wearing his sweater, a symbol of our relationship. I stepped into my room, and when I turned back to him, he was pulling his phone from his pocket and closing the door in my face.

I can just imagine he was calling his friends. I wonder if they all had a good laugh about it afterward. Let the chubby girl think you're into her, and then dump her at her door. Was it some kind of cruel prank? One nasty rumor spread around my dorm after that night certainly had suggested that.

Goddammit, I was such a cliché.

Stop thinking about him.

Needing to clear my head, I begin humming, but no matter how hard I try, I can't get that man out of my thoughts. A laugh I have no control over bubbles in my throat. I went out of my way to avoid him on campus until he graduated at the end of that year. But there's no avoiding him here, now is there? Nope. We're in the same bridal party, for God's sake.

After the introductions, I panicked and pretended not to know him. He didn't correct me, which leads me to believe he doesn't remember me. Why would he? Since graduating law school a few years back, I lost the weight and changed my hair. Inside, I'm no longer that shy, self-conscious girl, either. Though I can't deny that even as I moved on, I never forgot him or that experience. It took me a while to feel confident on a date afterward. Meanwhile I'm sure he hasn't given me a thought. As I consider that, my mind races down a dark path, calculates all the ways I could get back at him for humiliating me. Maybe I could get him to take me back to his place and then walk away, the same way he walked away from me. It's juvenile for sure, but maybe revenge would help me finally get him out of my head once and for all.

Exhausted, I stop swimming and climb from the lake. I shiver as the cool mountain air washes over me. I should have brought a towel but I ran from the hotel so fast, needing a reprieve from Luca, I never thought to grab one. I fold my hands over my naked body and go in search of my clothes. Wind whips over me, and I dart a glance around, combing the exact spot I left them.

I shake my head when my hunt comes up empty. "What the hell?"

"Looking for these?"

My head jerks up to find Luca standing close, his outstretched arm holding my clothes.

"What are you doing here?" I ask and snatch the clothes from his hand. At least he has the decency to keep his eyes closed. "Turn around," I say. He does as I ask, and I struggle into my clothes, a difficult task with my body dripping wet. I fight with my skirt and finally get it over my damp hips.

"I didn't mean to interrupt," he says. "Bri, isn't it?"

Okay, he's either messing with me, or he really doesn't remember who I am. "Brianna. My friends call me Bri. What are you doing here?"

"I came for a swim. I didn't expect anyone else to be here."

"How do you know about this place?"

"Tate showed it to me."

I nod, even though he can't see me. I hurry into my blouse and button it. "Okay, you can turn around now." He slowly turns, and his heated gaze rakes over my body, a slow, leisurely inspection that steals the air from my lungs. He presses his thumb to his bottom lip, and when his head lifts and his eyes meet mine, I damn near bite off my tongue.

My mind quickly revisits my juvenile plan. From the way he's looking at me, I have no doubt I could get him to take me to his bed. But isn't that just like this type of guy? Only interested in me now because I fit his standards. My ex, Ryan, was the same way, telling me I was beautiful one day and then hounding me when I gained a pound or wore something he didn't like. I squash my anger and slowly blink my lashes, trying my best to be flirtatious, but that's so out of my wheelhouse, I'm not sure I can pull it off.

"I should get out of your way then, let you have a swim," I say and let my lashes fall slowly, hoping I'm giving him all the right signals.

Curiosity moves into his eyes as he angles his head, his gaze raking over my face. He probably thinks I've escaped the asylum. One minute I'm raging on him, and the next I'm doing my best to be flirty.

A cool breeze washes over me, and my teeth clamp together. "You're freezing," he says. While I want to shoot back with, way to state the obvious, I bite my sharp response and hug myself tighter. "Come here."

He steps up to me and drags me to him. My face goes to his chest, and I breathe in the clean, soapy scent of his skin. His natural aroma, combined with a hint of cologne—likely named Panty Remover—makes me want to do just that. Holy God, no man should ever smell this good. I breathe deeply, fill my lungs with his scent, and then hold my breath.

He runs his hands up and down my arms, creating heat with friction, but I only shiver harder. Although I'm not so sure the goose bumps breaking out on my flesh are from the cold this time.

"You need to get off this mountain and inside somewhere warm," he says and steps back. I wince at the dismissal. So much for my efforts. His fingers go to the last buttons on his shirt. I turn toward the path, giving him his privacy to undress and swim. "What are you doing?" he asks.

I turn back toward him. "Going back to the..." My words fall off when he peels the shirt from his shoulders, exposing a beautiful bronzed body and a six-pack my fingers suddenly itch to touch.

"Here." He closes the distance between us and wraps me in his shirt. Warmth sinks into my bones as he throws his arm around me and guides me down the hill.

I probably shouldn't be touched by the gentlemanly gesture. Once an ass, always an ass, right? Which begs the question: Now that I've got his attention, should I go through with my plan of payback?

The air warms as we descend, and night is fully upon us by the time we reach the village. My body is still quivering, and so is the needy juncture between my legs. Jeez, with the way I'm reacting, I'm not so sure I could seduce him and walk away.

You hate this guy, Bri. He humiliated you.

"I'm still so cold," I say.

"Let's hurry. You're staying at the hotel with the others, right?"

"Yes, aren't you?"

"No, I'm in one of the chalets." He points off in the distance, but I know where the chalets are located. I've stayed in them many times over the years.

"Maybe we should go there," I say. "It's closer, and I'm afraid I'm going to freeze to death."

He goes still, and his brow furrows as he stares off into the distance, like his mind is a million miles away.

"Luca?" I ask. "It is Luca, right?"

"Yeah, that's what my friends call me," he says, a small grin on his face. Touché. "Come on. I'll get you warmed up and then see you back to your hotel."

With his arm still around me, he guides me down a narrow path leading to his chalet. He opens the door for me and guides me in. The place is perfectly neat, much of what I'd expect from a guy like him.

"So tidy," I say, walking down the hall leading into the main area, which has a kitchen, island and dining table on one side of the big room. I glance to the left to take in a sofa facing a fireplace. Beyond that there is a big king-size bed and a door leading to an outside deck. "How long have you been here?"

"Got in yesterday." His gaze moves over me again. "Do you want to get out of those clothes?"

My pulse leaps. But then it settles quickly when I realize what he's asking. Oh, how I wanted to hear those words from him all those years ago.

"Yeah, I probably should," I say. *Okay, Bri, this is the perfect opportunity for seduction.* "Do you have something I could slip into? A pair of sweats, maybe."

"I have a T-shirt," he says. "And gym shorts. No sweats."

"That should do."

He goes to the dresser and comes back with a

T-shirt that will float on me and a pair of shorts with no drawstring. I point to them. "Ah, those won't work."

"Probably not." He puts them aside and hands me the shirt. He gestures with a nod. "Bathroom is in there."

"I know where it is," I say as I saunter across the room.

"That's right. Your granddad owns the resort, doesn't he?" I nod as I step into the bathroom and leave the door slightly ajar as I change. "What's with you and him, anyway?"

"What do you mean?"

"You seem tense around him."

Luca always was a smart guy. Very astute. I'll have to play it careful around him. "He won't stop pushing me to get married," I say truthfully. No need to fib about that.

"Ah," he says.

I take off my wet clothes—bra and panties included—and shrug into his warm shirt. "Ah, what?"

"Nothing," he says, but before I can press he continues with, "So, you're not interested in marriage?"

"Hell no."

I come out from the bathroom and walk to the closet housing the washer and dryer. I bend slightly and toss my clothes in. When I stand and turn around, Luca's glance is slowly lifting from where my ass had just been.

Okay, girl, here goes nothing.

CHAPTER FOUR

Luca

MY EYES LIFT from her ass, and when I catch a small smile on her lips—clearly I'm busted—I tear my gaze away. What is going on with her? One second she's acting like she doesn't know me, and the next she's aiming her sexy ass my way. I'm pretty damn sure she's aware of what she's doing and is trying to get a rise out of me.

Well done, Brianna. It worked.

I turn from her and pretend to do something in the kitchen sink as I adjust my cock. Her bare feet graze the wooden floor as she walks around the chalet and it's all I can do to keep my shit together. A whooshing sound reaches my ears and I turn to find her flicking on the propane fire.

"Still not warm?" I ask, even though the sun's been beating in through the windows of the chalet all day and it's a million degrees. She holds her hands out in front of the fire to absorb the heat.

"Not yet," she says.

"Maybe you should jump in the shower," I say as beads of perspiration dot my bare chest.

"You think a warm shower will help?"

"For you, yes. Personally I need a cold one," I say, and when she wipes her tongue over her bottom lip, I groan. "It's so hot in here," I explain, not wanting her to think I need a cold shower to cool down my dick, which just happens to be the truth.

"Well, you weren't swimming in an ice-cold lake," she says and pokes the air with the tip of her finger.

I shrug. "You're right, I wasn't."

"Go ahead and take a cold shower if you want." She turns back to the fire. "My clothes will probably be ready by the time you get out."

"No, I'm good, but I'm going to change into shorts." I grab the pair I'd offered her and make my way to the bathroom. As I pass Brianna, she's adjusting the thermostat, turning it up higher.

"Keep that up and I'm going to end up in my birthday suit." I say without thinking and close the bathroom door. *What the hell?* Get your mind off nakedness. Her soft chuckle reaches my ears and I wonder if she's really that cold, or if she's just jacking up the heat to get me out of my clothes. Shit, all she has to do is ask.

Wait, no. I am not going to have sex with Brianna. No way. No how. Not even if she asks.

Okay, maybe if she asks.

Cazzo!

I kick off my pants, and as I glance at my swollen dick, I take it into my hands and consider rubbing one out. In my current state it wouldn't take long, and Brianna would be none the wiser. I pull from the base to the crown. Heck, I should probably ease the tension before something ruptures.

"Maybe the hot tub will help," she calls out. The click of the patio door opening reaches my ears, and I close my eyes and try not to visualize her in that hot tub naked.

Again with the nakedness.

"Good idea," I say. Fuck, is that my voice? I open the bathroom door and walk to the patio just in time to see her peel my shirt from her shoulders and climb into the water. Naked.

My God, she has a beautiful body. Her curves are less pronounced than they were years ago, but she was as breathtaking then as she is now. She settles into the tub, leans her head back and stares up at the night sky.

Not wanting to startle her, I speak quietly, avert my eyes even though she's covered now by the water frothing from the jets. "Can I get you a drink?"

"Do you have any wine?"

"Yeah, I'll be right back." I hurry to the kitchen, and my hands are a bit shaky as I pour her a glass of wine and grab a beer from the fridge. I pop the cap and down half of the liquid in one swallow. With my cock jumping in my shorts, I step outside and the heat of the night falls over me.

"Join me," she says as I hand her the glass.

I wipe moisture from my brow. "I'm too hot as it is."

She presses the glass to her parted lips and takes a drink. A drop settles on her bottom lip, and it takes every ounce of strength I possess not to lean in and lick it away.

I clear my throat and her gaze settles on me. "So, your grandfather is after you to get married," I say for lack of anything else.

"Yes."

"And you don't want to."

"No." I settle into one of the Adirondack chairs, and her eyes narrow in on me. "What?"

I shrug. "I'm not sure I believe you."

She lifts her chin slightly. "You don't know me well enough to make that call. In fact you don't know me at all."

I take a pull from the bottle. "I know a few things."

"Oh?" she says, an almost worried look crossing her face.

"I know you went to Oxford, and that you're a lawyer. I know you're Tate's cousin, and that you two were close growing up. I know you make a mean apple pie."

"I guess I know a few things about you, too," she says, almost under her breath.

I lean toward her. "Such as."

She waves her hand and water splashes over me. "You're a corporate lawyer and work for my cousin."

I settle back in my chair. "So, really, you know nothing about me," I say, a bit relieved. The less anyone knows, the better.

"Well, I also know you like to sneak up on girls when they're swimming naked."

I laugh at that, and she laughs with me. "You said you were going back to your room. How was I to know you'd be in my spot?"

"Your spot, huh?" she says.

"Yep. Let's just say next time you use it, be warned that I might not be such a gentleman."

Stop fucking flirting, man.

She sits up a little straighter in the tub and I want to punch myself in the face for engaging in sexy banter with her. I need to end this now and get her out of my chalet before I do something I can only regret later.

I open my mouth to tell her it's time to go but stop when she says, "Maybe I don't want you to be such a gentleman."

Perspiration breaks out on my body as her nipples pop above the water line. "Brianna…" I begin, but as my cock thickens, my brain cells stop functioning.

"I think I'm warm now," she says, and lifts a little more, water splashing around her bare body. Unable to help myself, my gaze drops to her beautiful breasts, and a groan I have no control over crawls out of my throat.

"If you're warm, then why are your nipples so hard?"

Holy fuck, what the hell are you doing?

My blatantly sexual question takes her by surprise, but she recovers quickly. "The night air. I should probably get inside to warm up by the fire."

Walk away, Luca. Walk away.

I stand, about to do just that, but my cock has other ideas. Before I can stop myself, I slide into the tub with her, shorts still on. A gasp catches in her throat as I go to my knees in front of her and my gaze latches on to hers.

"Or I could use my mouth to warm you," I suggest, and when her chest rises and falls, everything in her eyes and her body saying yes, I lean into her and close my lips around her hard nipple.

At first she stiffens beneath my touch, and I wonder if I've made a colossal mistake. Have I read this situation wrong? Has she not been coming on to me? I'm about to pull back, but then my name is spilling from her lips, and her hands are circling my head, gripping my hair and holding me to her.

Hell yes.

I swirl my tongue over her turgid bud and draw her deeper into my mouth, sucking and tasting until she's murmuring something incoherent. A small part of my brain warns me not to start this, but at the moment, the throbbing head between my legs is the one calling the shots. I've wanted this for so fucking long, it would take this entire village to pull me off her.

Warm water heats my already hot body, and I lift her a bit higher, wanting to see all of her. The night air is warm, so I'm not worried about her getting cold, plus it's easy to tell she's burning up. I break the kiss and inch back, take in her glossy, lust-filled eyes.

"Where else are you cold?" I ask as I press my lips to hers. Her mouth parts, welcoming me in, and the second my tongue enters her sweet mouth, need grips my balls.

She moans into my mouth and kisses me back, and I take everything she's willing to give. I move my mouth to her neck. "You cold here?"

"Yes, very," she murmurs and leans her head back to give me better access. I lick the long column of her neck and then burrow my face into the soft hollow there. Her hips move restlessly beneath the water, telling me what she wants, and I grip them, hold her still. "Don't worry," I whisper. "I'll warm all your cold spots."

I slide my hand down her hips, grip her thighs and widen them. She whimpers, and her hands go to my shoulders. Her fingers are warm and soft against my skin and I can't wait to feel them on my dick.

Breathing heavily, I nuzzle her ear and run my fingers up her inner thighs. I touch her clit, circle it, slowly, methodically.

"Yes," she says on a breathless whisper.

"Cold here, Brianna?" I ask, everything in me dying to get between her legs.

"Freezing," she says, and unable to wait a second longer, I stand and pull her up with me. Her eyes go wide, and I put my hand back between her legs. "You need my mouth here," I say, a statement not a question, but she answers with a nod.

"Then we need to get you inside, and get you spread wide open so I can warm you up properly." I scoop her up, carry her into the stifling heat and set her on the bed, which is facing the fire. "Legs open," I command in a soft voice.

"Bossy," she says, and it's clear to me she's used to giving orders in the bedroom, not taking them.

"Do it." Her nipples quiver as she spreads for me, and I meet her glance as I pet her sex lightly. "So cold. It might take hours for me to warm you up."

"My cousin never said you were bossy, but I do remember hearing something about you being meticulous and working long and hard into the night to get a job done."

I grin at that, and ever so slowly inch a finger into her. She's so fucking tight and wet, I nearly explode in my shorts. I finger her for a second and she grows even wetter. "Is this helping?"

"A little…" she murmurs, as her body tightens around my finger. My God, she's so close, I can't believe it. I pull my finger out, wanting to prolong her pleasure, and tear my shorts from my body. She goes up on her elbows to see my dick, and her eyes widen when I take my cock into my hands.

"Smart, meticulous and totally *equipped* to stay up all night to finish the job. I might have just won the man lottery," she says, and smiles up at me. I smile back, pleased that she likes what she sees.

I climb onto the bed and find her mouth again. As I kiss her, I ease her back until she's beneath me. She reaches out, captures my dick in her hand and gives me a little squeeze. I brush my thumb over her nipple and make a tsking sound.

"Hard again." I fall over her, press her into the mattress and find her nipple. I take a long, hard suck until she's scratching at my back, dragging skin with nails. Damn, that feels good.

"Heating up, Brianna?" I ask around a mouthful of pink sweetness.

"So hot," she murmurs and lifts her hips, moving her pussy against my stomach and leaving me soaking wet. I shimmy lower and press openmouthed kisses to her stomach and belly button, and when I reach her hot little sex, I blow on it.

She quivers and I press my mouth to her clit, suck it in until she's jerking beneath me. She swells even more beneath my ministrations, and I slip one finger into her tight core.

"Luca," she cries out, and bucks against my mouth, a shameless display of need that turns me on even more.

"That's it," I say, lifting my mouth from her sex.

"No, please. I'm still—"

Her words fall off when I roll onto my back and drag her until her pussy is positioned right where I want it. "Work your pussy over my mouth. Get it nice and warm for my cock," I say and flick my tongue out to taste the sweetness dripping from her center.

"Oh God." She presses down on me and moves her hips, writhing and rotating and soaking my face unabashedly. She's no sedentary passenger along for the ride between the sheets, and I love that about her. For a buttoned-up girl outside the bedroom, inside, Brianna is a girl who knows what she wants and takes what she needs.

I fuck her with my tongue, and she rubs her clit all over me until her breathing changes. I dip a finger into her core, brush it back and forth over the hot bundle of nerves as I eat at her with all the need unraveling inside me—far too many years in the making.

"Luca," she cries out as her body breaks, her hot release splashing out of her and dripping down my chin. I drink her in, lap at her, not wanting to miss a drop. She tries to move, but I slide one hand around her and grip her ass. No way is she going anywhere until I've had my fill. Then again now that I've tasted her, I'm not sure I'll ever be able to sate my appetite.

She's panting and her nails are tugging at the sheet as I take my time, despite the fact that my dick is so hard I'm in agony. I finally clean her and slide out from beneath her body. She rolls over onto her back, and I have to say, that sexy, well-fucked-woman look she's wearing totally suits her.

My gaze falls to her hard nipples, and she cups her breasts, squeezes them together. "They need my mouth again?" I ask. She shakes her head, mischief in her eyes, and my gaze roams her face. What is she up to?

"They need this," she says and sits up to grab my throbbing cock. Instantly understanding what she wants, I climb up her body, and she squeezes her beautiful breasts together for me. I do love a woman who doesn't hold back and makes no qualms about what she wants. I slide my cock between her breasts and thrust forward, into her waiting mouth. Fucking her like this is so goddamn hot, pre-cum spills from my tip, and she laps at it with each upward thrust.

"So good," I growl as the dual pleasure takes me to the edge fast. I stroke her like this a couple more times, then tear my dick from her perfect tits.

"Time to really warm you up," I say and grab my pants. I pull a condom from the pocket and rip into it. Brianna goes up on her elbows again to watch me, her gaze latched on to my dick. *Gesù*, I really like the way she looks at me, like when she finally gets her mouth on my cock, she's going to worship it.

She crooks her finger, urging me back to her, and I don't waste any time getting between her legs again. I fall over her, and she wraps her legs around my back, trying to force me inside. But I need to go slowly, or I'm going to blow my load before I even get started.

I give her an inch and her head rolls back. "Yesss," she hisses, and puts her hands on my shoulders.

"You're fucking hot," I say.

"So hot," she murmurs, her lids falling heavily over dark eyes.

"Maybe you don't need my cock, then," I tease, and her eyes open wide. When she catches my grin, she relaxes. "So, you do need it?" I ask, wanting, for some strange reason, to hear her say it.

"Yes, I need it," she says, and lifts her hips. "I need your cock, so don't make me wait any longer."

"No?"

"No," she repeats, and before she even finishes, I power forward, driving my entire length into her, and seating myself so goddamn high, I'm sure I've reached heaven.

"Luca," she cries out, and curls forward as I fill her. Her muscles tighten around my girth, her liquid heat coating my cock.

I move my hips and slide in and out of her, creating friction until we're both panting, our skin ridiculously hot to the touch.

"This," she begins and then swallows hard. She tries to speak again, but her words catch in her throat.

"This feel good?"

She nods and whimpers as I angle my body for deeper thrusts. "Oh…" she manages to get out as I slide a hand between our bodies and toy with her clit. Her body vibrates around my dick, and I clench down on my teeth, struggling to hang on. I want this to be amazing for her, because this is a one-time thing. Some working brain cell reminds me it has to be.

"Are you going to stay out of my swimming hole?"

I ask as I slam home, my balls slapping her body with each thrust. She shakes her head and a groan catches in my throat. "What about my warning?"

"Don't…care," she croaks out, her voice broken.

"I told you I won't be a gentleman next time." She quivers harder, liking this little game I'm playing with her.

Her eyes flash. "And I told you I don't want you to."

"Then I won't be so nice again."

"What…what will you do?"

I drive into her, slam her against the mattress, my dick ready to explode. Heat zaps my balls and they tighten as I think about bending her over a log and taking her in the woods. "A naked woman in the woods, warned to stay away and choosing not to. Well, that woman might just find herself up against the Big Bad Wolf if she's not careful."

As soon as the words leave my mouth, she comes all over my cock. I pinch my eyes shut as her heat seeps into my body, burns me from the inside out.

"Fuck," I murmur, and bury my face in her neck as she rides out the gripping waves. I pull out, slam back in again, and with her last few clenches, I let go on a growl.

As I come and come and come, I collapse on top of her and breathe in the sweet smell of her skin. We're both panting, taking deep, labored breaths, and we stay like that until my cock grows soft. I inch out of her, then I pull her to me, hold her close.

For the last few months I've been all work and no play, but now that I've played with Brianna, I can't help but want more. As I think about that, my cock starts thickening again. Brianna shimmies away, but I reach for her.

"Where do you think you're going?" I ask as I pull her on top of me.

She looks over her shoulder, glances at the door. "I was—"

I drag her mouth to mine, kiss her deeply. No way is she getting out of here tonight. My cock grows against her body and she moans her approval. Oh yeah, we're going to fuck until the sun comes up.

CHAPTER FIVE

Brianna

How could I have been so stupid?

I shake my head and give myself a good hard lecture for falling for Luca's charm and letting him seduce me into his bed. Or was it the other way around? I'm not sure. All I know is I was supposed to turn him on and leave him hanging, like he did to me all those years ago. I groan and pound the bed, but settle myself back down when Luca comes back from the bathroom. Shit, I wanted to be out of here before he finished. I close my eyes, pretend I'm sleeping until I can figure out what to do next, how to get myself out of this.

Yeah, I made a mistake last night, but goddammit the sex was good. Better than good. It was fan-freaking-tastic. The best sex I've ever had. The second he put his mouth on my nipple, I had planned to put a stop to things, tell him who I was and bolt. But did I do that? Of course not. How could I? No one has ever worked my nipples quite like that before. I knew I had to see it through. Why shouldn't I take what I want, on my terms? Unfortunately those terms weren't supposed to include a stupid sleepover.

The edge of the mattress dips, and I inch one eye open to find Luca sitting on the bed, a cup of coffee in his hand.

"Morning," he says. "Coffee?"

"Like you even have to ask." He grins and hands the mug over. I take a much-needed sip. "Thank you. You will be rewarded in heaven," I say. He stands and my gaze roams his body. This morning he's dressed in nothing but his jeans. Dammit, what is it about a guy in nothing but jeans that turns me on? Okay, maybe it's just Luca in jeans that does that.

Time to go.

I push the blankets off me, and that's when I realize I'm stark naked. I grab the sheet and haul it back up.

Luca angles his head. "I've seen you naked, Bri," he says.

"It's Brianna."

He grins. "I've seen you naked, Brianna. And I've been inside you. It's a little late to cover up, don't you think?" He grips the sheet and slowly drags it down my body. "You're beautiful, you know."

Old hurts come back in a crushing wave. He didn't think so years ago, couldn't see that I was more than just a chubby freshman. "I should go."

He frowns. "Was it something I said?"

"No. I should go. Tate and the others will be wondering where I am." I climb from the bed, and Luca's moan of appreciation fills the room as I saunter to the dryer and grab my clothes. I hurry to the bathroom and dress. Great. I'm wearing yesterday's clothes, and from one look at me it's easy to tell I've been up having sex all night. I somehow have to get to my room without anyone seeing me. This…whatever this was…is not something I want to explain, or repeat.

Liar.

Okay, okay, maybe I do want a repeat—why bother denying it?—but it's not going to happen.

Oh, but it did once, and it was so damn good.

All righty then. On that note I step from the bathroom and glance around to find Luca in the kitchen. I take another sip of coffee and set my cup on the counter. I'm about to slip out when Luca points a spatula at me.

"Sit."

Ribbons of need swirl through me at his assertiveness. I'm not sure what that's all about. I'm the one who's always in control, always calling the shots, but last night when he took charge of me, it awakened something needy inside me, something I never even knew existed.

"You're not going anywhere until I feed you. What kind of guy do you think I am, anyway?"

Oh, if he only knew.

"I don't normally eat breakfast," I say, but glance

over at the counter to see what smells so good. My stomach takes that moment to grumble.

"Maybe not, but we worked up quite the appetite last night and you're going to eat."

"Maybe I work up an appetite like that every night," I say, having no doubt he does the same himself. I remember his reputation back at Oxford.

He flips the pancake, turns and leans back against the counter, crossing his feet at the ankle. Seriously, could he make the pose look any sexier? I want to tell him to put a shirt on already, but I don't want him to know the true effect his near nakedness has on me.

"Is that right?" he asks.

"That's right."

"Is that why you don't want to get married? You like having a different guy in your bed every night?" He shrugs. "Not that there's anything wrong with that, I'm just curious." He flips the pancakes again and then plates them, sliding them across the island. I breathe in the delicious smell as he grabs the syrup.

"Why so curious?" I ask as I pour a generous amount of syrup over my pancakes.

"It's the lawyer in me."

"It's the lawyer in me that keeps me single."

He forks a big bite into his mouth, chews and then says, "How so?"

"I'm a divorce lawyer. I see the worst in people all the time, and if you know anything about my family, the guys move from woman to woman constantly."

Tate's dad, Uncle Don, is the latest example. He married his fourth wife several months ago. Half the family didn't bother skipping work to attend. Carson family weddings have become so run-of-the-mill... Sounds scornful but it's the truth.

"Tate's not like that."

I smile. "No, he's one of the good guys."

"Then you're saying there *are* good guys out there?"

I laugh. "Way to twist my words. You must win a lot of cases."

"I win enough." He takes another bite, lounging against the island.

"You really don't want to get married. I never would have guessed that about you," he says, redirecting the conversation back to me.

"I don't do relationships, don't do love and I don't sleep with the same guy twice. Believe me, I know happily-ever-after doesn't exist. I see that every day."

A moment of silence as he absorbs that, and then he says, "Your job is doing a number on you. Do you even like what you do?"

I take a long moment to think about it. "Some days, I guess."

"You did family law at Oxford?"

A question, not a statement, but I answer anyway. "That's right."

"I wonder if we ever ran into each other, attended any of the same parties."

"The guys in their Oxford hoodies." I wave my

fork. "I couldn't tell one apart from the other. You all looked alike."

"Ah, the hoodies. They were all the rage back then. I wore mine to every party."

"I remember," I say. Then when his eyes lift to mine, I add, "I mean I remember the hoodies. I don't remember you in one at any party." Wow, for a girl who hates to lie, I'm really nailing it here. "By the way, these pancakes are delicious," I add, wanting to change the conversation.

"Come back for dinner. I make a mean carbonara."

I reach for my coffee and take a sip. "I wouldn't have taken you for a guy who could cook."

He quirks one brow. God, could he be any more adorable? "No? What kind of guy would you take me for?"

"A guy who has others cook for him." On campus, rumor had it he was extremely wealthy, but no one really knew much about him. Funny, now that I think about it, he really kept his private life…private. I'm guessing that hasn't changed, since he chose to stay in the chalet, away from the rest of us. "I guess I just assumed."

"Assumption is the mother of all screwups," he says with a wink, then adds, "I've been single a long time. It was either learn to cook or starve."

"You made the right choice, and now, lucky for me, I'm reaping the benefits from it."

"My mom is a true Italian who loves to cook. I spent hours in the kitchen with her when I was

young. We're still close." I look down at the mention of his mom, as memories of my own fill me with
heartache. "Brianna? What's wrong?"

"Oh, nothing. What about your father?" I ask,
and then kick myself for veering into the personal.

He looks down, pain ghosting his eyes. "We lost
Dad and my brother at the same time. Car accident."

I touch his arm. "I'm so sorry."

"It was a long time ago." His gaze meets mine.
"What about you? Are you close to your parents?"

I sigh… No point in lying in this regard. "My
Dad left when I was young, and my mother sort of
checked out after that. She died a couple of years
ago."

"I'm sorry. That must have been very hard on you."

"I miss her terribly. Miss who she was before it
all happened." Long before she was physically gone,
she was both emotionally and mentally gone from
my life. I try to inject a bit of humor into my voice.
"Unlike your mother, she wasn't Italian or a good
cook. At least I didn't have to eat her food after she
checked out on me."

He smiles at me, and I get the sense he can tell
I'm making light of things. "You did the cooking?"

"Yeah, and I wasn't very good at it, either. A chip
off the old block," I say and slide another piece of
pancake into my mouth. The taste explodes on my
tongue.

"But you can make a mean apple pie, right?"

I can't help but laugh at that. "No, Tate was kidding. I actually burnt down the kitchen the only time I tried. I mean, the pie might have been good, before the firemen doused it."

He laughs out loud. "You're kidding me?"

"I wish I was." We both go quiet for a moment. "You said you've been single for a long time. Are you anti-marriage, too?"

He looks down, stares into his coffee cup like it holds all the answers in the universe. His muscles bunch, the tension in his body taking up space between us. God, he's suddenly strung so tightly, I'm afraid something is going to pop.

He leans away from the countertop, presenting calm even though there is a storm going on in his eyes, and his nostrils are flaring. "I'm not opposed to marriage," he says. "If it was with the right person, you know?"

What the hell does he mean by that? Was he married before, to the wrong person? I wouldn't judge— I was nearly engaged to the wrong guy once. Ryan was so temperamental, it was almost a relief to catch him cheating on me with his sister's friend. Good riddance, asshole. I'm curious about Luca but it's not my business, nor do I want to make it mine, so I don't ask.

A noise outside the chalet gains my attention. As the guests wake up and begin their activities, I finish the last bite of my breakfast. "I'll help you with the dishes and get out of your way."

"You're not in my way, Brianna," he says, and

my gaze flies to his when he takes my hand. "I was serious about tonight," he says, his mood changing. "Come back. I'll cook for you, even give you a few lessons."

My gaze meanders to his bare chest, and I take in his bronzed skin, the hard grooves my fingers itch to touch again. "I…" Oh God, how tempting. But this has already gone too far. I'm out of my element as it is. I pull my hand free, stand and take my plate to the sink. "I can't. I told Granddad I'd have dinner with him tonight. I haven't spent a lot of time with him lately, and he's not well."

"I want to keep fucking you."

I turn and grip the counter at his bold statement. "Last night was a one-time thing, Luca. And like I said, I don't date the same guy twice."

"Last night was a date?"

"Last night was sex, or rather 'fucking' as you put it."

He grins. "Really good fucking."

"Yeah, really good, and I never screw the same guy twice, unless it's Mr. Right," I say and wonder why I'm telling him any of this.

His eyes search mine, and my stomach clenches with desire. "Mr. Right?"

"My battery-operated boyfriend."

He laughs at that, but it quickly morphs into something else. "You probably shouldn't have told me that. Now I'm going to want to see you use it."

Holy God, did he really just say he wanted to see me pleasure myself? "Not going to happen."

I make my way to the door, and he's hot on my heels, his closeness heating up my body again. My nipples quiver, and the juncture between my legs begs me to take him up on his offer. But I can't. I don't want to get involved with this man. I don't even like him.

He reaches past me and opens the door, and his bare chest brushes over my back. "Enjoy Mr. Right, but if you decide you miss the real thing, you know where to find me."

Heat rips through me just that easily, and I clear my throat. "It was nice meeting you, Luca."

"You too, *Brianna*," he says, drawing out my name.

With that I step outside, close the door behind me and nearly melt to the ground in a puddle of need. But no matter how my body reacts, no way, no how am I stepping foot in his chalet again.

I don't think.

CHAPTER SIX

Luca

DUSK FALLS OVER the village as I make my way down a long cobblestone path leading to the main bar, Diamond Peak, where I plan to grab a much-needed drink with Tate—maybe two. I spent most of the day going over some work I brought with me, and thinking about what happened last night. I never meant to go down that path with a woman who could make me forget all about my obligations. A woman who doesn't believe in marriage or even second dates. It's a shame, really. I might not be able to have her long-term, but I'd hate to see her go through life without ever finding love.

A fresh strip of anger curls through me as I think about the stipulations placed on me. What I'd like to do is rip up my father's will and stomp it into the ground, but if I do and the conglomerates go to my cousin, we could lose everything. I have my mother to think about, not to mention all the things I want to do for my people once I take my rightful place.

This morning I should have run the other way instead of telling Brianna I wanted to continue sleeping with her. But now that I've gotten a taste of her, I want more. I want to keep her in my bed until I have to go back to Italy. Hell, maybe a week in her bed will help me forget her once and for all. I can only hope, because once I step into my position as duke, I can't be with her. As I think about that, I wonder what Brianna would make of it all. Most think the Italian nobility are nothing but a joke, thanks to some of Marco's over-the-top playboy antics. They've gotten worse in recent years.

I glance around the bar in search of Tate. Tonight it's just the two of us, and we plan to kick back and down a few brews to celebrate the last of his bachelorhood. I step into the bar where I once worked as a bartender and nod to Henry, the aging manager who should have retired ages ago. He waves back, and I make my way over to him.

"How's life treating you, Luca?" he asks.

"Good, I'm enjoying New York."

"Sure do miss you working back here with me. Hard to get good help these days." He pours me a draft and slides it across the counter.

I take a sip. "Perfect as always." He smiles at that. "How's Marion?"

He smiles when I mention his wife. "She's good. Still nagging me to retire."

"Maybe it's time to take her on that American vacation she's been wanting," I suggest with a raised brow.

He winks at me. "It's in the works."

"Nice. If you make it to New York, you have to look up me and Tate," I say, but then swallow down the knot jumping into my throat. Soon enough I'll be packing up and heading back to Italy. My thirtieth birthday is around the corner and I won't be able to put it off any longer.

Henry turns to another customer and I spin on my stool and glance around, looking for Tate. Instead I find Brianna and her grandfather, seated near the window. I can't hear what they're saying from here, but from the intense look on her face, I'd guess it's a pretty serious conversation.

I look her over, revel in the way her jeans hug her curves. My eyes go to her buttoned-up blouse, and how she's toying with the top button. As I gaze at her, and think about last night, every instinct I possess tells me she remembers me from Oxford. So why is she pretending otherwise? Why the secrets? I'm not sure what sort of game she's playing, but I'll let her play it, for now.

I pick up my beer and head farther into the room, about to grab a table, when her big blue eyes meet mine. She runs a hand through her hair, and I can almost see the wheels turning in her head as she stares at me. I stop walking, my gaze going from her to her granddad, and then back to her. She's clearly agitated about something.

Before I even realize what's happening, she jumps from her chair and crosses the room, coming at me fast. She reaches me, goes up on her toes and throws her arms around me. "Just go with it, please," she begs, and presses her lips to mine.

I slide my free hand around her back, tug her sexy body against mine and breathe in the floral scent of her shampoo as we kiss. She finally breaks from my hold, and I dip my head, waiting for an explanation.

"Please, just follow along." she says, and grabs my hand to drag me over to her grandfather.

"Well, well. I knew there was something going on with the two of you," James says.

Brianna gestures for me to sit, and she grabs the chair next to me and shimmies closer. She reaches for my hand. "Look, Granddad, we didn't want anyone to know. This week is about Tate and Summer, and we didn't want to take any of the attention off them."

James folds his arms and assesses us. "I guess that's where you were last night. With Luca in his chalet." Damn, for a guy who swears he's on his deathbed, he sure has his ear to the ground and knows everything going on around him.

Heat crawls into Brianna's cheeks, and her gaze jerks to mine. Her mouth opens and closes again, like she can't quite figure out how to answer. Coming to her rescue, I say, "Yes, she was with me. But like Brianna says, we'd prefer not to steal Tate and Summer's thunder by announcing we're together."

"I suspected you two knew each other." He taps the side of his head. "An old man knows these things."

"You're very astute," I say.

His grin is cocky as his head bobs. "Can't keep anything from me."

"Apparently not."

"You'll keep our little secret, Granddad?" Brianna asks, leaning toward the elderly man.

"How did you two meet?" he asks.

"Back at Oxford," I say honestly. "At a party. Isn't that right, Brianna?"

"Ah…that's right."

"I was wearing one of those popular blue hoodies. Brianna had a thing for them. I guess that's why I caught her eye."

Brianna toys with her straw and looks down, like she's recalling our first spoken words. I smiled at her, and she glanced behind herself, unsure. I'm not sure what this was all about. But hours later she came at me with liquid courage.

"We went our separate ways after Oxford, and when I found out he was working for Tate, well… here we are."

"Here we are, indeed," James says, a sly look on his face. He taps his cane and stands. But then he glances at Brianna's bare ring finger and frowns. "Where's the ring?"

Ah, so she told him we're actually engaged.

"Getting sized," I say quickly, and she gives my hand a thankful squeeze.

"When we get back home, I'd better see that ring on her finger," James says to me. He taps his cane.

"Well then, I don't want to be a third wheel. You two kids have a good night." He zips his lips. "And don't worry, your secret is safe with me." His eyes sparkle when he adds, "At least I'll try. Sometimes I just blurt things out without thinking. Senility."

Senility my ass. The man is a sharp son of a bitch. Why is it no one can see it but me?

Brianna frowns as she watches him go. It's easy to see how close they are and how much she wants to make him happy. James slowly makes his way across the polished wood floor, and when the doors close behind him, Brianna shrinks into herself and cringes.

"I'm so sorry, Luca. He was giving me a hard time about meeting the fiancé I lied about, and I saw you there, and before I could even think better of it, I decided to pretend we were a couple."

I grin at her and think about all the fun ways we can be a couple, all the benefits of a pretend engagement.

"Wait, why are you smiling. Aren't you mad?"

"A beautiful woman kisses me in a crowded bar—how could I be mad about that?"

"What about the lie, and me dragging you in to my problems?"

I give a casual shrug and stretch my legs out. "I don't mind helping."

Relief comes over her. "Really?"

"Sure, but I have a condition."

Her smile falls and her eyes narrow. "I should have known."

"What's that supposed to mean?" What is it with her? One minutes she's all sweet and kind, and the next she's full of anger. I guess I have a week to figure her out.

"Nothing," she says and grabs her drink. She takes a pull from her straw and then clamps down on it. Hard. My dick shudders, and I squeeze my legs together. "What do you want, Luca?"

"You stay with me at the chalet, and we live and act like a real engaged couple."

Her gaze jerks to mine. "You've got to be kidding me. Why would we do that?"

I tap my thumb on the table, take in her exasperated expression. "You only do one-night stands, right?"

"Right?"

I lean toward her. "I want you to spend the week with me, try it on for size. See what it feels like to be with someone longer than one night. I bet you won't find it so bad."

She shakes her head. Hard. "No, no way."

I take a sip of my beer and set it on the table. "Those are my terms, Brianna."

Venomous eyes I remember from our college days latch on to mine. "Things are always done on my terms, Luca. I'm always the one in control. Always."

"Last night I remember you losing a bit of that control, and if memory serves me correctly, you quite liked handing yourself over to me."

"Oh God," she says, a pink blush crawling up

her neck and making her look so sexy. "Why…why would you want me to do this?"

"Maybe I think deep down you really do want to find Prince Charming and live happily-ever-after. Maybe I think you're just scared."

"I'm not scared. I'm a big girl, Luca. I know what the real world is like. I see the worst in people every day." She glares at me, her eyes searching my face. "What's in it for you, anyway?" I'm about to answer, tell her that I'm just helping a girl out, but she holds her hand up to stop me. "Never mind. I get it. It's all about sex, isn't it?"

I shift closer, put my mouth near her ear. "Oh, there's going to be sex, Brianna. Lots and lots of sex. That's what couples do."

Her body quivers, and no matter what words come out of her mouth next, I know sex between us is pretty fucking great and that she wants it again, just as much as I do.

"There you are," Tate says, and I inch back to find my best friend and his fiancée grinning at us.

Summer's gaze narrows in on me. "What's going on?"

I turn to look at Brianna. It's her call whether we tell them or not. She exhales loudly and buries her face in her hands.

"Hey, what's wrong?" Tate asks, and takes the seat next to her.

She groans. "You're not going to believe what I did."

Summer sits next to me, a worried look on her face.

"What did you do?" Tate asks.

"Granddad was harassing me again, so I told him Luca and I are engaged."

I press my thumb to my bottom lip, recalling her sweet taste. "She's even thinking about staying with me for the week to prove it." Brianna glares at me from between her fingers.

Tate leans back in his chair and gives a slow whistle, while Summer sits there with a smirk on her face. "It was a stupid thing to do, but I panicked," Brianna says, and finally drops her hands. She takes another drink and finishes it off.

"I'd say," Tate says as he gestures the server.

"It's not so bad," I pipe in. "We told him we were keeping it a secret because we didn't want to take the focus off you two."

"Good thinking—but he's a meddler, so pretending to stay together might not be a bad idea." He glances at Brianna, who flushes again. "What are you going to do when we go back home? Granddad is frail and weak, a breakup just might…" He lets his words fall off, unable to vocalize them. His mouth turns down and Summer reaches out and takes his hand in hers. She gives him a warm, understanding smile.

"He's expecting to see a ring on my finger," Brianna says and holds her jewelry-free hand up.

"As hard as it might be on your granddad, you'll have to pretend a breakup sooner or later," Summer says. "Or not."

"Or not?" Brianna practically shouts. "Of course, we have to, but that will destroy him. All he ever does is worry about me. He says it's not healthy to be alone. He just…he just wants to see me happy, and…" She pauses and waves her finger back and forth between the two of us. "And I did this to make him happy."

"Then you'll have to just keep on pretending," Summer says, like there is absolutely no problem with the two of us staying together forever, to keep an old man happy.

"Summer," Tate says, quietly. "They can't do that."

"I can't hurt Granddad, either," Brianna says.

Summer squeezes Tate's hand. "You know, sometimes things just have a way of working themselves out. Just ride the week out, act like you're in love with each other and try not to stress out about it too much. Doctor's orders." With that she stands and reaches for Brianna's hand. "Come on. These two are going to drink beer and get stupid, and you and I are going shopping. There's this great little boutique I found last time I was here. They have the best lingerie."

"Nice," Tate and I say at the same time, and Brianna shoots daggers my way. I hold my hands up in surrender and laugh. "What, a guy can't appreciate lingerie?"

"This isn't real," she says. "And I'm not wearing lingerie for you. Ever."

"Hey, you're the one who sprung this on me. The

least you could do is consider it," I say, and Tate laughs as he punches me in the arm. I know he's secretly loving this. In the first month I worked for him, he mentioned Brianna often, even joked once about setting up us two workaholics.

"Dude, are you not fond of your nuts?" Tate asks and shakes his head at me like I'm insane. Yeah, I get that Brianna is confident and a take-charge kind of woman—a woman a guy should never mess with—but the blush on her cheeks when I tease her is so goddamn sexy, I can't seem to help myself.

I cross my legs to protect my nuts. "I just might give up one to see her in lingerie," I say, and Brianna opens her mouth, likely to shoot back with some kind of profanity, when Summer captures her arm and gives a little tug.

"Ignore him, Bri." Summer winks at me. "It's the beer making him stupid." She puts her purse over her shoulder. "Behave yourselves, boys."

"See you tonight, Bri," I say and then fish my key from my pocket to hand over to her. "Just let yourself in."

She looks it over before shoving it into her purse. "It's Brianna."

"I know."

CHAPTER SEVEN

Brianna

THE CHALET'S OUTSIDE solar lantern is on, brightening the path as I drag my suitcase along the walkway. I grab my key card from my purse and stare at it for a moment. Truthfully I can't believe I accepted Luca's terms and agreed to live with him for the week. Things are always done on my terms. I set the rules. Then again I got him into this, so he should have some say on how it all plays out, right? As I consider that, my mind goes back to the incredible sex we had, how he said he wanted to keep fucking me. I shut him down at the time, which begs the question: Why did I throw myself into his arms and kiss him hours later? Was it really all for show, my way to let Granddad know I was okay? Or was there some other reason behind it—like the fact that I wanted back in his bed, and this was the perfect excuse?

Oh Jesus!

I quietly let myself in and listen for sound at the

door. The light above the sink in the kitchen is on, and I leave my suitcase in the foyer and tiptoe farther into the chalet. It's late but it's possible Luca is still out drinking. After we went shopping, Summer and I met up with her friends Cara and Amber. We all went out to the wine bar for a drink—my idea. I kept them there longer than I normally would have—I'm still exhausted from the travel—but I was hoping Luca would be asleep when I returned.

I'm half to blame for this situation, I realize. I did get myself into this mess. Honestly, I could be the poster girl for screwed-up good intentions. I walk down the hall and find Luca stomach down on the bed, stark naked and sound asleep. The sheets are a crumpled mess near the footboard. My heart picks up the pace as I let my gaze roam the long, hard length of his beautiful body. He must work out a lot to be in such good shape. Which reminds me, I need to hit the gym in the morning for a good cardio workout.

There are other ways you can work off the calories, Bri...

I reluctantly tear my gaze away and go back to my suitcase. I carry it into the room and unzip it. All the goodies I purchased earlier spill from the overstuffed bag. The pretty pink package with the silk ties tumbles to my feet, like it wants my attention. I lift the bag and shake my head. How I let Summer talk me into buying lingerie is beyond me. That girl can be persuasive when she wants to be. In the end I caved. But I'm not wearing it in front of Luca and giving him the idea I want sex again—even though I totally do. I guess I can always wear it on a date when I get back home. Oh, who am I kidding? I've been so busy trying to prove myself at work, I haven't been out with a guy in ages. Maybe that's why my revenge plan backfired. One touch, and I was putty in Luca's hands. I shove my purchase to the bottom of my suitcase—out of sight, out of mind—but then something starts to buzz.

"Oh crap," I say under my breath when I realize what it is. I start tearing clothes out, desperate to find Mr. Right. Dammit, I must have accidentally turned it on just now. I finally pull it free and struggle to turn the damn thing off. I exhale when the buzzing stops, and I'm about to put it away until I hear the bed squeak behind me.

Oh hell no.

"Well hello, Mr. Right."

"Shit," I say under my breath, and quickly bury the vibrator in my clothes.

"Hey, don't let me keep you from him."

I turn slowly to find Luca up on one elbow, grinning at me. "It accidentally turned on. I wasn't about to use it." Although now, after getting a full frontal and seeing his thickening cock, my body is heating, screaming for a little attention. Sadly, after a night with Luca, I'm not so sure my vibrator is going to cut it anymore.

"That's too bad." Luca rolls to his back, and without a hint of modesty, sprawls out, showcasing his gorgeous body. "I'd love to watch you use it or, better yet, use it on you."

My pulse pounds against my neck. "Not going to happen," I say quickly, as the visual floods my body with lust.

He puts his arm over his head. "Do you have any idea how badly I want to fuck you again?"

Heat zings through me. I've never had a man talk so blatantly before, and the hardening of my nipples is a testament to how much I like it. Instead of answering, I shoot back with, "Do you think you could cover up?" I grab my nightgown and cosmetic bag from my suitcase.

"You've seen me naked," he says casually, and my body warms at the memory of him on top of me, inside me, taking me to places I've never been before.

"Which means I don't need to see it again."

"Once was enough?" he asks.

"Once is always enough for me," I say and stomp into the bathroom. I close the door behind me and lean against it. My entire body is on hyperdrive, fully aware there is a willing man in the bed I'm about to slide into.

Go for it. Have sex with him. On your terms.

I unbutton my blouse and shrug it from my shoulders. As I slip off my jeans, I think about Mr. Right. Dammit, I should have taken him into the bathroom with me. The toy is waterproof, and with the shower running, Luca would've never been the wiser. I could have taken the edge off and fallen into a sound sleep.

Now I'm going to be a quivering mess and trying to pretend otherwise. I open the glass shower door and turn on the spray. Once it's lukewarm—a little more cool than hot—I climb in and let the water wash away the lust building inside me. I stay there for a good long time, until my skin is shriveled and I'm shivering.

Praying Luca has fallen back to sleep, I dry off and grab my nightgown. Dammit, in my hurry I forgot panties. Not that I ever wear them to bed, but with Luca in there, I don't want him to get the wrong idea—or the right one.

Oh God, what am I saying?

I slip into my nightgown, brush my teeth, quietly leave the bathroom and then slide into the bed, being careful to hug the edge so we don't accidentally bump into each other.

Touch him, already.

A frustrated moan catches in my throat and I put my hand over my mouth to stifle it, but it's too late.

"Everything okay?" Luca asks, his deep, rumbly voice vibrating through me and stroking the needy spot begging for his attention.

"Fine. Just tired." I fake a yawn as my body stirs with need.

The bed moves as he rolls toward me and I hug the blankets tighter. "Did you have fun with Summer?" he asks, his breath hot on the back of my neck.

"Yes."

"I had fun with Tate, too. He's a good guy."

My mind goes back to when I first heard about Luca, Tate's new junior partner, and how much Tate wanted me to meet him. I'd just been so busy working, I hadn't met him before now, and never would have thought he was *my* Luca. Well, not *my* Luca, but the Luca from Oxford. I think back to the stories Tate told me, and how he met Luca when he was here in St. Moritz six months ago. "Wait, if you're a lawyer, why were you working at the bar?"

He goes quiet for a moment—too quiet—and I'm about to turn, but stop when he says, "Just wanted to experience other things, you know?" My stomach tightens. There is something he's holding back. The lawyer in me sees this kind of hedging in couples all the time. What is it that Luca doesn't want me to know? I consider it for a moment, but is it really any of my business? One night of sex and this week-long pretend engagement doesn't mean I'm privy to his secrets and vice versa.

"I can't believe he's getting married in four days," he says, bringing the conversation back to Tate.

I don't answer; instead, I pretend I'm asleep.

"After the bar, we walked to the golf course. We ran into your grandfather there."

"Granddad was golfing?" I ask. Darn, I'm supposed to be sleeping.

He scoffs. "Strange, right?"

I slowly turn to see if he's kidding me or not. My eyes meet his and there isn't an ounce of humor on his face. In fact he's frowning. "What?" I ask.

He rolls to his back, shoving one arm under his head. "He was with your uncle Bill. Bill congratulated me on our engagement. So much for James keeping our secret." Damn, no doubt Uncle Bill would tell his sons, my cousins Alec and William. They're both expected at the end of the week, along with Uncle Don and his new wife.

"Dammit." I pound the bed. "Now we'll have to pretend in front of everyone."

"I know." A moment of silence and then, "Are you sure we're going to be able to pull this off? He's pretty good at reading people and situations."

"That's what made him so successful on Wall Street."

Luca moves his leg and it touches mine. I suck in a fast breath and jerk it back, hoping he doesn't notice my reaction.

"That right there is what's going to tip him off," he says, his voice a bit deeper, huskier than it was a second ago.

I'm so on edge, it's hard for me to think straight. "What are you talking about? What's going to tip him off?"

He slowly slides his leg toward mine again, and I flinch when he touches me. Not because I don't like the connection, but because I like it too damn much. I shouldn't have sex with this guy again. It goes against my rules. And those rules are in place for a reason.

"The way you react to my touch," he says. "You're all jumpy."

"Then stop touching me."

"Ah, but if we're going to pull this off, your grand-dad will expect us to touch. Tate and Summer are getting married, and they can't keep their hands or eyes off each other."

With my stomach tightening, I roll onto my back. He's not wrong, of course. Granddad will expect to see us gazing at each other, touching lovingly, acting like Tate and Summer.

His hand slides across the bed, his fingers lightly brushing over my arm. I'm about to pull away but stop myself, not just to prove we *can* pull this off, but because I like what he's doing. Dammit. I'm off my game, not as in control as I'd like to be. Then again it was fun sleeping with him. Why can't I do it again? Break my rules just this once. It's not like my heart is going to be involved. I'm too smart for that.

"If we're out and I touch you like this, you have to pretend you like it," he says. "You might even want to touch me in return."

Touch him, Brianna. Do it already. Take what you want.

Before I can stop myself, I roll toward him. I place my finger on his shoulder and then drag it downward, stopping near the tiny hairs forming a V-shape at his pelvis. His hips jerk, and the sheets tent just a little more. "You mean like this?"

He moans. "Yeah, like that."

"You think I'll have to touch you like that in public?"

"I can't say what kind of situation we'll find ourselves in, but I think we need to be prepared for anything, don't you?" He smirks. "Your granddad is a smart man, and we wouldn't want to do anything to make him suspicious, or upset him."

"You're right. We do have that to consider," I say, going along with this game he's playing.

He turns on his side to face me and I take in his chiseled face and sculpted jaw. Simply put, the man is gorgeous. "I think we should practice," he murmurs. Dark eyes full of possession search mine as his hand goes to my side and traces my curves, stopping on my hips. I shiver at the heat of his touch, the way my nightgown is lifting higher on my legs. I can't believe I'm playing along. Then again I'm drenched with desire.

"I don't think we have a choice," I say casually, even though there is a storm going on inside me. The black in his eyes bleeds into the brown. My God, the hungry way this man looks at me is insane. This crazy lust between us is unlike anything I've ever felt before. It's volatile, explosive and I pray to God it doesn't blow up in my face.

It's just sex, Bri. Nothing more.

He puts his hand on my thigh and then slowly slides it upward, his face searching mine, like he expects me to tell him to stop.

I won't.

I can't.

I want this more than I'm willing to admit.

I inch my legs open and a sexy smile tugs at the corners of his mouth. The rough pad of his thumb goes to my clit, circles it, but never touches. I give a frustrated groan and lift my hips.

"I'm not so sure I'll have to touch you here in public, but I think we should cover all bases, don't you?"

"Absolutely," I say, and Luca chuckles at the eagerness in my voice, but suddenly all I can think about is sex in public. It's not something I've ever done before, ever had the desire to do. It's risky and inappropriate, but if it were with Luca, I'm sure it'd be a mind-blowing experience that I'd never forget.

He strokes my clit, and I let loose a blissful moan. "That is so good." He slides over me, presses his mouth to mine as he beautifully manipulates my clit with deft fingers. His magnificent cock, fat and heavy, presses against me, and as his tongue slides into my mouth, I can't help but want something else in there. He presses one finger inside me, thick and long and demanding as he fucks me with it. I'm already so wet, I instantly soak his hand, and his low groan of approval awakens every nerve in my body. His palm bangs my clit, and as his touches and kisses consume me, I try to remain in control but soon find myself drowning in him. I swallow a cry as my muscles clench hard around his finger, and my body shakes violently.

I have never come so fast before.

He lifts his head, like he's as surprised as I am, and I gasp for my next breath. Giving me no reprieve, he says, "On your knees." He helps me up, until I'm on shaky knees and he flattens himself out on his back. "Straddle me." He reaches out and pets my wet sex. "I've wanted back in here so badly, it's all I could think about today. I nearly fell into the sand-pit at the golf course."

"You sure it wasn't the alcohol?"

"I had two drinks. Didn't want anything to mess this night up."

"So you had this planned, did you?"

"Let's just say I didn't want to be messed up in case you changed your mind." He sits up, rubs his hand across my cheek, and there is a gentleness about him as he lightly rubs his thumb over my flesh. "I'm glad you changed your mind," he says softly, ten-derly, as his warm breath falls over my face.

My heart does an odd little flip at his sweetness, and I lower my head. *This is just sex, Bri. He's an asshole who hurt you, and you're just taking what you want, what you were denied all those years ago.*

With that in mind, I gaze at his throbbing cock, and my body burns hotter. I wet my bottom lip to prepare my mouth, and his growl curls around me. "What if I have to touch you here in public," I say, making this all about sex as I take his thick cock into my hand. It jerks, and pre-cum spills from the crown.

He falls back to the bed. "You think it will come to that?" he asks, his tortured voice stroking my wet sex. I straddle one of his legs and rub my sex all over him. His cock hardens to steel. Every muscle in his body tightens and he moans as I bend forward, lick the cum from his tip.

"*Cazzo*, Brianna," he says and grabs a fistful of my hair.

I take him deep, deeper than I've ever taken any other man, and his soft curses curl around me. I slide a hand between his legs and cup his balls. I breathe in, loving the tangy scent of his skin as I massage his balls gently, until they tighten in my palm.

He thickens even more in my mouth, stretching my lips, and I love every second of it. His hips move, and I work one hand over his long length as he fucks my mouth.

"Stop," he grumbles, and I reluctantly inch back. His eyes are dark, intense, when they meet mine, and his nostrils are flaring. He grabs a condom from his nightstand and quickly puts it on. "Come here," he says and captures my hips to lift me. He positions me over his cock, and I cup my breasts as he slowly lowers me, giving me one glorious inch at a time. Closing my eyes, I cry out shamelessly and wiggle until he's seated deeply inside me.

"You are so beautiful," he says, and I open my eyes to see him. His eyes are locked onto mine, and my belly flutters at the desire I see blazing in the dark depths. His hands tighten on my hips and he slowly lifts me, then pulls me back down onto his long length.

"Luca," I cry out, as he fills me the way no man ever has before.

I pinch my puckered nipples, but they are eager for his touch. My sex trembles around his cock. We move together, create a rhythm, and then taking me by surprise, he sits up, swats my hands away and takes one breast into his mouth, and the other into his palm. He licks and kneads, and sensations flood my system. My toes curl with pleasure, and I rake my nails over his back. I push down harder, wanting to feel every damn inch of him inside me, and he growls around my nipples. Pleasure vibrates through me, centers between my legs. He releases my breasts, grabs my hips and takes over, pounding into me wildly, until I'm so delirious, I can barely see straight.

With control now a thing of the past, I let him take charge, let him lift me up and pull me back down with a force that sends waves of pleasure surging through me. I gasp and break around him, my hot juices dripping down his fat cock and heavy balls. He growls and thickens even more as he fucks me with fierce, blunt strokes. His fingers bite into my skin, and he holds me still, his cock hidden in the depths of my body, as he spurts into the condom. I collapse on top of him and revel in his fast heartbeat against my cheek as I work to breathe. A long time later, I lift my head, meet his intense gaze and my pulse jumps into my throat.

He's not nearly done with me.

CHAPTER EIGHT

Luca

I SIT ON the side of the bed and look at the beautiful woman sleeping silently beside me. It's early—before dawn—and I hate to wake her, considering we were up having sex most of the night, but if we're going to make it to the summit before sunrise, I have no choice.

"Hey," I say quietly and brush her hair from her face.

Her eyes open one at a time, and a small smile that rocks my world forms on her face when she sees me.

"What time is it?" she asks, her voice hoarse.

"Early, before dawn. Here, I have your coffee ready."

She sits up, and the blankets fall from her body, exposing her beautiful breasts. She doesn't bother trying to cover up. Instead she reaches for the coffee and takes a sip. "Mmm, a girl could get used to this. Wait, why are you waking me up before dawn?"

"We're going on an adventure."

She groans. "Luca, I want to sleep."

"Sleep is overrated. Come on."

She takes another sip of coffee. "I hate morning people," she says, and I laugh.

"I'll let you sleep in tomorrow. We only have one week, and I want to make the most of it."

"Are you going to make me spend every minute with you?"

"That's kind of the plan. Like I said, I want you to see that you can spend more than one night with a guy. Prove it's not so bad." As I think about that, my stomach tightens. When it comes right down to it, I'm grooming her for another man. I might want her, but I can't have her. Yet I want to see her find happiness in life. She groans and I run my finger over her pert nipple. "Has it been so bad, Brianna?"

"If you find a fork in your thigh by the end of the week, remember it's no one's fault but your own." She grins at me and I laugh.

I pull the sheets off. "Come on, get dressed." Although now that I've exposed her entire body, all I want to do is crawl back into that bed with her.

"Change of plans?" she asks and cocks her head, no doubt catching the lust in my eyes.

I adjust my thickening cock. "I think you'll like what I have in mind."

She taps the bed. "I usually do."

I scrub my face and it takes every ounce of strength I have to turn from her. "Move it," I say, and she grumbles as she climbs from the bed. "I boiled us some eggs, and I have protein bars for energy. We'll have a real breakfast when we get there."

"Get where, and why do we have to go so early?" she asks.

"Piz Nair sunrise. We're going to bike up the mountain, watch the sunrise, then have breakfast."

She gasps and I turn to face her. "Are you serious?" she asks.

"Yeah, I arranged it last night."

"I haven't done that since I was a kid."

"Tate told me you loved it."

Her eyes go wide. "You and Tate talked about me?"

Teasing her, I give a low whistle and shake my head. "The things I never knew about you."

She grabs a pillow and throws it at me. "Liar. You don't know anything about me." She lifts her chin. "And I prefer to keep it that way." With that she grabs her clothes, hurries to the bathroom and comes back after a few minutes, dressed and ready.

Thirty minutes later we're at the meeting point and have been given our bikes and helmets. She tugs hers on and I help her clasp it.

"Maybe we should have taken the cable car. This is going to kill me," she groans.

"Yeah. Me too."

She gives me a look that suggests I'm dense. "Yeah, right, you're in good shape."

I put one hand on her hip. "And I love your shape." She looks down, fast. "What?" I ask.

"Nothing. We'd better get going if we want to see the sunrise." She starts up the hill and I follow behind her. Up ahead there is another group on the go, and more bikers follow behind us. The air is cool this morning but soon enough we're hot as we exert ourselves.

I breathe in the fresh mountain air, and it makes me think of home. Deep down I miss Italy, my family. I talked to Uncle Gio a couple of weeks ago, and he sounded tired. Running the family business is taking its toll on him, but he's terrified of his son being at the helm one day. It might not be my thirtieth birthday yet, but I can't stay away much longer. The last letter he sent me—he's old-school like that—reminded me of the will and explained Marco's latest antics. I'm needed back home. I told Gio about Tate's wedding, and that I'd be making plans to return afterward— once I talk to Tate and clear my things from the office. Fuck, how is Tate going to take the news of my leaving his firm? I'd agreed to the job because I wanted to help him launch his practice, thinking there'd be time later to tell him it wasn't permanent. My uncle urging me home early was unexpected, though.

Brianna stops up ahead and I slow my bike. She's winded but she has a huge smile on her face. She moves to the side as a few bikers greet us and go past.

"I need to catch my breath," she says. The enthusiasm on her face is adorable and I lean in and press my lips to hers. I give her a quick kiss and when I inch back, she quirks a brow. "What was that for?"

"For agreeing to go on this ride with me."

She glances around and I follow her gaze. "I miss this place. I used to come here with Tate and Granddad all the time."

"Was it just the three of you? You don't have any other cousins? Tate only ever talked about you. He was anxious for us to meet, I think."

She nods at that. "No, we have other cousins. Some of them are coming in later this week for the wedding. Most got tied down with work. It's a wonder I made it so early. But Tate is the oldest, so he was closest to Granddad, and they both sort of took me under their wing. Of all the cousins, Tate and I are the closest. He's like my brother." She exhales a sigh. "I owe those two so much. I guess that's why I jumped at the chance to make Granddad happy—as stupid as that was." She glances around like she's looking for a change of subject. "I'd forgotten how much I love it here."

"Not quite the same as New York, is it?"

She laughs. "Not quite the same at all." Contentment comes over her. "I wish I could live here. Or at least live closer."

I take in the pink on her cheeks, the way her shoulders have relaxed slightly. "This place is good for you."

"Why do you say that?"

I touch her shoulders. "Because these…" I begin, as my hands go to her ears. "Were here when you arrived."

She nods. "You're not wrong." She sits back on her seat. "Come on, I'll race you to the top," she says and takes off fast.

I go after her. "What does the winner get?" I ask.

"Does there always have to be something in it for you?" she asks breathlessly as she stands up on her pedals.

"Always," I say.

"What more could you want, Luca?" she asks, her breathing coming faster. "Since I arrived, you seem to be getting your way with everything."

Gesù, there are so many things I want with her, things I can't ever have.

"What do *you* want, Brianna?"

"I want to move out of your chalet and back into my hotel suite," she says, but I'm not so sure I believe her.

"It's on, and after I win I'll tell you what I want," I say and then pass her. She whacks me as I go, trying to push me off the bike, and I laugh when she scoffs at me. I glance at her over my shoulder. "Doing okay back there?"

"Oh, you're so going to get it!" she yells.

"I'll be sure there are no forks at our breakfast table," I say and put a great deal of space between us. Although I do keep checking over my shoulder in case she needs me. She finally catches up with me, and she opens her mouth, likely to shout a few profanities, when I touch her shoulder and turn her. Her eyes go wide as night surrenders to morning and the first rays of sunlight creep over the mountaintops. It's a spectacular view, enjoyed by many every summer here in St. Moritz, but I can't seem to take my eyes off Brianna and the childlike enthusiasm on her face.

I tug her to me, and her hand goes to my stomach. Dozens of people are gasping around us, all enjoying the same view, but it feels very much like it's just her and me right now, the two of us all alone at the top of the mountain, experiencing something unique together. She leans her head against me, and a gust of wind blows her hair. It tickles my face. I dip my head, kiss the top of hers and just hold her to me, wanting nothing more than to enjoy this week with her.

"Thank you," she says quietly as the long rays touch the snowcapped peaks and dance on the evergreen trees. "I needed this." I hug her tighter and we remain like that until daylight is fully upon us. She lifts her face to mine and smiles. "But please tell me I can sleep the afternoon away."

I laugh. "You can go to bed, sure. But I can't guarantee that you're going to get any sleep." Someone beside me chuckles, and Brianna's eyes go wide. I glance at the guy and grin. "Recently engaged," I say. "She's so beautiful, I can't keep my hands off her." I turn back to Brianna, take in the almost confused look on her face. "No one can blame me for that, I'm sure." I drop a soft kiss onto her mouth. "Come on, let's go get breakfast. I'm starving."

"Me too."

We set our bikes in the rack with the others and make our way into the restaurant. We're seated by the window, where we can see out into the mountains, and the hostess hands us our menus.

"How was the sunrise?" she asks and then narrows her eyes. "Wait, Luca, I didn't realize that was you. What are you doing here?"

"Hey, Jess. How are you? We're here for Tate's wedding. This is his cousin, Brianna."

Jess flicks a glance at Brianna, barely acknowledging her. "How long are you here?" she puts the end of her pen in her mouth and grins. "We should get together for a drink."

"Pretty busy week," I say.

"Here." She scribbles her number on a pad of paper and hands it to me. "I'm still in staff-housing, building number four, in case you forgot."

"Okay," I say and put the number in my pocket.

"See you soon. I hope," she says when our server comes to the table to get our drink orders.

"Coffee?" I ask Brianna, who is staring at me. She nods and I order two. When the server leaves, I turn back to Brianna. "What?"

"Old girlfriend?"

"Old friend."

"She was rather friendly."

I set my menu down and lean toward her. "Jealous, Brianna?"

She huffs. "No, of course not. You can date who-ever you want."

"Why would I want anyone else in my bed when I only want to fuck you?"

Pink crawls up her neck. "You took her number."

"I didn't want to be rude. When I get back to the chalet, I'll toss it. I didn't want to do it in front of her. I'm not a *stronzo*."

"Stronzo?"

"Asshole."

She makes a strange sound and turns her atten-tion to her menu. As she studies it, I think about calling her out, asking her why she's pretending not to know me. The words sit on my tongue, but I bite them back. I'll eventually get to the bottom of things, but right now I don't want to wreck what started as the perfect day by pissing her off and ru-ining my chance of getting to the bottom of *other* things later on.

The server comes back with our coffee, and I drink mine black as Brianna pours a dab of milk into hers. She takes a big sip and leans back to look out over the mountains.

"I haven't been up here since I was a teen."

"Did you bike it?"

She nods and lifts her cup. "Yeah. I was a bit on the plump side, needed the exercise." She stares at me over the rim of her cup, like she's waiting for me to comment on that. I'm not sure what she considers plump, but in college she had curves that drove me insane.

"Tate said you guys all spent a lot of time here when you were young."

"We did." She gives me a wobbly smile. "Granddad was very good to us."

I take a sip of coffee and set it on the saucer. "I'm glad to hear that. Every girl needs a male influence in her life."

She looks out the window, her gaze misty. She's obviously worried about her grandfather's health. "After Dad left us for a much younger woman, Granddad really stepped up, for all his grandchildren." She puts on a smile but there is pain behind it.

"A much younger woman?"

She shakes her head and rolls her eyes. "Early twenties. Like I said, the guys in our family do that. Which is why Tate thought Granddad had fallen for Summer."

What Granddad was doing was matchmaking, and while I'd like to tell her that I don't think he's as frail as he lets on, I keep my mouth shut. She adores the man and I don't want to say anything that might upset her, or lead her to believe her granddad is messing with her in any way. He simply wants to see her settled down and happy. I can't blame him for that.

"I'm sorry," I say.

"Where exactly are you from?" she asks me, redirecting the conversation.

"Italy," I say.

"Obviously." She rolls her eyes at me. "Where in Italy?"

"Massara, small town. You probably never heard of it."

She crinkles her nose and looks out into the distance again. "Actually I have."

I swallow. "Yeah."

"There was some guy—I think he was an aristocrat or something—in the news when I was at Oxford. Everyone was talking about it. He crashed a billion-dollar boat or something like that, and he was connected to some sex cub. I think he was married, too."

"Still is," I say without thinking.

"You know of him?" She shakes her head. "The guy sounds crazy."

"Yeah, crazy." Crazy that my father would want his conglomerates to go to him. He was my father's attorney for years, so I know he trusted Marco, but I need to save Dad's legacy from him. That means marrying Valentina—another mystery I can't understand. Dad was a generous man—was this his way of taking care of his friend's family, even in death? I can't shirk my responsibility, and I don't want to. I want Dad and Matteo to be proud of me. But I wish I could run my life and the business on my terms.

"We don't hear much about him back in the States. Is he still making the papers here?"

"All the time," I say and exhale a heavy sigh.

"Why Oxford?" I redirect. "Were you hoping to find yourself a British Prince Charming?"

"Very funny."

"Seriously, why so far from home?"

"I don't know. I guess I just wanted a change of scenery. Experience something different." She laughs. "God, I was so innocent and naïve back then."

"How so?"

"I went into law school thinking I was going to change the world."

I nod. "We all did." When I go back to Italy, I plan to take my place and do good things for my community. *Bisnonno* built a hospital many years ago, and I want to bring in top-notch specialists, as well as increase tourism in the area, which will benefit all. I just don't want to do it with an arranged wife.

"Yet all I do is battle with couples who hate each other. How is that changing the world?"

"I understand exactly what you're saying. There is a lot I want to do to help others and leave this a better world for my kids."

She quirks a brow. "Really?"

"That surprises you?" I ask.

"I guess. Maybe. I don't know." A beat and then, "You want kids?"

"Yeah, if it was with the right woman." She frowns and opens her mouth like she wants to ask something but then closes it again. I reach across the table and take her hand in mine. "It's not too late to make a change."

"You think?"

"You're in your twenties, Brianna. You can still do whatever you want."

She looks at my hand holding hers. "I guess."

"What is it you want?" I ask.

"I'd like to be doing things for the people. Maybe use my legal skills to help needy organizations, or to build schools in third-world countries. Or maybe champion causes like Artscape, where they transformed streetcars into homes and businesses for artists." Her eyes light up as she talks, and this…this is the kind of legal work she should be doing. "But I chose family law, thinking it'd be a stable career, and I fell into a firm that specializes in divorce law, where I work sixteen-hour days and have little time for anything else," she says and glances out the window. There's silence between us for a moment, and her voice is low when she says, "Hey, you won the race up the hill."

"I know. Sorry you didn't win. I know you're desperate to return to your room."

She casts a quick glance my way. "Are you going to tell me what you want?" she asks, sounding like she's miles away.

I stare at her as she turns back to gaze at the mountains. I think about that for a moment, but I can't tell her what I want. I can never tell her that. "Eventually," I tease, and she laughs, no doubt thinking I'd like to tie her up or something. Which I totally do.

She goes quiet as the server comes, refills our coffee cups and takes our orders. "Beautiful day," she says and glances at Brianna, who is staring out the window. "The scenery doesn't get much better than this, does it?"

"It's perfect," I say and look at Brianna as she pours a bit more milk into her cup.

We thank the server, and when she leaves Brianna says, "It's strange how I've always been drawn to Europe."

"Have you ever considered living here?"

"Yes, but then I remember I have a life in New York and I want to be close to Granddad."

I nod. "Family is important." She smiles at me, and while we come from different worlds, we both value family and hold them in our hearts.

Our food arrives and we both pour a generous amount of syrup on our waffles. "These Belgian waffles look amazing," Brianna says.

"Did you know that in Belgium they just call them waffles."

She laughs, then stifles a yawn as she picks up her fork. "It must be all this fresh mountain air making me tired."

"Or all the sex," I say and reach for my knife. "Oh, but wait, that's nothing new for you. I forgot."

She picks up her fork. "What was that about you not being an asshole?"

I laugh and hold my hands up in surrender as she stabs her waffle. "Speaking of sex, we kind of look like we've been in a marathon."

"Yeah, it's written all over us. That should be enough to convince Granddad," she says.

"And everyone else," I add.

"As long as Summer and Tate don't get the wrong idea about us and think there is more going on."

With a bite of my waffle halfway to my mouth, my hand stills. "No, you're right. None of us can forget this is a ruse."

Myself mainly.

CHAPTER NINE

Brianna

I SLIDE FROM the bed and leave a very tired Luca sleeping as I tiptoe across the wood floor. After our early-morning bike ride and our afternoon sex-a-thon, we need to get ready for the wedding rehearsal, followed by a romantic sunset horse-drawn carriage ride. I'm really looking forward to it. I can't remember the last time I saw a sunrise and sunset in the same day. Normally I'm in my office before dawn and after dark. Honestly I haven't had this much fun since I was a teen.

I make my way into the bathroom, pull back the sliding glass door to the shower and turn it on. It's a huge marble creation that spans one length of the room. Muscles I didn't even know existed tighten as I bend forward and adjust the spray. I hold my hand under the rain showerhead for a moment until the temperature is perfect, and I'm about to stand when a low growl curls around me. I grin as my body comes alive, even after all the sex we just had.

How the hell am I going to go back to my crazy, sex-less work schedule after this week? I have no idea, but I'll have to find a way. I'm not looking for anything more from this man, and he made it blatantly clear he wasn't either when he said earlier, *None of us can forget this is a ruse.* And I have to say, I'm happy about that. Neither of us has any expectations and that's perfect. Absolute, 100 percent perfection.

I stay bent over, showcasing my backside, and his feet slap the floor as he approaches. Warm hands go to my hips and he presses his cock to the crease of my ass and lets loose an agonized moan that settles deep between my legs. Other than that one morti-fying time, Luca never paid me any attention back in college, but he's sure making up for lost time now. That thought brings another. Does he really not know who I am, or is he pretending, like me? If he knew, he would have said something, right? Then again why bring up past hurts and ruin all this amazing sex?

He's not the ass I thought he was. He's fun to be around. And today, surprising me with the mountain biking at sunrise and then having breakfast, after finding out how much I like it. That was sweet, right? It kind of makes me want to surprise him with some-thing he'd like.

Oh Jesus, Brianna, get it together. This is tem-porary.

Big hands slide around my body and draw me up until my back is pressed against his chest. "I didn't like waking up and finding your side of the bed empty," he murmurs in my ear.

"You were sleeping so quietly, and you exerted yourself so much today, I didn't have it in me to wake you."

"Aren't you thoughtful."

"I try to be."

His lips press against my neck, his heat going through me. "Do you ever get rewarded for your thoughtfulness?" he asks, his breath warm on my flesh as he nudges me forward under the hot spray.

"Never," I say, and his hands go to my breasts. He brushes his thumb over my nipple and I let my head fall back to his chest. "Is this my reward?" I ask.

"It's just the beginning, Brianna." His hand slides lower, gently pets my sex, and his cock thickens against my back. It's crazy to think he wants me again, after all the times—and ways—he took me on the bed earlier. His hand stills, and he turns me around. I take in the frown on his forehead and my heart leaps. What's going on? Has he changed his mind, or did it finally dawn on him who I am?

Dark eyes full of worry move over my face, assess me. "Are you too sore to take me again?"

Warmth flows through me at his concern. "I'm a bit sore," I say honestly. "But I'm okay." I glance down, reach for his cock, run my palms over him. "I want you again."

He touches my chin, lifts it until we're eye to eye.

His head angles, his eyes slightly narrowed. "You'd tell me, wouldn't you?"

"Yes."

"I want you, Brianna, but we won't do anything if it's going to be too much."

My heart wobbles, a little overwhelmed at his thoughtfulness. "I want you inside me, Luca."

His cock grows impossibly thicker in my palm. "Then I'm going to fuck you right now, here against this wall, but I'll go easy. After we return tonight, you sleep. At the end of the week, I don't want you going back home exhausted. That's not what this trip is about for you."

I swallow and try to appear casual, unaffected by his concern, when I throw his words back at him and say, "Sleeping is overrated." His deep laugh wraps around me, cocooning me in a blanket of warmth. Dammit, I'm starting to really like this guy.

Shit.

But I can't think about how bad that is right now, not when his mouth is closing over mine and kissing me with a gentleness that seeps under my skin and awakens something I've kept buried for years.

"Did I ever tell you how much I like kissing you?" he asks as he devours my mouth.

"You just did," I manage to get out as my knees weaken.

He pushes my damp hair back. "You've got one hell of a beautiful mouth."

"Oh yeah, and where else do you like it?" I ask,

and he growls his response as I rub the long length of him.

"I don't have to ask where you like mine," he says and slides a hand between my legs. "I've been paying attention."

"So you have," I say and widen for him.

"I'm a detail-oriented person," he murmurs between hot, openmouthed kisses that turn me inside out and make me forget there is a world outside our chalet.

"I must say I like that about you." He strokes my aching clit, a soft, barely there touch, and I lean in to him, wanting more. He removes his finger and I groan in disappointment, but it turns into a soft moan when he easily picks me up and presses my back to the tiled wall. I wrap my arms and legs around him to hang on, and he bends slightly, then slides his big cock all the way inside me.

"Yes," I cry out, and we both go still, holding each other with his cock seated high inside. But that's when reality hits. "Shit, Luca. We didn't use a condom." How the hell did I forgot about protection? I never forget protection. Then again this man has the ability to shut down my mind just by being in my presence.

"*Cazzo*, I'm sorry," he says. "I took one look at you bent over the shower, and lost the ability to think logically."

He's about to pull out but I stop him. "I'm clean, and I'm on the pill," I say.

Oh, Brianna, this isn't smart.

"I'm clean, too. And if you want to know the truth, I haven't been with anyone in a long time. I've been swamped helping Tate get his business up and running."

A strange thrill zings through me, and I silently lecture myself as I clamp down on my teeth. *Don't feel anything other than physical pleasure.*

"I haven't been with anyone in a long time, either," I admit. "I've been too busy with work, too."

He arches a brow, and it's so goddamn odd that we're having this easy, open conversation with his beautiful cock buried inside me, unmoving. It's kind of weird…yet insanely intimate.

"Not a different guy every night?" I shake my head and the movement stirs his cock inside me. Our moans mingle. "It's okay for a woman to own her sexuality and sleep with whoever she wants, but I didn't take you as the type." With one hand beneath my ass, holding me against him, he touches my face with the other and brushes his thumb over my cheek. "I'm glad I'm the guy you broke your dry spell with."

Oh God, I should tell him. I should tell him who I am and why I seduced him that first day. He's being so damn sweet and honest with me, and he deserves that in return. But if I do, he may want nothing to do with me. What kind of grown woman, a professional at that, does something so juvenile? Sure he hurt me, but everyone makes mistakes, right?

"Hey, you okay?" he asks quietly.

I shake my head to pull myself together. "I'm good."

"You sure you want to do this?"

I'm not sure of anything anymore.

"Yes. I like the feel of skin on skin."

"It's incredible," he practically shouts, and we both laugh, tension easing out of me.

He readjusts and cups my ass with both hands as he presses me harder against the wall. He bends, pulls halfway out of me and slides back in again. I hug him, bury my mouth in his neck as he moves in and out of my body—slower, softer movements, but I want it hard. I want all of him, unleashed, wild, giving me everything he has.

"Fuck me harder, Luca," I cry out and he goes still for a second. "Harder," I demand.

He pulls out and plows back in again, and my teeth slam together from the blunt force of it all. His balls slap against my body as he buries every glorious inch inside me. My God, I love the way this man fucks me. Truthfully, before him, I'm not sure I ever knew what it was like to be properly fucked.

"Yes, like that," I say. I don't care if I wake up chafed and sore tomorrow. In fact I want the sting. Every time I move, I want to be reminded of this moment, this man.

He pummels me with his cock, and his sweet groans vibrate through me, race over my clit like I've got Mr. Right working away between my legs.

Everything about this is perfect. So perfect, I could stay like this forever.

"Luca," I cry out, wanting to but unable to hold on a second longer. I give in to the pleasure pulling at me and cry out as I let go. I come and come and come some more, and Luca finds my mouth, muffles my cries. My body trembles and massages his cock with each powerful, mind-blowing spasm.

He pumps harder, giving me no reprieve. "Your cum is dripping down my legs, baby. I should have eaten you first. I'm dying for a taste."

As soon as the words leave his mouth, I come again and he chuckles against my ear. The man knows exactly how to get to me, how to wring out another orgasm when I thought I was spent. I curl into him, and greedy for his own release, he bucks against me, grunts a few times, and when his cock thickens in my pussy, I tighten my legs and hold on. He throws his head back, and I whimper as he spills his seed into me, filling me with heat, pleasure, a new kind of need.

"I feel you," I murmur and run my fingers over his wet body, reveling in his hard muscle and deep grooves. "I feel every drop of you."

"Feel good?" he asks thickly as his hips curl into me so he can deposit the last of his lust into my body.

"Soo...hot," I say. "I don't ever want to use a condom with you again."

His body jerks and spasms, and I hold him tighter

until his release is complete. His breath is hot on my face as he pushes my hair back. "I lied," he says.

My heart seizes and air leaves my lungs in a rush. "Lied?" I ask, not at all sure I want to know what he lied about.

"I'm not going to let you sleep when we come back here tonight."

CHAPTER TEN

Luca

I STAND AT the altar in the glassed-in octagon-shaped gazebo, with Tate shifting restlessly beside me. I search the room for Brianna and find her at the back, talking to Summer's other bridesmaid, Amber. My gaze moves over her, takes in her lush curves. My dick stirs in my khaki shorts and I turn my focus back to the minister, who is going over the upcoming ceremony with Summer.

"How was sunrise this morning?" Tate asks me, and I don't miss the knowing grin he has aimed my way.

"It was great. I missed this place."

"Yeah. Me too." He scans the crowd, and I follow his gaze as Summer's maid of honor, Cara, and Brianna and Amber all rehearse their entrance. Tate's two college buddies, Jared and Carter, are his groomsmen. With Cara leading the way, they walk the other two down the aisle, and when Jared puts his arm on Brianna and says something to make her laugh, a surge of jealously rises up inside me.

"You and Bri made Granddad a very happy man. He seems to have his energy back."

I nod, but my stomach tightens. Soon enough this pretending will be over, and I hate the thought of hurting James—of walking away from Brianna.

"You okay?" Tate asks.

"I just don't want to see James hurt by all of this."

"What are you going to do when we go back?"

I scrub my face and think about that. "I'm not sure how Brianna will want this to play out. I'm letting her take the lead on this." It was foolish to agree to this plan when I'm returning to Italy soon. We can't fool James much longer, even if we wanted to. But how could I have said no to Brianna when she asked?

"You've been good for her," Tate says, taking me by surprise. "I haven't seen her this happy in a long time."

"She works too much."

Tate laughs. "You're one to talk. I'm going to have to hire a new associate, just to get you out of the office once in a while."

Shit. I need to tell him.

"About work," I begin, kicking my ass for not doing it sooner. "Now that you're up and running, I'm not sure how long I'll be staying."

Tate's head rears back with a start. "Are you serious?"

I grip the back of my neck. "I'm needed at home,"

I say and avoid the details of why I'm needed. "Family."

"Damn, I had no idea." Tate puts his hand on my shoulder. "Of course family comes first."

"I'll stay long enough for you to find a replacement, though."

His blue eyes narrow in on me. "Does Bri know you're leaving?"

"No. Why?"

His brow furrows. "You might want to tell her sooner, rather than later."

I glance past Tate's shoulders and my breath stalls when Brianna walks toward the altar, toward me, in a dress I can't wait to peel from her body. She's so damn gorgeous. I'm not sure how I'm going to walk away. I only know that I have to, and in the end, hopefully she realizes she can count on a man for more than a one-night stand.

For the next fifteen minutes, we all learn where to stand and what to expect from the ceremony. Once we're done, we're led outside to a waiting horse-drawn carriage. I help Brianna up and take a seat beside her. James is watching us carefully, but that's not why I put my arm around her and draw her to me. She glances up at me, a warm, loving smile on her face—no doubt for show. Still, it does something weird to my insides.

The wagon shakes and bumps as the horses lead us through a trail, a mixture of pink and purple bruising the sky as day bleeds into night.

"So pretty," Brianna says and then exhales slowly.

Lights strung along the many ski hills pop to life as darkness falls, and St. Moritz comes to life like a Christmas tree. The air changes as we follow a trail along the mountain, and I pull Brianna in closer as she shivers. Conversation picks up around us as everyone participates in idle chitchat, but right now I'm only interested in talking to Brianna, learning more about her.

"What other fun things did you used to do here when you were a teen?" I ask her.

"I did a lot of things. In the winter I skied, of course, but in the summers I swam, did stand-up paddle and went boating. Once Granddad even took us on a helicopter tour. That was fun."

"I bet."

She crinkles her nose. "Mostly though, I read."

"Really."

"I was a total bookworm."

"That doesn't really surprise me."

"I...was a bit of a loner, I guess. I didn't have a lot of friends," she says, her voice low, and I get the sense that she's telling me something very important about herself.

Her eyes meet mine and the sadness I see guts me. "I'm sorry."

"That's okay. I had my stories."

"What kind of books did you read?" She turns her head away and glances out over the lake as we pass it. I wait a long moment and then ask, "Are you not going to tell me?"

"No."

I laugh. "Why not?"

"Because you'll make fun of me."

I touch her chin, draw her eyes back to me. "I would never make fun of you, Brianna." She looks off into the distance again, like she's remembering something, something hurtful. "Tell me," I say.

"I read romance. Okay?" she blurts out.

I lean in to her and press my lips to hers. The girl who doesn't believe in happily-ever-after reads romance. I knew it. Deep inside I knew she was the kind of girl who wanted the white picket fence, and goddammit she deserves it. Still, I can't help but wonder about her fears. Is it her job that has her too frightened to commit, or is it something else altogether?

"There is nothing wrong with a good romance story," I tell her. "My mom reads them all the time." That seems to relax her.

"What did you do for fun when you were working here?" she asks.

"When I wasn't working, I was kiteboarding."

Her eyes go wide. "That seems like so much fun. I've never tried it. I was too scared. You're way more adventurous than me." She taps her head. "I recall Tate saying something about that. Didn't you guys go skydiving?"

"Yeah, we did, once." She smiles up at me. "I can make the arrangements for us to go kiteboarding if you'd like. We should always face our fears, Brianna."

"I'm not sure about that."

"I am." The heavy scent of pine and moss falls over us as the horses take us below a canopy of leaves that blocks out the night sky.

Her hand goes to my thigh, and as it rests there, I wonder if she even realizes she's doing it. Nevertheless I really like the easy intimacy growing between us.

"I'd probably kill myself if I ever tried," she says. "Best for me to stay on land."

"I won't let anything happen to you."

She sags against me, and a quiet, comfortable silence falls over us as we sit back and enjoy the view. Half an hour later the horses drop us off where we began and we all climb off.

"It's still early. You guys want to hit the club?" Tate asks as he pulls Summer into his arms.

"Brianna?" I ask. "What do you think?"

"Sounds like fun."

"We're in," Cara and Amber say.

Jared and Carter also nod in agreement.

"I'll get Granddad settled into his room and meet you all there," Tate says. He drops a kiss onto Summer's lips and walks away.

We all make our way to the club, and the place is alive when we enter. The scent of alcohol and perfume clogs the air, and Summer snags us a big table. We all order drinks, and Brianna begins swaying in her chair. I'm about to ask her if she wants to dance, but Jared jumps at the chance.

Her gaze goes to me, and I give a casual nod, showcasing indifference. At first it seems to take her by surprise, but then she accepts Jared's outstretched hand. I stare after them until they're lost in the crowd, and when I turn back I find Summer grinning at me. She shifts closer and puts her hand on mine.

"You like her," she says after the others all go off to find dance partners.

"Of course I like her. I wouldn't be helping her out if I didn't."

"Oh, is that what you're doing? Helping her out?"

"Yeah."

"And sleeping with her. That's helping her out, too?"

I shake my head and Summer goes quiet when the server comes and distributes our drinks. I pay for them all and glance up to see Tate arrive. Thankful for the distraction, I ask, "How is James?"

"Good. I didn't get him to his room, though."

Summer, who used to be his doctor, frowns. "What happened?"

"We entered the lobby, and Deloris, an old friend of the family, stopped us. Apparently the two are going to the rooftop for a drink."

I laugh at that. "Leave it to James. In his nineties and still getting action."

Tate holds his hands up, palms out. "I don't want to even think about this."

"Luca," someone screams, and I turn to see Jess

rushing toward me. She's wearing a tight black dress that barely covers her ass. "You didn't call," she says. "I've been waiting."

"I…uh…lost your number," I say and don't miss the way Tate and Summer are watching me, their eyes narrowed.

"Well, you're here now and that's all that matters." Before I can protest, she pulls me out of my chair and drags me to the dance floor. She wiggles her ass at me and shakes her breasts, and I move to the music and glance around for Brianna. When I find her, her eyes are locked on mine, a surprised look on her face when she sees Jess. The music changes, slows, and I'm about to walk off the dance floor when Jess drags me to her, sliding her arms around my body and touching my ass.

Jared pulls Brianna to him and moves her hair from her neck to whisper something in her ear. A vicious growl catches in my throat, and Jess must mistake it for something else. She rubs up against me, and I feel her hard nipples through her dress.

I put my hands on her shoulders and pull her off me. She pouts and places her palms on my chest. One hand slides lower and closes over my cock, giving me her best massage. My gaze flies to Brianna. Our eyes meet, hold for a second, then she's back to laughing at something Jared says to her. Sparks of jealousy fire my nerves, and I bend, put my mouth to Jess's ear and excuse myself.

I stalk through the dance floor and then slide my

arm around Brianna's waist, tug her to me. "I need to talk to you," I say, acting like a goddamn caveman.

Incredulous, her eyes go wide. "Can't it wait? I'm dancing."

"I need to talk to you now," I say.

Our eyes lock, hold and then something in her softens. "Okay." She apologizes to Jared, and I lift to my full height as I face off against the other man. "Come on." She begins to lead me back to the table, when I give a little tug to change directions.

"It's not what you think," I growl.

"What are you talking about?"

"With Jess and me. It's not what you think."

"What is it I think?" she asks.

"She grabbed my dick, making it clear what she wants from me. You saw it."

"Hey, you can do whatever you want with her," she says with a tip of her chin. "Leave with her if you want, for all I care. Granddad isn't here to see it, and we're not really engaged, remember?"

"I asked for a one-week commitment from you. It's obvious to me you've been hurt before and don't trust guys. I'm not an asshole who's going to go off with someone else and deepen that distrust." Trust? Who the hell am I to talk about trust? She doesn't even know who I really am. "Besides, I told you I'd be ending tonight by keeping you up and totally satisfying you, and I meant it."

I cup her elbow and lead her down the long hallway to the staff lounge. Once inside I set the lock, grip her by the waist and spin her until she's pressed against the door. Her eyes are wide, her shock evident in the way her chest is rising and falling erratically, but I don't miss the lust as I step back and take in her curve-fitting dress, consider what she might be wearing underneath it.

She slides her hand along the door and grips the doorknob. "Don't," I warn in a soft but commanding voice.

"What…what are you doing?" she asks.

"Following through with my promise to you."

She's about to push off the door, likely to flee, but I press my hand to the center of her chest and pin her there. Her eyes grow impossibly wider, and her breathing quickens even more. She might be a lawyer with a poker face in the courtroom, but I can read her like an open book. This girl does things on her terms, but goddammit she loves it when I take charge.

My eyes leave her face, travel the length of her quivering body. "I want you naked."

"Luca, we're in the staff room. Anyone can walk in on us."

"The door is locked."

She shakes her head, and her chestnut hair sweeps over her shoulders. "I'm sure the manager has a key."

"Then we'd better get on with this before someone goes on break and asks for it, don't you think?" My hand slides down her quaking, needy body, and I reach her outer thigh. I rub the hem of her short dress between my thumb and finger. A little groan catches in her throat, and I dip my head, my mouth inches from hers.

"I…I don't have sex in public places," she says, but the lack of protest in her voice makes me chuckle.

"Define *sex*," I say, and slide my hand between her warm, inviting thighs.

"Luca…" she moans as her hips push off the door, her body seeking more of my touch, despite her objections.

"Do you consider this sex?" I rub her clit through her silky panties, a slow, easy caress that fires my blood. I take a breath to keep myself in check. Brianna's glazed eyes briefly close, and her tongue snakes out to wet her bottom lip. As she loses herself in my touch, it's all I can do not to bend her over the back of the sofa and slide into her heat. "Well, do you, Brianna? Do you consider this sex?" I ask, pulling her back from whatever erotic journey her mind just took her on.

She takes a fast breath and her lids flicker open. "Well… I guess… I don't know."

I dip a finger into her panties and rub her sopping-wet clit. A moan crawls out of her throat and she clasps her hand over her mouth to quiet herself.

"I don't consider it sex," I say. "I consider it foreplay."

I push my finger in deep and her eyes roll back in her head. "It's sex," she whimpers as I fuck her with my finger and take her higher and higher. She grows wetter, and I have to say, I love the sexy look that comes over her when she's aroused.

"You're saying any kind of touching is sex, then?" I ask.

"Yes," she whispers.

"Doesn't matter how you get off? Once you come, you're sated?"

I change the tempo, stroke her faster and deeper. "I… This…" She stops talking to take a deep, gulping breath. "This…this won't be enough. Not with you. I'm not sure what you're doing to me, but I need more from you."

"Not quite the same as Mr. Right?"

"No," she whimpers and bucks against my hand.

My chest swells with pride as I revel in the lust on her face. She's already so far gone, I'm not even sure she knows what she's saying.

I finger her for a minute longer, but I'm dying to see her body, so I pull my hand away.

"No, don't," she cries out and reaches for me.

"Naked. Now."

I take hold of her shoulder and spin her until her breasts are against the door and I have access to her zipper. She takes a breath and holds it as the hiss of her zipper fills the silence. Her dress falls open and when some working brain cell flashes red in the back of my brain, I briefly pinch my eyes shut.

What the fuck am I doing?

First I act like a jealous lunatic on the dance floor, and now I'm about to bury my face between her legs in the staff room to prove she is the only girl I want to be with—that I can't stand the thought of her with another man. Honestly, I need to get myself together. By rights I should have left her on that dance floor with Jared, let her see he could be the guy for her, because I'm certainly not. I exhale, and I'm about to put a stop to this, to send her back out to find a guy worth dating, when her dress hits her ankles. I go completely still, and as my mind registers what she's wearing, my heart stalls.

"Accidenti."

She slowly turns my way. My gaze leaves her face to take in her body, but not before I notice the way she's playfully nibbling her bottom lip.

"What does that mean?" she asks.

It means *damn*.

I take a fast breath, barely able to fill my lungs. "You wore this for me?" I ask. I touch the lacy strap on her sexy white camisole and as my chest constricts I note the tiny buttons lining the length of the outfit. It must have taken her forever to fasten. I don't have that kind of patience, and this lace is going to bear the brunt of that.

She shifts from one foot to the other. "Do you like it?"

The air around me grows thin, and it feels as if time has suddenly stopped as I slowly lift my gaze to hers. "Did you wear it for me, Brianna?" I ask again, my voice a bit deeper than it was moments ago.

She stiffens, and her lashes flash rapidly over

wide eyes. "Yeah. Why? Don't you like it?" she asks, her words coming out fast, a hint of worry behind them as she plays with the top button on her camisole. That little nervous gesture, combined with her vulnerability, softens something inside me. I reach out, take her hands in my palms and carefully place them at her side.

I shake my head. "Don't ever cover up with me," I say, my pulse beating double time against my throat as I struggle to wrap my brain around the fact that she purposely wore sexy lingerie tonight.

"But—"

"I thought you said you wouldn't wear lingerie for me. You seemed pretty adamant about it."

She works to give a casual shrug like she's trying to pass this off as nothing. But it's not nothing. Not to me, anyway. Her dark lashes fall and she flicks a shaky glance around the staff room. The nervous laugh that rises in her throat massages my aching cock.

"Must be the mountain air." She taps her head. "Messing with my ability to make rational decisions."

I run my hand down her arm, and a shiver racks her body. "Am I an irrational decision, then?"

"Yes… No… I…I don't know…" Her words fall off as I shape her sexy curves and press my fingers into her hips for leverage as I push my cock against her, letting her know, in no uncertain terms, what she does to me.

"You don't take me as the type to make irrational decisions," I say, putting my mouth close to her ear, mainly so I can breathe her in.

"I have. A time or two," she answers, and beneath the lust there is real regret in her voice.

"Haven't we all," I say, to let her know she's not alone. Truthfully, what I'm doing here with her right now isn't rational or smart, yet here I am, unable to keep my hands off her. One hard nipple pops through the lace, and I brush my thumb over it.

I inch back and take a long, leisurely inspection of her lingerie, even though I'm dying to rip it from her body. "Did you know white lace is my favorite?"

"No." She looks down, her gaze sliding over the lace. "I just thought it was so pretty."

When her gaze lifts, meets mine, I catch the heat backlighting her baby blues. "You bought this recently, then?"

"When I went shopping with Summer."

I stand there for a moment longer, my pulse pounding in my ears. *Brianna bought this for me.* "You know you're the sexiest woman on the planet, right?"

She curls into herself, an insecure gesture that reminds me of the young schoolgirl from Oxford—before she came to me with liquid courage that one night.

"You don't have to say that," she murmurs.

"I wouldn't say it if it wasn't true." I touch the buttons lining the camisole, desperate to show her just how beautiful she really is. "I hope you didn't pay a lot for this."

Her shoulders tighten. "You don't like it, do you? Oh God, I shouldn't have—" Her words turn into a gasp when I grip the lingerie and tear it wide open. The buttons pop, scatter to the floor and then roll away.

"Yes, you should have," I say and then bend to take her nipple into my mouth. I suck her in, revel in the honeyed flavor of her skin. "You definitely should have," I say around a mouthful of pink sweetness. Her body relaxes and her hands go around my head as I indulge in her pebbled hardness. "And I'll replace this."

"You don't have to," she whimpers. "I bought it for you."

As her words touch something inside me and squeeze around my heart, it urges me on, and in this moment I want nothing more than to give her everything her body needs. I devour her, unable to get enough as I swirl my tongue over her firm bud until she's practically crying with need. Eager to taste all of her, mark every inch of her body, I sink to my knees and grip the lace on her panties. One quick tug, I tear them away from her hips and she gasps, not from surprise but from excitement, judging by the way she's trembling beneath my touch.

"I'll buy you a new pair," I murmur.

"And I'll wear them if you promise to do that again."

A tortured noise catches in my throat as I grin up at her, taking pleasure in her boldness, the way she's playing along.

"Guaranteed," I say, and she sighs with contentment. Goddammit, I love the way her face is flushed with lust, the way her eyes are unfocused as she awaits my kisses. I grip her thighs and widen them, so ready for her to come all over my face. Once I have her fully open, mine to do with as I please, I press my lips to her clit and suck her in. I bite down gently, and her entire body quivers. My eyes slide shut and I moan, savoring the flavor of her on my tongue. *Gesù*, how will I ever be able to taste another after her?

Impossible.

"Yes…please," she murmurs and moves her hips to grind against me.

Intense hunger curls through me and I eat at her like a man starved. I insert a finger, and then another, wanting to fill her up until she's screaming my name, which probably isn't wise, considering our location. We don't need anyone to come running and breaking down the door. As I consider that, think about another man's eyes or hands on her body, rage builds inside me. How the hell could I have thought it was a good idea to groom her for someone else, to prove she really does want the happily-ever-after? Oh, because I care about her, want what's best for her, despite what it's going to do to me.

Her walls tighten around me, and she bucks

against my mouth, taking what she needs. I honestly love how she lets go and loses all control with me. Her fingers curl in my hair, and she tugs, a firm grip that drives me mad. Her voice is a low murmur, saying things I can't decipher from deep between her legs.

A thin sheen of sweat coats my body as I pleasure her with my mouth and fingers, increasing the tempo, until her legs are quaking. She moans, low and deep, and her body begins to twitch, her sexy noises a little louder now as she gives herself over to the orgasm pulling at her.

"That's it Brianna. Rub that hot pussy against me," I say as she rolls her hips toward me. "Show me how much you like me fucking you with my fingers, and how much you like my mouth on your body."

"Luca," she murmurs as the floodgates open, and her sweet juices fill my mouth and drip down my chin. I lap at her, but she keeps coming and coming and coming. I can't believe I can do this to her. I stay on my knees and lick her clean, and by the time I stand and press against her to keep her upright, her boneless body is a limp mess, the epitome of a well-pleasured woman.

I brush her hair from her face to see her. She swallows, and from the rough, scratchy sound it's easy to tell she's parched. I press my lips to hers, share the moisture on my tongue.

"Mmm," she moans.

I break the kiss and brush my thumb over her hot

pink cheek. "What do you think of sex in a public place now?" I ask.

She moves her hips, massages my dick with her stomach. I want to be inside her, but tonight is about her, which means I'll have to take care of myself in the shower later.

She arches her brow. "Didn't you clarify that this was simply foreplay."

"Yeah, I did."

"Then I can't answer your question, now, can I, since technically we didn't have sex in a public place." She bats long lashes over innocent eyes, and I love this playful side of her.

I laugh at that. I'm sure she's one hell of a great lawyer. "Something tells me you'd like to have sex in public," I say and then push my thumb into her mouth. She sucks it for a bit and a groan I have no control over escapes me. "That you'd like to try it on for size."

"Wouldn't you like to know," she says, her answer coy, playful.

"Goddamn right I would." She reaches for my button and I shake my head.

"I want to touch you," she says. "I want you in my mouth."

I want that too, but I wanted this to be all about her. "Oh, you will. Later I'm going to feed you my cock, and you're going to take it deeper than ever before," I tell her. A whimper catches in her throat and turns into a gasp when someone knocks on the door.

"Just a second," I say and grab her dress from the floor. I help her into it and toss the ripped lingerie into the nearest bin. Then something comes over us. We both start laughing like two teenagers who've just gotten away with something illegal. Maybe we're both tired, or maybe this is all just so insane, all we can do is laugh. I don't know the reason, but what I do know is, for the next week, I want to do everything with this woman. Everything. And after that I can never set eyes on her again.

CHAPTER ELEVEN

Brianna

I STRETCH OUT on the bed, my body warm, heating up at a rapid pace as arousal hits me hard, like a bullseye between my legs. Halfway between awake and sleep, I work to open my eyes, figure out what the hell is going on. Am I having a sex dream? I'm not sure, but the pleasure between my thighs is delicious and intense and I'm in no hurry for it to end. My temperature continues to rise and I take deep, gulping breaths, so close to orgasming, I can hardly believe it.

A buzzing sound reaches my ears and wakes me a little more. I lift my head, glance down and find a grinning Luca between my legs, waking me up with none other than Mr. Right.

"Oh God," I laugh. He wasn't kidding when he said he wanted to use it on me, and while I would have let him, I never expected him to surprise me with it like this. I have to say, I'm glad he did. You'd think I would be mortified, but after everything we've been doing, embarrassment is the last thing I'm feeling.

"Good morning," he whispers.

"Luca, I can't believe…" My words fall off as pleasure grips me. I sink back down onto the pillow and widen my legs even more for him. Mr. Right vibrates against my clit, and I curl my hands, grip a fistful of the sheets to hang on to. "Luca," I cry out. After all the sex we've been having, how can I still be so aroused, still so needy for more?

He puts the toy inside me and I clench around it, but I fear Mr. Right just isn't going to cut it anymore. Not after having Luca in my body.

"So good," I murmur and toss my head from side to side, my hair a tangled mess beneath me. "But it's you I want inside me."

He lays the toy over my clit and falls over me. In one smooth motion he enters, and just like that I come all over him.

"*Gesù!* You are so hot," he growls. I wrap my legs around him, Mr. Right vibrating against our bodies as he moves his cock in and out of me, making me feel so gloriously full, my mind shuts down. I wrap my legs around him, and he groans into my mouth before kissing me deeply.

I run my nails over his naked back as he takes me higher and higher. In no time at all my body lets go again, and Luca stills inside me, orgasming right along with me. He lifts his head and his eyes meet mine as he completely depletes himself.

I smile at him. "What a way to wake up. A girl could get used to that." I rake my hands through his hair, and he pins me to the bed. I suck in a breath of contentment as I angle my head to glance at the clock.

"I know I was fast, but you didn't have to time me," he says, his voice muffled against my skin.

I laugh. "Sometimes fast is good, and I wasn't timing you. We have to be somewhere."

"Where?"

"You'll see when we get there." I shove him to the edge of the bed. "Now get showered and dressed."

"Only if you'll join me."

I laugh. "If I join you, we'll never get out of here, and I think you're going to like what I have planned. Now go." Grumbling, he disappears into the bathroom, and I keep my gaze locked on his perfect backside until he disappears. Water running reaches my ears, and my body, so relaxed after sex, is completely boneless. I'm not sure I'll be able to use my muscles today, despite the fact that my plans involve the use of almost every muscle in my body. When the shower turns off, I jump in for my turn and wash quickly. Once we're both dressed, I tell him what to pack in a bag, and we head to the main lodge, where I rent a vehicle for our excursion. Thirty minutes later we finally reach our destination and I turn to catch Luca's expression.

"When you told me to pack swimming trunks, I had no idea you had this in mind. In fact it's the last place I ever thought you'd want to go," Luca says, a wide smile splitting his lips, his dark eyes glancing around to take everything in like he's seeing the place for the first time, even though I know he spent a lot of time at Lake Silvaplana when he worked here. I still don't know the real reason he was bartending at Diamond Peak, and while I'm a bit curious, I suspect I never will. He seemed to hedge a bit last time it came up.

"Why not?" I ask as I park the rental between two huge trucks and look out over the lake as the rippling waves glisten in the late afternoon sun. My gaze skates over the towering mountains, hugging the lake from three sides, and the rushing waterfall smoothing the rough edges of the jagged rocks as it spills into the pond below. At least twenty kiteboarders play in the breeze as their boards skim the water.

He removes his seat belt and shifts to face me. "You said you were too scared to try it."

I shrug. "And you said I should always face my fears. Maybe you were right about that."

His face softens, making him look so damn adorable, I can't help but want to kiss him. I release my belt, lean across the seat and press my mouth to his. His lips part, welcoming me in, and his hand cups my face as he gives me the softest kiss—a kiss so touching and profound, there isn't a girl alive who could come back from it easily. I exhale a soft sigh and inch back.

"Besides," I say. "You surprised me with the sunrise trip up the mountain, so I wanted to do something nice for you."

His grin turns mischievous. "You don't think you've been doing nice things for me?"

I whack him, and he fakes hurt. "You know what I mean."

"Tonight, when we get back to the chalet, I'm going to do something nice for you, too."

From the look on his face, I'm sure my surprise has something to do with sex, and I'm happy about that. His thoughtful gestures, like my sunrise surprise, awaken things in me, things best left buried.

"Ooh, can't wait," I say and glance at the kiteboarders again. "But right now I need a lesson."

"Okay, come on. I'll teach you everything you need to know."

He reaches for the door handle but I touch his arm to stop him. "No, it's okay. I booked a professional lesson."

He frowns. "Don't trust me?"

Trust him? Trust a guy who made a fool of me back at Oxford?

Oh God, I just might.

"We're only here for a few more days. I want you to enjoy the kiteboarding and not waste your time with me." He scrubs his face and looks off in the distance, like I'd just sucker punched him or something. *What the hell?* "Luca."

He reaches for the door handle. "Let's do this."

I climb out of my seat, and we grab our bags from the trunk. I hit the fob to lock the doors, and a cool breeze ruffles my blouse as I follow him to the rental lodge. We sign in, and the clerk gives us our gear and keys to our lockers. He points down the beach, to the spot where the instructor is giving lessons.

"Once you're changed, check in with Beck," he says.

I'm about to head to the locker room when Luca captures my arm, and I turn back to him. Concerned eyes meet mine, examine my face. "Careful, okay," he says quietly. "Don't take risks or do anything you're not comfortable doing."

"I'll be okay," I say and then swallow down the knot jumping into my throat. God, when he acts like this, like he really cares for my well-being, it makes me forget that what's between us isn't real. He leans down and drops a soft kiss onto my mouth. I'm breathless when he breaks it.

I stand on boneless legs when he peels his shirt off and makes his way into the changing room. I head into the girl's locker room, on the other side of the hut, and quickly change into my swimsuit, thankful I tossed one into my suitcase at the last minute before leaving New York. I shove all my things into the locker and pin the key to my suit.

Luca is waiting for me near the beach when I come out of the lodge, and his gaze leaves my face to travel the length of me. He frowns, and I fold my arms over my chest.

"What?" I ask, suddenly self-conscious in my suit. Which is ridiculous. The man has seen me naked, for God's sake.

"You're gorgeous," he says and scrubs his chin as he glances around. "I'll do my best not to be an asshole, but I can't guarantee it."

I shade the sun from my eyes and follow his gaze, trying to make sense of things. "What are you talking about?"

"Do you really not know how beautiful you are, or what goes through a guy's mind when he looks at you?"

"I…" I might not be that chubby girl from my younger days, but there is a part of her that still lives inside me. "I don't notice things like that, I guess."

"Well, I do. And Brianna, if a guy so much as touches you, and I lose my shit, you can't hold that against me."

Feeling playful, and maybe even a little giddy at the way this man makes me feel—like I'm the most beautiful woman in the world—I step into him. "The only thing I want to hold against you is my body, Luca."

His teeth clench with an audible click. "*Gesù!* You can't say things like that when I'm in my swimming trunks."

I move against him, feeling him thickening. His fingers close around my shoulder and he steps back. "Unless you want me to take you behind the hut, you'd better stop."

"Maybe I'd like that."

His dark growl swirls in the wind. "Brianna—"

I laugh and turn, giving an extra shake to my ass as I walk away. "Go. Have fun. I need to get to my lesson."

"Tonight," he calls out. "We're going to pick right back up here."

I glance at him over my shoulder as he carries his equipment to the edge of the water. He goes about preparing his sail, and I kick my sandals off and squeeze the warm grass between my toes. Shading my eyes, I walk toward the instructor, but as I do, nervousness jolts through me and I begin to second-guess this idea. Am I really going to go kiteboarding? The idea of flying across the lake, carried by a kite, terrifies me. As I mull that over, I think more about what Luca said to me.

I need to face my fears.

He wasn't wrong when he said I was afraid of commitment, and part of him agreeing to pretend to be my fiancé was my trying on a relationship for size. So far it hasn't been so bad. Well, that's not the best way to put it. More like, so far it's been amazing. I've never had so much fun in my life, and being with Luca has made me rethink everything in my life. Are there good guys out there? Ones who aren't going to hurt, lie to or cheat on me?

Even if there are, do I want any of them?

My stomach clenches at that thought. Oh God.

If I'm not careful, Luca could very well ruin me for another.

I stop at the edge of the embankment and admire Luca as he sets off. I can't help but smile as I watch him. He's totally in his element as he takes to the air, doing tricks and turns that would result in a trip to the emergency room if I ever tried them.

I follow the rocky path, and the instructor is just finishing up with a student when I arrive.

"You must be Brianna," he says and checks his watch. "I'm Beck."

I smile and take in his Australian accent as I shake his hand. He's a handsome guy. Tall, with windblown blond surfer hair that looks like it hasn't seen a comb in decades. "Nice to meet you, Beck." I take in the equipment he's laying out for me, and he must sense my nervousness.

"No worries, mate," he says. "I'll have you up and flying in no time."

I glance toward the water and search out Luca. Unlike me, he's athletic and brave. But I want to do this. I want to step out of my comfort zone here in the Alps and do something fun. I'm not sure why Luca brings that out in me, but it's certainly not a bad thing.

For the next half hour or so, Beck talks about the clock position and the wind window, as well as neutral, intermediate and power zones. He goes over all the equipment, explaining the kind of kite I'm using, the steering bar, training harness and struts. I take it all in, a little fascinated by it. Once the land lessons are over, he takes me to the water and I slide my feet into my board, waves lapping at my face and body as I try to position myself.

"Okay, remember," he says as he walks away, holding the kite, ready to get me in the air. "You give me the thumbs-up when you're ready to try, and when you're ready to come down, you tap your head. Got it?"

"I got it," I say, little bubbles of excitement welling up inside me.

"Don't forget the eject button if you get in trouble." I nod and run my finger over the word *eject* on my handle.

"Hey, Brianna. I'm right here," Luca calls out as he comes boarding my way.

I give him a nervous wave.

"She's got this, mate," Beck calls out. "Quick learner."

Luca stays close, and I appreciate it. If I go down hard—and I fully expect I will—he might be able to fish me out of the water before I drown.

I hold my handles, making sure the red bar is on the left like I was taught, and wind catches my kite, tightening the harness under my backside and dragging me deeper into the water. Before I know what's happening, I'm lifted clear into the air. As I go higher and higher, fear grips me and I can't seem to catch my breath. From the corner of my eye, I catch sight of Luca, and I let loose a loud cry. Panicking, I hit the eject button. I drop into the water, sink like a stone, and when I come up, Luca is right there.

"Brianna," he says and swims to me. "You okay?"

I gulp air and put my arms around him. He holds me, and I instantly calm down. "I'm okay," I say. "I panicked."

"We all do the first time," he says softly.

"How embarrassing."

"Nah, nothing to be embarrassed about. You were far more graceful hitting the water than I was my first time."

I cling to him, and he treads water to keep us both up. "I doubt that."

He grins at me. "Would I lie to you?" he says, but then something comes over him, and he averts his gaze. "You okay to swim?"

"Yes," I say and let go of him.

He keeps an eye on me for a second, to ensure I'm okay. "Just remember your wind window, and when you gain power, pull down on the bar, and it helps lessen it."

As we tread water, he brushes my hair from my face. "Come on, let's go back in and start again." He angles his head. "That is if you want to."

"I do want to. You make it look like so much fun."

"It is fun once you get the hang of it. Next time you're here with Tate, you can show him up."

"I'm not sure when we'll be back again. Tate has Summer now and we have Granddad's health to think about."

We begin to swim back in, and Luca says, "How do you want to handle things with James when this week is over?" His brow is furrowed, and oddly enough I get the sense he's worried about a lot more than breaking off our fake engagement.

"I haven't thought that far ahead. I don't want to hurt him, but I'm not about to drag this thing on any longer than needed. I'm sure you're anxious to end the ruse."

He opens his mouth like he wants to say something, but then turns his attention to Beck as he waits for us on the embankment. "You okay, mate?" he asks me.

"Panicked," I answer. "Nothing to do with you. You're an excellent instructor."

I climb out of the water, and Beck checks my lines and readjusts the harness on my backside. A low, strange noise, like a dog growling, catches my attention, and I angle my head to see Luca glaring at Beck. *What the hell?* He's acting like a jealous boyfriend, but that can't be right.

"Let me get your lines fixed and get you up again," Beck says.

"If you don't mind, I'd like to help her." Luca turns to me. "That's if it's okay with you?"

"I don't want to take you away from boarding. I set this up for you."

He steps toward me, cups my chin. "I can board anytime. Right now I want to help you."

I swallow, never having seen him so intense before. "If you're sure."

"I'm sure," he says and sits on the ground, cross-legged, dragging me down with him. I feel a little breathless as we stare at each other. Luca says, "Beck went over everything with you, but you panicked, and you panicked from fear. It happens." He takes my hands in his. "What you need to know is I'm right there with you, and I won't let anything happen to you. When I get you up, I'll stay by your side and guide you through the motions, letting you know when to pull and push until you're comfortable trying it on your own, okay?"

Good lord, why is this guy still single?

He said he wasn't opposed to marriage, if it was with the right person. Could that right person be me?

My God, what am I saying!

He's doing me a favor, and we're having some great sex. That's all. Right?

Beck stands by, offering occasional words of encouragement as Luca goes over a few more things with me; then Luca leans in and presses his lips to mine. "All set?" he asks, his mouth lingering on mine.

"I am."

"Nervous?"

"Not really. I think I got this."

"Okay." He stands, and we take up our positions. I tap my head to let him know I'm ready, and once the wind picks me up, and I'm in the water, I start to lift fast again. I pull down on the bar, and I'm instantly lowered and in more control of my kite. I glance over my shoulder to see Beck helping Luca get into the air.

I turn my attention back to my kite, and water zings around me as I let the wind pull me along.

Luca zips by me and I grin at him. "Doing good?" he yells out.

The wind takes me up again, and I let it this time, just a bit. Excitement wells up inside me, and I adjust the bar to lower myself. Now that I've gotten the hang of it, it's kind of fun. A little scary, but exhilarating, just the same. We play on the boards for a good long time and, show-off that Luca is, he does tricks as I keep my board in the water. I laugh at his antics and soon enough my arms grow tired. I catch Luca's attention and tap my head to let him know I'm tapping out.

I let the breeze carry me to the embankment and adjust the bar so the kite falls into the water. I'm breathless and exhausted by the time I climb out. Luca comes in behind me, and he's grinning like a child on Christmas morning.

"That was a blast," I say. "You can go back up if you want."

"Nope." He slides one arm around my waist and drags me to him. The cooler mountain air rushes over us and I shiver. His stomach grumbles and I laugh.

"That really builds up an appetite," I say as my own tummy grumbles.

Luca gives me a smack on the ass. "Let's get going."

"Do you want to grab some lunch on the way

back?" It'd be more like dinner; we've been here for most of the day.

"Nope."

"But you're hungry." He gives me a mischievous grin. "Wait. What are you up to?"

"You'll see."

"Luca…" I warn in a playful voice as he helps me from my harness. I'm about to press but Beck runs over to us. He gives me a high five and helps us gather our equipment. We return it to the rental shop and go to the locker rooms to change back into our clothes.

A yawn pulls at me when I step outside and find Luca waiting for me. He captures my hand, brings it to his mouth and gives it a kiss. "Thanks for this, Brianna."

"My pleasure," I say.

His gaze narrows and then moves over my face. "Want me to drive?"

I stretch my arms out. "I'm a bit sore actually. I've used muscles I haven't used in ages." I fish the keys from my bag and hand them to him. We walk back to the car, toss our bags into the trunk and he opens my door for me. Another yawn pulls at me, and after I buckle myself in, I close my eyes. All the sex, fresh mountain air and late nights have been getting to me. By the time I open my eyes again, Luca is shutting off the ignition.

"Where are we?" I ask and blink my eyes open.

"You slept the whole way back."

"I'm sorry."

"Don't be." He shifts in his seat, rests his arm on the back of my seat and gently brushes his thumb over my cheek. "Feel better?"

I stretch out. "I didn't realize how tired I was."

"Tonight, I'll let you sleep."

"But I thought you had a surprise," I say. I might be tired, but I want to enjoy every possible moment with this man. I'll sleep when I return home. But the thoughts of returning to New York bring a knot to my gut. How the hell am I going to deal with Grand-dad and get out of this situation without hurting him?

"I do," he says and opens his door. He comes around my side of the car and holds his hand out to me. I graciously accept it and let him pull me from my seat. We snatch our bags from the trunk and make our way inside the chalet. I go still when I see a counter full of food and grocery bags.

"What's going on?" I ask.

"Special delivery."

"What are you up to?"

"I'm making us dinner, and then if you're up to it, I thought you might want to try your hand at baking an apple pie." He points to the fire extinguisher in the hall. "I'm prepared for the worst."

I laugh and hit him in the gut. "Not funny."

"A little funny?"

"Okay, maybe a little."

He pulls a chair out from the island. "Sit."

"Bossy," I say, but sit down anyway. He reaches

into the fridge, grabs a bottle of wine, and pours us each a glass. I take a sip.

"Mmm," I murmur and twirl the liquid in my stemware. "Although if I drink any more on an empty stomach, I can't be held accountable for my actions," I say, tossing his words back at him as the wine warms me all over.

He pours another splash into my cup and wags his brow at me. "Drink up?"

"Why, do you plan to take advantage of me?"

He goes perfectly still, the smile falling from his face. "Tonight, I'm letting you sleep, remember?"

"I remember," I say. Here I thought his surprise had something to do with sex, yet he's cooking a meal for me. I wish I wasn't so touched by the gesture.

He pulls food from a brown paper bag. "What are you making?" I ask as I look over the ingredients.

"My mother's famous carbonara."

"Mmm. Yum. Is there anything I can do to help?"

"I've got this. But if you want to peel apples for the pie, you can." He gestures to the bag on the counter. I ordered pie crust from Hauser's. All we have to do is roll it out. It's too much work to make it from scratch here."

He pulls a box of pasta from the bag. "What, you're not making the noodles from scratch?" I ask, feigning shock as I relax in my chair, contentment falling over me.

"Hey, be nice to the people who cook for you. You

don't know what they can do to your food." I laugh at him. "My mother always used to say that."

"She sounds like a great woman."

He nods and smiles, then turns his attention to the fridge. He pulls out a couple of different kinds of cheese and reaches for the grater.

"You must miss her," I say as I slide off my chair and grab a knife from the table. I tear off some paper towel, spread it on the island and then reach for the bag of apples.

"I do."

"Do you get home to visit her much?"

"Not as much as I'd like," he says and puts a pot of water on the stove.

I don't want to pry but I kind of want to know more about him. "I'm really sorry about your father and your brother, Luca. It must have been so hard on you and your mother."

He nods and turns on the burner. "I was away when it happened. By the time I got home, Mom was a mess."

"When did it happen?"

"When I was at Oxford, my final year of law school."

I pause for a second. I remember. He'd disappeared for a while and I made up all kinds of things about his absence. My final conclusion—or maybe at the time it was just wishful thinking—was that he was out being treated for a bad case of herpes. I'm such a jerk.

He exhales a slow breath, and a small smile touches his mouth. "I miss fishing with him." Remaining silent, I take a sip of wine and go back to peeling apples as his mind trips down memory lane. "He taught my brother and I to fly-fish. We were all pretty competitive." He laughs. "This one time, I caught a huge bass. Record-breaking," he says and eyes me like I'm going to call him out on that. "I was only around ten, and it was almost as big as me. I yelled to Dad, and when I turned I lost my footing, and the rapids took me down the river."

"Oh my God, were you hurt?"

"Only my pride."

We both laugh and he says, "Never let go of the fish, though. I can prove it was big if you don't believe me. Mom took a picture."

"Hey, I never said I didn't believe you." I reach for another apple. "What else did your dad do? Besides fish with you."

"He actually ran many big conglomerates. My brother was being groomed to take over." His frown returns and he reaches back into the fridge, like he doesn't want me to see his sadness.

"Who runs it now?"

"My uncle," he says quickly, and I get the sense he doesn't want to continue with the conversation. "You like cured meats, right?" He pulls a package from the fridge.

"I do. Although I don't really eat it."

"Why not?"

"Fattening."

"You're perfect," he says and unwraps the meat. "You can't have carbonara without authentic Italian guanciale. My mother would disown me if I used anything else. In fact she'd probably beat my ass with her wooden spoon."

I laugh at that. "I really like this woman. I kind of missed..." I let my words fall off and his dark lashes lift over even darker eyes.

"Missed what?"

I cut a slice off the apple, take a bite and hand it to Luca. He tosses it into his mouth and we both chew for a second. "My mother gave up on everything after my dad left, and I never really had a female role model. I guess I miss that. I'm a little envious of what you have with your mom."

"You want your ass beaten with a wooden spoon? I can do it for you," he says, and I get that he's trying to lighten my mood. I chuckle, but then he goes serious. "Mom would really like you, Brianna. She'd mother the hell out of you if she had a chance. I think she secretly wanted a daughter."

"She'll get one when you marry," I say, then curse myself when he turns from me, fast. Good God, does he think I'm hinting at marriage? As I take in his back, the tightening of his shoulders, my stomach knots. The two of us are playing house. I'm never going to meet his mother. Never going to have a loving family of my own.

Do I want that?

Oh God, I think I might.

"What about you—still anti-marriage, no kids, no family?" he asks.

"Yes," I say quickly, not wanting him to get the wrong idea, that I might want just that with him.

"I don't think it's been so bad, Brianna? You've been sleeping with the same guy night after night, we've been having fun together, sharing meals, and I've yet to get a fork in my leg," he says, his voice low, soft.

"None of this is real," I remind him and ignore the tightening of my throat. "We're doing it to fool Granddad." Redirecting, I scan the counter. "Can you pass me a bowl?" I say and inwardly curse myself when my voice hitches. Luca places a big glass bowl on the counter, and I concentrate on cutting the apples into thin slivers as he slices guanciale and drops the pasta into the water. He turns his attention to the sauce.

"Do you need a recipe for the apple pie?"

"Of course I need a recipe," I say, and he chuckles.

"I have it on my laptop. I called it up earlier when I put the order in for the groceries." He gestures with a nod to the coffee table, and I cross the room and grab it.

"Password," I say after opening it. I spin the laptop, and he types something in. I turn the computer back to me, and the website with the recipe pops up. "If I burn this place down…" I say as I read the ingredients off and go in search of them. I put everything on the counter and grab the measuring spoons and cups.

"This is going to be ready in a minute. We'll make the pie after we eat and maybe we can watch a movie while it's baking."

I look at the sauce on the stove and breathe it in. "That smells amazing."

"Tastes even better. Grab us a couple of plates." I search the cupboard and pull out two plates.

Luca puts a generous portion on each plate and I carry them to the table. He refills our wine and we both dig in.

"Luca, this is amazing." He grins at me. "Are you good at everything you do?"

"Pretty much."

"And modest, too. I like that in a guy." We laugh, but deep down, the truth is I do like everything about this guy, and that scares the hell out of me. We can't be together. We set the terms for this ruse, and falling for each other was not part of the plan.

Oh God, I'm falling for this guy.

We settle in to easy conversation as we eat, and Luca talks more about his fishing days with his father and brother. I love hearing his stories, love the enthusiasm in his voice as he recalls those happy days. I, in turn, talk about my days with Granddad and Tate, and all the summers and vacations we had here in St. Moritz. Once we finish eating, we clear the dishes and, working together, we build a big apple pie, although I fear I'm too full to eat any.

We put the pie into the oven, and Luca flicks on the television. I plop down onto the sofa and he settles in beside me. Our legs touch, and he puts his hand on my thigh, giving it a little squeeze as he flicks through the stations.

"Let me guess, romantic comedy?" he asks.

"Of course."

He goes through a few more stations, and as I settle into the cushions, someone knocks on the door, hard. I sit up straighter, a measure of panic. "Who could that be?"

"I don't know," Luca says and stands.

"I hope Granddad is okay." I should be spending more time with him, but every time I look at him, guilt swamps me. I stand and follow Luca to the door. With my hand on his back—for some reason I need the connection—he opens the door.

"Is that pie I smell?"

I step around him to see Granddad on the stoop. "Are you okay?" I ask and take his hand to usher him in.

He looks around, sniffs the air and elbows Luca in the gut. "At least she didn't burn the place down this time."

"I was prepared," Luca says and nods toward the fire extinguisher. As the two laugh, I put my hands on my hips.

"I'm right here, and I'm not amused."

"Are you going to cut me a slice or what?" Granddad asks.

"What are you doing out? How did you get here?" I ask and look outside before Luca shuts the door.

Gnarled fingers close around his cane as he lifts it. "I walked."

"You shouldn't have."

"How else am I going to see my granddaughter and her fiancé," he says, the deep lines around his mouth curling upward as he smiles. "And hear all about their wedding plans."

I cast a quick glance at Luca, a wave of guilt hitting hard. "Come on in. The pie won't be ready for a bit. Have you eaten? Luca made carbonara and there's some leftover."

He gives Luca a wink, then coughs into his elbow. "Had dinner with Deloris."

"Granddad, you need to be taking it easy."

"Just needed to see if my granddaughter is okay. You've been scarce, girly."

"I'm okay."

"Good, then let's sit and we can talk about this wedding of yours."

"No," I say firmly. "This week is about Tate and Summer." Just then my phone rings. "Hang on." I rush to my beach bag, pull my phone out and check the caller ID. "It's Tate," I say and slide my finger across the phone.

"Hey," I say. "What's up?"

"Hey, Bri. Have you seen Granddad? I went to his room, but there's no answer."

"He's here," I say and hear the relief when Tate exhales. "Apparently he smelled pie."

"You're making pie? Is the fire department on call?"

"Very funny. Why don't you and Summer come over?" At least with the two of them here, it might take Granddad's focus off us and our wedding plans. "We'll play a game. Make a night out of it." Tate calls to Summer, and for a second his voice is muffled.

When he comes back he says, "We'll be right there."

I end the call as Luca leads Granddad to the sofa. "Looks like we're having company," I inform them.

"Fine by me," Luca says.

"As long as I get the biggest slice of pie," Granddad says, and Luca and I just shake our heads. "Now, where's the brandy?"

By the time Tate and Summer show up, I'm taking the pie from the oven. "Just in time," I say as Luca greets them at the door. It's odd how this all feels, really. Like Luca and I are a real couple and having family over. It's not a bad feeling. In fact I kind of like it. Could very well get used to it.

"Smells amazing," Summer says. She joins me in the kitchen, setting a bottle of wine on the counter, along with a couple of bags of potato chips. *Is everyone trying to fatten me up?* She pulls a deck of cards from her purse and a few board games from her shoulder bag. "I wasn't sure what you guys might want to play." I look them over as she takes in the dirty dishes on the stove. "Did you cook?" she asks.

"No, Luca made me his mother's famous, authentic carbonara."

She grins at me. "Oh really. How nice of him."

"He's a great cook, and a great kiteboarder," I say without thinking, my mind going back to earlier today.

"Tate said you were going there today. That must have been fun. I've never tried it myself. I'm too afraid of heights."

I laugh at that. "It was fun once I got the hang of it. Luca stayed by my side and helped me out."

"Sounds like you guys are really hitting it off."

I glance past her shoulder, in time to see Luca help Granddad to the kitchen table. He pours him a glass of brandy, and then comes my way to get a couple of beers for him and Tate.

He stands behind me, his breath hot on my neck as he leans into me. "Would you ladies like wine?"

"Sounds good to me," Summer says, her eyes narrowing in on us, like she can see right through me, see how much I like this guy. He pours us each a glass and heads back to the table. I can't seem to tear my eyes from him as he goes.

"Look how happy Granddad is," Summer says, lowering her voice for my ears only. She gives me a nudge. "I think the news of your engagement added years to his life."

As I think about that, think about the sparkle in

his eyes tonight, I can't help but wonder if it's because of me. Now that I'm *engaged*, has it put his worries to rest, given him new life? God, if so, how the hell am I ever going to tell him the truth? Worry gnaws at my gut. Worry for Granddad's health. For the things I'm starting to feel for Luca.

"Yeah, I know. He's full of life tonight, isn't he?"

She takes a sip of wine and sighs. "You're never going to be able to tell him the truth."

My gaze flashes to hers, takes in her grin. "I have to tell him, Summer. This is all just pretend."

Her gaze goes from me to Luca, who's laughing with Tate and Granddad, and then back to me again. "Are you sure about that?"

CHAPTER TWELVE

Luca

I'M NOT SURE what Brianna and Summer are talking about, but from the way my pretend fiancée is fiddling with the top button on her blouse, I'd guess it's something unsettling, and probably something about this situation we've all found ourselves in. I'm a little troubled by it myself and I'm not sure how I can just walk away once the wedding is over. I care about this family, but I've been keeping secrets from them, too. How would they feel about me if they found out I was a duke, with an agenda laid out for me, one I must follow for my family's sake?

"Fill me up," Granddad says and sets his glass on the table with a thud. I exchange a look with Tate and he just shrugs. At this point in his life, the man's blood is half brandy, so I guess a few more glasses won't hurt him.

Pushing from the chair, I grab the brandy bottle and spill a bit into his glass. When I sit again, Brianna and Summer join us and set an old game of Snakes and Ladders on the table.

"Where did you ever find this?" I ask. The game takes me back to my childhood and the happy days I spent playing with my brother. I miss those times. I miss my family.

"At the lodge. They let us borrow a few for tonight," Summer says.

"We used to play this all the time when we were young, Bri," Tate says, and a smile comes over her. A warm, soft smile that curls around me, pinches my heart. I hate that her father left when she was young and her mother checked out. At least she had Tate and her granddad. But her time with them has been scarce with her long work hours, James hounding her about marriage—even though he only has her best interests at heart—and Tate spending more and more of his time with his soon-to-be wife.

Tate unpacks the game and hands out pieces. "The oldest goes first, I believe," James says as he scoops up the dice and tosses them onto the board. He moves his piece and slides up a ladder. "I always did like this game."

"Watch him. He cheats," Tate says, and we all laugh.

Indignant, James lifts his head. "I do not. You're just sore because you can never beat me."

Soon enough we're all laughing and playing, and I glance at Brianna, take in the smile on her face. She's in her element here, surrounded by family. Just like I knew she would be. She might be cynical, but deep down this is what she wants, and this is what she should have. If only we could have it together.

I let my mind go for a second, envision sweet Brianna as my duchess. It's a role where she could do the charity work she wants, become more involved in projects that interest her and benefit society. Then again does she even want more with me? She's given me no indication.

What the hell am I saying?

I can't have more with her. If I don't follow through with my father's stipulations, my family could lose everything. I could never do that to my mother. I work to block out those disheartening thoughts, and when my turn comes up, I roll the dice and hit a ladder. I climb it and land on the same square as James.

"Oh, it's on," I say to him, and he waves a gnarled hand at me, as if to shoo me away.

"Beginner's luck," he says. "Nothing more."

"This isn't the first time I've played," I tell him.

"First time you've played with me."

As I look at James, my thoughts stray to Uncle Gio. He told me once that arranged marriages weren't so bad, it was done all the time in the past and that my bride would serve me well. I want to take my place, live up to my responsibilities, I just can't do it with a woman I don't love by my side. If only I could get the stipulation removed. If only there was a way around it. Maybe Uncle Gio could help me find some grounds to contest it. A seed of hope blooms inside of me, and I draw in a deep breath.

Brianna rolls the dice and her groan pulls my focus back to the game at hand when she hits a snake and slides down.

"I don't think I like this game anymore," she says, and I stand to refill her wine. Without thinking, I lean down and press my lips to her cheek, and when I stand again, all sets of eyes are on me.

"What? Can't a guy kiss his fiancée?"

"You can kiss her all you like, once I see that ring on her finger," James says, and Brianna's body tightens.

She worries her top button again as I pull the wine from the fridge. I fill Brianna's glass and then Summer's. "Beer?" I ask Tate.

"Sure, I'm not driving."

I hand Tate a beer and pour myself a soda. "I'll be driving James home, so I'm switching."

"I don't need you driving me," James says with a snarl. "I can walk."

"I'm driving you," I say, and give him a hard look that lets him know this isn't up for debate. When I turn back to Brianna, she's smiling at me. So warm, soft and appreciative, it's like a shot of adrenaline to the heart.

"Fine then," James says. "If you like driving so much, tomorrow I'll let you drive the golf cart. Tee off is at eleven. Don't be late."

"You're going golfing?" Brianna asks.

I open my mouth to tell her no, but James pipes in. "Of course he is. I want all of my sons on the course with me."

James considers me his son.

A knot clogs my throat and my heart wobbles a little. I haven't been anyone's *son* in a long time, and dammit I like the sound of that.

"If the guys are golfing, why don't we plan a girls' day?" Summer says. "I'll text Cara and Amber. They went to the spa last time we were here and they loved it." She pulls her phone from her back pocket and shoots a text off to her friends.

Brianna looks at me, and while I want to spend all my time with her, I hold my hands up in surrender, pretty sure I'm not getting out of golfing with James, and that an interrogation as to our wedding plans might be on his agenda.

We continue to play the game, until James wins. As he gloats a little, Brianna yawns. It's been a long day, and I promised her a good night's sleep tonight.

Reading the room, Summer stretches. "We should probably get going, Tate. I'm getting sleepy." She turns to Brianna. "Don't forget all the girls are staying together at Raydolins tomorrow night after the rooftop cocktail party. We have four adjoining suites booked for us, so we can hang out and then get ready together in the morning. It will be fun to spend the day together, then watch some chick flicks at night." She grins at Tate. "With no one complaining."

"That's right," Brianna says. "The groom can't see the bride before the wedding."

Tate finishes his beer and stands. "All right. Come on, Granddad. I'll help you into the car."

James grumbles under his breath, finishes his brandy and stands. Summer packs the game back up and puts it in her bag as Brianna clears the glasses and takes them to the sink.

"Luca, I forgot. I have your suit jacket," Summer says. "You left it at the restaurant after our bridal party dinner. It's back at our place. I keep forgetting to give it to you."

"Right. I forgot about that. I'll get it from you later." I step up to Brianna, run my hands along her arms. "Leave the dishes. I'll do them tomorrow."

She turns to me and smiles. "Thanks for driving Granddad. It's a long way for him to walk."

"Why don't you crawl into bed. I'll be back soon," I say, torn about leaving her when I'd like to undress her and put her between the sheets myself.

"Okay," she says.

"You don't need to drive me," James grumbles again.

"Yeah, I do," I say. Not just for him, but for myself, too. Selfish bastard that I am, I love the way Brianna looks at me when I help her grandfather out. "I'll make sure he gets to his room." I grab the keys and lock up behind me as Tate helps James into the passenger seat of my rental.

"We're going to walk to the lodge to return the

game," he says as he closes the door and captures Summer's hand. As they stroll off, I jump into the driver's seat and back out of the driveway.

"Brianna seems very happy," he says to me. "You seem to make her happy."

I nod and consider the changes that have come over her since first arriving in the Alpine town. "She needed this vacation."

"She works too hard," he grumps.

"I agree."

He nods like he's happy we concur on that. "Once you two are married and have a dozen kids, she'll want to cut her hours."

"That's up to her," I say and drive the narrow road until I'm in front of Raydolins. I park, and James doesn't make a move to leave the vehicle.

He turns to me, his cloudy blue eyes serious. "You won't hurt her, will you, Luca?" he asks, his voice low, troubled as he zeroes in on me.

For a minute I'm sure the man can see into my soul, see our lie. Does he know we're pretending? If so, wouldn't he call us out on that, or is he hoping something more will develop between us?

"I'd never purposely hurt her," I say truthfully, and James nods his head and reaches for the door handle. I jump from the car and circle it to help him get inside. The front door of the hotel opens and the cool air-conditioning falls over us. I slow my pace to match his as we go to the elevator and take it to his suite.

He uses his key card to open the door and waves me away. "I'll see you on the golf course tomorrow," he says. "Don't be late."

I wait until he closes his door, and then I hurry back to my car. I drive the vehicle to the rental shop to return it, and then I jog back to the chalet. I let myself in, lock the door behind me, kick off my shoes and then quietly pad down the hall, not wanting to wake Brianna if she's already fast asleep.

The light over the sink is on, giving me enough light to walk past the sofa and find her curled up in the bed. I peel my shirt off, kick off my pants and then lift the sheets to slide in next to her. A soft moan crawls out of her throat as I settle in behind her and wrap one arm around her to hold her to me. Being with her like this is definitely something I could get used to. While I'd like nothing more than to make love to her tonight, we both need sleep. I let my lids fall shut and when I open them again, Brianna's side of the bed is empty.

I jackknife up and rub the blur from my eyes as I glance around. "Brianna?" I call out, my gaze going to the open bathroom door. I listen for a moment but the place is silent. *What the hell?* I kick the sheets off and that's when I see her note.

Gone shopping with the girls before we hit the spa. You were sleeping so soundly, I didn't want to wake you. Enjoy golfing with Granddad.

The note brings a smile to my face, but I still wish she had woken me up so I could at least have given her a good-morning kiss—and hopefully a little more—before she left. As I think about having her in my arms again, just holding her next to me, my heart beats a little faster.

I am in so much trouble here.

I throw my legs over the side of the bed and work to get my shit together. I take a couple of fueling breaths and check the time. After hurrying to the bathroom, I take a fast shower, pull on a pair of shorts and a T-shirt, grab an apple from the fridge and then head outside. The warm morning sun beats down on me as I walk through the Alpine town and make my way to the golf course. I finish the apple by the time I get there, and find Tate and James loading their clubs into a cart.

"I need coffee," I say. "Got up later than I meant to."

Tate gives me a knowing look, but there is concern in his eyes. "Come on, let's go get you some clubs, and we'll grab a coffee in the lodge."

I shove my hands into my pockets and we make our way inside. He keeps casting fast glances my way, like he's got something on his mind.

"What?" I finally ask when we reach the rental counter.

"Have you talked to Bri? Told her you're going back to Italy?"

"No." Would it matter? Would she even care?

She's not talked about extending this pretend en-gagement past this week, and even if she wanted to, no way can I go back to New York and turn my back on my family and obligations. Torn between love and duty, I nod to the man behind the counter.

Wait!

Love?

I love Brianna?

"Clubs?" the man behind the rental counter asks.

I take a deep breath and let it out slowly. "Yeah, thanks," I say and sign my name and room number on the sheet of paper he slides my way.

He comes around the counter and gives me a bag full of clubs, which I hike over my shoulder. As we leave and head to the restaurant inside the lodge, un-ease takes up residency in my gut.

"You're falling for her," Tate says, taking me by surprise.

"Look," I begin. "I'm doing her a favor, and she isn't looking for anything more. Even if she was..."

Tate puts his hand on my shoulder. "I think you two need to have a long talk."

I nod, but what would I say to her? Oh yeah, did I forget to mention I'm a duke and I have to go back home to marry? If she did want more with me, that would be a deal breaker and I'd be lucky to leave here with my nuts intact.

We grab three coffees to go, and I turn the sub-ject back to Tate as we walk back to James. "Big day tomorrow," I say.

The smile that comes over his face squeezes my heart. "I've only known Summer for six months, but when you know, you know, right?"

I nod. I've known Brianna a lot longer. Well, I didn't *know her* know her. I'd seen her around on campus numerous times. It wasn't until now that I'd gotten a glimpse into the girl who I was always drawn to. But that does take my thoughts back to our initial meeting during dinner, when she pretended not to know me. I've been waiting for her to come clean on that, but she hasn't yet. I can't quite figure out why. I mean, there's a possibility that she really doesn't remember me, but everything in my gut tells me different. There was a flash of familiarity in her eyes when they first met mine, before she quickly blinked it away.

We reach James, and Tate hands over his grandfather's coffee. "You driving?" he asks, and I nod and climb behind the wheel. For the next few hours we play, and I'm grateful that James hasn't brought up Brianna or our wedding plans.

After eighteen holes, which took forever under the scorching sun, we grab a bite to eat in the restaurant. Once done I make my way back to the chalet, hoping to find Brianna. I unlock the door and push it open, listening for sounds of movement.

"Hey, you here?" I ask when I enter, but my question is met with silence. I walk through the chalet, which has traces of Brianna all over it. Her clothes are strung everywhere, but I don't mind it. I like seeing her things in my space.

I'm about to turn my attention to the dishes as I wait for her, but a note on the counter catches my attention. I pick it up and read it. *So hot I thought I'd cool down.*

My pulse jumps in my chest, and I can't help but smile as I set the paper down. As my mind races with possibilities, I remove a tie from the closet, shove it into my pocket, and hurry back outside. I lock up and practically run to the path that leads up the mountain, to my favorite, off-the-beaten-path swimming spot. In my hurry I trip over a few tree roots and scare a bunny out from beneath the underbrush.

"Sorry, little guy," I say, need pulsing through me.

Humming reaches my ears as I approach the small lake, and my cock thickens in my shorts. I stand back from the edge of the pond, take pleasure in the sight of Brianna swimming and humming. I grin, loving this game she's encouraging me to play with her.

Play we will.

"What do you think you're doing?" I ask in a harsh tone.

She gasps at the sound of my voice and sinks into the water, up to her chin. "I could ask the same of you," she says.

"You're in my spot." I glance at her clothes on the ground and bend to pick up her panties.

"I don't see your name on it," she says. She feigns

anger and points to the slip of lace in my hands. "And put my clothes back." I spin the panties on my finger for a moment, then shove them into my pocket. "Hey, put those back."

"You want them, come and get them."

"I'm naked," she announces with a lift of her chin, portraying an innocence that turns me on even more.

"You were warned what would happen if I found you in my spot," I say, playing along. "I told you I wouldn't be a gentleman next time."

Her breathing changes and she lifts from the water, just enough to expose her nipples. "I'll scream," she announces, her voice deep, sensual.

Heat sparks through me, and my muscles clench. "Go ahead, no one can hear you up here."

Her wet hair falls forward, falls over her creamy skin, as she takes a slow, measured step toward the embankment. "Turn around and I'll get out."

I widen my feet, stand my ground. "No." That one word and the forcefulness behind it brings lust to her eyes. "You're invading my space. You don't get to call the shots."

She huffs at me, and my gaze goes to her beautiful body as she climbs from the water. "Fine, take your spot then," she says and tries to walk past me.

"Where do you think you're going?" I ask and spin her back to face me. Heat crawls into her cheeks, letting me know she's as turned on by this game as I am.

"I—"

Her words fall off as I bend my head, press my

lips to hers and back her up until she's pressed against a smooth rock. I break the kiss and inch back.

"What do you think you're doing?" she asks.

I let my gaze go the length of her, rake down her lush body, which is writhing, beckoning my touch. "Anything I want." I grip her shoulder, turn her and pull my tie from my pocket. Before I secure her wrists, I put my mouth to her ear.

"Trust me?" I ask.

Her chest rises and falls with her heavy breaths. "Yes," she murmurs without any sort of hesitation. The low rumble of her voice vibrates through me and wraps around my dick. For a fast second I feel a measure of guilt. I'd never do anything to hurt her, but I haven't been totally honest. My omission of the truth would shatter her trust in seconds flat.

"Hands behind your back," I say, and when she angles her head to see me, I show her the tie. Her eyes go wide, brim with the hottest flames I've ever seen. This take-charge girl who does things on her terms is excited about me taking care of her body, having my way with her. I'm floored by it, really, and take the responsibility seriously. For a girl who had to do almost everything on her own, it can't be easy to just relinquish all control.

She puts her hands behind her back, and my dick thickens even more at her eagerness. "A pretty girl like you, out in these woods alone, I can't help but think you're looking for trouble."

"Are you trouble?" she rasps, her voice breathless

as I secure her hands, binding them loosely so she
can get free if she wants to, but from the way her
body is quivering, I'm guessing she doesn't.

"Yeah, I'm trouble," I say, putting my mouth
close to her ear to breathe in her sweet scent. It tears
through me, fires every nerve in my body. "And I'm
going to do all kinds of dirty things to you." Once
I have her tied, I turn her to face me and step back,
my gaze raking over her body once again. Her nipples are rock-hard, and my mouth waters for a taste.
"You're cooled off then?" I ask.

"Yes," she says, regarding me with suspicion, all
an act, because this is what she wants.

"What if I told you I was going to make you so
hot, you're going to start panting, begging me to
fuck you?"

"How…how do you plan to do that?" she asks.

Instead of answering, I say, "What if I don't answer your pleas? What if I leave you aching for my
cock, punishment for not listening?"

She gulps, her body quaking with excitement.
"You wouldn't?"

"Open your legs."

"Why?"

"Because I told you to, and you're going to do everything I say." I nod toward her tied arms. "It's not
like you can run."

Her chest rises and falls as she widens her legs,
and I grin at her compliance.

I step up to her, put my hand between her legs and

insert one finger. Our moans merge as her hips jerk forward to force me in deeper. Her tight walls close around me, and my dick throbs against my zipper.

"Hot," I say. "But not hot enough. Not yet, anyway."

"Luca…" she says, and goddammit I love the sound of my name on her tongue.

I pull my finger out and she groans. Reaching over my head I pull my shirt off and drop it onto the ground before her. "On your knees," I command. She goes down, and I tear into my shorts, releasing my dick. "Open your mouth." Her eyes heat even more at my bossy commands as she widens her lips for me. I run my cock over her bottom lip and she whimpers. My God, seeing her on her knees like this, eager to take my cock in her mouth, is a total mind fuck. I feed her my cock, an inch at a time, and she widens her mouth even more. Gripping a fistful of her long, damp hair, I hold on as my cock slides into her throat. She chokes a little and I pull back, but she won't have any of that. She leans into me, and I let loose a groan that frightens a bird in a nearby tree as I slide into her throat.

"Gesù," I murmur as she fucks me with her ravenous mouth. She sucks me in, and I grow impossibly thicker. I give a low, deep groan and she inches back, my tip bobbing in her mouth. She swirls her tongue around my crown and licks the cum from my slit, and then she moans like she's never tasted anything better. The sight of her worshipping my cock and enjoying every second of it stirs the want that I have for this woman. She continues to pleasure me, and I tug on her hair. "Brianna," I murmur. If she doesn't soon stop, I'm going to come down her throat and right now my dick wants—no, needs—to be inside her body.

I pull my dick from her mouth, bend down and help her to her feet. She wobbles a little and I hold her to me, and her glazed eyes flicker to my shirt as I retrieve it and toss it over my shoulder. After a quick glance around I find the perfect log to bend her over. I guide her to it, toss my top back on the ground and remove my shorts, laying them over the rough bark to protect her body from injury.

"On your knees, ass in the air," I command, and she drops to the ground, understanding exactly how I plan to take her—like a goddamn animal in heat. She obliges and I take a minute to look at her. Wide-open and bare. Totally handing herself over to me. She's so perfect, and no way could I leave her hanging, begging for my cock. No, this woman, well, I want to give her everything she never knew she wanted. Those dirty words were just to heighten her arousal.

I drop down behind her, run my hand along her back and then go lower to squeeze her beautiful ass. She wiggles and I nearly shoot my load off. I run my hand between her legs and brush my finger over her wet clit to prepare her for my girth. She moves against me, her sweet ass swaying as she takes what she needs. I slide a finger into her, and she bucks against me, so damn ready for me to slam home.

"More," she cries out, and I grip my cock, stroke it a few times and position it at her hot entrance.

I give her my crown. "Is this what you want?" I ask as her fingers twist in the binds behind her back.

"Yes," she murmurs. "I want all of you inside of me. Fuck me, please. Hard. Punish me for invading your spot."

I grip her hips for leverage, curl my body into hers and then drive high inside her. Breath leaves my lungs in a whoosh as her tight channel squeezes me, messes with my ability to take this slow, draw it out and savor the moment.

But the way she's moving, the dirty words on her tongue, well, a man only has so much control. I pull out and slam back home, hard, punishing, blunt strokes so raw and needy, it's all I can do to hang on. In seconds her hot release is coating my throbbing dick, and my balls tighten.

"That's it, fuck me just like that," she groans, as she unleashes the animal in me. When I said she might find herself up against the Big Bad Wolf, I wasn't kidding. Everything about this setup has brought out the beast in me. Then again maybe it's because I know our time is almost up, and I've yet to get my fill of her, yet to get deep enough into her body. *Gesù*, will I survive this?

She begins panting, crying, and I pound into her,

giving her everything, every part of me until I'm lost in her, so lost I'm not sure I'll ever find my way out.

My eyes fall shut, suddenly overwhelmed with the intensity of our lovemaking, the loss of control that's come over me. But when it comes to Brianna, this is all too much…yet not nearly enough. She lets loose a keening cry and comes again, all over my cock, and euphoria surges inside me as my orgasm approaches.

"I'm there," I say. "I'm going to fill your beautiful body with my cum."

"Yes, I want that."

I let go and spurt high inside her, liking that I'm leaving a part of me in her when we finish here. My cock spasms again and again, pleasure rocketing through me as I hold her body to mine, never wanting to let her go, never wanting this moment to end. I hug her for a long time, and neither one of us seems to be in a hurry to move. My cock grows flaccid inside her and I sense she needs to get off her knees.

"You okay?" I whisper in her ear as I lift her and untie her hands.

She slides her arms around me. "I'm… My God, Luca. That was… What was that?"

I laugh. "That was a game and it was insanely hot."

"I need to play games more often," she says, her lips turning up into a sexy grin.

While I don't deny that's true, I hate the thought of

her playing these kinds of games with someone other than me. I grab my clothes, lay them on the ground and then I settle her on them. I spread out beside her, the two of us naked, completely bare as we stare up at the sky and catch our breaths. She rolls into me, places her cheek on my chest. My heart pounds hard as she trails her finger over my damp flesh, curls the tip of it around my nipple. I cup her chin, bring her mouth to mine. I kiss her softly, passionately, and her moan of satisfaction fills me with a new kind of need that I shouldn't let myself feel.

Goddammit, deep down I knew that after one taste, she'd ruin me for any other girl. I never should have touched her, kissed her, played sexy games with her. No, I should have stayed strong and kept my distance.

I totally fucked everything up.

CHAPTER THIRTEEN

Brianna

LEANING AGAINST THE BAR, I take a sip of my champagne as my gaze roams around the rooftop lounge. A mountain breeze rolls in through the open windows, and off in the distance, high above the snow peaks, darkness falls over St. Moritz. My mood should be high, euphoric even, but instead it matches the somber night sky. Amber steps up beside me. She's saying something but my brain is on hyperdrive and my stomach is knotted so tightly, I'm having a hard time focusing.

After our lovemaking all afternoon, Luca has been acting a little distant. Both emotionally and physically. I'm not sure what's come over him, but there's definitely something wrong. Maybe this is his way of telling me he's done pretending. We did after all agree to one week, and with the wedding ceremony taking place tomorrow afternoon, most will be preparing to return home, to their real lives.

The thought of going back to divorce court sits heavily on my shoulders. Maybe Luca was right. Maybe it's not too late for me to try something else. I can't deny that he was right about other things, too. Things like the fact that I *can* be with a guy for more than one night, that I might just want a family of my own. I had so much fun sitting around the table, playing board games the other night, it's not something I'm ready to turn my back on. I think back to the young Luca from Oxford. I spent years hating him, but he's not that guy who hurt me. He's grown, changed, has become a caring man who's treated me to surprises, cooked for me, taken me to heights of pleasure I've never before known. Would he have done all that if he didn't care about my well-being? I think not. Which makes his sudden distance all the more confusing.

Amber says something again, and I turn to her. It was fun spending time earlier today with the girls at the spa and getting to know Summer's friends better. I really don't get much girl time, or have that many girlfriends, so it was a special day for me.

"I'm sorry, what was that?" I ask.

"Who's the cutie Tate and Luca are talking to?"

My gaze slides to my two favorite guys again, and I smile when I see that my cousin Alec has joined them. "That's Alec. He couldn't get here until today."

"Where have you guys been hiding him?" she asks with a smack of her lips.

I laugh at that. "Watch yourself with that one, Amber. He'll eat you alive."

She takes a long swallow of her champagne and then grins at me. "Well now, that just makes me all the more interested." I laugh at that. "Is he a lawyer, too?" she asks.

"No. Worse," I say, and she snorts.

"What could be worse... Oh wow, who's *that* guy?" she asks, getting sidetracked as she points to the guy sauntering into the room like he owns it.

"That's cousin Will. Alec's younger brother." I wave to him and he gives me a *GQ* smile as he comes my way. Behind him, in walks Tate's father, Uncle Don, and his much-younger wife.

Amber gives a low, slow whistle. "Did your family win the gene pool or something?"

I laugh at that. If only she knew the battles I had with weight when I was younger. She wouldn't think so then.

"Bri," Will says and bends down to kiss me on the cheek. He takes my hand, stands back and looks me over. "Still the most beautiful woman in the room, I see."

I whack him. "Oh, cut it out." I roll my eyes at Amber. "Don't believe anything he says." But that's when I catch the way Luca is watching us. I meet his gaze, and we stare at each other. For a second I think he's going to come over, take me into a back room somewhere and go wild on me, like he did the night I was dancing with Jared.

Why did he do that? Was it for show, to let everyone know I was his possession? Or did it stem from something else, something like jealousy? If so, could that mean he feels more for me, too? After our staring contest, he tears his gaze away and goes back to talking to Tate and Alec, and a giant lump fills my throat.

"Oh, I'm so sorry," I say as Will and Amber wait for an introduction. "Amber, this is my cousin Will. Will, this is Amber—she's Summer's bridesmaid."

As the two begin to talk, Granddad comes up to me, his friend Deloris on his arm. "Found my plus-one for the wedding," he says with a cheeky grin.

"Hi, Deloris. Nice to see you again," I say and take her frail hand in mine. It's nice to see that Granddad has found someone to keep him company. And she's not half his age like Uncle Don's new wife. I wonder when I'll be settling their divorce. I nearly laugh at that, even though it's not at all funny. No, a breakup is never funny, which is why I always avoided anything serious…until now.

"Where's your plus-one?" Granddad asks.

I fake a smile. "We're not joined at the hip, Granddad." I point. "He's over there, talking to Tate and Alec."

Granddad turns, stares at the men for a good long moment. When he looks back at me, his astute blue eyes moving slowly over my face. I catch a hint of worry lingering in the depths. I stiffen, my back pressing into the oak bar top. Oh God, is he onto us? Does he know we've just been pretending?

He glances at his watch. "Well, we must go mingle. Then I'd like to turn in early." He grins at Deloris, and I shake my head. I do not want to know the details of their relationship.

"Night, Granddad," I say and give him a kiss on the cheek.

I finish the champagne in my glass and take in the long length of Luca, who looks incredibly handsome in his suit. Is he ever going to talk to me tonight? Then again maybe he's waiting for me to go to him. I push off the bar, but that's when Summer comes over, a big smile on her face, oblivious to the storm raging between Luca and me.

"You ready?" she asks.

I rack my brain. What the heck am I supposed to be ready for? Oh right, girls' night. "You bet," I say, injecting enthusiasm into my voice that I don't feel. This is Summer's week and I refuse to let my emotions ruin anything for her.

She waves Amber and Cara over, and they excuse themselves from the men they were talking to. "I'm so happy I get to spend tonight with my girls," Summer says and links her arm in mine. "Champagne, facials and chick flicks," she says as she leads us toward the bank of elevators.

I take a quick look over my shoulder and find Luca watching me. When my eyes meet his, he tears his gaze away, and it hits like a slap to the face. I honestly have no idea what's going on with him. The only thing I know is what's going on with me.

I've fallen hard for a man I thought I hated.

We take the elevator to our floor. Apparently all the guys are staying in the suites one level up from us. Summer hands us key cards to our respective rooms.

"I love you guys, but I need my own bed when we go to sleep."

Amber laughs at that. "That's so you can get your snore on without anyone throwing socks at you to shut you up."

Summer laughs. "I do not snore."

"The last time you came to Palo Alto to visit me and we shared a room, you woke up with twelve pairs of socks on the bed. Are you forgetting why?"

I grin at the two, then let myself into my room. It's beautiful and spacious, but it feels so empty without Luca in it. The bag I'd packed earlier and left with the concierge is on my bed. I open it and pull out the nightshirt I bought the other day. A knock sounds on the adjoining door, and I open it to find Cara there. I look through her adjoining door and see Summer popping a bottle of champagne in the honeymoon suite.

"Get in your pajamas and get in here," Summer says.

"I'll be right there," I say and pull my phone from my purse. The only messages awaiting me are from work, and I'm in no mood to deal with them right now. I drop the phone and head into the bathroom, walking by my plum bridesmaid dress hanging in the closet. I strip off my little black dress, and I exhale slowly. Dammit, this is so not the way I wanted it to come off my body tonight. The nightgown wisps over my skin as I slide into it, and I gather my dress and toss it onto the bed.

All the girls are dressed in pajamas when I meet them, and I put on my best smile. Summer falters for a minute as she hands me a glass of champagne.

"Everything okay?" she asks.

"Fine," I say and then take a big sip.

Cara grabs the remote and flips through the stations as Amber looks through the packages of facials.

"Everything okay with you and Luca?" she asks, lowering her voice.

I tug on the collar of my nightgown. "Perfect."

She steps a little closer to me. "You two barely spoke tonight."

"Busy night celebrating." I lift my glass of champagne.

A long pause and then, holding no punches, she asks, "Are you going to tell him how you feel?" Leave it to Summer to see right through me.

I glance down for a second, my mind going a million miles an hour as I think about everything that's happened this week, and where Luca and I are now. "Summer, it's not like that. I don't think… Look, he was just helping me out."

"You say that, and it might have started that way,

but have you seen the way he looks at you?" My heart leaps at that. Is it possible that there really could be more between us? "You like him. He likes you. I think before this week is up, you two need to talk. It's that simple."

Nothing about this is simple, but I nod because she's right. We do need to talk. Am I really going to just let this week end? Even back in college, when I was an insecure, overweight girl, I still found the courage to talk to Luca. Albeit liquid courage, but courage nonetheless. Then again look how that turned out. But we're not college kids anymore, and I'd be a damn fool to leave here without at least finding out how he feels.

With a renewed sense of purpose, and a bubble of hope welling up inside me, I lift my champagne glass to Summer. "I will talk to him," I say. "Tomorrow, after the ceremony."

"Good." She taps her glass with mine. "Somehow these things always have a way of working out. Oh, hang on." She crosses the room and comes back with a suit jacket. "Can you give this to Luca tomorrow? I keep forgetting." I take the jacket and put it over my arm.

"Well, you do have a lot on your mind," I say, then lean in to hug her. "I'm so glad you're going to be my cousin-in-law. I couldn't have found anyone better, and you make Tate so happy." I pull back and Summer has tears in her eyes. I wipe mine away and hurry back to my room for a second, to toss

Luca's jacket over a chair, and to quickly pull myself together. Honest to God, I'm not normally such an emotional person, but this week has been like a roller-coaster ride. Before I set his jacket down, I bring it to my nose and inhale his familiar scent. Warmth moves through me, and my heart beats a little bit faster. I'm so crazy about this guy, it's insane. I just pray to God he feels the same way about me.

I get myself in order, then go back to find the girls have settled on *Made of Honor*. It's one of my favorite romantic comedies, so I grab a seat in the big love chair and stretch out to watch it. We drink more champagne, stop the movie a million times to gab, and by the time it finishes, it's past midnight. Summer stretches out and yawns.

"We'd better let you get some sleep. Don't want bags under your eyes when you walk down the aisle tomorrow," Cara says.

We all say good-night, and I make my way back to my room. I wash up, brush my teeth and check my phone again. Still nothing from Luca. Tomorrow, though. Tomorrow after the wedding we're going to have a talk. I crawl between the sheets and spread out in the big king-size bed. My hand snakes across and emptiness engulfs me when I find the other side cold. It's almost scary how much I've grown accustomed to crawling into bed with Luca every night, and more important, waking up with him each morning. I smile as I envision us doing that until we're Granddad's age.

I close my eyes, and sleep pulls at me. Just as I'm about to doze off, a soft knock comes from the main door. My heart leaps into my throat and I sit up in the dark room. Could it be who I think it is?

CHAPTER FOURTEEN

Luca

I SHOULDN'T BE HERE. I shouldn't be doing this. But I can't seem to help myself. I'm not sure what tomorrow brings, or even if we have a next week. I only know that tonight I need Brianna in my arms more than I need breath in my lungs.

The door inches open, and the heat that moves into her eyes wraps around my heart and lets me know how much she wants me inside her again.

"Brianna," I whisper as she melts into me. She opens her mouth to speak, but I'm right there, my lips on hers, kissing her deeply, devouring her mouth like a man denied the pleasure too long. Her tongue plays with mine, and in the dark room a small lamp casts soft shadows in the corner. I back her up and kick the door shut behind us.

She moans into my mouth and it's all the encouragement I need. I pick her up, carry her to the bed and gently set her down. She sits there quietly as I tear off my suit jacket, remove my tie and unbutton my shirt. I shrug out of it, and she reaches for my pants. I touch her face, run my hands through her hair as she releases the button and opens the zipper.

My cock springs free, and her little whimper of need strokes my aching balls. With my dress pants dangling around my knees, she draws my cock into her mouth like she's been starved of it for too long. She works her mouth and hands over me, the slide of her tongue a thing of beauty against my throbbing appendage. I push her hair from her shoulders to watch, and my breath catches in my throat at her beauty. No woman on the face of this earth will ever be able to touch my heart the way this one has.

Needing to get my mouth on her, I ease my cock from her lips and give her a little nudge. She falls backward, her arms splayed on the mussed sheets. I take in her beauty, the long mess of her hair, as I kick off my pants and drop to my knees. Driven by need, I grab her legs, put them around my shoulders and shove her nightgown to her stomach to give me better access to the spot my mouth intends to ravage.

Her breath hitches, and her soft, sexy moans of pleasure cut the silence of the room as I take her clit into my mouth. I suck and nibble until she's wet and squirming, moving in all the sexy ways that toy with my arousal. I deepen the kiss, slide one finger inside her tight opening and fuck her with it, loving the little gasping sounds she makes. She's so goddamn responsive to my touch, her muscles begin a slow tremor, a telltale sign she's right where I want her. Needing her desire on my tongue, I change the pace and tempo, forcing her over the edge, even if she's desperately dangling by her fingertips. If only I could bind her, keep her in this bed with me forever and forget that there's a real world out there, forget that there's a different world calling each of us, pulling us in opposite directions.

"Ooh," she breathes out as she explodes on my tongue, coming and coming and coming like we haven't been having sex like two hormonal teenagers all week. Her pussy shudders against my lips, and I continue to eat at her, wanting all her cum in my mouth, determined to taste her on my tongue a week from now.

I work my mouth over her and run my hands along her hips as her quakes subside, but soon enough I plan to have her break for me again. She goes up on her elbows, her chest heaving as I climb up her body, pressing hot, wet openmouthed kisses to her sweet-smelling flesh. I take her nightgown with me, pulling it to her shoulders and lifting her slightly to remove it all the way.

Gazing at her nakedness, the way she so readily opens for me, I toss the nightgown aside and pay homage to her marbled nipples. She moves beneath my ministrations, her body so damn alive from my touch, it does the craziest things to me. Need like I've never before felt tugs at me, and I draw her tight peaks in deeper, my palms on her breasts, massaging them gently. Everything I feel for her burns through me, intensifies when she places her hands on my shoulders, drags her nails across my skin. Tomorrow the marks will remind me of this profound moment.

I move up her body, bury my face in the hollow of her throat, kiss her earlobe, her eyes and nose, before finding her sweet mouth again. She widens her legs, and my cock presses against her hot center, and even though I'm desperate, I need to touch her all over first.

I turn her over, shove a pillow under her hips until her sweet ass is in the air. I run my hands over her back, the beads of her spine, until I reach her backside. I massage her lush cheeks, knead them between my fingers until she's crying out for more. Parting her cheeks, I lightly rub her puckered passage until I'm near the point of breaking, coming all over her trembling body. I lean over her, kiss her shoulders, her back, and run my tongue along her ass. While it would be easy to take her like this, fuck her hot pussy with her ass up in the air, I need to see her face when she comes all over my cock. I drop to the mattress, flat out on my back, and reach for her.

Understanding what I want, she sits up and tosses one leg over my body. I hold her hips, and my cock is like a missile as she lowers herself onto me.

"Cazzo," I cry out as she takes every inch into her body. Her head rolls back, and I cup her breasts as she wiggles like she's trying to get me balls-deep.

I capture her hips, lift her up and down, moving

her slowly so I can savor this moment, burn it in my brain for later. As I lose myself in her, give her a part of myself I've never given another, my dick swells even more. Half-lidded eyes, steeped in desire, meet mine. Adrenaline pulses through my veins, and I take her a bit faster, powering into her with hard, blunt strokes, until she's dripping down my thighs.

As my cock pulses, drenched in her liquid desire, my balls scream for release, but I struggle to hang on, wanting to wring one more orgasm out of her. I wrap my arms around her and shift until she's on the mattress beneath me. I brush her hair from her forehead and search her eyes. Warmth, openness and honesty wrapped in a hint of vulnerability stare back, and my heart squeezes. This woman deserves the world, and I want to be the man to give it to her. I move inside her, slow my pace, and she puts her hands on my cheeks as a whimper climbs out of her throat. Minutes pass, and time slows as I kiss her mouth, her shoulder, the two of us moving together in perfect sync. Our lovemaking is a little softer this time, a little slower than it was moments ago, with everything in what we're doing holding a great amount of meaning.

Passion and desire swirl around us, pull me into a vortex of need. I press my dick in higher, slide my body against hers as I reach between us to stroke her clit. A weening cry catches in her throat and once again she's exploding on my cock, soaking my entire length. I clench down on my jaw as her muscles bunch, squeeze, seduce an orgasm out of me. Unable to get any closer or deeper, I press my mouth to hers and give myself over to the pleasure, filling her in my release. We cling to each other, hold on like it could very well be our last night. My throat tightens, hurts like it's been scraped raw as I press down on her. We stay like that for a long time, and when she shifts I fear I just might be crushing her. I slide off her to give her air, but she reaches out for me.

"Luca," she moans, her body boneless, spent, completely sated from our lovemaking.

I roll her to her side, facing away from me. "Sleep," I say and shuffle in close, needing the contact, the feel of her naked body against mine. I hug her to me, flesh to flesh, and when her breathing changes and she falls asleep, I quietly pull away. I ease from the bed, dress in the dim light and take one look at the girl who stole my heart. The girl I want desperately to make mine but can't.

So what the fuck am I going to do about that?

CHAPTER FIFTEEN

Brianna

I'M NOT SURE what last night was about, but after waking up, my body sore and my heart full, I can't stop smiling. I love that Luca couldn't stay away, that he needed to be with me as much as I needed to be with him. It's true we have to talk, and I wanted to last night, but I didn't want to break the magical spell between us. And when it came right down to it, Luca didn't appear to be in the mood for talking.

I kick my sheets off and stretch out. Noise comes from the other side of the adjoining door. I guess everyone is up but me. Probably because they weren't up having the best sex of their life last night. Glancing at myself in the mirror, I try to wipe the smirk from my face. I'm not up to answering a million and one questions. No way would Amber let it go. But then another thought hits. When I talk to Luca, I have to be completely honest with him, and that means telling him I knew exactly who he was when we were introduced, and why I seduced him. Will he laugh it off, or be angry that I would do something so juvenile? I hurry to the bathroom, make myself somewhat presentable and brush my teeth before meeting the girls.

"What's all the commotion in here," I ask as I open the adjoining door. "You'd think someone was having a party."

"Just in time," Amber says and pours me a mimosa.

"This is going to go straight to my head," I say and make my way to the tray of food that must have been delivered earlier. I pick up a strawberry, pop it into my mouth and reach for a muffin. I don't usually eat like this, but…

Summer comes out of the bathroom in her pajamas, looking happy, radiant and a bit jittery, as one would on her wedding day. I smile at her, so happy for her and Tate.

I glance at Cara, who is sitting on the bed, sipping her drink and flipping the pages of the newspaper.

"Hair and makeup will be here within the hour," Summer says. "Until then we can relax. Although I'm finding that hard to do."

I settle onto the sofa and nibble on my muffin. Beside me, Cara chuckles. I glance over at her as Amber and Summer talk hairstyles.

"What's up?"

"This guy. What a douchebag. His name is Marco L. Marino, from Massara, Italy." My mind races—

Luca's last name is Marino—as she glances up at me. "I think the *L* must stand for loser."

"What did he do?" I ask and stand to sit beside her. Is it possible he's related to Luca? She shuffles over and I sit cross-legged next to her on the bed.

"He got caught having sex with his kid's nanny, who is barely legal." She angles the paper for me to see, and I scan the article. Something niggles in the back of my brain and I grab on to it. "I know this guy. When I was at Oxford, he was all over the news—some sex-club thing and crashing a yacht." Luca and I talked about it when he told me where he was from. I take a look at the elderly man with Marco as he steers them away from the paparazzi. The gentleman, who appears mortified, is most likely his father, considering their similar features.

"When did this happen?" I ask.

"Yesterday's paper," she says, and flips the page. I make a mental note to bring it up with Luca when I get the chance.

I finish my muffin and mimosa as I pour over the pages with Cara. When we're done, I slide from the bed. "I'd better jump in the shower before the stylist arrives," I say.

"Same," Cara says, and we go to our respective rooms. I hurry to the shower and run my hands over my body, reminiscing about the way Luca touched me last night, and hoping that come tonight, after our talk, he'll be touching me again.

But what if he doesn't want the same things?

I reach for the shampoo and shut down those thoughts. Today's wedding is about love and happiness, and I refuse to let any negative thoughts ruin it.

By the time I finish showering and tug on a robe, the makeup artists and hairstylists are here. I go back to Summer's suite, and for the next couple of hours, all four of us get prettied up for the wedding.

Our lunch is delivered, and after we eat, it's nearing Summer and Tate's one o'clock ceremony. I carefully slide into my plum dress, and Amber zips it for me. After giving myself a once-over in the mirror, I glance at Summer in her white dress. Tears pool in my eyes.

"Do not cry," she warns. "If you cry, I'll cry and I don't want my mascara running down my face when I marry my Prince Charming."

We all laugh at that and my heart misses a beat. How many times has Luca asked me about Prince Charming? Never in my entire life did I think I'd find one for myself, or that he'd be a guy I thought was so different at first.

"Limo is here," Cara says. It's not far to walk to the outdoor gazebo, but it's hot and sticky and we want to look our best when we arrive. We all pile into the elevator and go quiet, an excited, nervous energy about us. We reach the lobby, and outside, the long stretch limo is waiting, the driver holding the door open for us. We all slide in, and my stomach feels like I'm about to go skydiving. I'm not sure what I'm more excited about: the wedding or setting eyes on Luca in his tux.

After a short drive, we step from the car, and inside the glassed-in gazebo, I search the gathering crowd for Luca and find him standing with Tate and talking to the minister. My heart misses a beat as I admire him from afar. As if feeling my eyes on him, he angles his head and our gazes lock. His eyes narrow, and he scrubs a hand over his clean-shaven chin. I take in his stance, the tightness in his body. I know that look. He was acting the same way at last night's cocktail party. He's agitated about something, that much I know. Is he nervous about standing up there in front of the guests? I know I'm anxious about walking down the aisle and doing a face-plant. Or is something else entirely bothering him?

I don't currently have time to think about it, as we're all arranged, ready to walk down the aisle. A couple of guests stop to take a picture of us as we head inside, and we all slowly make our way to the altar. I smile and concentrate on putting one foot in front of the other. Tate smiles at me, and I return it and then look to Luca, who is staring at me with heat in his eyes. For a minute I envision I'm the bride and he's waiting up there for me. My heart rushes a little faster, and I'm certain my cheeks have turned a deeper shade of pink.

I take my place, and Cara stands beside me. Amber comes down next, and after she positions herself, the music changes and everyone stands. I glance at Tate and hear an audible gasp as his beautiful bride makes her way toward him. With a tight throat, and tears threatening, I gaze at Summer in her gown, her arm on Granddad's. With no family of her own, she asked my grandfather to walk her down the aisle, and as I look at him now, a huge smile on his face, I'm so happy she did. Will he give me away to Luca someday? With that thought pinging around inside my brain, I turn my head and find Luca staring at me. I draw my bottom lip between my teeth and turn to the minister when Summer takes her position.

The guests sit, and the minister begins the ceremony. I hold my flowers tighter, the sweet scent teasing my senses as the vows and rings are exchanged. Tate leans in for a kiss, and we all clap. The newlyweds turn, huge smiles on their faces as they walk out, and we all follow. The next hour races by in a blur as we get pictures taken in the gardens. I need to talk to Luca, but now is not the time or place. It will have to wait until the reception later on.

Soon enough we're all back in the Raydolins' ballroom, seated around the head table, with our meals being served. I make small talk to Cara and Amber, and nibble on my food even though I don't have much of an appetite. I'm both excited and nervous to talk to Luca, to find out where we go from here.

After the cake is served and the dishes are cleared, the lights dim, and Summer and Tate make their way to the dance floor. I sniff back the tears as the newlyweds hold one another, begin their new life to a beautiful song. The waltz ends, and Summer calls everyone to the dance floor. I sit back for a second, and when Summer and Tate come my way, I give them both a big hug.

"I need to change," Summer says.

"I can help," I say.

"That would be great." She gives Tate a kiss.

"Hurry back," he says. "I have plans for us."

"I can't wait," Summer says.

"Get a room already," I tease, and Tate laughs.

"That's the plan," he says.

I help Summer with her train as we head to our rooms, and once we get inside, I work all the tiny buttons free on the back of her dress. She slides out of it, and I hang it for her as she slips into her going-away dress.

"You look beautiful," I say.

"So do you. I can't believe Luca hasn't torn that dress off you by now."

I laugh at that and catch my reflection in the mirror.

"You go on down. I'm going to freshen up a bit," I say, wanting to look my best for when I talk to Luca. I go through the adjoining door and reach for my makeup case on the dresser, but when I do I notice the little piece of white paper sticking out of Luca's jacket pocket. The jacket Summer had been meaning to give him.

Excited and thinking he left me a note last night—since I've left a couple for him—I pull it out, but the bottom drops out of my world when I read the plea scribbled on the page. I back up until my knees hit the bed, and I fall onto the mattress. Tears prick my eyes, and I try to breathe but can't seem to fill my lungs. I swipe at my face, sure I'm misreading this, sure that Luca doesn't have to return to Italy, to his fiancée, and marry before his thirtieth birthday, taking his rightful position as duke—or his father's conglomerates will go to his cousin.

What. The. Hell.

I lift my head, gaze around the room, recalling the way he came to me last night, making sweet love to me on this very bed. Could I have been so wrong about him? Could he still be that same selfish, arrogant guy I met at Oxford? I shake the letter in my hand and read it for the third time. Is this some kind of joke?

Desperate for answers, I run to the bathroom, fix my face and grab Luca's suit jacket before heading back down to the dance, determined to find Luca and get to the bottom of matters. I tap a restless foot, but the elevator seems slower than usual, and when I finally reach the main lobby, I step off. My footsteps slow when off in a corner—like he doesn't want to be seen—I catch a glimpse of Luca and a man who looks familiar. Why do I feel like I know him? I blink once, twice and then suddenly the tumblers fall into place. Holy shit! It's the man from the newspaper. The elderly gentleman escorting Marco L. Marino to his car. They must all be related.

My heart leaps into my throat and a noise beside me draws my attention. I turn to find Granddad coming my way, his cane hitting the ground with a monstrous thud with each hurried step.

"Brianna," he says, deep concern edging his cloudy eyes.

"Granddad," I say and turn back to see Luca, take in the concern etched on his face. His head lifts, and he goes stiff when he sees me with his jacket draped over my arm, his letter in my hand.

He stands, and so does the man with him, and I don't even realize my feet are moving, crossing the wide expanse of marble, until we're face-to-face.

I open my mouth to speak but stop when he says, "I can explain." He takes the letter from me. "My father, his will—" he begins, but the man with him cuts him off.

"Luca, I'll be in the rental outside, waiting," the elderly gentleman says. He nods at me, turns to say something in Italian to Luca and then walks off, his gait tired, crooked, much like Granddad's.

I stare at Luca and realize he's not denying what's in the letter; he's trying to explain it. I take that moment to wrap my brain around everything that's happened between us, from our college days until this very moment, and what it all means.

Luca is a duke, has a fiancée waiting for him in Massara, and nothing between us was real, not back at Oxford and not here in the Alps. He wasn't falling for me; he was just having sex. The fact that he has a girl waiting for him makes him a two-timing jerk. I've had one too many of those in my life already.

"Brianna—"

I hold my hand up to stop him. "You don't need to explain anything." I force out a laugh, determined to portray indifference. "Don't you get it?" I ask.

He reaches for me and I inch away, unable to have his hands on me. "Brianna," he says. "Listen to me."

"No, you listen to me. I know who you are, Luca. We met back at Oxford, at a party."

His head drops, and he nods. Jesus, so all along he knew who I was, too.

"I was wondering why you were pretending you didn't know me," he says.

A laugh bubbles in my throat, and it comes out almost manic. "Oh, because I was just playing with you. The same way you played with me that night."

His brow furrows as he stares at me. "What are you talking about?"

"Give me a break," I say and roll my eyes. "Have fun with the pudgy freshman, pretend you like her, walk her home and close the door in her face. I bet you and the guys had a good laugh over that."

He steps toward me, and I take a measured step back, tears pounding against the back of my eyes. "Brianna, you don't understand—"

I poke his chest and wish I hadn't touched him. "No, Luca, what you don't understand is I set this up as payback. That first night at your spot." I do air quotes around *spot* as heartache wells up inside me.

I'm not normally spiteful or mean—then again I've been doing a lot of things this week that I've never done before—but I strike back with, "I decided to seduce you, take you back to your place and leave you hanging." I give a casual shrug even though there is a storm going on inside my stomach, tossing the contents around and making me nauseated. "Then I thought, why not just use him for sex. Take from him now what I thought I was going to get from him back then."

His shoulders sag, and his lips part, his eyes dark, pained. The sound of him swallowing as he digests my words curls around me. "Are you serious? This was all a game to you?"

"Of course it was." I wave a dismissive hand. "So go, marry your fiancée. Or don't. I don't care one way or another." I shove his jacket into his arms, and with my head held high I float past him on my heels. Fearing I'll never make it to the elevator before the floodgates open, I walk back into the dimly lit ballroom and search for a quiet, dark corner where I can give myself a good, hard lecture and cry my eyes out in private.

CHAPTER SIXTEEN

Luca

IN MY LATE father's study, I pace to the window and pull back the curtain to see my mother tending to the weeds in one of her many flower beds. Tall trees line the long driveway of our massive family estate, and bright flowers burst from the gardens throughout. But not even the vibrantly colored foliage, or the bright sunshine feeding them, can lighten my mood.

Brianna was playing a game with me?

I've been home for a little over ten days, and I still can't wrap my brain around that truth, still can't quite loosen the knot in my gut. While one part of me is angry, there is another part that tells me I have no right to be. I kept things from her, too, important things.

A dark car slowly crawls up the driveway, and my mom stands to wave to my uncle Gio. It shouldn't have surprised me when he showed up at the wedding that night, begging me to come back sooner rather than later. After Marco's latest antics, which were splashed in every newspaper, Gio needed me home, taking my rightful place at the head of the family so I could get things in order and prepare for his retirement.

I drop the curtain and pace around the room. I glance around, and my father's presence hits like a physical blow. Grief presses down on me, heavy, suffocating, squeezing the air from my lungs. I miss him, goddammit. I miss my brother, too. As I catalogue the room, my throat tightens, and I fist my hands, shove them into my pants.

This office has been waiting for me to stand up and be the man everyone needs me to be. I want to live up to my dad's expectations. Make him proud. But how the hell can I do it without the woman I love beside me? Dad was a free thinker, a man who stood up for what he believed in, even if it went against tradition. Putting a stipulation like marriage on his surviving son makes no sense to me, doesn't seem like the sort of thing he'd do at all. None of this adds up.

As I think about that—and something niggles in the back of my mind, something just out of reach— Uncle Gio comes into the office. He'd been looking into the marriage clause, trying to find a way around it. Even if he does, the only woman I really want with me has been playing a revenge game, payback for something she thinks I did.

But was it really all a game to her?

There is a part of me that doesn't believe that. How could a woman touch and kiss the way she did if deeper feelings weren't involved? She even did special things to please me, like a day kiteboarding when she feared it herself. Something isn't adding up there, either.

As Uncle Gio takes the chair on the other side of the desk, my thoughts once again wander to Brianna. My heart beats a little faster, pounds harder against my rib cage. I love her. I love her so goddamn much, it hurts. I pinch my eyes shut, recall the adventures we took, the games we played, the way she touched me, kissed me. The way her body opened up for me, welcomed me in like we were made for each other.

We are made for each other.

I slowly open my eyes, and the frown on Uncle Gio's face is a good indication that he's not been able to find a way around the marriage clause.

"I'm sorry, Luca," he says. "It's ironclad. Marco and I went over the details these last few days. Your fiancée is aware that you are home, and she's waiting for you."

"Why did she even agree to this?"

"I'm sure her father pushed her to do the right thing after the reading of the will. He was your father's best friend, and this will make her a duchess."

"It's not the right thing." I lean forward, brace my elbows on the desk and grab a fistful of hair. I pinch my lids shut again and work diligently to find a solution to this. I can't marry some girl when I'm in love with another woman, even if she doesn't reciprocate those feelings. I just can't. As betrayal eats at me, rakes my insides raw and leaves me bleeding, my mother steps into the room. I straighten, not wanting her to see me like this. My gaze meets with dark eyes identical to mine, and I force a smile.

"Your flowers look lovely," I say in a light tone I don't feel.

Mom's eyes narrow, her gaze bobbing back and forth between me and Uncle Gio. "Does someone want to tell me what's going on?"

"Nothing," I say. "Everything is fine."

"Everything is not fine," she says and puts her hands on her hips. "You've been traveling from one place to the other for years, and now you come home and you're miserable."

"I'm not miserable. I just—"

"Do you not want to be here, Luca?"

"I do," I say. "I want to be here. I want to be here for you and make Dad proud. It's just that…"

She takes a step closer, those astute eyes moving over my face. "Who is she?"

"What are you talking about?"

"Who is this woman who has you twisted into knots."

I shake my head. I never could get anything by my mother. "It doesn't matter."

Her lips pinch. "I'd say it does matter."

"There are some…obstacles." Although I'm beginning to second-guess everything, including what

Brianna told me. I can't help but think what started as payback turned into something more. After discovering all my secrets, did she lash out to protect herself? The truth is, I never meant to hurt her at Oxford, and I never meant to hurt her now.

Fight for her. Go to New York. Apologize. If that doesn't work, tie her to the bed until she sees things your way.

But what about obligation?

I do a quick mental tally of my trust fund. If Marco drains the businesses, I could use my personal funds to ensure my mother stays in the family estate, make sure she's taken care of for the rest of her life. I might not be able to do all the charitable work I want, not yet anyway, but if I join a practice I could do some pro bono work and give back to my peerage. My heart beats a little faster as I consider that scenario. It might not be ideal, but it's a solution, at least for now.

Wait, what am I saying?

I'm saying I'm choosing love!

I suck in a fast breath, my adrenaline pumping, urging me to run to the airport and catch the next plane to New York. Fight for the woman I love.

"Do you have any idea how many obstacles stood in the way of your father and me?" she asks. "He was an aristocrat, with certain expectations placed on him. I was the gardener's daughter. We were from different worlds, but despite it all, we weathered the storm and had a beautiful life together."

I scoff. "Then why did he put a stipulation in his will that I marry his friend's daughter?"

My mother's head rears back. "I have no idea what you are talking about." She looks at Gio. "Do you know what he's talking about?"

Gio runs his hand along his balding head and sinks a little into his seat. "He must marry before his thirtieth birthday, or the conglomerates go to Marco. You were too distraught after the accident and weren't in Marco's office when he went over the will with us."

"If you'll excuse me for a moment," she says and disappears from the office.

I glance at Uncle Gio, searching his face for some sort of explanation, but he shrugs. We sit in silence, and a few minutes later my mother comes in with a large envelope, yellowed from age.

"Here," she says and hands it to me.

"What's this?" I ask as I open it and pull out the papers. Uncle Gio sits up a little straighter in his chair and leans over the desk.

"That is your father's will. I was with him when he wrote it up many years ago and signed it in front of me. Believe me, I'd know if he'd changed it. There is no marriage stipulation in it, Luca. I suspect if you take a look at the will Marco showed you, and compare the signatures, you might find some discrepancies."

I flip through the pages, then slowly sink back into my chair, the pieces of the puzzle all falling into place. My eyes meet Uncle Gio's and we both sit there, shocked, staring at one another. I knew something was off, but I didn't think Marco would ever go so far as to forge the will. How could he do this? In my grief over my dad and brother, and then trying to get away from it all, I missed what was happening right in front of me.

"Luca, is this why you've stayed away so long— you thought you had to marry?" my mother asks. I nod, and tears form in her eyes. "We've lost so much time, my child."

I swallow hard. "I just couldn't understand why Dad would want that for me. Why he wouldn't want me to marry for love."

She sits on the edge of the desk and cups my cheeks. "He would want you to marry for love, and if he were here now he'd tell you to go fight for the woman who has you a mess."

I stand, and my chair slides backward. "I have to go."

"Yes, you do. Now go bring that woman back. Do you have any idea how long I've been waiting for a daughter?" she asks, grinning.

I give my mom a hug. "You're going to love her."

"I already do."

I glance into my mother's dark eyes, and as I reminisce about my childhood, my heart fills with all the love I have for her. She is going to spoil Brianna something terrible, and no one deserves it more. "She never really had a mother growing up."

My mother touches my cheek. "Then hurry, because we have a lot to make up for."

I turn to my uncle, and our eyes meet. "Uncle Gio—" I begin.

He holds his hand up, looking pale and a million years older. "I'll deal with my son. He'll be disbarred for this and his hands will never come close to running the conglomerates your father built over the years," he assures me as he shoves the real will back into the envelope. "Now go."

I take a deep breath and let it out slowly. "I'm going, but there is one thing I need before I do."

"You're right. There is," my mother says with a twinkle in her eyes.

I'm not sure what she's alluding to, but the only thing I know is I have to fight for Brianna, convince her how good we can be together. I want to offer her everything she's always wanted. I just pray she's willing to accept it.

CHAPTER SEVENTEEN

Brianna

UMBRELLA IN HAND, I hurry down the sidewalk and check my watch. Dammit, I'm late for dinner. I hate being late, but once again court kept me tied up for hours. Granddad is probably holding dinner for me, which means Tate and Summer are likely starving, too.

I haven't really been avoiding Granddad after St. Moritz; I've just been busy. Tonight he was adamant that I come for dinner, and while I like the idea of it, I don't want to see the worry on his face. Nor do I want him pushing me to call Luca. After the truth came out, he said he understood why I did what I did, even going so far as to take responsibility for it, saying it was his fault for pestering me so much. Despite that, he still won't let up about Luca.

Footsteps pound the pavement on 64th Street as I hurry into Granddad's mansion and shake out my umbrella before closing it. Voices sound from the large dining room, and for a fast second I'm certain I'm hearing things. God, I still can't get Luca's voice out of my head, the scent of his body off my skin—no matter how many times I've scrubbed my flesh raw.

"That you, Bri?" Granddad asks.

"Sorry I'm late," I call out. "I'll just wash up and be right in." I hurry to the bathroom and glance at myself in the mirror. Today was a stressful day—as most of them are—and I look like I'm amped up on Red Bull. I try to smooth my hand over my mussed hair, but it just springs back up again. I wipe under my eyes to remove the mascara that ran down my face in the rain. An almost hysterical laugh catches in my throat. My reflection is identical to the day I got out of the taxi in the Alps. I thought I had no one to impress that night, and look how that turned out.

I wash my hands quickly and leave my hair in a tumbling mess. This time I really don't have anyone to impress. Granddad, Tate and Summer have all seen me at my worst, and they still love me. Then again Luca saw me at my worst that day we re-met, and he still made sweet love to me.

It was sex, Brianna, nothing more.

My shoes tap on the floor as I make my way into the dining room, and my stomach grumbles at the smells coming from the kitchen. Delicious smells that take me back to the time Luca cooked for me. Is someone making carbonara?

Stop thinking about him already.

I round the corner, and my feet come to a resounding halt when I see the extra person seated around the table. No. Frigging. Way.

I swallow, falter, sag against the door frame, my knees going weak beneath me as I glance at my family, as well as the man I hate—love—to find them all staring back. Have I just walked into an intervention or something?

"What is this?" I ask, anger welling up inside me.

Luca stands and his eyes meet mine. "Can we talk?"

"No," I shoot back. "I'm leaving."

"Brianna, please. Wait."

"I don't want to hear any more of your lies," I say, and chairs shuffle as Granddad, Tate and Summer all move into Granddad's study to give us privacy. I turn around, head back to the door, but Luca is right there, so close I can feel his breath on my neck.

He touches my shoulder, and I spin to face him. My heart wobbles when I see the pain in his eyes. Is he hurting as much as I am? *Don't go soft now, Bri.* He's messed with you twice. Don't let him do it again.

"Where's your fiancée? She must be missing her *duke*," I say, and that's when I realize he's wearing his blue Oxford hoodie, which is now two sizes too small. But it does remind me of the sting of his rejection. "Why?" I ask and then touch the cotton, stare at it through watery eyes. "Why are you wearing this?"

"I made a mistake," he says softly.

"You made a lot of them," I shoot back, my stupid voice hitching.

"You remember I once said assumption is the mother of all screwups?"

"I don't want to do this, Luca. I can't." I swallow against the tightness in my throat, the love squeezing my heart. "I just want to go home."

"Can I walk you?"

A laugh bubbles up in my throat. "Is that why you're in this hoodie, so you can walk me home and reenact the night I finally got up the nerve to talk to you?"

"Yes."

I shake my head, hardly able to believe what I'm hearing. "You don't think I've been humiliated enough? Who are you, anyway?"

"I made a mistake back then and I want to rectify it."

"What—"

"Brianna, you know me. Whether you think you do or not, you know me. Do you think I'm the kind of guy who would go to bed with a girl who had as many drinks as you had that night?"

I blink once, twice, and I consider what he's asking. From what I learned about him in St. Moritz, he's not the kind of guy to take advantage of a woman. "No, I guess not."

"You read the whole situation wrong. You made assumptions that weren't true."

Oh God, did I? Was I so insecure about myself

that I assumed I was the butt of a joke and hadn't stopped to think he was just trying to get me home safely. I take in his handsome face, the way he's gazing at me through eyes that look like they haven't had rest in weeks. Had he really been taking care of me? I mull that over for a second and shake my head. I really shouldn't find it so hard to believe now, not after the way he took such care of me during our week in the Alps.

"That week was about more than sex," he says, and reaches out to touch my cheek, brush his thumb lightly over my jaw.

"You said it was about me trying a relationship on for size." I frown up at him. "Why? Why would you do that?"

"You're jaded, for many reasons, but deep down I knew you wanted your own Prince Charming. I wanted you to find him, Brianna. Except it killed me to think about you with any other guy but me."

"You have a fiancée," I whisper, my heart breaking a little more.

"I sure as hell hope I do," he says, and I stumble backward, his words cutting me a little deeper. Catching me by surprise, he gathers me in his arms. "Know this—back at Oxford I wanted to be with you. I wanted you more than I'd ever wanted any other woman. I still do. I left you in your dorm for two reasons—one, you were drinking, and two, I knew if I touched you, made love to you, it would screw me over. You were the one girl, the only girl, who could make me forget my obligations. After my father and brother died, the responsibility of running his million-dollar conglomerates was left to me. I take that very seriously. I want to ensure people stay employed, want to help my peerage, want to make sure my mother stays in her home and see to her well-being. But my father put a stipulation in his will, that I must marry his business partner's daughter by the time I am thirty, or everything goes to my cousin Marco. I only met her once, Brianna. When we were young. I've never even touched her. She can't want this any more than I do."

Fighting back the tears pounding against my eyeballs, I nod and recall Marco's latest antics. No way can he let a guy like that take over the company. He has responsibilities and he needs to live up to them. "Then what are you doing here?" I ask, shocked that I'm not all cried out by now, considering I woke up to a soaked pillow every morning for the last two weeks.

He peels off his hoodie. "I want you to be my girl."

I shake my head and push it away. "That's stupid."

And sweet. So very, very sweet.

Wait!

"Why are you asking me to be your girl when you have a fiancée?"

He drops to his knees and produces a velvet box. "When I said I sure as hell hope I have one, what I was really saying was I hope you say yes and agree to be her. I love you, Brianna. Marry me."

Luca loves me.

I shake my head and fear moves into his eyes. "What about your obligations? You can't let everything go to Marco. I won't let you. Not for me. I could never forgive myself."

He smiles up at me. "That's one of the things I love about you." I gulp, and tears spill down my face. "I chose you, Brianna. I chose love."

I sniff and back up until I hit the wall. "No."

"Even before I knew the will had been tampered with, I chose you."

My heart leaps into my throat. "What? What are you talking about?"

"It seems my cousin, who was Dad's lawyer, put that stipulation in there after Dad died. He knew I would never marry if I wasn't in love, and the businesses would go to him."

"You...you...mean..."

"I love you, and I was going to find another way to take care of my obligations. Now I don't have to, but there is no other woman I want at my side, Brianna."

"No, don't. Don't say it like that."

His brow furrows. "Brianna, please. I love you. I want you. I want you to come to Italy, be my duchess, the daughter my mother always wanted. This is her ring. She already loves you as much as I do."

My throat squeezes so tight at that, it's all I can

do to hold it together. A mother like his is something I've always wanted and never knew I could have.

I wave my hand toward the study. "My family... my work."

"Your family wants this for us. I already asked James for his permission. We can travel back here any time you want to see him, and your work, is it what you really want?"

"No," I say, feeling completely sure of that.

"Together we can do all the things we want," he says. "You can help build schools in third-world countries and champion projects like Artscape."

I drop to my knees, and my gaze goes to the ring. His mother's ring. I've never been more touched.

"Brianna?"

"Don't say it like that," I whisper again, and slowly lift my head until our eyes meet. I smile at him. "If my friends call me Bri, my future husband probably should too, don't you think?"

A huge smile lights up his face, and my heart nearly explodes with the love welling up inside me. His lips find mine, and he kisses me with two weeks' worth of pent-up hunger. I know the feeling.

He breaks the kiss, and he lightly brushes his thumb over my bottom lip. "You remember I won that bike race to the top of the mountain."

"I remember," I say, my voice a breathless whisper.

His grin is sexy, mischievous, and my entire body lights up. "I never did tell you what I wanted."

I laugh, wondering where he's going with this. "What do you want, Luca?" I ask and touch his face.

"Put on that sweater, say yes to my proposal and let me walk you home. Let's reenact that night from Oxford and have it end the way we both wanted it to back then."

I reach for the hoodie and tug it on. When my head pops through the hole, Luca is removing the ring from the box.

"Yes," I say, pushing that one word from my tight throat and holding my shaky hand out for him. Tears pour down my face as he slides the huge diamond solitaire on.

"It's beautiful," I say as he wipes the water from my cheeks.

"You're beautiful," he whispers and drops a tender kiss onto my mouth. I sigh and put my arms around him. I might not have found my Prince Charming, but I found my duke, and that's a million times better.

Luca stands and pulls me up with him. "Let's go," he says.

"Wait." I breathe in, catching lingering scents of dinner. "Did you make carbonara?"

"Yeah. I wanted to do something special for you and your family."

Teasing him, I say, "We should stay and eat it with the others, don't you think? It would be rude just to take off."

He rakes a shaky finger through his hair. "Ah, okay. If that's what you want."

I step into him, feel his erection. Grinning, I go up on my toes and press my lips to his. "No, it's not what I want, and I think Granddad, Tate and Summer will understand."

He exhales a relieved breath, as anxious to be alone with me as I am to be with him. "Thank God!"

I touch his collar. "What I really want is to go back to my place, where things will be done on my terms."

He grins at me. "What are your terms?"

"You, having your way with me."

"Accepted," he says and then slides his arm around my waist.

"Then we'll come back later and eat," I say, laughing as I open the front door.

Forgoing an umbrella, we step out into the rain. "You really love that carbonara, don't you?"

Water soaks our clothes, but it doesn't matter. Soon enough we'll be out of them. "I do, but not as much as I love you."

"I love you, too, Bri, and I plan to spend the rest of our lives proving it."

A happy laugh rises in my throat. Never in my life have I felt so giddy, so loved. "Good, now let's hurry to my place so we can get naked and start on that right away."

* * * * *

COMING SOON!

LET'S TALK
Romance

For exclusive extracts, competitions
and special offers, find us online:

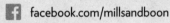 facebook.com/millsandboon

@MillsandBoon

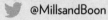 @MillsandBoonUK

Get in touch on 01413 063232

For all the latest titles coming soon, visit
millsandboon.co.uk/nextmonth